CW01465062

Malcolm Richards crafts stories to keep you guessing from the edge of your seat. He is the author of several crime thrillers and mystery novels, including the PI Blake Hollow series, the award-nominated Devil's Cove trilogy, and the Emily Swanson series. Many of his books are set in Cornwall, where he was born and raised. Malcolm credits authors such as Stephen King, John Connolly & Agatha Christie as major influences on his writing.

Before becoming a full-time writer, he worked for several years in the special education sector, teaching and supporting children with complex needs. After living in London for two decades, he now lives in the Somerset countryside with his partner and their Miniature Schnauzer.

Author website: www.malcolmrichardsauthor.com

Books by Malcolm Richards

PI Blake Hollow

Circle of Bones

Down in the Blood

The Dark Below

The Devil's Hand

The Devil's Cove Trilogy

The Cove

Desperation Point

The Devil's Gate

The Emily Swanson Series

Next to Disappear

Mind for Murder

Trail of Poison

Watch You Sleep

Kill for Love

Wish Me Dead (*prequel novella*)

Standalones & Shorter Works

Prey for Night

After Midnight

The Hiding House

PI BLAKE HOLLOW BOOK FOUR

Malcolm Richards

THE DEVIL'S HAND

Copyright © 2024 Malcolm Richards

This paperback edition published by Storm House Books

The right of Malcolm Richards to be identified as the Author of the Work has been asserted by him in accordance with the Copyright, Designs and Patents Act 1988.

All rights reserved. No part of this publication may be reproduced, stored in a retrieval system, or transmitted in any form or by any means without the prior written permission of the publisher, nor be circulated in any form of binding or cover other than that in which it is published and without a similar condition being imposed on the subsequent purchaser.

All characters in this publication are fictitious and any similarity to real persons, living or dead, is purely coincidental.

ISBN 978-1-914452-63-5

www.malcolmrichardsauthor.com

For Xander

Prologue

Fire. Blood. Screaming. The town was ablaze and no one could save it. The girl was frozen to the spot, watching flames as tall as people ravage the street. Heat seared her face. Thick black smoke choked the air. She stood, mesmerised, at once enchanted and horrified by the carnage before her. A terrible shrieking on her left pulled her attention from the burning houses. A man in his thirties writhed on the ground, hands raised in defence, as three knife-wielding figures in red devil masks stabbed his chest, stomach and face. On her right, a middle-aged couple sat slumped in the front seats of a silver estate car, silently staring into space. The front of the vehicle was burning, yet neither adult tried to escape.

Someone, she did not see who, let out a terrible, guttural wailing that grew to a crescendo then was immediately silenced. The girl sniffed the air, smelled ash and burning meat. She tasted sea salt and death. Looking down at herself, she saw the T-shirt and jeans hanging from her malnourished, pubescent body were caked in dirt and blood. The blade in her hand had been wiped clean. It was as if she were in a dream or underwater, a viscous film separating her body from reality.

She stared at the blazing houses, saw a front door open and a burning man stumble out. She watched him take two silent steps before collapsing to the ground. She should have felt horror, disgust, but she only felt a vague awareness. The man was dead because of her. And so was the one in the street and the couple in the car. And all those people down at the seafront. She was responsible, along with the others. But for what benefit? She had been given the answer, over and over again. It had been drummed into her like a mantra until she could recite it in her sleep. To show the world what a dangerous thing it was. To demonstrate how chaos was a terrifying, unstoppable force. To prove that the innocents in this cruel world could be just as vicious and unforgiving towards the people who longed to hurt them.

But standing there, death and violence swarming around her, the girl questioned the point of it all. She heard their leader's voice in her ear. 'We are clearing a path to the New Dawn so that we may cross over.' The girl had never understood the meaning behind those words, but now, despite the haze that blanketed her mind, despite the numbness that slowed her limbs and kept her heartbeat steady, she understood exactly what they meant. She just didn't know if she was ready.

Someone was calling her name. Footsteps were approaching.

'Hey! What are you doing? Come on, we have to go.'

Slowly, she turned. A boy stood before her, similar in height and build. Like hers, his clothes were soiled and bloody, and his face was obscured by a red devil mask. But she knew exactly who he was.

The boy held out a hand. When she didn't take it, he gripped her by the wrist. 'Everyone is gathering in the wood. They say it's time. But I don't want to cross over. I want to go home!'

He pulled off his mask and dropped it to the ground. And there he was. Her kin. Her everything since they'd shared their mother's womb. And he was as terrified as she was numb.

The boy tugged the girl's arm, but she did not budge, even when he begged her with his eyes.

'What's wrong with you?' he said. 'Don't you get it? If we stay here we're going to die. Do you want to die?'

The girl shrugged. The boy lunged at her, tearing off her mask and tossing it away.

'No!' he bellowed. 'I'm not going to let that happen!'

He pulled on her arm again. When she still didn't move, he took her by the wrist and began dragging her along the street. The girl did not fight back, but she did not help him either.

They passed more destruction. More bodies and burning things. The boy's breathing was heavy and erratic, each terrible scene making him babble under his breath. The girl was afloat on a sea of nothingness. Even though the knife in her hand had been cleaned, blood was still smeared on the blade, close to the hilt.

Up ahead, a car skated around the corner, tyres screeching on the tarmac as it shot towards them. A woman was behind the wheel, her expression twisted with terror, and in the back seat a girl no older than five or six years old. The boy leapt to the side, dragging the girl out of the vehicle's path. Then they were on the move again, the boy pulling the girl along, the girl staring blankly.

Reaching the end of the road, they turned right and began climbing the hill. The boy slid to a halt. The girl slammed into him. Up ahead, more figures in red devil masks and bloody clothing were making their way towards the wood. He twisted around and saw more masked figures close behind.

The boy wailed and looked back at the girl with desperate eyes.

'Where do we go?' he cried. 'How do we get out?'

She stared at him, offered another shrug.

'This way!' one of the masked devils called, pointing up at the hill. 'Salvation is at hand!'

And then hands were upon them, helping them along, guiding them to the top of the hill, towards the wood, where the New Dawn was waiting. Where they would finally cross over.

The boy was helpless, too weak to fight them. Too scared to say no. But he did not loosen his grip on the girl's wrist. Soon, they were cresting the hill, where they were swept along in a sea of red, leaving the town behind and entering Briar Wood. Even from up here, they could feel the heat from the fire below and smell the stench of death.

The girl stared at the army of masked devils that surrounded her. Something stirred inside her body, beginning to wake. It started with a tightening of her chest, followed by a quickening of her heartbeat. Her stomach convulsed, as if she'd swallowed a bird and now it was trying to get out. What was this feeling?

They were moving deeper into the woods, feverish chatter reducing to a low hum. The girl was breathless now. She stared at the boy's terrified face, at the clearing up ahead, where they would enter the New Dawn.

'No.' The word was a whisper. The first word she had uttered since the first life had been taken. 'I don't want this.'

She squeezed the boy's hand, who looked wildly around him. He squeezed back. The girl's heart thumped in her chest. Blood rushed from her extremities, towards her brain. She tried to move to the left, but the crowd surged around her.

'Let me out,' she said, her voice a little louder this time. 'I need to get out!'

And then she was shoving with her shoulder, pushing people out of her way while dragging the boy behind her. No one tried to stop her; every masked face was pointed at the clearing. The girl pushed and shoved, all the emotions she had been suppressing suddenly flooding her cells. Panic choked her. Tears sprang up in her eyes. Crushing guilt threatened to drag her to the ground. But she pressed on, cutting a path through the bodies, the boy following closely behind.

And suddenly they were free. The girl fell to her knees, panting and sobbing. The masked mob continued on, oblivious to the deserters.

The boy placed a hand on her shoulder and said, 'Get up.'

But she could not move.

'What did we do?' she moaned. 'What did we do?'

Pulling her to her feet, the boy gripped her shoulders. 'It doesn't matter now. If we stay here we're going to die. Do you want to die?'

The girl shook her head.

'Then get moving.'

Taking her hand, the boy turned away from the clearing, away from the town. Then froze.

A masked devil stood before them, blocking their path. She was bigger than them, older. She carried a sharp looking sickle in her left hand.

No one spoke. The boy pushed the girl behind him. He would fight to the death if he had to, would happily lie, bleeding out, if the last thing he saw was his sister escaping to freedom.

He quickly scoured the ground, looking for a rock or stone that could be used as a weapon. The devil reached up and removed her mask, and they saw she was no devil at all. It was Julia, one of the older teens, who had always been kind to them. Who, like the boy, had always hovered on the perimeter.

He opened his mouth to speak, but Julia pressed a finger to her lips.

'If you want to leave,' she said, 'I know a way out.'

The boy and girl stared at her, then back at the clearing, where hordes of red devils were now gathered, impatiently waiting for the arrival of their revered leader. In the near distance, the low wail of sirens could be heard.

Panic flickered in Julia's eyes. She turned to leave.

'It's now or never,' she said. 'I'm not waiting.'

The girl tugged on the boy's hand.

'Can we trust her?' she said.

The boy shook his head. 'We can't trust anyone. But we're still going with her.'

And then they were on the move, ducking and weaving between the tree trunks, away from the clearing and the insanity that lay within. Away from the burning town and its dead and dying inhabitants. Away from the Dawn Children and life as they knew it.

'It's going to be all right,' the boy said over his shoulder, attempting to sound reassuring. 'Everything is going to be fine.'

But even before they had left the wood, skipped across the road, and slipped into the neighbouring fields, the girl knew that nothing was fine. And never would be again.

1

Summer had arrived in Cornwall and, for once, had not brought rain. The sun was the colour of honeycomb, rich and golden, the azure blue sky marred only by occasional contrails from passing jet planes. The green waters of Falmouth Inner Harbour were calm. Hundreds of moored yachts with pristine white sails swayed gently to and fro on the surface. They had been arriving in droves for days, in anticipation of Falmouth's regatta, a full week of fleet racing and shore-side events, which included an annual street carnival and pink wig parade. Also arriving in droves were holidaymakers. On the Prince of Wales pier, hundreds of brightly dressed tourists milled up and down beneath strings of colourful bunting, snapping photographs and eating ice cream. Every few minutes, a ravenous gull would swoop down to snatch tasty treats from unsuspecting hands. The birds had waited patiently for the holiday season to begin. Now that it was here they were not disappointed.

Blake Hollow watched the summer day unfold from the small

window of her third-floor office. She was sweating profusely, the portable electric fan in the corner doing little to appease the heat. Air conditioning was as rare in the UK as the white rhinoceros, although Blake fancied the rhinoceros would handle the rising temperature better than her. Her black jeans and boots were not exactly helping, but she had compromised and worn a grey short-sleeved T-shirt. She had even tied her dark hair in a ponytail, which was something she rarely did because it left her feeling exposed.

Much to her chagrin, Blake had recently turned forty, and she'd been having all kinds of intrusive thoughts ever since. Should she finally trade in her battered old Corsa and treat herself to a new car? Should she finally try to settle down with someone even though she was perfectly happy alone? Or should she get a dog for company, or worse still, a cat? Had she achieved enough at the age of forty? Was she happy with her career as a private investigator? Was she successful enough? Had returning to Cornwall after years away been a smart move or the worst mistake of her adult life?

All of these thoughts and more left Blake anxious and wary; emotions she thought she'd finally buried since Dennis Stott had last month finally been sentenced to life in prison. Blake had been the one to apprehend the serial killer, had almost become his eighteenth victim but had escaped with a knife wound in her shoulder and lasting nerve damage in her right hand. She had waited a year and a half for his crimes to go to trial, which included the murder of Blake's childhood friend. Now it was all over and Stott would rot behind bars until he was dead. Now Blake was meant to forget about him, maybe even rid herself of the terrible images that still plagued her at night. And yet she couldn't.

She peered down at the ice cream vendor at the foot of the pier, who was handing out cones and glistening ice lollies from his cart. Blake's mouth watered. But there was no time for ice cream. She had an imminent appointment with potential clients.

Blake checked the analogue wall clock: 1:59. As the minute hand struck twelve, the room filled with a loud buzzing. She arched an eyebrow. In that instant she had learned two things about her prospective clients before even saying hello. First, that promptness was important to them. Second, that their intentions were serious.

Crossing the room, she reached for the intercom and buzzed them in, then stood waiting as their footfalls on the stairs grew louder. She quickly checked her appearance in a small wall mirror and brushed a few lunchtime crumbs from her T-shirt. Silhouettes loomed on the other side of the door glass, where stencilled letters announced: *Hollow Investigations.* She waited for them to knock before opening the door.

Standing before her were a man and a woman who looked to be in their fifties, although Blake already knew from running background checks they were both in their mid-forties. But that was grief; it not only tore apart your heart, it aged you quite cruelly.

'Ms Lander? Mr Teague?' Blake said, even though she already knew who they were.

The woman smiled. The man gave her a sheepish look.

Stepping aside, Blake welcomed them in and directed them to the two chairs in front of her desk. She offered them iced water or coffee. Despite the heat of the day, Owen opted for coffee. Bronwen asked for water. As Blake set about making the drinks, she observed her potential new clients.

Owen Teague was dressed in dark trousers and a crisp white short-sleeved shirt, with just one open button at the neck. He was of average height and build, with a slight paunch. He had dark hair that was beginning to recede, with flecks of grey at his temples. His body lacked tone and his skin was sallow, signs of an unhealthy man who needed to take better care of himself. In spite of his obviously poor health, Teague sat with a confident posture, spine straight, eyes forward. Yet Blake could see a wariness in the way he repeatedly adjusted his shirt collar, and in the way his tongue unconsciously darted out to touch his upper lip.

Standing, Bronwen Lander barely reached five feet tall. Sitting, she looked almost childlike in her knee-length summer dress and red sandals. But there was nothing childlike about her demeanour. She sat upright, one leg crossed over the other, hands folded neatly in her lap, glancing furtively about the room. Like her ex-husband, she had dark hair, which was cut short, but that was where the similarities ended. Her complexion was tanned and glowing, her shoulders and limbs sculpted and lithe. This was a woman who enjoyed the outdoors and valued her health, and who clearly put time into it. Unlike her ex-husband, if Bronwen Lander was anxious about being here she showed no outward signs.

Finished making the drinks, Blake set a mug and a glass before them, and took her seat on the other side of the desk. From her background checks, she'd discovered that Owen Teague worked as a warehouse manager for a supermarket in Launceston, while Bronwen worked as a bank cashier in Newquay, where she also lived, in the same house she and her now ex-husband had once resided. Their marriage had lasted fourteen years and had ended seven years ago. In the second year of their marriage, the Teagues had become parents to twins, a girl named Sandra—Sandy for short—and a boy named Morgan.

It was why they were here today. Because of the twins.

'So, how can I help you?' Blake's notebook lay open in front of her, her favourite pen resting on top.

Owen Teague and Bronwen Lander glanced uncertainly at each other, as if psychically deciding who should speak first. It was quickly decided that Bronwen would do the talking.

'As you know,' she began, her voice soft but by no means meek, 'we're here about our children. They've been missing for eight years now. Eight years, four months, twenty-three days.' She glanced at her ex-husband, who nodded but remained silent. 'The police gave up on them a long time ago. The case is still open but no one is looking for them. I suppose it's because they're adults now and have a right to anonymity. But we haven't given up on finding them. We never will.' She glanced at Owen, who gave her another rallying nod. 'Today is their twenty-first birthdays. It feels so wrong to still not know where our babies are or if they're okay. That's why we're here.'

Blake leaned back slightly on her chair, which creaked. 'And you're hoping I'll be able to find them.'

'We're hoping you'll try. That's all anybody can do, isn't it? Try?'

Blake did not disagree with the sentiment. 'Tell me about how your children disappeared. I'm aware you will have gone over this countless times with the police, but I'm a fresh pair of eyes and ears, so please try not to leave anything out.'

She already knew some of the details, but it was always important to hear it first hand from potential clients. They could provide information that news archives could not, small intricacies that might not seem important to them but could lead to case-breaking revelations.

Taking a long sip of water, ice cubes clinking against the glass, Bronwen Lander retold the story of the day her children disappeared.

Every so often, Blake would interject, asking questions or confirming facts, while jotting into her notebook, but mostly she let the woman speak. Owen Teague remained quiet, his expression hardened and stony, years of torment and guilt buried just beneath the surface in a shallow grave.

Morgan and Sandy Teague had been twelve years old at the time of their disappearance, which had occurred eight years ago on Saturday, 14 April, an unusually sunny day after weeks of rain. There had been no family activities planned that weekend. Their parents had been having relationship problems for some time and were dealing with it by avoiding each other as much as possible. Which left Morgan and Sandy to entertain themselves.

After several weekends of being stuck indoors, the nearby park beckoned to them. With neither parent around to ask for permission, Sandy had left a handwritten note on the kitchen counter, informing them of the twins' intended whereabouts. Brother and sister had left the house together. Never to return.

It had been confirmed the twins had made it to the park. Eyewitness accounts had placed them there between 11 AM and midday. One woman had seen them talking to a small group of children and young people aged between ten and eighteen, and a young white man who could have been in his early twenties. The group did not seem threatening. In fact, the woman remembered seeing the twins laughing and joking with them. She'd thought nothing more of it at the time, until photographs of the twins had appeared on the regional evening TV news.

Armed with the eyewitness's statement, the police scoured local CCTV footage and located the group on the outskirts of Newquay, seemingly leaving the town on foot. Morgan and Sandy Teague were still with them. The young man in his early twenties became an immediate person of interest, then very quickly a suspect. Great effort was made to identify him, including several public appeals for information. It wasn't until Morgan and Sandy had been missing for more than a year that the man's identity had finally been revealed.

His name was Heath Monk.

Blake looked up from her notes. 'Why does that name sound familiar?'

Shifting on her seat, Bronwen stared at her hands and shook her head.

'Do you remember what happened at Devil's Cove?' she said.

There was a long pause before Blake spoke again. 'Of course. I don't think anyone will ever forget.'

2

It had begun with a missing boy and ended with a town razed to the ground. Blake had been living in Manchester at the time, but the story had been one of such horror and intrigue that it had made not only the national news but had spread far and wide via media outlets across the globe. One newspaper had branded it "Jonestown 2.0", which Blake had thought tasteless at the time, reducing two awful tragedies to a gimmicky moniker, even if the body counts were somewhat similar.

A young boy named Cal had vanished one day from the coastal town of Porth an Jowl, known to locals as Devil's Cove. An extensive search proved fruitless, and it was solemnly concluded that Cal had got into trouble in the water and drowned, his body swept out to sea by the current. That was, until some years later, the boy miraculously reappeared.

Blake's recollection of what happened next was patchy at best, but she remembered the boy's return was shrouded in mystery, and that he was unable to explain where he had been due to what doctors believed was trauma induced muteness. Fast forward a little, and it was revealed that Cal had been taken by a serial killer, with ties to a cult called the Dawn Children. And even though the killer was eventually apprehended, it did not stop the Dawn Children from exacting bloody revenge on the town of Porth an Jowl. Hundreds were murdered and the town was burned.

As for the Dawn Children cult, those who had not been killed or taken their own lives, were rounded up by the police. Mass murder aside, the most shocking element of the story was that the majority of cult members were young people and children under the age of eighteen.

The air in Blake's office was already thick and cloying, but in the past few minutes had grown even heavier. Getting up from her desk, she flicked a switch on the standing fan in the corner, increasing its rotation speed, then returned to her seat. Owen Teague and Bronwen Lander sat slightly turned away from each other, their eyes pointed at the floor. Blake considered her next words carefully.

'So, are we saying—and correct me if I'm wrong here—that your children became involved in the Dawn Children cult?'

'They did not become *involved*. They were *taken* by them.' Other than asking for coffee, it was the first time Owen Teague had spoken since entering the room. His voice was low and controlled, but Blake could hear the anger puncturing each word.

'My apologies,' she said. 'You believe Sandy and Morgan were abducted by the Dawn Children cult. Specifically, by Heath Monk.'

If Blake remembered correctly, Heath Monk had been heavily involved in the cult, and was presumed to be one of its main figureheads. If she also recalled the news stories correctly, Monk had met a particularly brutal end.

'The police came to the same conclusion, that Sandy and Morgan were taken in and brainwashed.' Bronwen's eyes were wet and the fingers of her right hand dug nails into the palm of her left. 'Then, about a year later, Devil's Cove happened. The police believe our children were there that day, even though they weren't among those arrested, or among the . . .'

Tears slipped from her eyes. Blake pushed a box of tissues across the desk.

'If there was no sign of them, why are the police confident your children were there that day? And I believe I'm right in saying that all the cult members wore masks, so identification would have been almost impossible.'

'Because of what happened in London,' Owen said. When Blake frowned, he continued. 'Although most of the cult members were arrested, some did escape. A year or so after Devil's Cove, a suspected member was found in a squat in Hackney. She'd been stabbed to death. The Metropolitan police believe she was prostituting herself, and that one of her clients turned violent.'

Blake picked up her pen. 'Do you remember her name?'

'Julia something. It's not important.'

Blake disagreed. All victims of murder deserved the dignity of being identified.

'Anyway,' Owen said, 'when the police searched the premises they found evidence of other people living there. Including this.'

He stared at Bronwen, who had finished drying her eyes and crumpled the tissue into a ball on her lap. Her gaze drifted from her ex-husband down to her wrist, where she wore a silver charm bracelet. Reluctantly unfastening the clasp, she removed it and handed it to Blake.

'We gave it to Sandy for her twelfth birthday. She loved it. Said it was the best present she ever had.'

Blake held the bracelet delicately in her hands, as if it were an ancient artefact. It contained three silver charms. A cat sitting on its haunches, its tail flicking. A love heart. And the letter "S". Blake recalled receiving her own first piece of jewellery, a gold plated necklace once owned by her mother. She had thought it pleasant at the time, but had never developed a love for such adornments, instead preferring a good pair of boots and hard-wearing jeans.

She handed the charm bracelet back to Bronwen, who quickly re-fastened it to her wrist and stared at it longingly.

'Is there a chance this bracelet might belong to someone else?' Blake asked. 'What I mean is, is it a standard charm bracelet that you picked from the shelf because of the "S"?'

Bronwen narrowed her eyes. 'No. We chose the charms specifically for Sandy. The "S" is obvious. The cat because ours had recently died and Sandy had been devastated. The heart because, well . . .' Her voice cracked. 'Because we love her very much, even though she might not have believed it at the time. Owen and I, we were fighting a lot back then, mostly over money, but I think it was really because we both knew our marriage had already come to an end.' She glanced at her ex-husband, who did not meet her gaze but instead let out a barely noticeable sigh. 'The twins suffered because of it. We neglected their feelings because we were so wrapped up in our own. Sandy was particularly sensitive. The bracelet was meant to show her that we still loved her, no matter what happened. I hope she understood that.'

Blake felt sadness and regret emanating from the man and woman sitting on the other side of the desk. Divorce was never easy on anyone, but for children it was particularly rough. Complex feelings of rejection, confusion, and guilt often led to self-hatred and acting out. Morgan and Sandy Teague's disappearance had spared them further pain caused by their parent's separation. Unfortunately, encountering the Dawn Children had led to much worse.

'How old would the twins have been at the time of the young woman's murder?'

Bronwen frowned. 'Fourteen. Why do you ask?'

Because two brainwashed fourteen-year-olds could easily over-power a woman if they wanted to, Blake thought.

'Just building a picture. So you believe your children possibly escaped with this Julia, made their way to London, where Julia was found murdered and Sandy's bracelet was discovered at the scene of the crime.'

Veins pulsed at Owen Teague's temples. 'I hope you're not insinuating our children had anything to do with that woman's death. She was a whore who picked up the wrong client, nothing more.'

'I believe the preferred term these days is "sex worker",' Blake said. 'And if what you're telling me is true, it seems this Julia may have been watching out for your children. They would have been, what? Thirteen, when Devil's Cove happened? Fourteen, when Julia's body was found. No matter how resourceful they might have been at that age, I highly doubt they made it to London without help, never mind survived in the city.'

Tension simmered in the room. Blake took a calming breath and relaxed her shoulders. The pinkie and index finger of her right hand were aching from taking notes, lasting effects of the nerve damage she'd been left with thanks to Dennis Stott.

'Tell me what happened next.'

'The police recognised the charm bracelet from photographs we'd given them when the children first went missing,' Bronwen said. 'And because Julia was suspected to be a member of the Dawn Children, the police put two and two together.'

Blake turned to a clean page and wrote: *Police suspect twins are members of DC. Suspected killers also?*

She glanced up to see both parents' gazes fixed on her note-book. She closed it.

'What happened after Sandy's bracelet was found?'

'Nothing, for a long time,' said Bronwen. 'The Met police focused on Julia's murder. Devon and Cornwall Police went about their business. There was nothing else found at the—where Morgan and Sandy were staying. Nothing to say where they'd gone. The trail went cold, as they say.' The woman smiled painfully. 'Until three and a half years later. He called, you see. My Morgan, he called me.'

3

Pain shot through Morgan's heels as he hurried along the busy street, weaving in between the pedestrians. Raindrops clung to his skin. His heart thumped in his chest. Shooting a glance over his shoulder towards the street corner, he saw none of his brethren, only the gloomy faces of rain-soaked shoppers. The old red phone box was just ahead of him. He would not have long before they caught up with him, maybe only a minute. They would have already noticed him missing. Thomas would have sent someone to look for him, most likely Kane. But Morgan could not bear it any longer. He had to make the call.

He reached the phone box and was relieved to see it empty. Hardly anyone used them these days. Why would they when nearly everyone carried a mobile phone? As he pulled open the door of the cramped booth and slipped inside, the acrid stench of stale piss filled his nostrils. Crushed beer cans lay at his feet, along with shards of glass.

He had passed this particular phone box several times during the past two months, walking from the train station to their spot in the Square, where they would attempt to sell handmade trinkets and hand out their leaflets. It was the first phone box Morgan had seen since they'd all left London together over a year ago, their departure shrouded in mystery. Newcomers like Morgan were not required to know reasons for why the group did anything, nor were they expected to ask questions. If they did, punishment was swiftly dealt.

Inside the phone box, he frantically shoved his hand inside his trouser pocket and retrieved the single coin he had kept hidden away for the past two weeks. He had shamefully stolen it from the upturned hat of a busking violinist, who had been temporarily distracted by an enthusiastic passerby. Thomas and the others had been six steps ahead of him as usual. Now, the coin felt heavy and unwieldy in his palm as he reached with his other hand for the telephone receiver. Pressing it to his ear, he was relieved to hear a dial tone.

He had never made a call from a public phone box before, but he had seen it done countless times in movies, back when he was young. Back before he and Sandy had encountered the Dawn Children in the park. All you did was slip the coin into the slot, punch out the number on the digit keys, then wait for the line to connect. For your mother to answer.

He shot another glance through the rain covered door glass. Visibility was poor from within the booth, but he knew they would be here soon, scouring the street, until they came upon him. Everyone knew Morgan was unhappy, that he was becoming a nuisance. His brethren had been warned to keep a closer eye on him, or they would be punished as a direct consequence of any misbehaviour. And they had watched him closely for a while. But recently their attention had begun to slip.

Morgan pushed the coin into the slot and carefully tapped out the phone number he had continued to memorise over the years. Their mother had forced both him and Sandy to learn the number, even though they'd both had mobile phones at the time. She had made them repeat it back to her, over and over, as if they were learning their times tables, until they could recite it in their sleep. 'It's for your own safety,' she'd told them. 'In case you're ever lost or in trouble, and you need our help.' Morgan was both lost *and* in trouble. And now, more than ever, he was desperate for his parents' help.

The line connected and the ringing tone droned in his ears. Morgan's breaths were fast and thin, his eyes searching the passing bodies outside. He counted the ringing tones. *Five . . . six . . . seven.* His gaze pulled back to the door, where a commotion was happening outside. Two figures were pushing through the crowd, making heads turn. Heading in his direction. *Eight . . . nine.* Morgan let out an exasperated cry.

The figures had stopped outside the phone box and were peering in, hands cupping their faces, noses pressed to the glass.

And then a woman's voice spoke in his ear, grainy and exhausted, as if she hadn't slept well in years.

'Hello?' she said.

The street fell away, along with the peering faces. Sounds muted, until there was only Morgan and the voice on the phone.

'Hello?' the woman said again, curiosity etched into the word. And there was something else. Something that, to Morgan, sounded like hope.

He opened his mouth to speak. No words came out. Only a dry, strangled croak.

On the other end of the line, the woman emitted a frustrated sigh. 'Is someone there?'

A frantic beeping sounded in his ear. Morgan glanced up at the phone box. His single coin had already been used up.

He opened his mouth again. Tried to force the word out. *Say it! For god's sake, just say it!*

'Mum?'

His voice was that of someone much younger, a frightened child waking from a bad dream. In his ear, he heard a sharp intake of breath. There was a trembling pause before his mother spoke again. 'Morgan? Is that you?'

And then suddenly the door was wrenched open and street sounds flooded his ears.

Morgan barely had time to hang up the phone before a strong pair of hands seized him roughly by his grey tunic. The same tunic his fellow brothers wore. It was the shoes that determined where you ranked in their group. Morgan's shoes had already been worn by at least three other people. The heels were almost gone, the soles flapping and holey. The man who stood before him wore shiny new shoes that glistened in the rain.

Kane's grip on him tightened. His dark, hateful eyes bore into him. But Kane was not alone. Thomas had come himself. He towered over Morgan, teeth mashing together as he leaned in close.

'Oh, you've really done it this time,' Thomas said, his sour breath flooding Morgan's senses, making him nauseous. 'Mother and Father are going to be so disappointed.'

He nodded at Kane, who released his grip on Morgan's tunic, only to take him roughly by the arm. Thomas took the other, and they marched along the street together, people complaining as the trio cut through the crowds.

Morgan did not try to fight. Nor did he cry for help; he was invisible to the people of this town. Morgan only thought of his mother and her soft voice in his ear, singing to him like a chorus of angels.

It didn't matter what happened to him next. Sandy had been lost to him a long time ago and he would never get her back. But now he had heard his mother's voice, and it was like a light in the dark. It would keep him safe as he was taken from this world and thrust into the next unknown.

4

Bronwen Lander took another tissue and dabbed her eyes with it. Outside, the sun continued to blaze, slowly baking the holidaymakers filling the Prince of Wales Pier. Beyond, a yacht was drifting out of the harbour, its white sails gently fluttering. When Bronwen looked up again, Blake saw only anguish.

'That was all he said before the line went dead. Just that one word. "Mum." His voice was different, older and deeper, and so sad. But I knew it was him. I knew it was my Morgan.'

Beside her, Owen Teague let out a faltering sigh. Blake could only imagine the loss he felt, to have missed out on hearing his son's voice after all those missing years.

'What happened next?' Blake asked, softly.

'I tried calling back,' said Bronwen. 'But the phone just kept ringing. I tried over and over, until eventually someone answered it and told me it was a payphone in the street.'

'Where, exactly?'

'Bournemouth. I don't know what he and Sandy were doing there.'

Blake was aware of the place but had never visited. Bournemouth was a large coastal resort town situated a couple of counties over in Dorset, southern England. She didn't know exactly how far it was from London, probably somewhere between a hundred and a hundred and fifty miles; still quite a distance for teenage twins to travel, especially without their murdered guardian Julia.

'Of course, the first thing we did was call the police, then drive up there,' Owen said, glancing at his ex-wife, who nodded in agreement. 'The call was traced to a phone box on Old Christchurch Road. The local police in Bournemouth searched the area and appealed for witnesses. We spent days there, looking for our children. But there was no trace of them.'

'What about the witness appeal? Did anyone come forward?'

'Just two. The first was one of those crazy people you hear about, who make stuff up just to get attention. They claimed they saw our twins down at the pier on one of the fairground rides. We should have known they were lying right then, but we were desperate. We spent day after day, hanging about the pier, showing the kids' photos around, all the while hoping to catch a glimpse of them. People who lie like that should be sent to prison.'

He swallowed hard and stared off into space. Bronwen reached out and gently patted his arm. Although they had been divorced for several years, Blake could see they still shared a close connection through the commonality of grief.

'And the second witness?'

Bronwen turned back to Blake. 'She thought she recognised Morgan from a group of young men she'd seen handing out leaflets in the town square a few times. She thought maybe they were Jehovah's Witnesses, or something similar. They were all dressed the same. She never took the leaflet so couldn't say exactly what they were preaching. We looked in the square. We went back day after day, waiting to see if they would turn up. But they never did. She wasn't lying about the group though. The police interviewed staff from the surrounding shops. People had seen them there several times but hadn't paid much attention. They only remembered them because of their clothing. No one seemed to remember faces though, including Morgan's.'

'What was so memorable about their clothing?'

'They all wore the same. Dark grey tunics that were short sleeved, and light grey trousers.'

Blake chewed the inside of her mouth as her gaze swept over her notes. 'So the group who the witness believes Morgan had been with suddenly disappeared after he called you?'

'We had the same thought,' said Bronwen. 'But when no trace of them could be found, the police decided it was a coincidence and that nothing more could be done.'

'It was a bloody disgrace.' Owen had rejoined the conversation, his anger still palpable. 'Our children had been missing for over three years by then. They would have both been sixteen at that time. Still minors. Yet those so-called police officers were content to call it a day yet again.'

Blake sympathised with the man, although she thought his sentiments weren't entirely accurate. Missing person cases stayed open for years, especially those of children. Even after time had passed and the leads had dried up, officers assigned to the case would continue to delve into any accrued evidence in the hope of discovering a new lead. It wasn't on a daily basis—other, more current, cases took precedence, and budgets assigned to older cases were invariably much smaller—but it didn't mean that the police gave up. And they were only human, which meant when all leads led to dead ends, there was very little they could do but check in now and again, and continue to hope.

Of course, Blake also knew that the cold hard truth of a trail gone cold wasn't what the parents of missing children wanted to hear. And why would they? They had birthed and raised those children, sometimes adopted them. In almost every case, they had loved those children more than life itself. To know that the police force could not find their children, the very force that was meant to protect and watch over them, must have felt like a knife to the gut. But no matter what, those parents would never stop looking for their children, even if it seemed, from an outside perspective, like the police force had.

She sat, staring at her notes, her mind mulling over everything she'd learned so far, which wasn't much at all. If the police with all their technology and connections had not been able to find Morgan and Sandy Teague, her chance of finding them was almost zero. She was just one person, whose technology consisted of the Internet, a laptop, and her mobile phone. Blake glanced up, meeting Owen and Bronwen's desperate eyes. Birthdays of the missing did nothing but rub salt into already infected wounds.

As if reading her mind, Bronwen smiled sadly and said, 'We're not expecting miracles. You may not find them, we know that. But we have to keep trying. We owe it to our children. They have a right to be found.'

She took her ex-husband's hand in hers, surprising him. He gave her a gentle squeeze back.

'Please,' he said to Blake.

She stared back at them. If Morgan and Sandy Teague were still alive, why hadn't they reached out to their parents after all these years? Why not pick up the phone again or hop on a train? Why stay stubbornly silent since that phone call three and a half years ago? It concerned Blake and, as always, her mind went straight to the darkest possible explanation.

Owen and Bronwen were still pleading with their eyes.

Blake shook her head. 'I'm sorry, but I'm not sure what I can do that the police already haven't. And I'm not one to take advantage of grieving parents. It would be a waste of your money.'

'Then it's wasted money,' Bronwen said. 'Better that than to never try again. I'm not giving up on them. I refuse to. *We* refuse to. All we're asking is that you try, Ms Hollow.' She leaned forward, hands clasped in front of her, as if in prayer. 'Please, Blake. Think of the lives you've already saved by simply deciding to try. Don't my babies deserve the same chance? I know you've risked your life before to help people. That girl you saved from the Stone Circle Killer. Those fishermen last year. It's why we picked you. We're not asking you to risk your life. We're just asking you to give us a chance, maybe even our last chance, to find our children and bring them home.'

Blake stared from one parent to the other, feeling hemmed in behind her desk.

'Please.' Owen's face crumpled as he fought off tears. 'I'm not a begging man, but I'll get down on my knees if I have to.'

A flurry of wings drew Blake's attention to the window. A gull had landed on the sill and was staring into the office. Its cold yellow eyes glared at Blake. She glared back, then returned her focus to the people at her desk. A tear had escaped from Owen's right eye and was sailing down his face.

Blake stared at the tear, which now clung stubbornly to his chin. She winced. If only men could get over themselves and cry more, maybe then she wouldn't be sucked in by their vulnerability.

She opened the top drawer of her desk, hesitated, then pulled out a fresh contract and laid it on the table. The relief that surged from Owen and Bronwen was almost physical, sweeping over Blake in a smothering wave.

'I'm not promising anything,' she said, pushing the contract towards Bronwen. 'As much as you won't want to hear it, you need to know that cold cases almost always come to nothing, especially when there's so little evidence to go on. Which means you need to lower your expectations right now. Both of you. All the way to the bottom.' She handed Bronwen a pen. 'We'll give it a week. If I find nothing, we'll review our agreement. If I do happen to find your children—and that's a big "if"—there's something you need to consider. For whatever reason, they may not want to come home or even have contact with you. If that's the case, I won't be able to divulge their whereabouts, no matter how much you beg or offer to pay. Your children are adults now, and the law says they can go about their business as they please. If you agree to that and understand the consequences, then read through the contract and sign it. My daily rate is on page two.'

'We understand,' Bronwen said, picking up a pen and signing the contract without even reading it.

She didn't understand, of course. Neither of them did. How could they? Hope was built into every parent's DNA. They would never give up on their children, which meant they would always try to find them and bring them home. Dead or alive. Blake hoped it would be the latter and that they would come willingly. But first she would have to find them.

Leaning back on her chair, she massaged her painful fingers. She was already troubled by this case before it had even begun. And that was never a good sign.

5

It was late. Blake had returned home several hours ago with a bottle of Rioja, a Thai red curry, and a hefty police file under her arm concerning Morgan and Sandy Teague. Their parents had recently requested the paperwork in preparation for hiring a private investigator. To Blake's knowledge, the police force's decision to act in favour of that request, was based upon several factors, the most important being how active the case was. The Teague Twins' case was now considered cold, and although it would continue to remain open, Blake imagined the police would be open to sharing if it meant someone was still looking for them.

Sitting on the living room floor of her rented country cottage, a mile or so outside of Falmouth, Blake sipped her wine as she stared at the paperwork sprawled before her. As expected, many of the files had been redacted, including the identities of several eyewitnesses, and information pertaining to what Blake imagined were potential leads that had gone cold but were still of interest to the investigating detective. This, in particular, frustrated Blake, but

she understood the decision to redact the details. The risk of exter-
nally sharing reports connected to an open investigation, even if it
had gone cold, could lead to mistakes being made, witnesses being
scared off, or potential leads being mishandled and lost. Blake was
a professional and believed she conducted her investigations with
the same integrity as any police detective. Yet she knew that, like a
professional poker player, a good police detective would hold their
cards close to their chest.

The file that Bronwen Lander had been given, who in turn had
passed it on to Blake, contained a series of written police reports
from over the years, starting with the twins' disappearance and
ending with the phone call made by Morgan Teague. At that
point, nearly five years into the investigation, the assigned case
budget would have been minimal, leading to a severe limitation on
the resources the investigating detective had at her disposal. And it
showed. Working in conjunction with Dorset police, two officers
were dispatched to search the areas of Bournemouth town centre
where the phone box was located and where Morgan was last seen
with the group of young men handing out leaflets. A few passersby were questioned, a few staff members of local businesses interviewed. With no further leads or any sign of Morgan, and with no
more money to fund an extended search, the case was once again
declared inactive.

Blake had already assembled these reports in chronological
order and lined them up in piles across the carpet. Now, she was
busy reading through the various eyewitness statements. There had
been several over the years, beginning with the day the twins had
encountered Heath Monk and the Dawn Children in the local
park, and ending with the sighting of Morgan in Bournemouth. In
between were various eyewitnesses alleging to have seen the twins
up and down the country. Each report had to be investigated, and
most were proved to be unfounded, wasting yet more police

resources and funding. It happened a lot with missing person investigations; members of the public genuinely trying to help, but often being mistaken.

There was also a minority of desperate, attention-seeking individuals who thought it funny to clog the helplines with deliberate lies and false sightings. Their selfishness not only wasted valuable police time but potentially endangered the lives of the missing. Of course, eyewitnesses were still a fundamental part of any criminal investigation. It was often the alertness of the general public that helped to apprehend any wrongdoers or find missing children like Morgan and Sandy Teague.

Next in the file was a series of dead leads the police had already investigated and deemed irrelevant to the twins' disappearance. Blake spent time reading through them, drinking wine and making notes. The lead detective had been thorough in her investigation and the subsequent dismissal of those leads. Blake could see no reason to pursue them further.

The only area of investigation that she thought warranted further exploration was that of the children's involvement in the Dawn Children cult. CCTV confirmed that Morgan and Sandy Teague had indeed met with Heath Monk and left the park with him, along with a group of unidentified young people. But despite the report's suggestion that the twins had been present that terrible day in Devil's Cove, and had potentially committed atrocious acts of violence against its townspeople, there was still no proof. Investigating the twins' connection to the Dawn Children might possibly lead to their whereabouts. But there was a darker side to treading this particular path. If by some miracle Blake happened to locate the twins, their involvement in the Devil's Cove massacre would have to be either proved or disproved. Too many people had died that day to let even missing children go free without scrutiny.

There was someone Blake knew who could help if she chose to

investigate Devil's Cove and the Dawn Children. Detective Sergeant Will Turner had been involved in the investigation of the crimes that occurred that day, and had even risked his life to save a child. Yet Blake was not one of the detective sergeant's favourite people. She had crossed paths and clashed with him on one too many investigations, although she liked to think that since last year's case at Porthenev Harbour, she and Turner had reached a truce. After all, Blake helped the man catch a brutal killer, one who had a taste for his victims' flesh.

Devil's Cove was not the only act of violence linked to the twins. There was also the murder of Julia King. Her body had been found at a vacated address in Hackney, East London. She had been stabbed in the gut and chest, and had died of subsequent blood loss. The report on her murder was heavily redacted, with only the barest of details shared. Blake did however learn that Julia's murder had been solved. DNA evidence had been extracted from her body, leading to the identification of her killer, a man named Joseph Fields, who not only had a previous conviction for grievous bodily harm but also had a reputation for treating sex workers roughly.

Although Morgan and Sandy were off the hook for the murder, the presence of Sandy's charm bracelet at the scene of the crime linked her to Julia King, a known member of the Dawn Children cult. It was possible that the twins had never made it to London or indeed lived in the squat; King could have stolen Sandy's charm bracelet at any time prior to the events at Devil's Cove. But Julia was not the only person living in the squat, and among the items seized by detectives during the murder investigation was clothing that would fit a young teenager perfectly.

Removing the final documents from the police file, Blake stared at the age progression images of Morgan and Sandy Teague. Constructed by a digital imaging expert using specialist forensic software, and drawing from family photographs, medical records, and other experts in the field such as forensic anthropologists and dentists, the images represented what Morgan and Sandy might have looked like at the age of eighteen. Which told Blake they'd been created about three years ago, around the time Morgan had called his mother. There was no indication in the police file that the images had been circulated to the public. Blake assumed that they had, otherwise their creation would have been a pointless exercise in wasting both time and money.

Her gaze moved back and forth between the pictures. Both twins had light brown hair with similarly coloured hazel eyes and prominent cheekbones. But there were also differences. Where Morgan had a square chin, Sandy's was slight and almost pointed. Her ears protruded a little, giving her an elfin appearance, whereas Morgan's were larger and sat closer to his skull.

Blake wondered how accurate the processed images were, and if they would be useful now, three years on. Perhaps circulating the pictures again might jog some memories.

She yawned, checked the time and saw it was almost midnight. Her gaze wandered to the plate of Thai food, which she had barely touched. Sitting up, she stretched her spine. A joint popped painfully, making her wince. Blake was forty years old. Even though she was an occasional practitioner of yoga, her days of drinking wine on an almost empty stomach, while hunched over like an old crone on the floor, were numbered. Especially when the files before her were not revealing much at all.

The instant regret she had felt for agreeing to take on the case returned to haunt her. Morgan and Sandy Teague had been missing for eight years. Despite Morgan's phone call three years ago, which could not be verified, there was little else to go on. Blake massaged her nerve damaged-fingers. She had promised to give the twins' parents one week. A week in which she would review all of the available evidence accrued over the past eight years in the vain hope that a fresh lead might reveal itself. Blake was still highly doubtful, but she was being paid to try, so try she would.

She reached for her notebook and pen and quickly jotted down an initial plan of action. Her first task would be to make a request to Devon and Cornwall Police to view CCTV footage from the day of the twins' disappearance. If they had access to it, she would also request CCTV footage from Bournemouth town centre, taken around the time of Morgan's phone call. If they did not have access, then Blake would contact the police force in Bournemouth. And while she was dealing with the police, she would attempt to connect with the detective in charge of Morgan and Sandy's case.

Devon and Cornwall Police did not have a Cold Case Unit, the department where unsolved cases would invariably end up like a slush pile of manuscripts on an editor's desk. Instead, CID, the Criminal Investigation Department, was responsible for them, along with all active cases involving serious crime. They were an extremely busy department, which made Blake suspect her privately hired assistance in a cold missing persons case would be warmly welcomed, as long as she played by their rules.

The next task she wrote in her notebook, although not necessarily in chronological order, was to reach out to Detective Sergeant Turner and request to speak to him about the incident at Devil's Cove. Blake's friend and former teen sweetheart, Detective Constable Rory Angove, happened to be Turner's partner and was therefore Blake's way in. But Rory had previously warned that Devil's Cove was not a subject Turner liked to talk about. He had witnessed terrible things that day, far more than any person, detective sergeant or otherwise, should have to see in a lifetime. Blake decided to put Turner on the back burner for now; there was one other task she could perform before asking to speak to him.

Scooping up her mobile phone, she made a call, which was answered moments later by a sleepy, irritated voice.

'Who died?' Kenver Quick said. 'Or is there a more pressing reason for waking me up?'

Blake smirked. 'I thought you were a night owl.'

'I used to be. Sobriety sucks.'

'I'm sure it has its benefits.' She stared into the dregs of her wine glass. 'Isn't whatshisname staying over? Trevor?'

'Travis. And no, he's seeing friends tonight.'

'Without you?'

Kenver cleared his throat. 'Why are you calling?'

'Just wondering if you fancied going on a road trip this weekend?'

There was a short pause before Kenver answered. 'A road trip to where?'

'Bournemouth. Epicentre of stag dos and hen parties.'

'Sounds like living hell. Why are we going?'

'I'm on a missing persons case and I need help with canvassing.'

'Do I get paid?'

'Isn't spending the weekend with your favourite cousin enough?'

'Don't flatter yourself. You want me, you pay for me.'

'You sound like an incestuous sex worker.'

'Sex workers get paid regardless of who they sleep with.'

Blake finished the wine in her glass. 'Yes, weirdo, you'll be paid. We're leaving early Saturday morning. I'll pick you up at seven.'

'Seven? On a Saturday? You live to torment me, don't you?'

'It's my civic duty. See you then. Be ready or I won't stop for a slushy on the way.'

Kenver drew in a sharp intake of breath. 'You wouldn't dare!'

'Try me.' Blake hung up.

A deep, sudden ache in her upper spine wiped the smile from her face. She stared at the piles of reports in front of her. Even with the beginnings of a plan, she did not feel hopeful. She doubted a trip to Bournemouth was going to change that.

6

The fine weather continued through Friday as Blake busied herself with contacting Devon and Cornwall Police to make requests for CCTV footage related to the disappearance of Morgan and Sandy Teague. The forms she needed to complete were tedious but necessary; the police weren't going to casually hand out potential evidence to anyone who asked, even a private investigator with a strong track record of solving her cases.

With the application submitted, she left a message for the detective in charge of the Teagues' case, a DS Amelia Rose, then took the age progression images of the twins to a local printing shop in Falmouth and made a hundred flyer-sized copies, ready for the trip to Bournemouth. Back at her office, she hopped on her laptop and searched for Facebook community groups related to Bournemouth, joined them all, then posted scanned copies of the images with a request for information. Three years had passed since the last sighting of Morgan Teague, so she didn't think it would amount to much. But every resource had to be exploited.

The rest of the day was spent on a potential fraud case for

Curnow Insurance, for whom she had been working semi-regular cases over the past six months. It wasn't exactly stimulating work, but the pay was good, covering the rent for both her office and home.

Recently, Blake had inherited a sizeable sum of money from the late Faith Penrose, a close friend who had been brutally murdered by a man connected to one of Blake's cases. She had been paralysed by guilt for the longest time. The only way Blake knew how to free herself was to donate the entire inheritance to several local charities. Her parents had thought her insane, but to Blake, that money was covered in Faith's blood. So here she was, back on the daily grind but working consistently now that she had finally re-established her private investigation practice in Cornwall.

Saturday came. As Blake had warned, she arrived outside of Kenver's cottage on the outskirts of Wheal Marow at precisely 7 AM. To her surprise, her cousin was not only dressed but waiting outside. She stared at his slim and heavily tattooed frame as he tossed his overnight bag into the back seat before climbing in next to her. Despite the summer heat, Kenver wore his trademark black skinny jeans and boots. He did wear a T-shirt, but it was black and sleeveless, with an image of a demonic creature perched upon a nest of human skulls.

'This is what you wear when I ask you to dress appropriately?' Blake said.

Kenver ran a hand through his nest of black hair. 'This is appropriate to me.'

'We're meant to be approaching passersby to ask about Sandy and Morgan. You're going to scare them away.'

'Look, if you wanted boring then you should have invited someone else. Christ, Blake. Reaching forty has turned you sour.'

He flashed a toothy smile and, for once, his large dark eyes didn't look so sad.

Blake glared at him. 'I may be sour, but at thirty shouldn't you have mastered basic hygiene? Your breath smells like fish paste.

She pulled away from the kerb, grinning to herself as a horrified Kenver breathed into the palm of his hand then brought it to his nose.

~

The four-hour journey to Bournemouth gradually turned into five thanks to roadworks and heavy summer traffic clogging the A30 and A35. The temperature was high, the Corsa's air conditioning non-existent. By the time they reached their destination, both Blake and Kenver were sweaty and irritable. Rather than immediately force themselves upon the general public, Blake thought it wise to first check into their pre-booked guesthouse, which claimed to have seafront views of the iconic Bournemouth Pier. What the guesthouse information had forgotten to add was that the seafront view was a tiny sliver of blue squeezed between two other guesthouses, and to see it you had to press your face to the bottom right corner of the window and cock your head at a seventy-degree angle, until your neck almost snapped.

As for the pier, Blake reckoned she'd have to be some sort of contortionist to snatch even the barest of glimpses, and if that were the case she would have run away with the circus a long time ago to make her fortune. But it was the height of summer, which meant she was lucky to have found any kind of bed for the night at such short notice.

She glanced around the room. In an effort to save Bronwen and Owen money, she had booked a twin room with two single beds. Kenver was currently perched on the end of his bed, upper lip curled in disapproval.

'Okay, so it's not the Ritz,' Blake said. 'But we're not here on holiday. Speaking of which, we should head out.'

Kenver ran his fingers along the duvet and shuddered. 'I can't believe you're making me sleep in floral print. With stains on.'

Twenty minutes later, they were out in the street and moving away from the seafront with its golden beaches. According to the police reports, Morgan Teague had called his mother from a payphone on Old Christchurch Road, which was in the heart of Bournemouth's town centre.

As they headed towards it, weaving their way between countless bodies of holidaymakers and disgruntled locals, Blake again wondered what had brought Morgan, if not both twins, to a large coastal town like this. Their parents were certain no relatives lived here, and didn't think either child had friends in Cornwall who had relocated to Bournemouth. Which meant if the twins truly had been here, it was for an altogether different reason. Had they simply drifted into town and perhaps stayed for a while? Or had they been here under duress?

Before leaving Cornwall, Blake had read up a little on Bournemouth, learning that it had a population of about half a million, and that it was the birth- and final resting place of Mary Shelley, author of *Frankenstein*. Bournemouth had also played an important role during the Second World War, with the Royal Air Force setting up operations here, with several hotels and guesthouses requisitioned to accommodate troops and serve as temporary military hospitals. During D-Day preparations, thousands of troops had marched through the streets of Bournemouth before heading to Normandy, where they battled on the front lines.

As for its iconic pier, the structure dated back to 1856 and began life as a simple wooden jetty. During Victorian times, the country had fallen in love with seaside leisure. Bournemouth Pier was completely rebuilt and extended with iron and steel. Today, it stood at a thousand feet long and offered all sorts of attractions to visiting tourists, including a zip line that ran from the very end of the pier back to shore. Blake had already decided not to tell Kenver about the zip line; the idea of flying through the air with her feet dangling above the English Channel made her queasy. Perhaps she really had turned sour.

'God, I thought tourism was bad enough in Cornwall,' Kenver said, as he pushed his way through heaving crowds. 'This is like a zombie apocalypse.'

They had reached Old Christchurch Road, which, according to Google Maps, was about half a mile long and housed several independent boutiques and cafés.

'You're not used to leaving the house,' Blake said. 'You should get out more.'

'Why would I do that?'

'Oh, yeah. That would mean you'd have to talk to people.'

As they continued to walk, Blake scanned both sides of the street, searching for the phone box. She found it three minutes later, a traditional red phone box, which was a rare sight these days, even rarer if it was still operational. Blake headed towards it, noting the missing panes of glass and the stench of human urine that tended to haunt every phone box in the country.

Kenver wrinkled his nose as they approached. 'If ever there was an argument for more public toilets . . .'

The phone box was vacant. Blake pulled open the heavy door and peered inside. She didn't know what she was looking for. Perhaps a sign that Morgan had been here, something he had deliberately left behind so his parents could find him. If that were the case, it meant Morgan was in some kind of trouble. But all Blake saw were a few faded flyers advertising local gigs, personal escorts, and phone sex chat lines. Blake was surprised the latter still existed, considering the sex industry had gone online a long time ago.

Stepping away from the phone box, she turned to look at the nearest shops. A barber, a newsagent, and a coffee shop that was closed and appeared to be undergoing renovations. Blake rifled through her backpack and pulled out the flyers she'd had made of the aged likenesses of Morgan and Sandy.

'You take the barber, I'll take the newsagent,' she said, holding out some of the flyers.

Kenver peered through the barber storefront and saw three men wearing tracksuit bottoms, muscle vests, and angry looks in their eyes. 'No way. Queer people like me don't go into places like that. Not if we want to come out alive.'

'Who cuts your hair then?'

'Since I've been back in Cornwall I've watched a lot of YouTube tutorials . . .'

'Fine. You take the newsagent. Show both images but focus on Morgan. He was the only one spotted in Bournemouth. Make sure to mention the leaflets and his grey clothing. It might help to jog people's memories.'

'Yes, boss.'

Blake watched Kenver enter the newsagent, then took a moment to look up at the area around her, searching for CCTV cameras. Finding one across the street, which pointed in the general direction of the phone box, she hoped the footage taken on the day Morgan had called his mother was still available, and that the police granted her access.

7

Canvassing the barbershop had not taken long. The men were wary of her but still answered her questions. None of them recognised Morgan Teague from the age processed image or recalled a group of young men in grey handing out leaflets three years ago. Thanking them, Blake returned to the street, where she found Kenver looking bored while eating an ice cream cone.

'Enjoying yourself there?' she asked.

He handed her a second cone, then licked his fingers. 'We may be working but that doesn't mean we can't have fun. How did it go at Homophobic Haircuts?'

'They offered me a free moustache wax. Apart from that it was a no-go. Anyway, you don't know for sure they're homophobic. They might surprise you.'

'Oh, please. You straight people have no idea.'

They got walking again, continuing along Old Christchurch Road, Blake's ice cream already beginning to melt and run over her hand.

'Any joy at the newsagent?'

'Nothing. I'm pretty sure the shopkeeper thought I was going to rob the place.'

'I bet you get that a lot.'

They soon reached the end of the street, which merged with Gervis Place. Following the directions from Google maps, Blake turned right. She ate her ice cream in silence, Kenver walking beside her. All around them pedestrians ebbed and flowed. A few minutes later, they exited Gervis Place and found themselves in Bournemouth Square. It was a pleasant area, with red and grey paving, green benches and old-fashioned street lamps, and a stone planter filled with attractive greenery, including Cornish palms. Not only did the square mark the centre of Bournemouth, it also separated the town's Victorian Central and Lower Gardens, which were designed and planted around the River Bourne. It was here in the square that Morgan Teague was said to have handed out leaflets with the mysterious group of young men.

Finished with her ice cream, Blake dumped the wrapper in a nearby waste bin and cast her gaze over the Obscura Café, which stood alone at the edge of the square, next to the road. A late twentieth century construction, the Obscura Building was an intriguing site, notable for its round shape and extensive use of steel and glass. Its lower tier housed the café, while a smaller upper tier contained offices. Capping the building was a cone-shaped clock tower. To Blake, it looked like a fascinating synthesis of a circus big top and an observatory, resulting in a coffee-serving UFO.

Kenver nodded at it approvingly. 'You wouldn't find that in Wheal Marow.'

Blake agreed. 'My mother would never get over it.'

They headed towards the café, weaving in between the packed outdoor seating, lively chatter filling their ears. Heading inside, they were welcomed by a pleasurable drop in temperature.

The decor was pleasant enough, pale yellow walls and a high

ceiling, round tables the colour of cherry wood, and vinyl floor-boards with a long train of grey carpet leading to a silver-blue bar at the far end. With most of the café's patrons preferring the sunshine, just a few of the interior tables were taken.

Telling Kenver to sit and wait, Blake made her way to the bar, where she joined the queue. It took a while, but at last she came face-to-face with a young barista, who looked to be in her late teens. Blake presented her private investigator licence and explained why she was there. The witness who had reported seeing Morgan handing out leaflets in Bournemouth Square was named Cassie Black. Blake asked if she was working today.

'I don't know any Cassie Black. Maybe she doesn't work here anymore.'

'I see. How long have you been here?'

'A few weeks.' The barista stared at Blake, then at the fast-growing line of people behind her.

'In that case, can I speak to your manager, or anyone who might have worked with Cassie Black?'

Behind Blake, a man in his forties cleared his throat impatiently. She slowly turned and shot him a steely glare. The barista asked Blake to wait, then vanished through a side door, leaving a male colleague of similar age to take her place. Blake stepped aside so that he could continue serving.

After a few moments, the barista returned, followed by a man in his mid-thirties who was dressed in an open white shirt and navy trousers.

'Can I help you?' His voice was pleasant, but his eyes were wary.

Blake introduced herself, waited for the manager to scrutinise her licence, then asked about Cassie Black.

'I remember Cassie,' he said. 'She left about two years ago. I don't know where she went, and even if I did, I'm afraid I can't tell you. It's company policy.'

Blake held up the flyer with Morgan Teague's age-processed face on it. 'In that case, perhaps you could tell me if you ever saw this boy hanging around. He's currently missing. Cassie told the police she'd seen him outside, leafleting in the Square with a group of other boys, perhaps a bit older than him, all wearing grey trousers and tunics.'

The man stroked his chin as he studied the image, then turned to stare out the window, at the Square beyond. 'Three years is a long time, but those boys sound vaguely familiar. I'm not sure I recognise the one in the picture though.'

'Did any of them ever come in here? Maybe to use the toilet or hand out leaflets?'

'We don't allow leafleting, and toilets are strictly for paying customers only.'

'Did you ever see one of their leaflets, or happen to know what they were about?'

The manager shook his head. 'Some religious rhetoric, I'd imagine. Do you have any more questions? As you can tell by the queue, it's our lunchtime rush, which means it's all hands on deck.'

Blake stared at the snaking line of people, then back at Kenver, who was slouched on a chair with his legs splayed and his eyes glued to his mobile phone. She turned back to the manager.

'Is there anyone else who might still be in touch with Cassie Black, or who might remember the boys?'

'It's the hospitality industry,' the man said. 'Staff come and go all the time. Now I really must get back to work.'

Blake thanked him, then handed him her card in case he remembered anything else or changed his mind about giving her Cassie Black's address. The manager assured her that he wouldn't, before returning to his office. As she had predicted, Bournemouth was already feeling like a wasted trip. But then, just as she signalled to Kenver that it was time to leave, an elderly man sitting alone at a nearby table waved her over.

'Couldn't help overhearing your conversation with Mister stiff trousers over there,' he said, nodding in the direction of the bar. 'I might know something that can help you.'

He indicated to the empty chair opposite him. Blake sat down and introduced herself.

'Harry,' the man said. He had a genuine smile and hands ravaged by arthritis. He offered one to Blake, who shook it gently.

'What do you know, Harry?' she asked.

The man pointed a knotted finger at the wad of flyers sticking out of Blake's bag. 'I believe I saw your boy, and that group of young men he was with.'

Blake leaned forward. 'Recently?'

'Recently could mean ten years ago if you've lived as long as I have. It was probably around the time you were asking about. I come here most days, have done for a long time. Not much else to do when you're on your own and tired of staring at the walls.' He smiled again, and this time there was a sadness to it. 'Anyhow, I reckon I remember those boys well enough. Used to see them in the square, day after day, selling things and handing out their leaflets.'

'What kind of things were they selling?'

'Trinkets, if I remember correctly. Bracelets, jewellery. It all looked handmade and a bit out there. You know, like what you might find hippies wearing back in the day.'

'What about the leaflets?'

'Those I do recall. I said they were handing them out, but the truth was most people steered clear of those boys. I was curious, and maybe I felt a bit sorry for them. So one day I took a leaflet off their hands. I don't remember too much about what was inside.

Something about walking a path of light through the forest. Religious talk, I suppose. But I'll tell you one thing I do remember. Something that got stuck in my head for the longest time. In fact, hearing you talk about those boys just now, brought it straight back.

'There was a strange picture on the front of the leaflet. A symbol, I suppose you could say. It was a picture of three moons: one waxing, one full, one waning. And inside the full moon was the skull of a deer, with vines growing out of its antlers. I remember that surprised me. It's not the sort of thing you'd expect from a group of nice young Christian folk, is it?'

Blake agreed. 'You wouldn't still have that leaflet, would you, Harry?'

The man laughed. 'I may be old and live alone, dear, but I'm no hoarder. It probably went straight in the bin as soon as I got home.'

Blake's mind raced as she removed one of the flyers and held it up. 'What about the boy? Morgan. You said you recognised him.'

Harry stared at the picture for a long time. 'I reckon that's him. Yes, I'm sure. I remember, you see, because he was different from the others.'

'In what way?'

'I can't say exactly. Only that he never looked happy to be there with them. In fact, if I think about it, it was almost like he was scared. Or nervous. Something, anyway.' He stared at Blake with milky blue eyes. 'That's all I remember. Don't know if it's helpful or not, but I thought I should tell you.'

'It's been very helpful,' said Blake. 'Let me buy you a coffee to say thank you.'

The older man leaned back and snorted. 'No thanks. Have you seen the size of that queue? I'll be dead in my grave before that coffee ever arrives.'

Smiling, Blake thanked him for his time and handed him her business card, in case the flyer happened to resurface. She made her way back to Kenver, who was busy staring at his phone screen.

'Flirting, are we?' he said, without looking up.

Blake ignored him. A deer's skull inside of a full moon. Harry had wondered if the leaflet had been Christian in nature, but Blake was not aware of any Christian iconography associated with the animal, or its naked skull. She would need to research it to make sure. Shutting her eyes for a moment, she tried to picture the symbol that Harry had described. In spite of the summer heat, she shivered.

'Come on,' she said. 'Half the day is over and we've barely started canvassing.'

Kenver stood and immediately caught the attention of a woman in her late twenties, dressed in black denim shorts and a tank top, sleeves of colourful tattoos on full display. She offered Kenver a shy smile. He smiled not so shyly back.

'Have you and Travis broken up or something?' Blake asked.

'Travis and I are casual. Besides, there's nothing wrong with window shopping.'

'God, you're a pig.'

'And you're a prude.'

Dragging Kenver through the exit, Blake shoved more flyers into his hand and left him to canvas the café's outdoor customers, while she worked on pedestrians traversing the square. Above them, the sun continued to irradiate the day.

8

The Tiien Thai restaurant on St Michael's Road was a hive of activity. Every table was full. Lively conversation flowed through the air, mingling with the traditional Thai music playing from hidden speakers. The decor was simple yet atmospheric: dark wooden floors and tables, wicker chairs and white walls, and lining one side of the restaurant, narrow shelves set in alcoves that were filled with hundreds of candles in colourful glass jars.

Blake and Kenver had managed to get a table late in the evening and now sat with full bellies and empty plates before them. Blake had opted for Thai fish cakes and a green salad. Kenver had opted for half the menu. For a tall, slender man who looked as if he weighed less than a loaf of bread, he could certainly eat. And because dinner was on Owen Teague and Bronwen Lander, he made sure to take advantage. Blake allowed him to; Kenver had worked the rest of the day in cloying heat, traversing the streets and handing out flyers of Morgan and Sandy Teague. He had even braved Bournemouth Pier, which was crammed with holidaymakers who were unlikely to have seen the twins or visited

Bournemouth before. Yet Kenver had persisted. Despite his appearance, which Blake thought might intimidate people, Kenver's good looks and charm had done quite the opposite. But his efforts had proven fruitless. No one recognised the twins from the age progression images.

Blake had ended her day with the same result. Now she was tired and her feet hurt, and she wanted nothing more than to kick back with a glass of wine or a tumbler of whisky, and sulk. But she was with Kenver, and when she was with him she didn't drink; it was easier to help him avoid temptation by abstaining herself.

Not so long ago, Kenver had suffered a relapse, thanks to Blake's use of him in a case. There had been naïveté and a degree of selfishness on her part. Kenver had a contact with access to crucial information that she needed, but the man wouldn't give freely. The plan was for Kenver to meet with the contact, an old school friend of his, while Blake "happened" to come across them by chance. Kenver had taken the meeting as an opportunity to go to a bar. By the time Blake arrived, the damage was already done. She still felt responsible now. Kenver was a grown adult who could make choices of his own, but sometimes Blake wondered if, for him, drinking wasn't a choice but a compulsion.

Was Kenver a full-blown alcoholic or was he still on a slippery downwards slope? The fact he could manage to abstain without any kind of support group or professional intervention suggested it was the latter. Blake supposed how fast he descended would depend on how oiled the slope was. Or perhaps she was in denial, just like he was. Throughout dinner, Kenver had eyed every tray of drinks that had passed by. When glasses of wine were brought to the adjacent table, he'd wet his lips with his tongue and forcibly turned his head away. Now, with a stack of empty plates and a full glass of cola before him, he seemed irritable and distracted, his left knee jigging furiously up and down beneath the table.

'Thanks for today,' Blake told him. Kenver looked up, and she saw thirst in his eyes. 'We covered a lot of ground, which I couldn't have done without you.'

'Yeah, well, it was all a waste of time, don't you think?'

'Maybe. But we had to try. After the amount of people we talked to, I think we can say if Morgan was ever here, he moved on a long time ago.'

'Not necessarily. How big did you say Bournemouth was? Half a million people? That's like looking for a needle in a haystack. Anyway, all of this is pointless. He and his sister are probably . . .'

'Probably what?' Blake knew what he was thinking because she had thought it herself. She just didn't want to be the one to say it out loud.

Picking up his glass, Kenver took a swig of cola and shrugged a shoulder. 'Well, they're dead, aren't they? Kids don't go missing for years just to turn up alive. Look at Madeleine McCann.'

A Thai waitress in her mid-thirties with a bright smile approached the table. She began clearing their plates, impressed by Kenver's effort, then asked if they wanted more drinks. Kenver bit his lower lip and stared hard at the tablecloth. Blake shook her head and asked for the bill.

When they were alone again, Kenver said, 'So, what's the plan now? Time to call it quits and go home?'

It was a question Blake had been asking herself for the past two hours. She had a few more places to check out in the morning, but with the CCTV request pending and nothing else in the way of leads, there was no reason to stay in Bournemouth beyond tomorrow.

'I'll keep to my word,' she said. 'I told the twins' parents I'd give them a week. That means I have until Thursday to find something. If by then I don't, then sadly it's time to pull the plug on their hopes.'

The waitress returned with the bill and a portable card reader. Blake fished out her wallet, paid for their food, and left a generous tip.

Kenver yawned and picked up his phone. Under the table, his knee jigged even more violently.

'Well, let's hope the next few days bring more luck. Because today gave you nothing.'

'Not entirely true. There was the old man, Harry, and the description of the leaflet he saw.'

'Doesn't sound like much.'

'Still, it's all we have.'

Blake was quiet for a moment, letting the conversations of her fellow diners wash over her as she thought about Harry's description of the leaflet. A design on the front cover, made up of three connecting moons: one waxing, one full, one waning. And in the centre of the full moon, the skull of a stag with leafy vines creeping around its antlers. The old man had thought the group of young men to be religious, maybe some sort of Christian sect. But to Blake, the image he had described sounded older. She didn't know much about paganism, but not too long ago she'd met someone who was very much attuned with nature and the old religions. Someone who also happened to be a twin of sorts. She wondered if it was worth paying her a visit.

A loud bang startled her from her thoughts. Kenver swore, pulled back his chair, and began angrily rubbing his knee.

'Everything okay?' Blake asked.

He glared at her. 'Fine. I'm just tired from walking.'

'How's sobriety going? Tonight must have been difficult.'

'Actually, it's easy. Like I told you before, I can control it whenever I need to.'

Blake sighed. Except when you can't, she thought, then decided to change the subject.

'So, what are your plans these days? You've been back in the homeland for a while now. Do you think you'll continue to stick around? Or will you be heading back to London?'

'Why? Hoping to get rid of me?'

Kenver's entire demeanour had changed at the mention of London. His body grew suddenly rigid and his dark eyes narrowed.

'Of course not,' Blake said. 'I like having you around. It's just that, well, you left London so suddenly and you've never really said why.'

'Yes, I did. I told you that place sucked the life out of me.'

'But you had a good job, friends, an active social life, which is more than you have in Cornwall.'

'Thanks.'

'And you never once gave any indication something was wrong.'

'That's because nothing *was* wrong. Why are you prying? I left London for the same reason you left Manchester—I outgrew it.'

'That wasn't why I left. And I didn't leave as abruptly as you did.'

'Then why did you leave? And don't say it was to take care of Aunt Mary because that was only a temporary thing.'

'I left because business dried up after the larger private investigation companies moved in. And anyway, you're deflecting. There's something you're not telling me. This isn't the first time I've asked you about leaving London, Kenver. You've never given me a straight answer.'

'Jesus. Can you spare me the interrogation? I'm tired and I want to go to bed.'

Kenver glowered at her, then leaned back on his chair and began chewing the inside of his mouth. Blake held up her hands in defeat. She wanted to press more because she knew something was there. Something Kenver had never told anyone. Whatever the secret he was keeping, it was nothing good.

'Okay, fine. Let's go back to the guesthouse,' she said. 'We don't have to check out until ten tomorrow morning, so you can lie in a little. But before we go home, I want to stop by a couple of places, homeless shelters mostly, and the local police station. Maybe I can speak to one of the investigating officers from when Morgan called his mother.'

Kenver continued to sulk in silence.

∾

The walk back to the guesthouse was brief. It was just after 10 PM, the summer evening still warm and balmy. The sun had set, but at this time of year darkness was rarely present in its purest form. Kenver was solemn and brooding, walking slightly ahead, the clomp of his boots echoing through the street. Blake worried about him, but what could she do if he would not talk?

Her thoughts returned to Morgan and Sandy Teague. She wondered if Kenver was right, if the twins were dead. It was entirely possible, although if she allowed herself to believe that right now, continuing with the case was pointless. Instead, she wondered if Morgan and Sandy had really been here, in Bournemouth. Only Morgan had been allegedly spotted. Did that mean he had come here without his twin? And if so, where had she gone? There had been no trace of Sandy Teague since the discovery of her charm bracelet near Julia King's murdered body six years ago.

Blake walked on, wondering if the twins' parents would ever see their children again. She hoped so. She really did. Even if that hope began to quickly dwindle with each step.

9

Sunday morning brought more relentless heat and sunshine, while Blake's path of investigation continued along an empty road. None of the workers at the homeless shelters Blake visited could recall Morgan or Sandy Teague ever taking a bed for the night. 'You tend to see the same faces in a town this size,' one of the volunteers had remarked. 'Those two would have still been minors, or just about. If they'd turned up here, we would have done something to help them. At the very least I'd remember their faces. Which I don't.'

Blake had no better luck with the homeless people she had managed to coax into talking to her in exchange for money. No one recognised Morgan and Sandy Teague, or recalled ever seeing them on the streets or in the shelters.

A visit to the local police station on Madeira Road yielded the same result. At first, luck seemed to be on Blake's side. PC Frank Lonsdale, who had been one of the investigating officers back when Morgan had phoned his mother, happened to be on duty. The officer working the station's front desk contacted Lonsdale by radio then gave Blake his location. Meeting near the town centre, Blake found the police constable to be an amiable man in his late thirties, who was pleased to hear that someone was still looking for the Teague twins. Sadly, his own involvement in the case failed to reveal anything new.

'It was a routine search that led nowhere,' he said, leaning against the bonnet of his patrol car while Blake stood on the pavement next to him. She had left Kenver, whose bad mood from last night had grown exponentially worse, in a nearby café. 'We did the usual, interviewing local businesses and the general public, but apart from that one eyewitness no one seemed to remember the boy.'

'What about the group he was with? I'm told they used to sell trinkets and hand out leaflets from Bournemouth Square. The leaflets had a picture on the front. Three moons with a stag skull in the centre.'

PC Lonsdale arched his eyebrows then frowned.

'I don't remember that, but I do remember those boys,' he said. 'I had to chase them out of the square a couple of times. If you want to busk or trade here you need to get a permit from the local council. They didn't have one. They were a strange lot, those boys. Young, but not like other young people their age. As for the Teague boy, I don't believe he was present the times I asked them to move on. But I can't say for sure. I certainly never met his sister. It was always boys and young men.'

'Do you know anything more about that group? A name, perhaps. Did they get into any other kind of trouble that would have led to identifying some of them?'

'If there'd been anything like that I would have followed it up at the time, to see if it led to the twins. But there was nothing else. And after we went looking for Morgan, the group did a vanishing act. Which we thought strange, but what could we do? We didn't have the resources to chase after them back then, and we have even less now. Of course, had the twins been younger it would be a different story. But all that was asked of us was to follow up on the Teague boy's phone call and canvass the area. We did that to the best of our abilities.'

Lonsdale folded his arms over his stomach and stared defensively at Blake. She understood the frustration of having your hands tied by red tape and limited funding in cases like this. She offered him a sympathetic sigh before handing him copies of the age processed images. 'Have you seen these before?'

The police constable nodded. 'They were sent to us when we were first asked to get involved. We circulated them, but if no one recognised the twins from these pictures back then, they're certainly not going to now.'

'I spent all day yesterday coming to the same conclusion.'

PC Lonsdale shook his head. 'I'm sorry I can't be of more help. If you ask me, that boy is long gone from Bournemouth. If he was ever here in the first place.'

10

The drive back to Cornwall was sticky and uncomfortable, the roads still jammed with traffic. They would stay that way for at least another month, until children went back to school and the holiday season came to an abrupt end. Blake's sullen mood was not helped by Kenver's persistent silence. Questioning him last night about his reasons for leaving London had clearly pressed on a nerve, but even though Blake knew there was something he was not telling her, she thought it wise to leave him alone. At least, for now. Besides, her mind was busy with Morgan and Sandy Teague.

Dropping Kenver at his front door, she told him she'd call, then watched Wheal Marow disappear in her rear-view mirror as she headed back to Falmouth. She did not go home right away but instead went to her office to type up a report detailing her lack of findings so far, which she then emailed to both Bronwen Lander and Owen Teague. When she was done, she leaned back on her chair and stared at the ceiling, tracing the splintered crack running from the central light to the window.

Frustration crept into her shoulder muscles. She had been

working this case for three full days now and all she had to show for it was a strange symbol that an old man had recalled from three years ago. Still, she supposed a lead was a lead. Until it wasn't.

Leaning forward, she opened her laptop and began researching. Outside, the sun began to set, searing the sky and painting the harbour waters in hues of amber and red. Eventually, Blake looked up from the laptop screen and rested her pen on top of her note-book. The nerve-damaged fingers of her right hand throbbed. But she had discovered several interesting facts. The most important being that the old man's description of the image on the leaflet was, in fact, not of one symbol but two.

First was the horned stag skull. It seemed, for many cultures, the stag was revered as a sacred animal. In Christianity, it repre-sented piety and devotion to God. In several examples of Christian artwork, the beast was depicted as a symbol of innocence and the desire to be free of mortal sin.

In Celtic traditions, the stag was known as the king of the forest. It represented purification, pride, strength and indepen-dence, and was associated with forest deities such as Cernunnos, the horned God and protector of the forest.

Pagans saw the stag as representative of nature and fertility, of renewal and the cycle of life, and the ever-changing seasons. In certain traditions, the stag's skull was a protective symbol used in rituals to stave off evil spirits and negative influences. In initiation rites, initiates wore stag masks as a means to shed their human characteristics and invoke the beast's primal nature.

In several ancient European folk traditions, the stag was the focal point of *The Wild Hunt,* a ghostly chase across land and sky, the stag hunted by the spirits of long-dead huntsmen, the hunt representing the untamed and mysterious aspects of nature and the spirit world.

And finally there was the Buck Moon, sometimes known as the

Stag Moon. Named by the Native American Algonquin people, who lived east of the Mississippi River, the full moon appeared in July, the same month every young buck's horns would regrow.

Stag research exhausted, Blake moved onto the symbol of the three moons. She quickly learned of its primary connection to Wicca. Also known as *The Craft*, Wicca was a modern, nature-centred religion founded in the mid-twentieth century. Drawing from folklore, ancient pagan traditions, and ceremonial magic, it formed the basis for contemporary witchcraft. Like the Eastern concept of karma, Wiccans believed in a threefold law, which meant that no matter what they put out in the world, be it good or evil, it would be returned to them threefold. They were also duotheistic, believing in two deities, the Horned God and the Triple Goddess.

Represented by the triple moon image that the old man had described, the Triple Goddess was a powerful representation of femininity and the feminine experience in all its complexities, connecting the female lifecycle to that of the moon, and represented by the Goddess's three phases: Maiden, Mother, and Crone.

The Maiden, symbolised by the waxing moon, governed over new beginnings, growth and youthfulness, purity and the promise of new life. Represented by the full moon, the Mother was the nurturing aspect of the Triple Goddess, and was associated with fertility and abundance, creation, stability, and fulfilment. Finally, the Crone, symbolised by the waning moon, represented wisdom and experience, transformations and endings, night and death.

In Wicca, each phase of the Triple Goddess was also sometimes linked with a Greek goddess of similar qualities. The Maiden was associated with Artemis, goddess of the hunt and the wilderness, protector of young women and children. The Mother was represented by Demeter, goddess of the harvest and mother-hood, while the Crone was represented by Hecate, goddess of magic and witchcraft, of crossroads, the underworld, and the night.

Her mind overwhelmed with information, Blake peered up from her research and saw that the sunset had come and gone. It wasn't quite dark outside but the sky had grown dim and shadows were creeping in at the edges. Blake mulled over what she'd learned. While it was all very fascinating, none of it told her where to find Morgan and Sandy Teague. What it did tell her, in relation to the imagery of the leaflet, was that the twins had perhaps become involved in some sort of group, possibly Wiccan in nature, if Wiccans insisted on wearing all grey outfits, which Blake didn't think they did. Beyond that, she felt as if she had opened a strange new door only to find yet another empty room.

Her eyes found her notes again. There could be something there, she thought. But what she needed was someone with specialist knowledge to make sense of what she had learned. Whether it would lead to new information, she didn't know. But right now, this research was all she had.

Picking up her mobile phone from the desk, Blake searched for a number that had been stored in her address book for almost a year. One that, until now, she had never called. Despite her reasons for that and the discomfort that came with it, she pressed the call button and waited for the line to connect. The phone rang for a long time. She was about to hang up when a familiar voice sounded in her ear.

'Blake? Is that really you? I thought you'd never call.'

Taking in a breath, Blake held it for a few seconds, and expelled it, along with the unwanted memories overwhelming her mind.

'Hello, Tegan,' she said. 'It's been a while. But I need your help.'

11

They met the next morning outside of Koffiji Bar and Café, which was located in Discovery Quay. Known locally as Events Square, the quay had undergone huge development some time ago and was now home to a vibrant mix of shops and small businesses, bars and restaurants, and the National Maritime Museum Cornwall. Falmouth Week, which included the regatta, was just days away, and that meant hordes of tourists and street merchants had already taken over the streets. The quayside square, in which Blake and Tegan now sat, was already full to the brim with holidaymakers enjoying iced coffees and perusing various stands selling locally made crafts. Just beyond them, a flotilla of moored yachts bobbed up and down in the harbour.

Blake was surprised that Tegan had chosen to meet somewhere so public. It wasn't so long ago the eighteen-year-old had lived an incredibly isolated life, locked away behind the sheer walls of a place called Saltwater House. Ten months had passed since then and much had changed for her. She no longer presented as much younger than her years, her immaturity mostly due to her father's insistence on keeping his family hidden from the outside world. Tegan had been treated like a young child, and so a young child she had continued to be. Until Blake was hired to investigate the family. Her subsequent findings led to the decimation of the Trezise family and its toxic legacy. Blake felt no guilt about it—the family had long kept a viper's nest of vile secrets and murderous antics. Antics that had led to their own inevitable self-destruction, and the death of an innocent woman, Faith Penrose, whom Blake had known since childhood.

Tegan and her brother Jack were now the sole survivors of the Trezise family, and heirs to a lurid misfortune that neither of them wanted. With nowhere else to go, they had been taken in by Ivy and Saul Bodily, the family's former housekeepers, who had shown the children more love and kindness than their own father ever had, which had been close to none at all.

Blake was happy that Tegan had survived her family, and that she appeared to be adjusting to a modest life devoid of sprawling mansions and Old Money. Yet she still couldn't forget Tegan's involvement that had led to the death of Blake's friend, even if her involvement had been under duress. As they sat outside Koffiji Bar and Café, Blake drinking black coffee, Tegan sipping chocolate milkshake, Blake couldn't help but feel a spike of animosity towards the young woman. But she pushed it down for now.

'I like the new look,' Blake said.

Tegen smiled and touched her white-blonde hair, which had once been long and flowing, and was now cut short and fell just below her chin, accentuating her sharp jawline and high cheek-bones. Where she had once found it impossible to be at rest, constantly fidgeting even when seated, there was now a stillness to Tegan's posture that was almost serene. Yet her eyes troubled Blake. Once, they had been filled with light and energy, darting around the room or staring at you with such intensity that it felt as if

Tegan could see into your mind. But now her eyes were full of shadows and heavy with sorrow. Tegan Trezise had witnessed terrible things and they would forever haunt her.

'How have you been?' Blake asked. Despite the hustle and bustle of the square, the silence between the two women had grown strained.

Tegan avoided Blake's gaze, instead focusing on a drop of milkshake that was slowly seeping into the grain of the table.

'I'm fine,' she said. 'College is going well, although it's weird being older than everyone else. I suppose that's what happens when your home schooling is apparently not up to the standards of the Secretary of State for Education.'

Even Tegan's voice had changed. Gone was the childish timbre, replaced by something more adult. More cynical.

'Well, it's good you're back in school, at least.'

'I suppose. I mean, education is subjective, isn't it? You could learn a hundred useful things just from taking a walk rather than sitting in a classroom and staring at a whiteboard. But what do I know?'

'Have you made any friends?'

Tegan shrugged and found another spot of milkshake to stare at.

'And Jack? How's he doing?'

Blake did not care for Tegan's brother. He had been a nasty and vindictive young man, who dealt out spite with glee. But even so, she didn't think he deserved what had happened to him.

'Jack's not doing very well,' Tegan said. 'We don't hear from him much since he moved to London. I suppose he needs time alone, to process everything. After all, it's not every day you learn your entire life is a lie. Or you watch people you love die horribly in front of your eyes.'

Her gaze momentarily flicked up to meet Blake's before shooting away again.

'And how are you doing with that, Tegan?'

'I try not to think about it. I try not to think about a lot of things these days.' She cleared her throat as she slowly rolled the straw in her glass between her thumb and forefinger. 'Anyway, you wanted to show me something. What is it?'

Blake gave a slow nod. It was clear that Tegan was still processing everything that had happened to her. The difficult truth was that she would be processing it for years to come. And even though Blake still felt animosity towards her, she reminded herself that Tegan was barely an adult and, in spite of the entitled life she had led, she had suffered a great deal. Blake chose not to pry further. Instead, she took out her notebook and from it produced a sheet of paper, which she had tucked inside.

Last night, Blake had attempted to draw what the old man, Harry, had described seeing on the leaflet handed out by Morgan and his group of strange young men. It was a rough sketch but accurate enough to spark a reaction from Tegan. Unfortunately, it was not the reaction Blake had been hoping for.

A look of panic fluttered over Tegan's face as she recoiled in her chair. She seemed to shrink in on herself, to grow younger. It was then that Blake understood this new, cool demeanour was nothing but a ruse. The Tegan that Blake knew was still very much present, hiding beneath the skin like a frightened child beneath bed sheets.

'I don't do that anymore,' Tegan said, a hint of her old voice returning.

'Don't do what?' Blake asked.

'The Craft. Magic. It's stupid and it's dangerous. It's not even real. No religion is.'

Blake was momentarily taken aback by Tegan's reaction. The young woman she had met last year had been obsessed with all things Wicca, and had even proclaimed herself to be a white witch, who was on the spiritual path of something she called the Red Serpent. At seventeen years old, she had already dedicated her life to the study of "The Old Ways", the practice of ancient magic rituals and traditions. But now, the Tegan sitting before Blake appeared to be rejecting her old self completely. It was unsurprising, she supposed. Tegan's devotion to magic drawn from the natural world had been the unknowing catalyst for the destruction of her entire family.

'I'm not asking you to practise magic, or whatever it is you used to do,' Blake said softly. 'I just need your knowledge and advice. I'm trying to find missing twins and this symbol is all I have to go on.'

Tegan looked up. 'Twins?'

Blake took her time to describe the disappearance of Sandy and Morgan Teague, and the subsequent failed search for them, then moved onto the symbols she had drawn on the page. As she talked, Tegan's expression began to change, shifting from panic and guilt to genuine curiosity. She peered at the drawing again, a small crease of concentration appearing between her eyebrows.

'So, to my limited knowledge,' Blake said tapping the sheet of paper, 'we have the triple moon, representing the Triple Goddess, and we have the stag's skull, representing the Horned God. Two deities, both worshipped as archetypal Mother and Father figures in the Wiccan religion.'

Tegan stared at her, a surprised smile on her lips, before turning her attention to the drawing. 'That's one possible interpretation of it, yes. It's most certainly not Christian like the old man believed. Your definition of the triple moon symbol is correct. And the stag skull could represent the Horned God, the second Wiccan deity, although it's not a typical representation. What's unusual is to see them linked together like this.' She paused, biting her lower lip. 'The merging of both symbols could reflect a joining of the natural and spiritual world, or the alliance of life, nature, and the divine.'

Blake arched an eyebrow, impressed by Tegan's intellect and knowledge. Perhaps there was some truth in the girl's view on education after all.

She leaned forward. 'Do I sense a "but"?'

'This was on a leaflet, you say? What kind of leaflet?'

'I'm not entirely sure. The old man thought it was religious. He remembered it said something about walking a path of light in the forest.'

'That could mean anything. But if you're talking about Wicca, it could mean the spiritual path that many witches walk. Not literally, of course. It's more a journey of self-discovery, of spiritual growth and alignment with both the natural and magical realms. But that's only witches who follow Wicca. Other witches, who practise more ancient rituals, don't follow a path at all.'

'So, do you think it's possible the twins have joined some sort of Wicca group?'

'No, I don't think so. As much as Wiccans respect other religious traditions of saving others or spreading their faith, they do not promote their own religious beliefs, and they certainly do not evangelise. Wicca is all about personal exploration and the self. Which is why you'll find nearly all true Wiccans like to keep their beliefs private or only share them with like-minded individuals. Part of the wish for privacy is clearly to do with the historical persecution and misunderstanding of witches. But mostly it's because we don't wish to impose our beliefs on others.'

Blake paused, noticing Tegan's use of "we".

'So, if you're saying this leaflet doesn't come from a Wicca group, why does it have Wiccan symbols?'

'I honestly don't know. The triple moon is undeniably

Wiccan, but the stag skull isn't exclusive. It's an ancient symbol that goes back thousands of years.' Tegan picked up the sheet of paper and studied Blake's drawing. 'All I know is that in this image you have a bringing together of mother and father, masculine and feminine, the natural and the spiritual. Beyond that, I can't tell you what it means. All I do know is Wiccans don't go around converting others. And they certainly don't wear a uniform. That's what you described the boys wearing, isn't it? Grey tunics and trousers?'

Blake had had the same thought. 'So if it's not a Wicca group, then what?'

'Perhaps another kind of group, pretending to be Wiccan?'

'You mean like a cult?'

Tegan sipped the last of her milkshake and said, 'I don't know. But this group wouldn't be the first to appropriate and misuse Wiccan symbology.'

'But why? To what end?'

'To create an air of mystique. People have long had a fascination with the occult. Some groups have used that fascination to attract followers and gain wealth in the form of voluntary donations.'

'If brainwashing someone into giving you all their money can be called voluntary donations,' Blake said.

Tegan was watching her carefully, her large eyes unblinking. To Blake's surprise, she suddenly got to her feet.

'I should go now. I have a class this afternoon, and I suppose I shouldn't be late.'

Blake could have asked her to stay a while longer, at least for another milkshake. But instead she nodded and thanked her for her time. 'I'm glad you're doing well, Tegan. It's nice to see you finally on the other side of those four walls.'

The young woman stopped dead, the fingers of her right hand

gripping the strap of her shoulder bag. She turned towards Blake, an unnerving smile etched on her lips.

'Yes,' she said. 'It's just unfortunate how I came to be here.'

She left then, turning her back on Blake and hurrying away until she was lost in the crowds. Blake watched her go, a confusing mix of defensiveness and guilt suddenly clouding her mind. Because as much as Tegan had played a role in the death of Faith Penrose, Blake was far from innocent. She had taken the life of one of Tegan's siblings.

Blake sat in silence for a while. Eventually, she picked up the drawing she had made and stared at the strange symbols. Was it possible? Had Sandy and Morgan Teague escaped one cult only to be swept up by another? She hoped not. But it was certainly an explanation for their years-long disappearance, and for the leaflet's mysterious symbology.

A cult, Blake thought. Who would be susceptible enough to join one?

12

Summer Abernathy sat in the back seat of the SUV, wondering if she had made a terrible mistake. She was twenty-one years old, small in stature, with a mane of red hair, porcelain skin, prominent cheekbones, and a constellation of facial freckles that accentuated her vivid green eyes. It was her striking Celtic looks that had first caught the attention of the three men with whom she was currently travelling. Or perhaps they had caught hers.

Summer had first noticed them two days ago, dressed in their drab grey outfits and huddled together on the high street, attempting to sell cute handmade bracelets and pendants to the tourists. They looked to be the same age as Summer, give or take a year or two in both directions, and all three were clean shaven with tidy but amateurish haircuts. When Summer first approached them, they looked up in unison and their eyes widened, as if bewitched. The leader of the three, who was slightly older than the others and whose name was Thomas, smiled at her. And it was such a beautiful, welcoming smile that she found herself smiling back.

At first, she had only been interested in their trinkets. Her wrists were adorned with several bands, bracelets, and charms that she had collected over the years, each one with a tale to tell, and she was always on the lookout for more. But their wares were quickly forgotten when she noticed the leaflet in Thomas's hand. It was the image that had caught her attention, or rather, the melding of images. She recognised the symbol of the Triple Goddess—she'd had a passing interest in all things Wicca since her early teens—but the deer skull sitting inside the full moon, its antlers covered in vines, was not meant to be there. Did it represent the Horned God, the male Wiccan deity? His symbol was a full moon with a crescent moon lying on top, pointing upwards.

Perhaps the deer skull was more for aesthetics. Or perhaps it pointed to something older than Wicca, something ancient. Either way, Summer had been intrigued.

Now, she was in the back seat of the SUV, beads of perspiration gathering on her brow and the nape of her neck. They had been driving along the A30 for some time, passing villages and hamlets, cornfields and giant wind turbines that loomed over the countryside like alien sentinels. With every mile they drove, the land grew more remote, until they were passing through a vast expanse of rocky moorland.

Summer turned to Thomas, who was sitting next to her. None of the men had spoken much since they'd climbed into the vehicle, which made Summer nervous.

'How long till we get there?' she asked.

'It's not far now.' Thomas's voice was warm and soothing, and laced with a smile. 'Try not to worry. It will be worth the wait when we get there. You'll see.'

Summer nodded, but the churning of her stomach did not relent. Thomas had promised her a place to stay for a few days, somewhere safe and welcoming, where she could bathe and sleep in a clean bed, where she would be well fed and even given new clothes if she wanted them. Theirs was a peaceful commune, Thomas told her, that rejected societal expectations and the fascist state, choosing instead to live peacefully together, where all were equal and none were forgotten.

To Summer, the commune sounded like a bohemian haven, one that aligned with her own anti-authority stance. People in power had never done anything good for her. People in power only helped themselves. Summer had learned that the hard way, after finding herself on the streets on her sixteenth birthday. Her stepfather, a despicably cruel man who had sexually assaulted her on a daily basis for two years, had drunk an extra bottle of vodka in celebration of her coming of age. Rather than render him useless, the alcohol had served to fuel his frenzy. For the first time since it had all begun, Summer had screamed for help, alerting not only her alcoholic mother, who was semi-conscious in the adjacent room, but their next door neighbour.

Police were called and Summer's stepfather was arrested. And what thanks did Summer get for eliminating such an odious excuse for a man, once social services had retreated and left her alone with her mother? A vicious slap to the face, bejewelled rings turned a hundred and eighty degrees so they would tear her delicate skin. Because it was Summer's fault that her mother's marriage was now in ruins. Summer's fault that her stepfather had repeatedly assaulted her—because why else would he have done it if she hadn't tempted him in the first place? And it was Summer's fault that her mother was to end up alone. Because on the night of her sixteenth birthday, she packed a bag, stole the meagre roll of banknotes her mother kept hidden under her bed, set fire to the kitchen, then walked out of the house and never looked back.

She'd been drifting through life ever since. At first she'd slept on friends' couches, until their parents became overly concerned and began making noises about calling her mother. So she began to travel, at first hitching rides through her native Scotland, touring its many parks and sleeping on its benches. When she was done with Scotland, she moved onto north England, then Wales, living off the kindness of strangers, and sometimes the cruelty. Eventually, she found herself in Cornwall. But still she found no place to settle; a place where she might finally rid herself of the rancid stench and taste of her stepfather.

Was this commune the haven she'd been searching for? Her sanctuary? She was attracted to its ideology and they clearly had an interest in paganism and Wicca. And she had met people like this before: carefree individuals or small groups who chose to live outside of society, swapping the laws of an oppressive government for the laws of nature. She had felt a connection with those wandering spirits she had previously met. Perhaps she would feel the same with the people of this commune.

But what of these young men with whom she was currently travelling? Did she feel that same connection with them? She wasn't so sure. Perhaps it was the plain clothing they wore, which was clearly handmade. Their simplicity suggested modest living. In all things Wicca, the colour grey represented neutrality and balance, maturity and wisdom. But with all three men in the same outfit, it was almost as if they were wearing a uniform—and Wicca was about fostering individuality, about following your own path, not the paths of others.

Something about these young men didn't quite fit with how Summer envisioned this community to be. Or perhaps, she was being overly cautious, and rightly so. It didn't matter how street-wise or hardened she had become, she was still a woman travelling to an unspecified place with three men whom she had only recently met and knew very little about.

She peered at Thomas, who had returned to staring out of the window, his hands resting neatly on his lap. Sitting in the front passenger seat was Matthew, who was perhaps a year or two younger than Summer, and had a nervous energy about him that was not present in the others. Driving the vehicle was Kane. Summer was wary of him in particular—he had not spoken a word since she had encountered the three of them in the street.

Summer drew in a breath and slowly let it out. The heat in the vehicle was becoming uncomfortable. Outside, the sun shone down over the increasingly remote terrain. There was still plenty of traffic on the road, which offered Summer a little comfort. If it came to it, all she had to do was hammer on the window and scream, or even kick her foot through the glass.

Or maybe she was overthinking it all. If these boys—she couldn't really think of them as men—were lying, they were weaving a particularly elaborate tale. Besides, people surely would have seen the pretty young woman with red hair climb into the back of an SUV, then disappear with three men in grey.

But if Thomas was telling the truth, if the community was a real place, then perhaps Summer would stay with them for a few days and enjoy their hospitality. She had been sleeping rough for too long now, and the constant aches and pains that plagued her were warning signs her body had grown tired of it. Maybe this commune, if it was real, would see her as a like-minded individual and invite her to stay.

Behind the wheel, Kane shifted gears and changed lanes. Then they were leaving the A30 behind, along with its traffic, and heading down a narrow B road, which dipped sharply before quickly beginning to rise. They were heading deeper into a vast expanse of granite moorland, which, to Summer, looked like a desolate alien landscape filled with threat. Large rocky outcrops rose up in the distance, overlooking rolling swathes of gorse and heather. There were no towns, no villages, no people. A weary traveller could easily get lost out here, especially when fog descended. One wrong turn, and that would be the end of you. Even the current glorious weather did little to warm the place.

Summer wasn't completely familiar with the Cornish land-scape, but she thought this place might be Bodmin Moor. And the only two things she knew about Bodmin Moor was that Jamaica Inn could be found here, made famous by the writer Daphne Du Maurier, and that a terrifying beast was said to stalk the land, attacking livestock and chasing unsuspecting hikers. There had been several sightings of it over the years, a hulking black cat with sabre-like fangs. When Summer had first heard the tale, she thought it was nothing more than a silly story—every county in England laid claim to its very own beast. But now, staring out of the window, the moors closing in on all sides, she could believe the beast was very real and was watching her from its hiding place.

Kane turned the wheel, manoeuvring the vehicle onto a winding dirt track. Still, they continued to climb, tyres running in and out of potholes, bodies being thrown from side to side. Fear wrapped icy fingers around Summer's windpipe.

This was a mistake. What the hell had she been thinking?

She glanced at Thomas, who smiled at her, his chestnut eyes conveying nothing but warmth.

'Not long now,' he said.

But despite his outward benevolence, there was something sinister about those words.

Kane turned the wheel again, and now they were leaving the dirt track and driving off-road, on the moorland, the terrain so rough that Summer had to hold on to the door handle for balance.

Something was wrong. She sensed it in her gut, in the voice

pleading with her to escape. But how could she escape? Did she throw herself from a moving vehicle, hope she didn't smash her head on a rock, then run for her life? To where? They were in the middle of nowhere. Besides, on this terrain, no matter how fast she ran, they could easily catch up to her in the SUV.

The alternative was to continue on. To reach their destination and see what happened. Because, either way, if these men were going to hurt Summer, they were going to hurt her whether or not she tried to run.

She leaned back against the seat and shut her eyes, sucking in a breath and steadily expelling it. There was no choice but to see the journey through. But if these men tried to hurt her, she would do her utmost to hurt them back. She had learned a long time ago what boys wanted, and how to manipulate them through their want. She kept a pocketknife in her bag for such times, and she was not afraid to use it to protect herself. She had done so before.

The vehicle continued to climb, gears grinding, engine roaring in Summer's ears. A minute later, it passed a tree that stood alone on the hillside, growing at warped angles, like a crooked old man reaching for the clouds. In the near distance on the right, a body of water shimmered in the sunlight, its mirror-like surface reflecting the blue sky.

The vehicle reached the top of the hill, then was over it and bouncing along uneven ground. There, in the distance, over-looking the moorlands and flanked by woodland, was a huddle of single-storey buildings.

Leaning over for a better view, Summer peered between the front seats. She could see at least five dwellings of various sizes, all surrounded by a tall chain-link fence. Perhaps the men had not been lying after all.

Intrigued now, she leaned further forward. As they drew closer, she saw the buildings were in fact log cabins with flat roofs and crooked chimneys, just like the fairy tale ones she had dreamed of living in as a child. And as the front gates slowly swung open and Kane steered the vehicle through, Summer saw people. Men, women, and even children. They did not wear grey like her three chaperones. They wore the colours of the forest.

She turned to Thomas, who smiled serenely.

'Welcome to Fortunate Keep,' he said. 'Our home.'

13

Stepping out of the SUV, Summer slung her bag over her shoulder and stared in awe at her surroundings. Only moments ago she had convinced herself that Thomas and the others had driven her to the middle of nowhere to rape and kill her. But they had been telling the truth all along. Before her was a scene like an illustration from school history books, a snapshot taken long before technology came along and changed the world forever. There were at least twenty people of varying ages standing in front of her, all eyes turned in her direction. Some regarded her with curiosity, others with welcoming smiles. A few with overt wariness. For a long time, no one moved, as if someone had pressed a pause button on the world. Then, one by one, the people began to return to their business.

Thomas and Matthew hopped out of the vehicle and stood next to Summer. Kane drove away, following the perimeter of the fence before disappearing behind the wooden dwellings.

'Try not to worry,' said Thomas. 'It's been a while since we've had a guest. Everyone is wondering who you are.'

Beside him, Matthew let out a contented sigh. 'When I first arrived, I was scared of everyone and everything. But Fortunate Keep taught me that to be afraid was to be a prisoner. No one will hurt you here. It's a safe space for all.'

'Then why the fence?' Summer's eyes were still glued to the people, who were no longer paying her any attention. Some were busy working in the large vegetable garden located on her far left, where an abundance of corn, potatoes, and squashes grew, while on her right a group of men worked to replace a broken wheel on an upturned cart.

'The fence is to protect us from the outside world,' Thomas explained. 'We may be remote here, but there are always others wanting to do us harm. Some people wish to destroy what they fear, or what they perceive as outside of the law.'

Summer glanced at him. 'What do you mean by "outside of the law"?'

'Nothing special. It sadly comes down to capitalism and the demand that we all pay taxes, even though it goes straight into the pockets of the people in power. People hate to see us living so freely, refusing to follow the rules when they can't help but comply.' Thomas reached out and lightly touched her arm. 'Come on, let me show you around.'

Leaving Matthew to join the men fixing the cart, Thomas began a slow walk, with Summer next to him. As they moved, she eyed the cabins, which were simple constructions of varying sizes with flat roofs and metal chimneys. At the centre of the compound was a much bigger barn-shaped building, which had a pointed roof and two large doors at the front. The air here was cool, and a gentle breeze teased the leaves of the surrounding woodland. The sound of a barking dog caught Summer's attention. She turned to her right and saw a couple of young children running barefoot on the ground, with a small terrier playfully dancing around them.

'That big building you see in the centre, that's the meeting house,' Thomas said. 'It's the beating heart of Fortunate Keep, where we all gather to give thanks each evening before dinner. The building on its right is the kitchen and dining hall. But if the weather is as good as it is today, we like to eat outside. We grow our own food, mostly. There's no electricity here—not yet, anyway —so our cook, Melissa, has to make do with bottled gas and a simple stove. Which means you won't eat fancily here, but you will eat well.'

No electricity. Summer wondered what it was like here when darkness fell. With no towns or villages for miles around, there would be no light pollution, which meant a night as pitch black as it could get, with thousands upon thousands of shimmering stars. She couldn't wait to see it.

'On your left is the medical room,' Thomas continued. 'We were blessed to have a doctor, but she recently passed, which leaves us in a bind. Accidents are rare here, but they do happen from time to time, especially among the carpenters. After all, blades have to be kept sharp.'

'How did the doctor die?'

'She was elderly and fell ill.'

'Did you take her to the hospital?'

'She refused to go. It's not anyone's place here to force someone to do something against their will. There are many like the doctor here, who, once they've made Fortunate Keep their home, do not wish to leave again. They've already rejected society, so why would they ever want to go back?'

'Not even when they're sick?'

'Not even when they're sick.'

Summer watched the children playing with the dog and wondered what would happen to them if they fell ill beyond the usual childhood coughs and colds.

'What about you then? And Matthew and Kane. You go out.'

'That's because we have a role to fulfil. We may be self-suffi-cient here, but we still need money to buy occasional supplies. So the women make bracelets and pendants, sometimes scarves and purses, and we go out to sell them. We don't make a lot of money, but it's enough to cover any additional expenses for things we can't produce ourselves here.'

'Why do you go out and sell them and not the women?'

'Because we've been tasked with it.'

'And the leaflets? What are they about?'

'You ask a lot of questions.'

'You've brought me to a curious place.'

'That's fair,' Thomas said, smiling. 'Well, to answer your ques-tion, as a community we believe in sharing our vision of utopia, so we hand out leaflets containing our ideas. Most people discard them because they're slaves to capitalism, so a better way of living is impossible for them to perceive. But once in a while, one of our leaflets will fall into the hands of a like-minded person who's looking for a way out of an uncaring world. A person who is searching for salvation. For a place like Fortunate Keep. A person like you.'

Thomas smiled again and pressed on.

Summer was still in awe of the community that had been created here. She wondered how it had come together, away from the prying eyes of authority figures.

'Here is the women's bath house,' said Thomas, pointing to one of the outbuildings. 'The one next to it is where the women sleep. The men's quarters are on the other side of the compound.'

Summer stopped walking. 'Men and women sleep separately? What about relationships? And the children you have here?'

'All in good time. Come on, we're going to be late.'

'For what?'

They reached the rear end of the compound, which housed three small paddocks containing pigs, sheep and goats. Animal shelters made of wood and corrugated iron lined one side, while three vehicles were parked on the other, including the SUV that had ferried Summer to Fortunate Keep.

Over in the far left corner, next to the fence perimeter was a narrow, windowless building with a sloping roof that seemed to disappear into the ground. On the other side of the fence was dense woodland populated by towering pine trees, which served to seal this side of Fortunate Keep from prying eyes.

Thomas walked past the paddocks, where a teenage boy and an older man were busy feeding the livestock. Summer followed him, making eye contact with the boy, who quickly turned away, before turning her attention at the oddly-shaped building in the distance.

'What's in there?' she asked.

'Nothing of interest. Tools and supplies.'

They had reached the final stop of the tour, a large log cabin that was more elaborately built than the others, with pots of flowers lining the porch and lacy curtains in the windows. It was also the only cabin with a second floor.

'Here we are,' Thomas said, coming to a standstill at the foot of the porch steps. 'This is Mother and Father's house. Mother is waiting for you inside.'

Summer looked up at the cabin, a sudden fluttering in her stomach leaving her uneasy.

'Who are Mother and Father?'

'They are who their names say they are.' Thomas watched her for a second, a strange expression on his face. He nodded towards the steps. 'Go on. You'll find Mother in the kitchen.'

'You're not coming in?'

Thomas shook his head. 'Only those invited are permitted. I'll see you at dinner. Oh, and take off your shoes before you go in.'

She thought he would leave then, but he remained, standing at the foot of the steps like a sentry.

The fluttering in Summer's stomach grew stronger. Slowly, she removed her shoes, which were holey and worn, the soles flapping like bird beaks. Then she began to ascend the stairs, towards the cabin. Towards Mother and Father's house.

14

Mary and Ed Hollow lived in a detached property that was surrounded by half an acre of land and a ten-minute drive from Wheal Marow. It was there that Blake had spent her formative years with her parents and younger brother, Alfie, slowly drowning in small town banality while dreaming of escape. When she had lived in Manchester, her visits to her parents had been infrequent at best. Since her return to Cornwall, Blake had been trying to visit her parents once a week—"trying" being the operative word. Her tumultuous relationship with her father had improved somewhat, but she still couldn't tell if it was all a facade. Seeing him on a regular basis sometimes proved too much, never allowing time for wounds to scab over, let alone heal. And then there was her job. The hours were sometimes long and often unsociable. And when she was chasing a lead nothing else mattered, even weekly dinners with her parents.

After saying goodbye to Tegan that morning, Blake had spent much of the day researching cults and organisations who used Wicca symbology. Tegan had been right, the list was long, including the neo-Nazi satanic terrorist group, Order of Nine Angles; the esoteric Egyptian god worshipping Temple of Set; the Family International; Heaven's Gate; the Solar Temple; and a wealth of unhinged individuals, the most infamous being Charles Manson and his psychotic "family". It seemed that none of these groups actively followed the Wicca religion, rather they used the symbology to either create an air of mystery or as bait to reel in new members. Either way, it was pure appropriation, nothing more.

None of Blake's research had made her feel better about the missing twins' safety. Yet, she knew her theorising was based on nothing but circumstance and educated guesswork. She needed much more than that if she was going to present a case to Owen Teague and Bronwen Lander on Thursday.

Now, she sat at her parents' dining table, Mary at one end, Ed at the other, picking at the lasagne her mother had made and drifting in and out of the conversation, although it was more of a monologue on her mother's part. Ed had never been one for talk, although he was trying more since he and Mary were back together, and Blake had decided to give her relationship with him one last try.

'How's the house, bird?' he asked her, as she sat with her elbows on the table and a forkful of pasta poised in the air.

It was strange that he would ask after Blake's house and not her own well-being. But that was Ed Hollow, rough around the edges and awkward as hell.

'The house is fine.'

'Anything need fixing?'

'Just those loose stair railings, but the letting agency said they're going to send someone out.'

'I could fix that for you,' Ed said. 'Wouldn't take more than a little while.'

'It's their responsibility, Dad. It's what they get paid to do.'

'Oh, right. But when will they do it? That's the question. Those railings have been loose for months. It's an accident waiting to happen.'

Blake looked away and stabbed more lasagne with her fork. Her father was always trying to find ways to help lately. Her mother would say it was Ed's way of showing Blake that he loved her. But all Blake saw was a man desperately trying to seek forgiveness from his unforgiving daughter.

Blake was trying, she really was. But she had come to the conclusion that she could perhaps try to forget Ed's past infidelities with her best friend, but she could never forgive him. Not when his actions had led to such devastating consequences.

Whether that meant her relationship with her father would get no better than it was now, Blake didn't know. Part of her was no longer sure if she cared. But she would still try.

She glanced at her mother, who returned her gaze with arched eyebrows. Blake heaved her shoulders.

'Fine,' she said, not looking at Ed. 'If they haven't got back to me by Friday, come over at the weekend and fix the railings.'

Her father nodded, the slightest of smiles tugging at his mouth.

'I do worry about you out there on your own, bird,' Mary said.

Blake rolled her eyes. This again. 'Really? I didn't know that. I must have not been listening the first three hundred times you told me.'

'There's no need for sarcasm, my girl. I'm allowed to worry about my daughter. It's my job.'

'Then I have some great news for you. You've almost reached retirement age.'

'You cheeky bugger!'

Mary shook her head and took a sip of water. At the other end of the table, Ed was doing a poor job of hiding his amusement.

'I'm fine, Mum,' Blake said. 'Seriously, stop worrying. You know I can take care of myself. Besides, it's not like I'm living in the middle of nowhere like you make me out to be. I'm a mile outside of Falmouth.'

'Well, it feels like the middle of nowhere. There's nothing but fields and trees and lakes.'

'Yes, but there's also a road that takes me straight into town. No one is hiding in the bushes. Jason Vorhees isn't lurking in the reservoir, waiting to drag me down into its depths. So, can we please stop with the broken record and let me enjoy this delicious lasagne you've made?'

Mary shrugged and let out a heavy sigh. Ed had returned to shovelling pasta down his throat. Quiet resumed for a while. But it never lasted in the Hollow household.

'How was your weekend?' Mary asked, as she refilled her glass with water from a jug. 'A little bird told me you and Kenver went to Bournemouth.'

'Did they now?' Blake said. 'And I suppose that little bird was Aunt Hester.'

'Did you have fun?'

'It was a work thing, we weren't there to party. And no, before you ask, Kenver didn't touch a drop of alcohol. You can tell that to Auntie Hester when you next see her.'

Ed wiped his lips with the back of his hand. 'That boy's been nothing but trouble ever since he came back from London.'

'I hardly think that's true, Dad. Or fair. Besides, you have no idea what's going on with him.'

'Nothing good, I bet.'

'You just don't like him because he doesn't fit into how you think a man should be. Men are allowed to have emotions now, Dad. It's perfectly legal.'

Mary cleared her throat. 'Right. Well, that's good he stayed sober, isn't it? Good for Kenver. And your Aunt Hester is only looking out for him. It can't be easy having a, well, you know, a son with . . . who likes to drink one too many now and then.'

'You mean an alcoholic, Mum.'

'No, no. I didn't say that. That's you putting words into my mouth. Kenver just likes a drink and sometimes it gets him into trouble. That's all it is.'

Blake stared at her half-eaten food, her appetite suddenly gone. The problem with her family was that when it came to difficult matters, no one could ever say what they were truly thinking. A problem had to be handled in a roundabout fashion, poking and prodding at it with a stick, or watering it down into something more soluble, or even sometimes pretending the problem didn't exist. It frustrated Blake, who had always believed the fastest way to solve a problem was to tackle it head on. It was the same when it came to sensitive topics that caused discomfort for the family, such as Kenver's over-dependence on alcohol. It was easier to blame him for causing upset and embarrassment than to try to understand why his drinking had got out of control in the first place.

'Kenver does have a problem with alcohol,' Blake said, staring at her parents. 'Whether that means he's an alcoholic, I don't know. All I do know is that he didn't touch a drop all weekend, even though I could see he wanted to. He's trying his best, and we should be celebrating that, and supporting him every step of the way. Because whether you choose to believe it or not, alcohol addiction is a disease. You should both treat it like one.'

Quiet fell over the room, as it always did when Blake barrelled into a family issue that her parents did not want to discuss. Her thoughts returned to Morgan and Sandy Teague, and her distinct lack of leads. All she had was the Wiccan imagery, but even that trail had gone cold; her afternoon's research had failed to reveal any group, occult or otherwise, that merged the imagery of the Triple Goddess and the Horned God.

Mary cleared her throat. 'So what are you working on now, bird? Anything interesting?'

'Do you remember the disappearance of Morgan and Sandy Teague?' said Blake. 'Twelve-year-old twins from about eight years ago. They went missing from a park near their home in Newquay.'

Ed frowned and shook his head. Mary pursed her lips.

'Sounds familiar,' she said. Then her eyes lit up. 'Oh, yes. Aren't they the twins who got taken by that cult? The ones responsible for that terrible business down at Devil's Cove.'

"Terrible business" was an incredibly polite way to describe mass murder, Blake thought. 'There's no evidence the twins were in Devil's Cove that day, but yes, they were taken by the Dawn Children cult.'

'They were probably brainwashed, poor things. Where were their parents when they were taken from the park? That's what I'd like to know.' Mary tutted. 'Is that what you're working on right now? Looking into their disappearance?'

Blake nodded but disclosed nothing more.

'Well, you be careful,' Mary warned, as Blake got up to clear the plates. 'Messing about with weirdos and cults sounds like dangerous work to me. Even if those kids weren't involved with Devil's Cove, they'll be adults now. Who knows what's been done to them, or what they've become.'

'That's if they're still alive,' Ed, ever the optimist, added. He eyed the pile of dishes Blake was amassing. 'I'll give you a hand washing up.'

Usually, Blake would accept the offer; Ed helping around the house was a rare occurrence. But this evening, Blake was not in the mood to conduct awkward conversation with her father.

'Don't worry, it's fine.'

As she carried the dishes to the kitchen and began filling the sink with hot water—the only dishwasher her mother had faith in was the human kind—she glanced at the calendar hanging on the wall. It was Monday evening. She would be meeting Owen Teague and Bronwen Lander at 11 AM on Thursday morning, which left just two full days to give them something palpable. Blake knew they had only asked her to try, but she also knew they wanted so much more than that. Of course they did. They wanted her to find their children and bring them home. The only problem was Blake didn't think she could do that, no matter how hard she tried.

As soon as she was back in her office she would chase up her CCTV request made to the police. Beyond that, there was the twins' link to the Dawn Children, followed by the massacre at Devil's Cove. The last time anyone had seen Morgan and Sandy Teague together was at the park in Newquay, where they had encountered Heath Monk and other alleged members of the Dawn Children. Then they had vanished from the face of the earth. Until five years later, when Bronwen Lander received a one-word phone call from her son.

Blake shoved the dishes into the sink of hot water. The heat scalded her fingers. Two more days. She eyed her mobile phone lying on the kitchen counter. There was one person who might be able to shed some light on the Dawn Children cult and what happened at Devil's Cove. Whether he would be able to help find the twins was another matter. Nevertheless, it was time to talk to Detective Sergeant Will Turner.

15

She had been expecting the interior of the cabin to be rustic and minimalist, thrown together from rickety furniture and threadbare carpets. But to Summer's surprise, the cabin was comfortably furnished, and was aesthetically pleasing. Despite its outward appearance of having two floors, the cabin had only one, with a high ceiling and several exposed rafters that gave the room a grand, airy feel. The extra windows higher up let in an abundance of light, illuminating motes of dancing dust particles.

Covering the floor was a large red and gold Persian rug, patterned with fine lines and intricate symmetrical designs of leaves and delicate petals. It was clearly expensive; Summer could feel her bare toes sinking into its lavishness. On top of the rug was a beautifully crafted coffee table, with plush sofas and armchairs positioned on either side. At the far end was a large fireplace with a stone hearth. It was currently unlit, but Summer imagined that when winter came around, which would be especially cruel in a place as remote and barren as this, the fire would keep this house warm and safe.

But it was neither the furnishings nor the fireplace that captured Summer's attention the most. It was the huge wooden carving to the right of the hearth. Reaching at least twelve feet tall, the stag stood on its hind legs and looked down upon the world, its sharp snout and probing eyes fixed on Summer. Its front legs hung at its sides, giving it an almost humanoid appearance, while its thorn-like antlers, which were not carved from wood but were very real, pointed up to the heavens.

Her mouth agape, Summer stared at the great beast. It stared back, challenging her to enter. So entranced was Summer that she had not noticed the kitchen on her left, or the woman sitting within.

'It's quite something, isn't it?'

Startled, Summer spun around to face the kitchen, which housed an old coal oven, a sink, and a rectangular table with four hand-carved chairs. The woman sat at the table, slowly pouring tea into a cup from a large teal-coloured pot. Her hair was long and silver, and her skin was weathered. Her cheekbones were high and sharp, her nose aquiline, and her jaw defined. But it was her eyes that captured Summer: grey-green, the colour of a stormy sea on a sunless day.

Summer stared at her, momentarily mesmerised, then back at the stag.

'The Horned God,' she said, quietly.

'Observant. You know your gods.' The woman smiled. Despite her silver hair, Summer found it difficult to age her. She was perhaps in her sixties. Perhaps even older. 'But which Horned God is it?'

'I—I thought there was only one. From Wicca.'

'There are many Horned gods, my dear.' The woman's smile grew wider, with a playful curve to it. 'Even the one you speak of is associated with many different names. Cernunnos; Pan; Pashupati;

Gwynn ap Nudd; to name but a few. Here, we simply like to think of Him as the Horned One, Guardian of the Realm, our protector who watches over us from the depths of His forest. He blesses us with the food on our tables and the clothes on our back, and the fires in the hearth come winter. He is a God of many, but the only one we revere.' The woman peered up at the towering stag and let out a contented sigh. 'Or you could say it's a wonderful piece of artistry created by one of our local carpenters, inspired by myth and legend. It all depends on your perspective.'

She leaned forward, beckoning Summer to the table. 'Come, sit and have tea with me.'

Summer padded across the Persian rug and entered the kitchen, where she slid into a chair opposite the woman. Her bag was still slung over her shoulder, but a look from her host encouraged her to put it on the floor.

'Around here, I'm known as Mother,' the woman said, pouring tea into a cup. 'What do we call you, child?'

'Summer.'

Mother smiled warmly as she set the pot down, then carefully slid the cup across the table. 'A beautiful name, and aptly chosen. I can see the light radiating within you, and the warmth.'

Summer peered cautiously into the cup, which held a light gold liquid, unlike any tea she had seen before.

'Go ahead and try it. It's not poison, just a little lemon balm.' As if to show her guest that the tea was safe to drink, Mother brought her own cup to her lips. 'It has a calming nature. I enjoy it most days.'

Summer tasted the tea. It was a little bitter but not unpleasant. She thanked Mother for her hospitality, who stared at her closely, like an entomologist analysing a new species of bug. Summer looked away.

'You've been on the road a long time despite your age. How

long has it been now? Four, maybe five years?' The shock on Summer's face made Mother chuckle. 'It's not magic or psychic ability. It's simply age and wisdom. When you're as old as I am, you can read people from all walks of life.'

'It's been five years,' Summer said blankly. 'I ran away on my sixteenth birthday.'

'It hurts my heart to hear that. What was it? Abuse?'

'Something like that.'

'And there were no friends and family to take you in?'

'No family. None that I know of anyway. And when you move around a lot, friendships are temporary.'

'It's not right for a girl your age to have no one to turn to. You've never tried to settle anywhere?'

'I've tried. But I've yet to find the right place.'

Mother drank more tea. 'Well, perhaps you'll find it here.'

'Oh. No. I mean, thank you for the offer, but I've been thinking about moving on again. I'm not sure Cornwall is the place for me either.'

'That may be true,' Mother said. Her face had grown serious, the lines around her eyes and on her forehead carving deeper into her flesh. 'But the hard truth is that you can travel the world three times over and it won't mean a damn thing when there's a black dog on your heels, following you no matter where you go. And it will never leave you. Not until you find the courage to turn around and confront it.'

The seat on which Summer sat was growing uncomfortable, the hard wood pressing into her buttocks. She didn't like it when people spoke in riddles, yet she knew exactly what the woman was talking about. That black dog had been following her around for years now. It was why she had moved from town to town, trying to lose it. But she never could. Because that black dog was a part of her. It lived in the darkest recesses of her mind, and it was fiercely loyal. It would never leave her, not even in a place like this. She stared at Mother, who stared right back, her mesmerising grey-green eyes unblinking.

'Do you know why they call me Mother?' she asked.

Summer shook her head.

'Because nearly all of the people who come here have been let down by their own. Whether it was through violence, complicity, rejection, or an inability to love, their mothers no longer wanted them. But I want them. And I love each one of our family as if they were my own children. I give them what their biological mothers never could. I pour into them love and compassion, warmth and understanding. Forgiveness and humility. I bring them happiness. I open them up to love again. It is what the Horned God commands of me, and I am His humble servant.

'I can tell you've been failed by your mother. I saw it as soon as you entered my home. It's in the sadness of your eyes. In the way you flinch at the very word. And I'm sorry for it. This is a cruel world that we live in, Summer, populated by cruel people who only care for their own gain. Fortunate Keep is a circle of protection from that world, for those who desire to leave its cruelty behind. It's nothing more than that. Nothing less. Fortunate Keep is what you make of it. Whether you choose to stay for a few days or a lifetime, please treat it as your home. And let me love you like a mother should, even if for a short while.'

Mother looked towards the open front door, where two girls in their young teens had appeared. Both were barefoot and wore sleeveless dresses and their long hair in braids.

Summer stared at them, surprised at their presence. She had not heard their approach.

'Stay as long as you need to,' Mother told her. 'But at least stay long enough to put some meat on those scrawny bones. If you feel the need to leave after a while, Thomas will take you back into town. All we ask of you is that you never tell anyone of this place. It's sacred to us. We decide who we let in and who we let go.' For the briefest of moments, lightning flashed in Mother's eyes. Then they were calm again. She smiled. 'But I'm hoping you'll stay. I think you'll be good for us.'

Summer finished her tea, which she decided she liked, after all, then found herself staring at the young women once more.

'Jenny and Joni will take you to the bath house, where you can bathe and wash your clothes,' Mother said. 'We'll eat soon, once we've had our daily meeting. You'll meet Father then. I know he's very eager to meet you.' She turned to Jenny and Joni, who were waiting patiently in the doorway. 'You'll take good care of our new guest, won't you? She needs gentleness and tact.'

Jenny and Joni nodded in unison. 'Yes, Mother. Of course, Mother '

'Off you go then.'

Mother gave Summer one last smile, then promptly stood and left the kitchen, crossing the living room to disappear through a doorway on the far right.

Summer remained seated, feeling overwhelmed and slightly perturbed. What was this place? Why show such kindness to strangers? She twisted around in the chair, staring at the empty doorway through which Mother had disappeared. She had not given Summer a chance to properly thank her.

Jenny and Joni were waiting, smiling at Summer in a way that unsettled her, like the creepy twins from *The Shining*. Reminding herself to be grateful, she reached down to pick up her bag, then got up and walked towards the young girls. Despite the heat, a bath sounded like a wonderful idea. It had been a long time since she'd thoroughly cleaned herself. And now that the idea of dinner had been impressed upon her, Summer could think of nothing but filling her stomach. She couldn't remember the last time she had eaten a cooked meal, or one that hadn't been a stale sandwich or a half-eaten burger pulled from a waste bin. But she would eat tonight. And she would eat well.

She reached Jenny and Joni, who held out their hands and beamed. Surprising herself, Summer took them in her own and allowed them to lead her away.

16

Detective Sergeant Will Turner was in his late forties, with dark hair that was starting to go grey, and brown eyes that were haunted by ghosts. He was above average height, conventionally good-looking, and wore navy trousers and a pale blue shirt with the sleeves rolled up to his elbows. His usual tie was absent that Monday evening, and the top button of his shirt was undone. He looked exhausted. But then, Will Turner always did.

Transferred to Devon and Cornwall Police after several years of working as a detective constable for the London Metropolitan, Turner had earned himself a long overdue promotion thanks in part to his bravery during the Devil's Cove massacre. He had been a hero that day, risking his own life to save a young girl from certain death.

Blake met him outside Truro police station, a drab brown brick building that could have been mistaken for a block of flats, if not for the signage outside. It was 6:30 PM. The sky was still blue, the air balmy with a pleasant breeze. Turner did not seem happy to see

Blake. Then again, he never did. At least this time their meeting had been prearranged.

'Turner,' Blake said, with a nod. She was leaning against the front of the building, hands inside her jeans pockets. 'I'm not used to seeing you without a tie. You almost look like a civilian. Almost.'

'Whereas you never look anything but,' the detective sergeant said with a dry smile. He paused to observe the street, which was quiet and free of conspicuous characters, if he ignored Blake's presence. 'You're lucky you caught me with time on my hands at such short notice. It's a rare thing these days.'

He stood, uncomfortably swaying on his feet, as if he wanted nothing more than to go home and sleep for three days.

'In that case, we should celebrate,' said Blake. 'Drink?'

'No, thank you. I wouldn't want you to get the wrong idea. Victoria Gardens is around the corner. Let's go for a walk.'

Blake smiled as she pushed herself off the wall. 'How romantic. I thought you didn't want me to get the wrong idea.'

'I should arrest you for loitering.'

Victoria Gardens was a five-minute walk from the police station. Situated near the city centre, the park was established in 1898 to commemorate Queen Victoria's Diamond Jubilee. Victorian in design, it featured many exotic plants and trees, water features, and winding paths, with a bandstand at its centre that was still in use today.

'Do you come here often?' Blake asked Turner, as they passed a bench filled with teenagers playing loud music on their phones.

Turner eyed them with disdain but let them be. 'When I have a free minute. I like nature. It helps to clear my head. By the way, the next time you want to talk to me about a professional matter, try asking me rather than going through Detective Constable Angove.'

Blake shrugged. 'It seemed like the easiest route. Rory is your partner, after all. Besides, I figured if I asked you directly, you would have said no. I know you don't think much of me.'

'That's not true. My opinion of you has changed somewhat over the last year. Although I'd still very much like you to keep your nose out of police business as much as humanly possible.'

'I'm flattered, Turner. And let the defence show that our paths haven't crossed for almost six months now.'

'Must be a new record. So, Rory said you wanted to talk to me about Sandy and Morgan Teague. I didn't work on that case. You're better off talking to Detective Inspector Jackie Hosken. I can put you in touch, but it's unlikely you'll learn anything more than you have from the reports. Which I suppose means you want to talk to me about the twins' involvement with the Dawn Children.'

Despite the brightness of the evening, a dark shadow fell across Turner's face. The path turned a corner and they came upon a pond with a fountain. Turner paused, staring at the cascading water, which was cast in a warm hue by the evening sunlight. Beneath the pond's surface, goldfish of various colours and sizes ducked and weaved beneath a network of lily pads. The air was heavy with the smell of cut grass.

'I know it's a difficult subject for you. One you don't like to talk about,' Blake said. 'But I do have to ask.'

The detective sergeant glanced at her over his shoulder. 'Remind me to reprimand DC Angove when I next see him.'

'The only reason he said anything to me was because he cares about you. He respects you. Rory's a good man.'

'If he's such a good man why haven't the pair of you resolved your issues and got together already, instead of subjecting the rest of us to this continual and, might I add, exhausting, back-and-forth?'

Blake's jaw dropped. For once, she was speechless.

'You and Rory aren't the only ones who talk,' Turner said with a wry smile.

'Well, for your information, Rory and I have resolved our issues, as he well knows. They're just not resolved in the way he wants.'

'You may need to explain that to him again.' Turner continued walking. 'Ask your questions.'

Blake caught up to him. 'What do you know about the Teague twins' abduction by the Dawn Children cult?'

'About as much as you do. I told you, it wasn't my case. All I know is that Morgan and Sandy Teague were accosted by Heath Monk and were never seen again. At a guess I'd say their involvement was voluntary at the time. It was how the cult worked. Send out young recruiters, promise all sorts of exciting things to vulnerable children in a bid to get them to follow. Once they had them, the brainwashing would begin.

'We never found out exactly how it all worked, but with Lindsay Church, the girl I rescued, she told us she was locked in a dark room for days and deprived of food and water. When they did feed her, the food was laced with what we believe were hallucinogens. But Lindsay was different from the Teague twins.'

'Different how?'

'For a start, the Dawn Children invaded her home, slaughtered her family in front of her, then abducted her. But she wasn't the reason the Dawn Children killed her family. The year before, her father had been found not guilty of killing three young siblings with his car. The Dawn Children disagreed with the courts and took it upon themselves to see justice served.

'You see, their modus operandi was to protect children at all costs from the evils that adults do, even if it meant committing equally atrocious acts of violence themselves.' He paused, staring off into the distance. 'Morgan and Sandy Teague had the utter misfortune of bumping into the Dawn Children in the park. I'm sure that once it was learned they were suffering the ills of their parents' unhappy marriage, the Dawn Children saw them as potential new recruits for their cause.'

'And Heath Monk. He was the cult leader?'

'Not at first. We believe the original leader was an older man named Jacob. We still don't know much about him, only that he vanished one day, leaving the cult vulnerable and alone. Heath Monk, who until then had been Jacob's right-hand man, and a vicious son of a bitch, stepped up to the role. We believe it was Monk who was behind the massacre at Devil's Cove. According to some of the cult members we arrested, it was an act of revenge.'

They reached the central bandstand, which was currently unoccupied. Turner sat down on the steps. Blake joined him.

'An act of revenge against whom?'

'Cal Anderson. I'll assume you've done your research on him.'

Blake said that she had. Cal Anderson was the boy who had come back from the dead. The nine-year-old who had vanished from the beach at Devil's Cove one sunny afternoon, only to return seven years later, traumatised and scarred, both physically and mentally. He had been unable to talk, with psychologists believing his muteness was a direct result of the horrors he had experienced.

It turned out that Cal had been abducted and kept in a cage for seven years by a depraved individual, who had beaten and starved him, slowly chipping away at the boy's humanity, until he resembled little more than a feral creature. Only Cal's mother had been able to bring him back from the brink, to help save him from himself. But not before Cal had taken a life.

The last news stories Blake could find about Cal Anderson

were dated five years ago, and detailed the outcome of his trial. Cal had been found innocent of murder but guilty of manslaughter due to diminished responsibility, and was to remain under the care of a psychiatric facility in Bristol until he was deemed fit to return to society. Blake didn't know if he was still in that hospital or if he was now back with his family, his return kept secret from the media.

'What was Cal's connection to the Dawn Children?' Blake asked Turner. 'And what terrible thing did he do to make them destroy his hometown and everyone in it?'

Turner took a while to answer, as if he was still trying to figure out the reason himself. 'Even after all this time, we're not entirely sure. From talking to other members, we believe that Cal spent time with the Dawn Children at a smallholding called Burnt House Farm—before and after his reappearance. Which means the man who abducted him had a connection to the Dawn Children that we don't know about and maybe never will, seeing as all of the main players are now dead.'

'You know the name of the man who took Cal,' Blake said. 'Why won't you say it?'

'Because he was a killer of children, and I don't want that kind of filth in my mouth.'

Blake thought that was fair enough, especially when the detective had been present at the exhumation of so many tiny bodies.

Turner continued. 'Whatever the explanation for Cal's connection to the Dawn Children, I suspect that Heath Monk hated him. Some of the cult members said Cal was Jacob's favourite, and that Jacob had plans for Cal, that he would lead them all into a New Dawn. Not one of them could tell us what the New Dawn represented, only that it was enlightenment and that they would all be saved.' Turner shook his head. 'It was pure cult mentality, the sheep following the shepherd without ever questioning why.

'Anyway, it's clear from interviewing surviving members that Heath Monk was desperate to be Jacob's favourite, but was rejected at every turn in favour of Cal. Then, when Jacob disappeared, Heath blamed Cal, accusing him of killing the man and poisoning his vision. But by then, Cal was in police custody and Heath couldn't touch him. So instead, he decided to lead the Dawn Children into his own version of the New Dawn, which turned out to be a bloody massacre.'

Turner was trembling slightly, his pupils dilated and downcast. It was clear to Blake that whatever he had been forced to experience that day had left an indelible mark that was likely to stay with him for the rest of his life. She wanted to tell Turner that she was sorry, but she had a feeling her sympathies would not be well received. So she continued with her questions.

'The file on Morgan and Sandy Teague suggests they were there at Devil's Cove that day. It's entirely possible, of course. Especially when we know they were led away by Heath Monk and other members of the cult. But there's no proof. Their bodies weren't found among the dead and they weren't arrested. Which means if they were there, they somehow managed to get away. Circumstantial evidence says they ended up in your old neck of the woods.'

'Sandy Teague's charm bracelet, found in East London near the body of Julia King, confirmed member of the Dawn Children cult,' said Turner, as if reading from a police report. Blake stared at him. He shrugged. 'I did my homework before we met. So it's possible the twins were in London. It's also possible that this King woman stole the bracelet from Sandy a long time before.'

'Exactly. Do you see how little I have to go on? Which is why I wanted to ask you a favour.'

Blake expected immediate refusal, but to her surprise, Turner simply said, 'Let me guess, you want to talk to some of the arrested members, see if they remember the twins. I'm told we already did that, and they either didn't know them or refused to say.'

'What about Cal Anderson? Can I talk to him?'

'No.'

'Why not?'

'Because he wouldn't be able to help you.'

Turner got to his feet and began walking away from the bandstand. Blake jumped up and quickly followed him.

'But he may know Morgan and Sandy. He may have been there at the same time. Did anyone ask him?'

'Back then, Cal was so pumped full of drugs that he barely recognised his own mother. And he still wasn't talking. No one asked him about Morgan and Sandy, but that doesn't mean you can.'

'You said he still wasn't talking back then. Does that mean he's talking now? And how would you even know that?'

Turner was irritated, his pace picking up speed. Blake felt a flutter of desperation in her chest; the conversation was coming to a swift end.

'Are you still in touch with the family? Rory told me you were close with them. Maybe you could put me in touch with Cal's mother? Her name's Carrie, isn't it? Carrie Killigrew.'

'No, absolutely not,' Turner said, whirling around. 'Carrie and what's left of her family have been to hell and back, in more ways than you can imagine. You can't just swan in there and drag all this up for them. They're trying to move on with their lives.'

'All I need is fifteen minutes with Cal, just enough to ask about Morgan and Sandy. I know it's a long shot. But their parents have asked me to try. This is their last attempt at finding their children. I can't let even the smallest of chances slip by.' She heaved her shoulders and held out pleading hands. 'I know what it's like to have your entire family torn apart. Maybe not on the same scale as Carrie, but believe me when I say I've been there. I'll be respectful. I'll ask my questions, then I'll leave. I don't want to interrupt their lives any more than I need to. But Bronwen Lander and Owen Teague have a right to know where their children are. To know they're safe and well. To know they're alive. Are we really going to deny them that right?'

Turner walked on in silence. Blake felt a sudden desire to throttle him, but kept her voice cool and calm.

'Please, Will. Could you at least ask? If Cal's mum says no, then I'll walk away and won't trouble you again. But if she says yes, there's a chance Cal may be able to help us find the twins. Do we really want to pass that by? To send their parents to their graves never knowing what happened to their children?'

Turner stood on the path, the setting sun igniting the trees behind him.

'God, you're intolerable,' he said, glowering.

Blake smiled. 'Is that a yes?'

'It's an I'll ask and see what Carrie says. But if she agrees, there's one mandatory condition. I'm coming with you.'

'Why would I need a chaperone? Don't you trust me?'

Turner arched an eyebrow.

'Fine, it's a date,' Blake said. 'I suppose you could even call it our second date.'

'Don't push it, Hollow. I'll call Carrie when I get home. I'll let you know what she says. Oh, and if you see DC Angove before I do, tell him he's fired.'

Blake thanked him, then Turner began walking away.

'One more thing, Detective Sergeant. While you're on the phone, could you give your friends at the police department a call, see if they'll expedite my CCTV access request?'

Turner continued along the path as if he hadn't heard her. The path twisted to the right and vanished behind a copse of silver birch, taking the detective sergeant with it.

Blake stood motionless, thrumming with excitement. She knew the chance of Cal's mother agreeing to let Blake speak with him was slim, but it was still a chance. And a chance, no matter how impossible, was still better than nothing.

17

Unlike Mother and Father's comfortable home, the women's bath house was a crude construct of wooden walls and a stone floor, with five tin baths placed equal distances apart. An open doorway on the right led to a second, smaller room for washing laundry. But there were no washers or dryers here, only more tin baths and primitive instruments such as scrubbing boards and a strange contraption consisting of two large rollers and a handle, which, even upon closer inspection, Summer had no idea what it was for or how to use it.

'It's a wringer,' Jenny had explained. 'For squeezing water out of wet clothes.'

Now, Summer stood before one of the tin bathtubs, which had been filled with water. Bending over, she dipped in her fingers and swirled them around.

'We draw water from the well, but we can only heat so much on the stove,' Jenny said.

Even though they'd arrived at the bath house five minutes ago, she and Joni were showing no signs of leaving.

'It's fine. Thank you.' Lukewarm was exactly what Summer needed on a hot day like this. She glanced at the soap in the dish sitting on the edge of the bathtub, and decided it looked home-made.

Jenny and Joni continued to hover.

'Well, I think I'll take my bath now,' Summer said. 'Should I meet you outside?'

'We need to wash your clothes.' Joni was quietly spoken, and she twitched with nervous energy as she stepped forward and reached for Summer's bag.

Summer held onto it. 'It's fine, I can wash them myself.'

'But Mother says we must do it. It's our duty.'

Joni glanced at Jenny, who nodded in agreement. 'It's true. Mother insists. Please, let us do as she asks.'

Summer heaved her shoulders. Anything to get rid of the Shining twins. Unzipping her bag, she pulled out a handful of clothes and gave them to Joni, who wrinkled her nose.

'Sorry, they haven't been washed in a while.'

Joni stared at Summer's bag. 'Is that it?'

'Yes.'

It wasn't, but it was all Summer was prepared to give them for now.

As if remembering something, Jenny turned and vanished through the open doorway into the laundry room. She returned moments later, a simple green dress draped over her forearm.

'Something for you to wear while you wait for your clothes to dry,' she said, offering the dress to Summer, who stared at it warily, as if she were being asked to handle a snake.

'Is it sleeveless?'

Jenny nodded.

'Thank you, but I'm not wearing that. Dresses aren't my thing.'

'But we must wash all of your clothes. Even the ones you're wearing. Mother has made it quite clear.'

Dipping her hand into her bag once more, Summer rifled around until she produced a pair of jean shorts and a faded yellow T-shirt. She lifted them to her nose and sniffed.

'These'll do.'

'But—'

'I said they're clean enough.'

Jenny opened her mouth to argue, but a warning look from Summer made her shut it again. She stared helplessly at the rejected dress, then at Joni, who shrugged. Even though they now had Summer's much sought after laundry, they still showed no interest in leaving.

'The clothes you're wearing . . .' Jenny said, in a weak voice.

Swearing under her breath, Summer turned her back to the girls and began to undress, first peeling off her filthy shorts and socks, then her underwear. Jenny and Joni were starting to feel a lot like annoying younger sisters; sisters that she had once longed for but was glad she'd never received. She hesitated, a wave of shame coursing over her, before removing her T-shirt. Even though she had her back turned to them, she heard both girls gasp at the multitude of thin scars and cuts that covered her upper arms and shoulders, some healing better than others.

'What?' Summer snapped, as she held out her clothes without turning around.

One of the girls took them, and then they were both off, scurrying away like mice into the laundry room.

Now alone, Summer gently eased herself into the bathtub. All of the humiliation and self-disgust she felt was instantly washed away. It was like floating in nectar, as if she were still in the womb, swimming in amniotic fluid. She sank into the water. It had been so long since she'd last bathed that she'd forgotten how tender it could feel, like a warm embrace from a loving mother, who hadn't chosen her rapist husband over her only child.

Soon, Summer's eyelids grew heavy, until she could no longer keep them open. Until they were sealed shut and she slipped beneath the water.

She shot back up, coughing and spluttering, eyes stinging and lungs gasping for air. When she could breathe again, she swept her hair back behind her ears and twisted around in the bathtub. Jenny and Joni were nowhere to be seen. The bathwater was cold and Summer was shivering, her fingertips turned to shrivelled fruit. How long had she slept? A glance out of the small upper windows revealed daylight tinged with pale orange. Summer shrugged. The bath had been warm and inviting, the tea that Mother had given her to drink so calming.

Climbing out of the tub, Summer stood on unsteady feet and reached for the towel that Jenny had left for her on a bench. It was old and coarse, but she made quick work of drying herself, dabbing gently at the cuts, then pulled on her shorts, T-shirt, and shoes. She reached for her bag. And froze. It was missing.

Panic rose from Summer's stomach. All of her worldly possessions were in that bag. The last of the money she had collected from begging in the streets; a dog-eared copy of *The Lighthouse* by Virginia Woolf, which she'd read many times over and covered its pages in handwritten notes; a photograph of herself as a happy young child, with her father, who had yet to hang himself in the garage, and her mother, who had yet to become a bitter and rage-filled woman; and lastly, her pocket knife.

Panic gave way to anger. Those little bitches had stolen her bag! Stomping over to the laundry room, Summer ducked inside. But except for a bathtub full of soapy water, the room was empty. Where had they gone?

She marched outside, throwing open the door, which banged

against the wall. The heat hit her hard and fast, knocking the air from her lungs. As she stood, catching her breath, she saw a group of children kicking a ball around. On her left, she saw washing lines filled with laundry. Jenny and Joni were there, chatting happily while hanging up wet clothing in hues of greens and browns.

Summer raced towards them, a finger stabbing the air.

'What have you done with it?'

Startled, Joni dropped the shirt she was holding. Jenny stared at Summer, open mouthed.

'Don't fuck with me. You took my bag. Where is it?'

'We—we washed it,' Jenny said, taking a step back. 'We wanted to ask but you fell asleep, and we didn't want to wake you. It's over there.'

She nodded towards a bench next to the bath house, where Summer's freshly laundered clothes sat in a neat pile. Her bag lay on top, months of dirt purged from it, leaving its colours almost vibrant.

'We didn't take anything,' Jenny said. 'Mother and Father say stealing from each other is the way of the outside world.'

Summer glared at her, then snatched up her bag. Everything was inside, even the pocketknife. She picked up her clean clothes and stuffed them inside.

Coming here was a mistake. She wanted to leave right away. Not because the girls had taken her bag. Not because there was a strangeness to this place that she couldn't quite perceive. But because she had humiliated herself in the face of kindness and consideration.

'You shouldn't have taken it without asking,' she said quietly.

'We're sorry.' Jenny's voice was small and childlike. 'Mother and Father will be ashamed of us. You won't tell them, will you?'

Summer glanced over her shoulder, and saw how frightened she had made both girls feel. Guilt crashed down upon her.

'I won't. And I'm sorry. I'm not used to people being nice to me. Thank you for taking such good care of my things.'

Jenny and Joni stood next to each other in silence and with their eyes downcast.

'Perhaps we can start over,' Summer said. 'I'd like it if we could be friends.'

Jenny looked up. Slowly, a smile spread across her lips. 'I'd like that too. Very much.'

Summer stared at Joni, hoping for a similar response. But when Joni finally looked up, there was no smile for Summer. Only fear.

18

Wednesday came. Blake was tired and irritable. She'd slept poorly, her mind refusing to settle. When she had finally slept, she'd dreamt she was lost in a dark forest, branches gouging her skin as she ran from a skeletal beast with huge antlers and a human face. She had spent the evening re-reading the police file on Sandy and Morgan Teague, hoping to unpick a thread or stumble upon a trail that she had previously missed. But Blake was nothing if not thorough, which meant she had already picked it clean. Now it was 11 AM, and she was sitting in front of a desktop computer in a small, windowless room on the second floor of Truro police station. On the screen was CCTV footage from the day the Teague Twins disappeared.

It was likely she had DS Turner to thank for the sudden granting of access, but she couldn't say for sure; she hadn't spoken to him since yesterday evening's meeting in the park, and he didn't strike her as the type to call her up and brag about his ability to pull favours. Though Blake did wish he'd call—she was desperate to know if Carrie Killigrew had agreed to let her meet with her son.

For now she focused on the CCTV footage, which had been spliced together from several cameras and followed the twins' movements, from the moment they entered the park until the moment they vanished from the face of the earth, somewhere on the outskirts of Newquay.

The timestamp on the screen read 11:56 AM. Blake had already spent thirty minutes watching the siblings meandering in the park, spending time on the swings or kicking a ball around. There were other children around, younger than them and chaperoned by parents. But the twins had seemed uninterested in others. Until ten minutes ago, when a group made up of eight young people, including prepubescent children, older teenagers, and one Heath Monk, had appeared and asked to play with their ball. There was obvious reluctance on Morgan Teague's part, his body language taut and standoffish, as if intimidated by the group, or at least by the older members. Sandy was more open, her posture more relaxed and welcoming. It was an interesting dynamic, how similar the twins had seemed in nature when alone, and then polar opposites when intruded upon by strangers.

The group were permitted to join their game, passing the ball around but without any form or structure, or enthusiasm, Blake noted. Even through the grainy black-and-white footage, she could see the game was nothing more than a ruse, a means of getting close to the twins so they could be assessed. Heath Monk did not join in the game, but observed from the peripheries, standing eerily still, his head slowly turning in the direction of one twin, then the other.

Accompanying the CCTV footage was documentation identifying the other young people in the group, along with their age at the time.

Alison Strand, 18, deceased.

Morwenna Thompson, 19, deceased.

Julia King, 16, deceased.

Bailey Mattison, 11, deceased.

Jack Harper, 10, deceased.

The list of names made Blake nauseous. They were just children, all now dead thanks to their indoctrination by a crazed cult leader. And they weren't alone. Members of the Dawn Children cult not apprehended by the police had either burned to death in the very fire they had started, or had been killed in retaliation, a few by their own hands.

'Children . . .' Blake whispered.

But the frightening truth was some children were very capable of committing atrocious acts. One only had to look to the deplorable case of Jamie Bulger, the two-year-old who was abducted from a shopping centre by a pair of ten-year-old boys and subjected to such heinous torture and brutality that, of the forty-two terrible injuries inflicted upon his body, the coroner could not determine which had been the fatal blow.

Children had killed scores of adults that terrible day in Devil's Cove. Children who were currently playing a game of football on the computer screen before Blake's eyes. Were Morgan and Sandy Teague to be counted among those killer children?

By 12:01 PM, the group had stopped playing with the ball and were now huddled around the twins as Heath Monk talked to them at length, occasionally looking up and around before returning his focus. At 12:03 PM, the group began to depart, moving as one, as if controlled by a hive mind.

Sandy Teague had already been absorbed by the group. Only Morgan lingered, standing frozen on the grass, his ball clutched between his arm and his side. But then Sandy re-emerged, took his free hand, and pulled him into the group's welcoming embrace.

The Dawn Children and their new initiates left the park and the prying eyes of the CCTV cameras. Until twenty minutes later, when they were spotted again on the outskirts of town, walking along Gannel Road. Then, like the ghosts they would later become, the children vanished.

Blake rewound the footage and hit the pause button. She stared at the group on the screen. They were pressed close together as they walked along, their backs turned to the overhead CCTV camera. Individuals could not be identified, but Blake counted ten bodies. Rewinding the footage once more, she counted again. Yes, ten bodies for certain, with one hanging at the back of the group, carrying a ball under his arm. Morgan Teague.

Back at the park, his reluctance to leave with the Dawn Children had been painfully clear. Now, as they walked out of town towards an unknown destination, he seemed no more willing. Yet, he was still complying with his sister's decision to go with the group, perhaps so he could protect her, or perhaps because he was afraid of what might happen if he tried to leave. Heath Monk was an intimidating man; even Blake could sense that through the grain of the camera footage. And he was at least ten years older than Morgan, and surrounded by a group of compliant followers. It didn't matter whether or not Morgan wanted to stay or go—the choice had already been taken from him.

Blake let the footage run its course, but there was nothing more to see. The twins and the Dawn Children had vanished into the ether. Which meant they either had transport waiting for them, or they lived somewhere nearby. Police records leaned towards the former; the Dawn Children had been linked to a homestead several miles away called Burnt House Farm, which later lived up to its name by catching ablaze and burning to the ground. Following the Devil's Cove massacre, one of the apprehended cult members had volunteered the location of a second compound, an abandoned military base found just a few miles along the coast from the ill-fated town. A police raid found several signs of habitation, written plans for the attack on Devil's Cove, and the decomposing body of an unidentified woman in her forties. But no definitive signs of Morgan and Sandy Teague.

Blake moved onto the second file of footage she'd been granted access to, taken from CCTV cameras in and around Bournemouth town centre, including the square where Morgan had been spotted with the mysterious group of young men. The bad news was that a network failure had occurred the day before Morgan had phoned his mother, causing several camera outages in the local area that lasted several days. Affected devices had included the camera in the square and the one Blake had spotted near the phone booth. The only available footage was from the two days before and after the outage.

To Blake's disappointment, the Teague twins did not appear in any of it, no matter how many times she re-watched the footage or scoured each pixelated face. Neither did the group of young men Morgan had been seen with, selling trinkets and handing out propaganda. Which told Blake that, even before they'd vanished for good, the group had not been a daily presence at Bournemouth Square, which perhaps made them less memorable to the casual passerby.

She leaned back on the hard plastic chair, frustration growing. How could a group of people, cult or otherwise, simply disappear without a trace? The UK was one of the most filmed countries in the world, with more than five million CCTV cameras watching its citizens go about their everyday lives. It seemed the only private space these days was your own home, but even that had begun to feel unsafe, with cyber criminals hacking their way into laptop screens and smart doorbells. Yet Morgan and Sandy Teague had been abducted from a relatively rural area, where cameras were fewer, more so once you got outside the towns. If they'd disap-peared from somewhere like London, Blake had a feeling they would have been found a long time ago. Whether that would have been alive or dead was debatable.

Picking up the phone, she opened Facebook and checked the local Bournemouth community groups where she had previously posted the age progressed images of the twins. There were lots of comments from mostly well-meaning people, but still no one in the area had seen Sandy or Morgan Teague.

More dead ends.

Blake just had to hope that Turner had followed up on his agreement to call Carrie Killigrew, and that Carrie Killigrew would allow Blake to talk to her son. Because whether he knew it or not, Cal Anderson was fast becoming the only lead she had left.

19

As Summer entered the meeting house with Jenny and Joni, she was immediately struck by how much it resembled a church. Rows of benches were arranged like pews with an aisle at the centre, all facing a raised stage at the front. A lectern stood at its centre, intricately carved from a single piece of wood, while two huge totems of bipedal stags, much like the one at Mother and Father's house, were stationed at each end of the stage, towering over the congregation. Candle holders lined the walls, their candles unlit due to the lightness of the evening. Between each window were paintings of woodland scenes featuring a mix of real-world animals and mythical creatures.

Summer was in awe. She hadn't known what to expect, but it wasn't this. Nearly all of the benches were already full. There had to be at least fifty people, many more than she'd seen when she'd first arrived. They were all dressed in forest colours, their attention directed at the empty stage, although a few heads had turned upon her entrance. There were even elderly people here, perhaps in their late seventies and eighties. Summer wondered if they had always been members of the commune, or if emancipation had come to them later in life. And what of the younger children? Had they been born at Fortunate Keep and never seen the outside world? Or had their families brought them here to escape from it?

'Let's sit down here,' Jenny said, in a hushed voice, pointing to the half empty back bench. Joni scooted in first, quickly followed by Jenny. Summer sat on the end. The people in front of her twisted around to take a look. She stared blankly at them. They smiled, before returning their gazes to the empty stage.

'So, what's this all about?' asked Summer. Her bag was resting on her lap with her arms wrapped tightly around it. 'Because it feels a lot like Sunday service.'

Joni, whose wariness of Summer had shown no signs of abating ever since the bag incident, ignored the question and turned to say hello to the woman on her right.

'It might seem that way, but it's not,' Jenny said. 'In a moment, Father will come on stage and we'll talk about joyful things. When he enters, we must all stand and bow our heads. Then we give thanks. You won't know the words, of course, so you should stand there quietly until it's over.' Her gaze drifted down Summer's body, paying particular attention to her exposed legs. Jenny frowned, opened her mouth to say something, then decided against it.

Summer shrugged. 'Still sounds a lot like church to me.'

Up ahead, a ripple of excited voices spread through the crowd. At the right side of the stage, a door opened. The ripple turned into a wave. Everyone got to their feet. Summer looked to Jenny for guidance, who gave her an emphatic nod. Summer stood to join the others. Along the bench, Joni squealed with excitement.

A man entered through the door and, despite the walking stick he used, strode confidently to the centre of the stage. He was a large man, possibly in his late sixties, with short salt-and-pepper hair, and a neatly trimmed beard. A large belly was bursting through his green collarless shirt, and many rings adorned his fingers. He had a kindly face, Summer thought, like Santa Claus. Yet at the same time, there was cunning in his eyes that she saw almost immediately, even if the others didn't.

More people were entering the stage: two women, quickly followed by Mother, who carried a bundle of material in her arms. All three women wore simple jade coloured dresses that reached their ankles, and many bracelets around their wrists, like the ones Thomas and the others had been selling in town. The women were all barefoot, as was Father. As they approached him, he stretched his arms out, forming a cross, then turned his back to the congregation.

One of the women took Father's stick, while Mother and the other woman unfolded the ceremonial robe that Mother had been carrying and slipped it over Father's arms, then his shoulders. It was a thing of beauty, Summer thought, fashioned from silk the colour of pine needles, the edges embroidered with patterns of trees and flowers, while at the very centre, covering Father's back, was the same stag skull Summer had seen on Thomas's leaflet.

With Father now fully dressed, Mother and her helpers descended the short flight of steps on the left of the stage and joined the congregation, one of the women still carrying Father's stick. Which was interesting to Summer—did it mean the stick was just for show?

Father continued to stand with his back turned and his arms outstretched. After a minute, he turned slowly to face his audience and deliver a beaming smile.

'Good evening, children,' he said, in a deep, hypnotic voice that seemed to roll like thunder across the space to rattle Summer's ribcage. He remained in his Christ-like pose, arms outstretched.

'Bow your head now,' Jenny whispered in Summer's ear.

Summer looked around to see everyone had bowed theirs. Huffing, she did the same.

Father stood on stage, staring expectantly down at the congregation. The chanting began, many humble voices creating one undulating chorus.

'The Horned One is God. The Horned one is Love. The Horned One is our protector. The Horned One is our Father. Father is Oracle. Father is protector. Father is love, true and pure. Forgive us, Father, for our sins. Love us, Father, in spite of them. Lift us up, Father, when we fall. Cast us off the precipice, Father, if we fail you.'

The voices dropped to a low whisper. '*Thank you father thank you father thank you father thank you father.*' Then rose up like a tide, 'Thank you for protecting us from the outside world! For saving us from damnation! For giving us a home in Fortunate Keep! For giving us new life! For all this, we thank you and are forever in your debt. *Thank you father thank you father thank you father thank you, father . . .*'

And so the chanting went on, repeating itself, over and over, building in a frenzy, until the congregation was almost screaming. Summer listened, equally alarmed and bemused. Only once did she look up, and saw Father staring straight at her, his outstretched arms trembling with effort. She quickly dropped her gaze and waited for the ritual to end. When it finally did, Father lowered his arms and walked to the lectern.

'Please, take a load off,' he said, with a fatherly smile.

Everyone sat. Summer shifted on the bench, feeling the hard wood beneath her. She stared at Jenny and Joni, but so enraptured were they by the man on the stage, the teenagers had forgotten her existence.

'Well, look at all of you,' Father said, his tone warm and playful. 'My beautiful, loving children. You really all do light up my life.'

'Thank you, Father,' the chorus came. 'We are honoured, Father.'

'It's been yet another glorious day, hasn't it? We've been blessed with cleansing sunshine and more joy than we could ever know what to do with. All thanks to the Man in the Trees.' He nodded to one of the sculptures of the Horned God and gave a knowing wink. 'Who, here, would like to share something joyful from their day?'

To Summer's surprise, all hands shot up.

On the stage, Father feigned astonishment; this was clearly a routine repeated several times over. 'So many of you! We are favoured this evening indeed. Now, who will I pick? Such a tough choice! I know, why don't we start with young Daniel?'

Father leaned over the lectern, powerful hands gripping its side, and smiled at a little boy in the front row.

'Today, me and my brother helped make the beds,' the child said.

'You did? What a generous, joyful thing for both of you to do. And which one is your brother?'

The child pointed to the adolescent boy standing next to him.

Father smiled. 'Of course it is. I know Adam. I know everyone here because you are all my children. Well done, Daniel. And well done, Adam. Now, who else?'

All hands went up again, including Jenny and Joni's. To Summer, they seemed like the annoying kids in class who always put their hands up before the teacher had even asked a question. But much to Summer's relief, Father did not pick either of them.

'Emerald, let's hear from you.'

A woman in her mid-thirties, with a wide grin on her face, got up.

'What joy did you experience today?'

'Well, Father, I baked four beautiful apple pies for all of us to enjoy at dinner. I poured all of my love into making them, and I gave thanks to the trees that bore the fruit.'

'Wonderful. And I'm sure we will all experience much joy at the dinner table later, with not a crumb left.' Father winked at the congregation, sending trickles of laughter through the benches. 'I'm glad to hear you gave thanks to the trees, Emerald. For they are gifts from the Horned One. To thank the trees for their abundance is to thank Him for his generosity.'

Pleased, the woman took her seat again. Father scanned the congregation. 'One more, I think.'

Hands went up. Jenny and Joni's faces flushed red and veins throbbed at their temples. Summer worried that if Father didn't pick at least one of them, they'd both die from a brain haemorrhage. But yet again, Father chose someone else.

'Thomas, we haven't heard from you in a while. What joy can you share with us this evening.'

Summer's stomach churned. *Please, no*, she thought. *Don't make me stand up. Please, don't make me stand up!*

Thomas got to his feet and momentarily turned in her direction. Facing the stage, he said, 'Today brought me great joy, Father.'

'And why is that?'

'Because Matthew, Kane and I helped to save someone from the horrors of the outside world. Someone who is here with us now.'

Father's unremitting gaze fell upon Summer. She was like a stray cat caught in the sudden beam of a motion sensor light, paralysed and unable to escape. All she could do was return his stare, her heart thrashing wildly in her chest. Ever since the strange opening chant, Summer had decided that Fortunate Keep and its curious inhabitants were perhaps not for her. Despite borrowing its imagery, it seemed they had little in common with Wicca, which was the very thing that had attracted her in the first place—that and the promise of cooked food and a clean bed. Her knowledge of Wicca was by far from extensive, but she did know that the Horned God and Triple Goddess ruled the universe in equilibrium, two deities equal in love and power. But here in Fortunate Keep, it was very clear that, despite its outward sheen of balance and harmony, there was only one ruler. The Horned One. Also known as Father. His grand entrance had made that very clear, as had the congregation's chants of adoration. Meanwhile, Mother, the Triple Goddess, was relegated to the benches with the rest of his followers.

No. Summer had had a stomach full of men telling her what to do. She wasn't about to make the same mistake here.

'Ah, yes, that's right,' Father said, still smiling at her. 'We have welcomed a guest into our home. Would you like to stand up and say hello?'

No, I would not, Summer thought. But all eyes were on her now, and, despite her feelings, she did not want to appear ungrateful for the kindness she had so far been given. Slowly, she got onto unsteady feet, while avoiding the many curious gazes of the congregation. Beside her, Jenny and Joni attempted to mask their disappointment at not being chosen to introduce the new guest.

'Everyone, please welcome Summer into the fold,' Father said.

A chorus of voices floated up to the rafters. 'Welcome, Summer. May the Horned One bless you, for you are now one of his children.'

Summer shifted her weight from foot to foot. She had never enjoyed being the centre of attention, and had spent much of her life invisible to others. The level of attention focused on her now made her skin itch and burn, and she wanted nothing more than to cut fresh lines into it and release those unwanted feelings. That, or run from the meeting house and never look back. Or, at the very least, sit down and cover her head with her hands.

Father was staring at her. 'Please, child. Come to the front and let everyone see you.'

Lead was filling her veins, leaving her immovable. She couldn't go onstage, even if she wanted to.

'Come on now, don't be shy.' Father's smile was wide, but straining at the edges. He was clearly not used to being disobeyed.

Summer felt pressure on her right thigh. She glanced down and saw Jenny jabbing at her flesh with two fingers.

'You have to go,' she hissed. 'You can't disobey Father.'

Now, heads were turning in her direction, offended eyes fixed on her. Summer dropped her gaze, saw that she was still clutching her bag to her stomach. She looked up again, and saw Father's smile grow white hot. Then melt.

He waved a dismissive hand. 'Not to worry. The overwhelm can be paralysing when first emancipated from the outside world. Please be seated, Summer. There will be plenty of time for everyone to get to know you. Plenty of time indeed.'

Summer's legs gave way and she collapsed on the bench. Jenny and Joni both shook their heads in disapproval. Father continued his sermon, but Summer was no longer listening. She felt awkward and humiliated. She should have known better than to come to such a place, regardless of the lure of a comfortable bed and hot food. She was better off alone, always had been, even if it left her back on the streets. At least on her own, she didn't need to worry about impressing others or making a fool of herself. Because that was how she felt now. Like a socially inept imbecile. The urge to cut returned. Her fingers itched for the blade.

The meeting was coming to an end. Everyone stood and held

hands, and sang an unaccompanied song about the Horned One, and Father being his vessel, about the trees and the beasts, about life and death. Summer stood with them, allowing Jenny to hold her hand and swing it gently back and forth as she sang from the top of her lungs. But Summer kept her head bowed and her eyes fixed on the floor until it was all over.

Someone opened the doors and the early evening light rushed in, bringing enticing food smells and the promise of escape. But as Summer tried to leave, Jenny gripped her hand.

'We always exit from front to back,' she said. 'Father goes first, followed by Mother. Then the rest of us.'

Up on the stage, the two women who had earlier helped Mother with Father's robe, now took his hands and guided him down the steps. Reaching the centre aisle, he stood before Mother, who bowed and kissed his hand, then gave him back his walking stick. He continued on down the aisle, with Mother and the two women following closely behind. As Father reached the last row of benches, he paused next to Summer. Up close, he was a towering, imposing man, a good foot taller than her and at least three times as wide.

'Walk with me, child,' he said, his midnight blue eyes strangely hypnotic.

Jenny immediately released Summer's hand. When Summer did not move, she gave her a small but firm shove.

Father was waiting, that eerie smile of his reminiscent of the Cheshire Cat from *Alice in Wonderland*.

Forcing one foot in front of the other, Summer slowly walked towards him.

20

As it happened, DS Turner called Blake later that afternoon, when she was back at her office and busy researching a new potential fraud case that had just come in from Curnow Insurance. She had earlier received another phone call, from Detective Inspector Jackie Hosken, who had been in charge of the initial investigation into the Teague Twins' disappearance. But, as Turner had predicted, there was little to learn outside of what Blake had already learned from the police reports. Hosken's personal opinion was that there was a reason the twins hadn't returned home to their parents in all this time and, whatever that reason might be, it was nothing good. She was, however, pleased to hear Blake was looking into the cold case and requested that she get in touch if any new evidence surfaced.

The call had left Blake feeling even more despondent. So it was to her utmost surprise to learn that Carrie Killigrew had agreed to let her question Cal.

'She was a tough nut to crack,' Turner said, over the phone.

'And believe me, I've worked on some real hard arses over the course of my career.'

'Thanks, Will. I owe you one.'

'Well, don't thank me yet because she has a number of conditions. One, that both she and I sit in on the interview.'

'Oh, come on. Really?'

'Two, that you submit your questions for approval before we visit. And three, any signs of upset in Cal and the interview is immediately terminated, no ifs, no buts.'

Blake was quiet, fighting the protestations that were clamouring to make themselves heard. She understood Carrie's wariness about letting a complete stranger question her son, who had been robbed of his childhood and left irreparably damaged. Yet the limitations she had imposed before Blake had even asked a single question, could potentially render the interview useless. If Blake was forced to sit and reel off a list of pre-approved questions as if she were interviewing a job applicant, how could she possibly find out what she needed if Cal was uncooperative? There would be no room to try other angles, other approaches that might get Cal to trust Blake enough to talk. But her hands were tied.

'Fine,' she said. 'When do we meet?'

'The weekend.'

'But my deadline is tomorrow, Turner.'

'I'm sure the twins' parents will wait a bit longer if it means a potential new lead.'

'That's a big if.'

'The only if from the sounds of it. So, what am I telling Carrie?'

'You tell her it's a date,' Blake said. 'And I'm bringing my chaperone.'

Turner sighed. 'You need to work on your material. I'll speak to Carrie and get back to you.'

The detective sergeant ended the call. Blake sat at her desk, thrumming with excitement, yet equally frustrated by the constraints Carrie Killigrew had put in place. But if that was what Blake had to work with, then so be it. She would just need to ensure her questions for Cal were as precise as they were non-triggering. Picking up her phone again, she called Bronwen Lander and waited for her to answer.

21

Father and Summer led the congregation from the meeting house and towards a long picnic table, which had been set up in front of the dining hall.

'This must all be new and strange to you,' Father said, strolling at a deliberate pace, his walking stick tapping alongside. 'Perhaps even amusing. But look around you. See all the happy faces. These people were all once like you, destitute and scarred by an uncaring, heartless world. Now look at them. Fortunate Keep is thriving. The Horned One has truly blessed us.'

Summer peered over her shoulder, glancing first at Mother, who acknowledged her with a slow nod, then at the long line of people, who were chatting animatedly and full of smiles. She couldn't deny that whatever went on at Fortunate Keep, its people seemed at peace.

'I'm sorry if I offended you earlier,' she said to Father. 'I've been on my own for such a long time, and I've never been good at being put on the spot.'

'No offence taken. I understand that coming from the outside world, where every minute is a living horror, to somewhere as archaic, even outlandish, as Fortunate Keep can overwhelm the senses. Especially, as you say, if you're used to living a solitary and loveless life. Sometimes even I feel overwhelmed by all the love surrounding us here. Sometimes I worry what would happen if someone tried to take it all away.'

He fell silent for a while, his heavy footsteps creating plumes of dust on the hard ground. As they drew closer to the dining hall, tantalising aromas teased Summer's senses, making her stomach rumble. She tried to remember when she'd last eaten. Had it been yesterday? Or the day before?

Father looked up again. 'Tell me, have you ever heard of the Fortunate Isles?'

Summer shook her head.

'In Greek and Roman mythology, the Fortunate Isles were a group of islands believed to be a kind of paradise on earth, where heroes and other favoured mortals were sent by the gods to enjoy a blissful afterlife free from turmoil, where food was in abundance, the sun always shone, and the landscape was a beauty to behold.'

'Sounds like heaven.' Summer's attention was fixed on the galley style picnic table, where baskets of bread rolls had been placed along the centre and covered with cloths to protect from flies.

Father laughed. 'Quite literally, I believe. As a child living within an unhappy, often violent home, I dreamt of being one of the gods' chosen, living a life free of hardship and terror. I promised myself that one day, when I was old enough and had the resources, that I would create my own Fortunate Isle for those who had suffered, just as I had suffered. It took me many years, and several attempts all around the country, but here it is at last.' He stopped in his tracks, bringing the line to a halt, and conversations to silence. He held up his hands as he looked around. 'This is my Fortunate Isle. My Fortunate Keep.'

He started walking again. They were just metres from the picnic table.

'Right now, you may not feel that our humble home is the right place for you. That our ways are unconventional compared to today's modern society. But all I ask is you stay for a few days. Enjoy our food and company, then re-evaluate. If you still wish to leave, well, we'll be sad to see you go. But I have a feeling once you've tried Emerald's apple pie, you'll never want to leave again.' He glanced over his shoulder, before dropping his voice to a conspiratorial whisper. 'But if I were you, I'd stay away from her cornbread. People have lost their teeth.'

He winked at Summer, who grinned, genuinely this time.

'There's just one more thing we need to discuss before we sit down to dinner,' said Father. 'The knife in your bag. While I understand your need to protect yourself, especially on the streets of the outside world, I promise no harm will come to you here.'

Tension returned to Summer's shoulders. Jenny and Joni had clearly been busy while she had fallen asleep in the bath.

'We do not allow weapons of any kind at Fortunate Keep. They are unnecessary and invite danger in. So I ask that you hand the knife over. It will be returned to you *if* you decide to leave. But why would you, when the food smells this good?'

Father held out one of his meaty hands, the palm upturned.

Summer's fingers gripped her bag. No knife meant no protection. No knife meant no cuts.

'You have my word, you won't need it here,' Father said in a gentle voice.

Summer stared at his open hand. She would stay overnight, get some food in her stomach and a good night's sleep. If the exchange for that was her knife, then so be it. And it wasn't as if she had a choice—the alternative was to leave now and wander off into the moors, with no idea how to find the road. Relaxing her shoulders, she unzipped her bag. One night only. Besides, she was nothing if not resourceful; all sorts of things could be turned into weapons if needed, or instruments to cut.

Summer took out the pocket knife and handed it to Father, who quickly slipped it between the folds of his robe.

'Good girl. Now, let's eat.'

They reached the picnic tables. An impressive throne-like chair sat at one end, with another, less ornate yet still handsome chair at the opposite end. Father waited for Mother to pull back his chair. He sat. The two women-in-waiting pulled back Mother's chair and then she sat. One by one, the people of Fortunate Keep took their places at the table. Summer felt Jenny's hand wrap around her own. She resisted the urge to crush it.

'You can sit with us,' the girl said. Next to her, Joni was perturbed but compliant.

Summer was brought to the centre of the table and seated between the teenagers. Faces swarmed around her, smiling and chatting, some greeting her warmly. Two large pots of mutton stew were brought out from the kitchen and placed on the table, where women filled bowls, bringing the first to Father and the second to Mother. The rest of the bowls were passed up and down the table towards hungry mouths.

Summer stared at the stew before her. She shut her eyes and inhaled deeply. Her stomach growled in response. But no one was eating yet.

Silence fell over the table. Father waited a moment before speaking. 'We give thanks to the Horned One, for the fruits of His forest and the yields of His land. As we are fed, may we nurture the land around us and the love in our hearts. So say Father. So say Mother. So say we.'

A chorus of voices rose up from the table: 'So say Father. So say Mother. So say we.'

Draping a napkin over his chest and tucking it into his collar, Father picked up a fork. 'Let us dine. There's an apple pie with my name on it.'

People laughed as they picked up cutlery and began to eat. Summer peered into the bowl of stew, anticipating the first bite of hot food that she'd had in days.

She began to eat. And immediately believed in the Fortunate Isles.

22

Saturday came quickly. The Teague twins' parents had agreed to delay their appointment until Monday morning. Both had sounded excited on the phone, as if Blake had uncovered a big break that would lead to finding their children, and she had to remind them that talking to Cal Anderson was not a guarantee of anything, that it was more likely to lead to nothing.

She spent the rest of the week working on the insurance fraud case and finessing her interview questions for Cal, before submitting them to Turner, who then passed them onto Cal's mother. She had heard nothing back, so assumed her questions had been deemed acceptable. Of course, there was only one question that really needed answering, otherwise the rest would be rendered useless: did Cal recognise Sandy and Morgan Teague?

Blake had also spent time familiarising herself with Cal's story, which was equal parts tragic and horrifying. Cal had been nine years old when he'd vanished, sixteen when he'd returned, transformed. Terrible things had been done to the boy and, in turn, he had done terrible things to others. Now, he was twenty-three years old, no longer a teenager but a man. According to Turner, Cal had spent three years at a secure mental health facility, undergoing intense rehabilitation, before finally being declared safe enough to return to society.

Since then, Cal had lived with his mother and his younger half-sister, eleven-year-old Melissa Killigrew. Cal's father, a deep sea fisherman named Kai Anderson, had occasional contact, as did Cal's paternal grandparents. His maternal grandparents were big travellers and rarely in the country. As for the rest of the family, they had all been lost in the Devil's Cove massacre.

Blake imagined Carrie Killigrew watched over her children with the ferocity of a lioness. It was no wonder she wanted to control Blake's interaction with her son with military-like precision.

Now, as she drove along the M5 towards Bristol, the motorway heavy with traffic but moving at an agreeable speed, she listened as Turner described Cal's previous muteness, which doctors believed was a direct result of the years of trauma he'd experienced. Even though Cal could talk now, his speech was infrequent, often monosyllabic, and for certain ears only. Whether he would talk to Blake, a complete stranger, Turner couldn't say.

'I haven't seen the family in a while,' he said, from the passenger seat of Blake's car. Despite the heat and being off-duty, he wore navy trousers and a short-sleeved light grey shirt. 'Sometimes Cal will say hi to me. Sometimes not. There doesn't seem to be any rhyme or reason to when or if he'll speak. I suppose it depends on whatever mood he's in when you see him.'

'Are there developmental delays?' Blake asked. Having been kept prisoner for seven years made it seem likely.

'I'm not an expert in the field but I'd say so. Of course, that's only an opinion based on observation. But Cal is definitely switched on. The way he looks at you sometimes, it's like he's peering into your very core.'

'And how is he readjusting to being back in the world?'

'I don't see him enough to comment. What I do know is last September Carrie enrolled him at the local college, on some sort of catch up programme. Cal lasted half a day. Too many people and too much noise. After that, Carrie hired a private tutor to work with him at home a couple of times a week. And Carrie tries to educate him as best as she can when she's not running her shop.' Turner paused, staring at the mounting traffic in the next lane. 'Cal may be back in the world, but I don't think he's ready for it. Not yet. Part of me wonders if he ever will be.'

Blake glanced at her passenger. She had always suspected that Turner had a sensitive side under that bad-tempered, gruff exterior. Now that it had shown itself, she decided that perhaps she quite liked him after all.

'Is this usual?' she asked. 'For you to develop personal relationships with civilians involved in a case?'

Turner shot her a glare. 'No, it's not. But what happened to that family . . . I was there for a lot of it. Carrie's lost so much. She needed someone to talk to. A friend. For some reason she picked me.' He gave Blake another wary stare. 'And that's all it is before you go thinking otherwise. A friendship.'

'Don't mind me, Turner. I was just curious. I'm sure Carrie is very grateful for your friendship.'

He relaxed a little, resting his shoulders against the back of the seat. Blake exited at junction 19 and merged onto the A369. It wasn't far now. Another fifteen minutes and Blake would be seated in front of the infamous Cal Anderson. She wondered if he knew how far and wide his name was known.

Blake felt a flutter of anticipation in her stomach.

'Is there anything else I need to know before going in there?' she asked.

'Just stick to your questions or you'll be out of that house faster than you came in. And don't expect miracles. Cal's a very damaged young man. He may want to help you, he may not. Either way, what he can offer may be limited.' Turner hesitated, drumming his fingers on his knee. 'Just go easy on them, okay? I'm still surprised Carrie agreed to the interview, considering what her family's been through. But she lost her child, just like your clients lost theirs. And even though she has her son back, he's not the same boy who disappeared that day on the beach.'

Blake let out a breath. 'Don't worry, Turner. I can be nice when I have to be. Sensitive too.'

'I'll believe it when I see it.'

'Funny, I'd thought the same thing about you until ten minutes ago.'

They drove the rest of the journey in silence, passing industrial buildings, which quickly gave way to suburban streets. And then Blake was pulling up in front of a semi-detached house at the end of a quiet cul-de-sac. They had arrived.

23

Carrie Killigrew greeted Turner and Blake at the front door almost as soon as the car had pulled up. She was slightly shorter than Blake, but was about the same age, with similar shades of dark hair and eyes. She was dressed casually in a summery sleeveless dress, open-toe sandals, and a thin silver necklace with what looked like a wedding band attached to it. Upon seeing Turner, Carrie smiled warmly and threw her arms around his neck.

'It's so lovely to see you, Will. How are you? It's been a while.'

To Blake's surprise, Turner hugged Carrie back. Another sign that he was more than just a jaded detective.

'I'm good,' he said. 'Work is keeping me busy, as always. In fact it's a miracle to have a Saturday off.'

'Well, maybe switch off that phone of yours, just in case.'

Turner laughed. 'Sometimes I wish I could throw it into the sea.'

Something flickered in Carrie's eyes, dark and unsettling. She stared at Blake, and her entire demeanour changed, like icy rainfall on a hot day.

Turner introduced the women.

'It's nice to meet you,' said Blake, holding out a hand.

Carrie shook it with a firm grip and offered a terse nod, before stepping aside to invite her guests into her home.

The Killigrew household was not what Blake had expected; although what she'd been anticipating, she wasn't quite sure. Perhaps chaos and disorder from a family who was so emotionally and physically scarred they could barely hold themselves together, never mind their home. But what Blake saw around her was clean and organised, economical yet comfortable. She felt ashamed for expecting less.

Carrie led Blake and Turner into an average-sized living room with neutral coloured furnishings and family portraits on the walls, then went to the kitchen to make coffee.

Blake perched on the edge of an armchair and stared at the young girl sitting on the carpet in front of a large TV, long blonde hair spilling down her back as she watched a cartoon. She had barely looked up when the adults had entered, giving Blake a cursory if not curious glance before returning her focus to the TV screen. But the look had lasted long enough for Blake to note how haunted the child's eyes were. Melissa Killigrew was eleven years old and she had already witnessed things no adult should ever have to.

Turner, who was growing increasingly unpredictable, sat down on the floor next to Melissa and glanced at the TV.

'What are you watching?' he asked, in a gentle voice.

Melissa replied with a shrug of her shoulders.

'Oh, I like that one. It's my favourite,' Turner smiled wryly. 'How are you doing, Melissa?'

The girl did not respond, only watched the cartoon.

Turner continued to attempt conversation for a while, earning occasional grunts and monosyllabic answers. Finally giving up, he got to his feet and sat down in the other armchair.

He glanced back at Melissa, a look of defeat in his eyes. It was obvious that he cared a lot about this family, and they, in turn, brought out a warmer side to Turner that Blake had not seen before. She wondered if he had his own family. Outside of his police work, she knew nothing about him. She would rectify that on the journey home.

Blake took out her notebook and pen from her bag and placed them on the coffee table in front of her. She had been forbidden from recording the interview. Turner said it was because Carrie didn't want the press getting their hands on a recording of Cal talking about the Dawn Children, only to throw their lives into chaos again. Blake had assured Turner that Carrie had nothing to worry about—the Killigrew family was last year's news, ever since Cal had been released and was no longer seen as a threat to society. The sad truth was murder sold newspapers, not rehabilitation.

The living room door swung open and Carrie came in, carrying a tray with three mugs of coffee and a plate of biscuits. She walked slowly and deliberately, with a slight limp that left her favouring her left leg. Turner had told Blake the limp came from a knife attack that day at Devil's Cove, and that Carrie had fought back harder than her attacker. That was something else she and Blake had in common: stab wounds and lasting trauma.

Setting the tray on the coffee table, Carrie proceeded to hand out drinks to her guests, then stood motionless, fixing Blake with a hardened gaze, as if trying to read her underlying intentions.

Blake squirmed on the sofa, which, for her, was an unusual sensation.

'Thanks for the coffee,' she said, 'and for agreeing to see me today. I know it can't have been an easy decision, especially when it risks bringing up the past.'

Carrie gave a stiff nod.

'Cal is upstairs,' she said. 'He's feeling worried about the interview, but I've assured him that you'll be kind and considerate, and thoughtful about how you ask your questions. I've promised him you won't ask anything that's not on the list.'

'Of course. You have my word. Has Cal seen the questions?'

'He has. I thought it might be good to let him sit with them for a while, so he can have a think. He doesn't like surprises, and he struggles to go back there in his mind. Too many bad memories. For all of us. Which is why you should know the only reason I've agreed to this interview is to see if we can help the parents of those missing children. That's it. Nothing more.'

Blake shifted on her seat again, feeling like a suspect in an interview room. Usually, she was sitting on the other side of the desk.

'We're all on the same page,' she said. 'It's the only reason I'm here as well. Everything I ask will be strictly related to Sandy and Morgan Teague.'

Carrie nodded. 'I know.'

Her gaze lingered on Blake for a while longer. Eventually, her body language softened as she turned to Turner.

'I just got off the phone with Nat. She says hi.'

Turner smiled. "How is that tearaway doing?"

'She's good. Although she still has no plans to move back here, not that I can blame her. Nat's very happy living in London among all the other freaks. Her words, not mine. You know how she is, always desperate to be seen living on the edge of society.' Carrie smiled warmly. 'She just sold another painting. And she's still seeing Stacey. Maybe I can finally worry about her a little less.'

Blake didn't know much about Nat Tremaine, only that she

was another young survivor of the Devil's Cove massacre, and that Carrie had taken her in when Nat had been left with no one to turn to.

'I'm glad she's doing so well,' said Turner. 'There was a minute there I thought she was going to give it all up.'

'You and me both.'

It was as if Blake had been momentarily forgotten. But then Carrie's body language shifted again.

'I'll bring Cal down now,' she said. 'If he doesn't want to talk to you, please don't push it beyond mild encouragement. I won't have him upset.'

'I promise.'

Carrie turned to her daughter, who still sat on the carpet transfixed by the television screen.

'Sweet pea, can you do me a favour? Can you go up to your room?'

Melissa did not move.

'Sweet pea, did you hear me?'

An exaggerated sigh came from the child's body, sounding like a deflating balloon. Slowly, she got to her feet, switched off the television, and walked out of the room without giving any of the adults a second glance.

Carrie's shoulders slumped.

Turner said nothing.

'I'll be one minute,' Carrie said, before following her daughter upstairs.

Alone, Blake and Turner sat in silence.

Then Turner said, 'Melissa's in therapy. Carrie doesn't think it's working, but I don't know. This time last year, Melissa wouldn't even say hello to me.'

'Was she there that day?' Blake asked.

'She was. Her father died right in front of her.'

Blake heard footsteps on the stairs. Her heart began to race. Anticipation thrummed in her veins.

The living room door opened and Carrie entered, hands clasped in front of her like a courtroom usher.

A moment later, Cal Anderson came into the room and stared nervously at Blake.

24

As Cal stood, staring at her, Blake felt waves of nervous energy emanating from him. He was a short, slim man, with dark hair like his mother, which he kept short. His below-average height had been caused by years of captivity in his abductor's cellar, which had left him severely malnourished and had stunted his growth. Medical and nutritional intervention following his return to the outside world had put some meat on his bones, but for someone who had recently turned twenty-three, Cal still looked as if he were in his mid-teens. Until, that was, you gazed directly into his eyes, which were black and hardened, like onyx stones.

Observing him, Blake wondered if he went outside much; after having spent most of his young life institutionalised, first in that underground hellhole, then at the secure facility, she assumed Cal would want to spend every waking minute outdoors. But his pallid complexion, which appeared bone white in contrast to the red shorts and vintage *WrestleMania* T-shirt he was wearing, declared otherwise. Maybe all of those vitamin D-deprived years living underground had left his skin hypersensitive to sunlight. Or maybe he'd grown used to living an indoor life.

As Cal hovered on the threshold, staring anxiously at the ground, Blake noted several old scars that ran up and down his arms and legs. They were not the results of self-harm, Turner had already informed her, but the results of the abuse he had suffered at the hands of his abductor. Blake shivered. Cal had been nine years old when he'd been taken. All of those terrible things that had been inflicted upon him, had been done to a little boy.

'Cal, why don't you sit down?' Carrie said, her tone gentle and light.

When he didn't move, she extended a hand to guide him, pressing it against the small of his back. But Cal darted away from her, heading for the sofa, where he quickly sat down and wrapped his arms around his ribcage. There was something animalistic about him, in the litheness of his movements, in the way his furtive eyes darted about the room. The only trouble was Blake couldn't tell if Cal was predator or prey. Perhaps he was a little of both.

Her brow creasing, Carrie sat down next to Cal and gave him a concerned, sideways glance. They looked alike, Blake thought, mother and son.

'Cal, this is Blake.' Carrie said. 'She's the woman I told you about. The one who's looking for those missing children.'

'Hello, Cal. It's very nice to meet you,' Blake said, keeping her voice soft and steady.

Cal's gaze was now fixed to the carpet, his arms still wrapped tightly around his body. He made no indication that he'd heard her.

Carrie continued. 'Blake is going to ask you some questions. The ones on the list I showed you. It would be really helpful if you could answer her. Okay?'

Cal said nothing. He remained resolutely still, as if he'd withdrawn inside a shell. Blake glanced over at Turner, who gave her an encouraging nod.

She cleared her throat. 'First of all, I wanted to say thank you for agreeing to see me, Cal. You don't know me and I'm sure you just want to get on with your life. But I'm here because I'm trying to find two missing children. A brother and sister. Twins, in fact. I believe it's possible you may have crossed paths with them a long time ago. Back when you knew a group of people called the Dawn Children.'

A sudden tensing of Cal's shoulders drew Blake's attention. She studied his face, saw his nostrils flare and his lips tighten.

'Their names are Morgan and Sandy Teague. I have photographs of what they looked like back then.' Reaching for her bag, she removed an envelope. 'It would be really helpful if you could take a look and tell me if you recognise them.'

Blake stood and began to cautiously approach, feeling as if she were moving towards a cornered lion. She was halfway across the room when Cal's head snapped up and he stared directly at her. Blake froze, his black eyes pinning her in place. There was menace there. A warning. *Come any closer and see what you get.*

Turner, who had been all but invisible until now, jumped up and plucked the envelope from Blake's hand. He handed it to Carrie and returned to his seat. Blake sat back down again, Cal still watching her.

'It's all right,' Carrie soothed in her son's ear. 'There's nothing to worry about. Blake is a friend.'

Removing the images from the envelope, Carrie paused to stare at the Teague twins. Morgan and Sandy, twelve years old at the time their pictures had been taken, both full of toothy smiles, without a care in the world. She had similar photographs of Cal adorning the walls of the living room, taken from a time before he had been stolen from her, along with his innocence.

She held up the photographs for Cal to see. 'Take a good look. Do you recognise them?'

But Cal would not look. Instead, he fixed his gaze firmly in front of him.

'I know this is hard for you, sweetheart. I know the last thing you want to do is look back into the past, but you see these children here? They're missing, just like you once were. Their parents are worried sick. All they want is for their children to come home. Will you help them? All you need to do is take a look.'

Cal's breathing had quickened. His hands, which were still pressed into his sides, curled into fists.

Blake shot a questioning look at Turner, who shrugged.

Carrie tried again. 'Please Cal. When you were gone, my life was so empty. I spent every minute of every day worrying about you. Were you okay? Were you hurt or getting enough to eat? Mostly I worried if you were still alive. Morgan and Sandy's parents, they've been waiting eight years for their children to come home. Eight years. That's even longer than I had to wait for you to come back to me. You found your own way back home. But these children . . . Maybe they can't. Maybe they need help. Please, Cal. Won't you help them? Just look at the pictures and say yes, you remember them, or no, you don't.'

Silence fell over the room. Blake held her breath. Ever so slowly, Cal turned his head. His fists uncurled and, one by one, he plucked the photographs from his mother's hands. He shot a glance at Blake, his glittering eyes chilling her to the bone. Then he bowed his head to study each picture. A deep line folded into his brow as he regarded them. After a minute, he wordlessly handed the photographs back to his mother and . . .

Nothing.

Blake felt hope collapse in her chest. Was that it? The end of the investigation? All leads gone cold? Did Blake now have the difficult task of meeting with Bronwen Lander and Owen Teague on Monday morning to inform them that their children were still missing and probably always would be? Or did she use the forty-eight hours she had left to try again? But where? And how? She still had the symbol of the Triple Goddess and the Horned One. Perhaps she should have sought out an occult specialist rather than rely on Tegan Trezise, despite her considerable knowledge of the subject. But would it have led her any closer to the twins? If she were honest, Blake didn't think it would.

Across the room, Carrie held the photographs limply in her hands, a look of defeat on her face. The women stared at each other, offering apologetic looks.

Cal stirred.

He opened his mouth and tried to speak. Then stopped to clear his throat.

'What is it?' Carrie said.

Cal tried again. This time he found his voice, but when he spoke it was at such a low volume that Blake had to lean forward

'I remember them,' he said.

Blake looked up. "You do?'

Cal flinched at the loudness of her voice. The urgency of it.

'Where do you remember them from?' Carrie asked. 'Were they at the farmhouse?'

Cal nodded. 'And from before.'

'Is that Burnt House Farm?' Blake's notebook was open and her pen was poised.

'Yes, but it's gone now.' Carrie turned back to her son. 'Sweetheart, what do you mean when you say you knew them from before? From where?'

Cal was shrinking again, his arms slipping around his torso. 'From the bad place.'

'You mean where you—the basement?'

'No. The other bad place.'

'I don't know where you mean. Are you talking about the army barracks? Sweetheart, you were never there. That was after you . . .'

The woman's voice faltered and her face flushed red. For a moment, she looked bereft and riddled with guilt. Blake knew why: Carrie had been the one to hand her son over to the police.

Cal was staring at Blake again, leaving her uneasy.

'They were in the bad place,' he muttered. 'In the forest.'

'Which forest?' Blake asked.

But Cal would not answer. He retreated further, leaning back on the sofa, putting distance between himself and this stranger.

Carrie frowned. 'Do you mean Briar Wood?'

The wood outside Devil's Cove, where they had once lived happy lives in what felt like someone else's dream.

Cal shook his head. 'The forest where the Bone Man lives.'

The adults in the room stared at each other.

'Who's the Bone Man?' Blake asked.

Now Cal was bringing his knees up and wrapping his arms around them, a look of fear in his dark eyes.

Carrie gently touched his shoulder. He flinched.

Blake leaned further forward. 'Was the Bone Man part of the Dawn Children? Was that what you called the leader?'

Carrie shot her a warning glance. She was going off piste, asking questions that were not on the list. But Blake pressed on. She had to.

'Cal, it would be really helpful if you could remember the name of the wood, where you saw Morgan and Sandy. Where this Bone Man lives.'

Cal shook his head violently.

'All right, that's enough for now,' Carrie said, tensing her jaw.

Blake knew she was crossing a line, but Cal was all she had left.

'Please, Carrie. It may not lead to anything, but what if it does? A minute of upset could save the twins' parents a lifetime of anguish. We have to ask for the sake of the twins.'

Across the room, Carrie glared. She swore under her breath because she knew Blake was right. She turned to her son. 'Sweetheart? Can you answer Blake? Do you know the name of the woods where you saw Morgan and Sandy?'

'No. I'm not talking about it anymore.' His voice was low and threatening, laced with signs of the old Cal that everyone was afraid of. Even his own family.

'Please, sweetheart. What if it was me asking someone else these questions so I could find you? Wouldn't you want that person to tell me where you are? *Please*.'

'The Bone Man is a bad man, living in a bad place, where bad things happen. We're not supposed to talk about him. So stop talking about him.'

But Blake couldn't stop. 'Perhaps if I show you a map, you could point to it. Or maybe describe to me some things you remember—landmarks that might help me find it.'

And then Cal was bellowing at the top of his lungs, his hands clamped to his ears, veins popping in his neck and at his temples. 'I said stop fucking talking about him or he'll tear off your skin!'

Blake flinched in her seat. Before her was no longer a scared young man, but a feral, dangerous creature that could easily lash out and harm anyone in this room.

Carrie put an arm around her son. He tried to shake it off but she persisted.

'That's it,' she told Blake. 'Interview over.'

Defeated, Blake gathered her things and got to her feet. She stared at Cal, whose face was pressed into his knees, and whose entire body trembled.

'One more question,' she said.

Carrie's eyes widened. 'Did I not make myself clear?'

'Cal, when you saw Morgan and Sandy, either at the bad place or at the farm, did they ever try to run away?'

Cal looked at her. He was impossibly pale, his face a death mask.

'No one ever tried to run away,' he said. 'They all wanted to stay in the end.'

Carrie stood. 'Okay, everyone out.'

Slinging her bag over her shoulder, Blake stared at Turner, whose expression was unreadable, then conceded defeat.

'Of course. Thank you for your time, Cal. I really appreciate it.'

Cal had already retreated into a protective ball, head resting on the tops of his knees, his hands covering his face.

Carrie walked Turner and Blake to the front door, leaving her son in the living room. On the doorstep, she paused to say goodbye to Turner. Her hug was briefer this time, Blake noted, perhaps punishment for bringing a stranger into the Killigrew household who didn't follow the rules.

'It was nice to see you, Will. Call me some time, okay?'

Turner said that he would and headed to the car. Alone, the two women stared at each other for a long time. Then Blake said, 'I'm sorry. I didn't mean to upset him.'

To her surprise, Carrie did not berate her, but instead seemed to collapse in on herself.

'It doesn't take much to upset Cal these days. Sometimes you can do it just by staring at him the wrong way. Or by breathing. But at least I have my son back. He may never be able to hold down a job, or have a relationship, or get a place of his own, but he's back where he belongs.' She paused, staring off into the distance, her eyes glassy and pained. 'What will you do now? He hasn't given you much to go on.'

'Honestly, I don't know. I find myself going continually backwards into the twins' past, when I need to go forwards. It's like I'm stuck in reverse. But Cal has just confirmed the twins were part of the Dawn Children cult, which means they were, in all likelihood, there that day at Devil's Cove. And now all I have to tell their parents is that their missing children are probably mass murderers.'

Carrie shivered, reliving memories she would rather forget, but never would. You weren't allowed to forget when your son was a killer. But Carrie was a killer too. She had been there that day at Devil's Cove, and had taken lives to save herself and her daughter.

'Don't tell them that,' she said. 'Let them remember their children as they were, before that damn cult poisoned their minds. At least give them that.'

They stood in silence for a moment longer, these two women. These killers.

'Maybe you're right,' Blake said, at last. 'Thanks for seeing me, Carrie. I wish you well.'

She said goodbye and returned to the car, where Turner was leaning against the bonnet.

'Everything all right?' he asked.

Blake used her key fob to unlock the car doors. 'Did you ever hear about this Bone Man before? He didn't come up in the police investigation?'

'Not to my knowledge. But then we didn't know about him to ask.'

Climbing into the driver's seat, Blake felt a sudden heaviness. 'Let's just go back to Cornwall, Turner. I've learned all I can here.'

As they drove away, she peered into the rear-view mirror and saw Carrie still standing on the front doorstep, while her broken children waited for her inside.

25

Time passed. Summer didn't know how much. The days at Fortunate Keep were blissful and sunny, the food plentiful, and the company eclectic. She had spent so long on her own that, at first, she'd found it difficult to be surrounded by so many people, particularly when they were all so curious about their guest. When they asked questions, she didn't know how to answer. She was ashamed of her life. Of her time on the streets, foraging in waste bins, fighting off rats to get a half eaten sandwich, or relying on the kindness of strangers, which had never been in bountiful supply, but lately had dwindled even further. Mostly, what she received from passersby who did not pretend she was invisible, was hostility in the shape of hurled insults or thinly veiled threats of violence. Sometimes not even veiled at all.

Get a job! Get a life! Get off your lazy arse and work for a living, just like the rest of us!

She knew it was misdirected frustration, and after a while she had grown numb to it. And yet she couldn't help feeling resentment. Of all her time in the streets, only two people had ever asked how she had come to be there. And when she had told them the terrible truth, they'd offered pitiful looks and moved quickly on.

Nobody liked the homeless because they were a reflection of a broken society. A threat of what would happen if you didn't go to work, pay your bills, pay your taxes. The homeless were a feared people, especially by those who believed they were nothing but junkies, alcoholics, whores, and thieves. And it was true, there were many addicts among the homeless, as well as disproportionate levels of mental illness. But did the people who feared them ever stop to ask why? Or if the addiction had begun before or *after* the destitution?

Summer had endured more pointing fingers than she could count, and she was only twenty-one. Why had no one ever tried to offer her help beyond a cup of tea or some loose change, especially in those early days when she had still been a child? Why was it that, in her brief time at Fortunate Keep, she had been shown more kindness, respect, and humility than she had ever been shown during her six years on the streets? In spite of the clear sexism on display when it came to certain chores, the laughable nightly meetings that made her squirm, and the questionable adoration of Father, who was revered as if he were a god on earth, Fortunate Keep was now chipping away at the hardened exterior of Summer's heart.

Her first few nights here had been difficult. Sharing the bunk house with the other women and children had not bothered her— she had slept numerous times in homeless shelters–but the comfortable bed with its downy pillows and soft mattress had felt so alien to her after years of sleeping rough that she'd taken to the floor and curled up like an animal. It was only with encourage- ment from the other women that she'd tried again. Now, she couldn't wait to go to bed each night and slip beneath the sheets, to sleep dreamless sleep in a room so dark it was as if she'd been pitched into a black hole. In those first few nights, when sleep had evaded her, she'd get up and go outside, where she was greeted by the magical sight of millions of stars in a sky so large her eyes couldn't take it all in.

Father had been right to name this place after the Fortunate Isles. Even if there wasn't a drop of ocean in sight, it was paradise, free from the cruelties and relentlessness of the outside world. A world which she had been intending to return to. But now, on this gloriously balmy day, while she hung wet sheets to dry on the lines and watched women laugh and children play, the idea of going back there made her sick to her stomach.

And so she found herself in a quandary. Should she return to the unforgiving streets, move on to another county and another town, where she would try and eventually fail to find her place? Or should she stay on at Fortunate Keep, where chauvinism ruled under the watchful eye of a patriarchal god, but where she felt safe and cared for, and possibly even part of a community?

Wasn't that what she had been searching for all this time? To be part of something? To be visible, not just a broken thing that strangers passed by on the street?

Summer drummed her fingers against her thigh. There was no rush to make a decision—Father had said she could stay as long as she liked. Perhaps she would give it a few more days and re-evaluate. In the meantime, there was fine weather and hearty meals to enjoy, and a cosy bed with her name on it at the end of the day.

Snatching up the last tunic from the laundry basket, Summer attached it to the washing line with two wooden pegs. She stared at the earthy, simple garments hanging limply before her, with no breeze to bring them dancing to life. She glanced down at her own clothes, denim shorts and a faded Green Day tour T-shirt. If she stayed, she would have to do something about the clothing situation in Fortunate Keep because there was no way on this green

Earth she would be dressing like a crazed villager from *The Wicker Man*. She smiled to herself. Then a large crease appeared on her brow.

The door to the women's bunk room swung open and Jenny came rushing out, all wide-eyed and taut shoulders. She began marching away at a brisk pace, pulling up the straps of her dress as she moved, and brushing down her hair. Her face was red and blotchy, sunlight bouncing off streaks of tears. On her right arm were the beginnings of finger-shaped bruises.

'Jenny, what's wrong?' Summer called. But it was as if Jenny hadn't heard her.

The door to the women's bunk room swung open again and Thomas appeared. Which was a surprise because men were strictly forbidden from entering the women's private spaces, and vice versa; it was something that still puzzled Summer because this wasn't a Christian summer camp and most of the community were adults, and most adults craved intimate relationships, committed or otherwise. But Jenny wasn't an adult. She was fourteen years old. Thomas, on the other hand, was at least twenty-one.

Summer watched his dark eyes scan left to right. He spotted Jenny scurrying towards the vegetable garden, where Joni and a few of the women were busy working, and took off after her.

'What's going on, Thomas?' Summer said in a raised voice. 'What happened to Jenny?'

Heads turned in her direction. Thomas stopped in his tracks and glared at her, his nostrils flaring, then at Jenny, who had made it to the vegetable garden and taken refuge behind the other women.

Summer watched Thomas closely. 'I thought you men weren't allowed in the women's bunk rooms. You better not let Mother catch you.'

The young man stepped towards her, fists clenched at his sides and his upper lip curling. He opened his mouth, as if to say something, then clamped it shut again. Turning on his heels, he marched away, flanking the meeting house before disappearing behind it.

Summer watched him go, then glanced over at the vegetable garden to see Jenny had re-emerged from behind the protective wall of women, and was wiping tears from her face. She briefly met Summer's gaze and shook her head—a warning not to come over. Picking up a gardening fork she began violently attacking a clump of weeds. Joni went over to her and placed a hand on her shoulder. Jenny shook it off. The women went back to work.

Picking up the laundry basket, Summer made her way to the women's bath house and laundry room. She would check on Jenny later, after dinner, if she could get her alone. If Jenny didn't want to talk about it, she could try talking to Joni. Summer already had a good idea of what she had just witnessed, and if she was correct in her assumptions, she would be having a strong word with Father. Because she knew from personal experience that when certain boys wanted something, and girls said no, those boys were going to take it anyway. Summer would not allow that to happen to Jenny, or any other girl, while she remained here at Fortunate Keep.

Except by morning, Jenny was gone.

26

The journey home from Bristol had been silent and sullen, Blake grumbling behind the wheel at the growing queue of traffic as they re-entered Cornwall. The fine weather was continuing to lure holidaymakers into the county, which was good news for local businesses, but not so great for Blake's patience. Picking up on her bad mood, Turner had mostly kept quiet in the passenger seat. When they reached Truro, rather than have Blake drop him off at his home, he requested she stop at the police station.

'It's Saturday night, Turner,' Blake said. 'I'm sure crime fighting can wait for one night.'

'You'd hope. But sadly the criminal underworld isn't as thoughtful. Anyway, I'm just picking up some reports before meeting a friend for dinner.'

Blake arched an eyebrow. 'A friend, eh? So the rumours are true — he does have a life outside of work.'

Hopping from the car, Turner brushed down his shirt then

leaned in through the open door. 'What can I say? I'm a man of surprises. Speaking of work, I'm sorry today didn't work out as you'd planned. But I did tell you Carrie will always put the welfare of her children before anything else.'

'As she should,' said Blake. She tapped her fingers on the steering wheel. 'But thank you for arranging the meeting. I appreciate it. Maybe you're not so terrible after all.'

Turner smiled. 'If only I could say the same for you. Have a good night, Blake. Don't mope too much.'

He patted the roof of the car, then headed into the police station. Blake drove home, her bad mood worsening.

～

Two hours later, Blake sat on the floor of her living room, picking at a carton of takeaway Singapore noodles while staring listlessly at the television screen, where an action thriller was playing with the sound turned down. Her laptop sat on the coffee table in front of her, next to a full glass of Rioja. Despite it still being light outside, she had shut the curtains and turned on the table lamps, creating the perfect mood lighting for sulking.

She was frustrated. Her meeting with Cal, as unnerving as it was, had proven almost entirely fruitless. The young man was deeply troubled, disturbed even. Blake felt sorry for him. He'd endured so many terrible things it was a wonder he could put a sentence together. But Blake was also frightened of him. Cal was clearly capable of terrible violence—he'd proven that in the past—and the way he'd almost exploded today made her wonder if that violence still festered inside him, despite his rehabilitation at the hospital.

Blake picked up her wine glass, took a small sip, then set it down again. Despite her wariness of Cal, she could still see the frightened little boy that was trapped inside a tortured man. It saddened her. She felt for Carrie too, who would spend the rest of her days trying to fix that little boy. Blake wondered if it was even possible.

Losing her appetite, Blake dumped the container of noodles on the coffee table. All she had learned from meeting Cal was that he remembered Morgan and Sandy at Burnt House Farm, but he had first met them somewhere else. Somewhere he called the bad place. A place where the Bone Man resided.

Carrie had suggested an abandoned army barracks. On the journey back to Cornwall, Turner had explained the barracks had been the Dawn Children's final hiding place before launching their attack on Devil's Cove, and that Cal had already been in police custody when they'd moved there.

So where was this bad place?

Cal had mentioned it was in a wood, but hadn't specified which one. Blake didn't know how many acres of woodland were spread over Cornwall, but she was willing to bet it was in the thousands, especially if you included private and unnamed wooded areas.

As for the Bone Man, who was he? Was he a real person, perhaps an unidentified senior member of the Dawn Children? Blake wasn't sure and Cal wouldn't tell her. All she knew was that when she'd pressed him on the man's identity, he'd grown terrified. But whether the Bone Man was real or a figment of Cal's imagination, his existence did not have any bearing on Sandy and Morgan Teague's whereabouts. She'd been right when she'd told Carrie her investigation was leading her continually backwards.

Taking a second sip of wine, Blake let out a heavy sigh. Cal's words came to her: 'No one ever tried to run away. They all wanted to stay in the end.'

If Sandy and Morgan had been indoctrinated by the Dawn

Children, perhaps it was possible that once the cult had been destroyed, they'd gone in search of another. Because indoctrination meant giving up choice and self-control. And if you'd been brainwashed into believing you couldn't make decisions for yourself, how did you function in the real world?

Blake supposed the answer didn't matter now, because what did she have to show Sandy and Morgan's parents come Monday morning? Nothing, that's what. Well, nothing and an invoice for her time. She had warned them though. She'd told them cold cases were almost always impossible to solve. And here she was proving it to them. Still, Cal's fear continued to play on her mind . . .

Opening her laptop, she booted it up and pulled up a web browser. In the search bar, she typed the words: *The Bone Man.*

The first link in the search results was for a 2009 Austrian private investigator movie of the same name. Below it were several results for Rag 'n' Bone Man, a famous British singer whose music Blake was unfamiliar with; she'd always been more of a grunge and rock aficionado growing up.

Further down the page were search results for "rag-and-bone men". Back in the nineteenth century, rag and bone men had been impoverished, often destitute, collectors of unwanted items, scavenged from the streets or acquired by knocking door-to-door. Any items they procured would be sold on to merchants, and the pittance made would feed the men for another day. It was a desperate way of living, collecting cloth and paper, scrap metal and broken glass. Even dead family pets could not escape the rag-and-bone man's hand—bones could be ground into fertiliser for farmland, and skin could be stripped and turned into leather.

Grimacing, Blake ran her fingers over the keyboard and added more words to the search bar: *Bone Man + Woods + Cornwall.*

The results appeared. She was about to start trawling through them when her phone began to vibrate on the coffee table. Picking it up, she saw Kenver was calling.

'It's getting late and I'm in a bad mood,' she said. 'What do you want?'

But Kenver did not reply. Blake listened, heard rustling, movement, the sound of a passing car.

'Kenver? Hello? Are you butt dialling me again?'

Heaving her shoulders, Blake kept the phone pressed to her ear while she returned her attention to the search results. She clicked on the first link, which took her to a website called *CornishGhostStories.com*. Scrolling down the page, she stopped and frowned. On the screen was a ghost story titled, *The Bone Man Cometh*. Below it was an introductory paragraph:

By day, Trevelyan Wood, near Newquay, is an ancient and idyllic woodland populated by oak and ash trees, where sunlight filters through the canopies to dapple the ground, and sparkling waters dance along streams and rivulets. It's a place enjoyed by dog walkers and hikers alike. But as night falls, when the bats are flying and the moon is rising, Trevelyan Wood transforms into a place of pure terror. Dare you seek out the dead tree at its centre and summon the spirit of the Bone Man? If so, read on and discover what horrors await you . . .

Blake's eyes grew wide. 'What the hell?'

Trevelyan Woods, near Newquay? The town where Morgan and Sandy Teague had grown up. The town they had been abducted from by the Dawn Children.

Was this the bad place Cal had spoken of? Where he had first met the twins?

A voice suddenly spoke in Blake's ear, startling her. She'd completely forgotten Kenver was on the phone.

'Blake? Are you there?'

He was crying. And he sounded drunk. Very drunk.

Blake's mind was a whirlpool, but the desperation in her cousin's voice dragged her from it.

'What's wrong? Have you been drinking?'

Kenver sobbed. 'Yes, I have. And it's all your fault.'

'My fault? How does that work?'

'Because back in Bournemouth you kept asking about why I left London. You wouldn't leave it alone. You kept pushing and prodding, and now I can't stop thinking about what I did.'

Blake's gaze wandered back to the laptop screen. She quickly closed it.

'What do you mean? What did you do?' Silence. Then the sound of cars racing by at breakneck speeds. 'Kenver, where are you?'

'On the bridge. Over the bypass. I did a bad thing, Blake. Ever since I've been back in Cornwall, I can't stop thinking about it.'

'Which bridge? The one outside Wheal Marow?'

But Kenver was sobbing now, his words slurring together to form one incoherent noise.

'God damn it, Kenver. Sober up! Are you on the bridge outside of town?'

'Yeah. I don't even know what I'm doing here.'

'Well, stay there and don't do anything stupid. I'm calling Ed. He'll come and get you.'

'No, no, no! Don't do that. Ed *hates* me. He'll tell Aunt Mary and she'll tell my mum. I only want you to come.'

Blake glanced at her wine glass. She'd only had a couple of sips so was fine for driving. The potential revelation on her laptop would have to wait.

Swearing, she jumped up and hurried to the hall, where she slipped on her boots and grabbed her car key. Kenver was family, closer to Blake than her own brother, whom she scarcely saw or heard from. But more than that, Blake still felt responsible for Kenver's recent struggles with sobriety.

'I'll be there as fast as I can,' she said into the phone as she opened the front door. 'And by the time I've finished with you, you're going to wish I'd called your Uncle Ed.'

27

Summer had watched Jenny climb into bed last night and pull the sheets over her head, in an attempt to shut out Joni's constant fussing. But come sunrise, her bed was empty and Summer was worried. Because Jenny had not been the same since leaving the bunk house yesterday, with Thomas in hot pursuit.

At the evening meeting, she'd worn a long-sleeved tunic over her dress in spite of the clammy heat, and she'd been sullen and withdrawn, chanting and singing with an unusual lack of enthusiasm. When the meeting ended, she'd left the building with her head bowed and her shoulders almost touching her ears. Thomas, on the other hand, exited the meeting house with his head held high and a smile on his lips that didn't quite reach his eyes. He made no attempt to interact with Jenny, not in the meeting house, nor at the dinner table. Summer watched him closely, making sure he was keeping his distance, but outwardly he seemed unbothered by whatever had transpired in the women's bunk house.

Joni continued to pester Jenny all through dinner. She was

worried about her friend and determined to find out exactly what had happened to her. Father had briefly intervened, bringing the dinner table to near silence as he told Joni to stop fussing and let Jenny be. It was unclear whether he knew about the altercation between Jenny and Thomas; Father was very good at keeping his secrets close to his chest.

After dinner, while on washing-up duty with a few of the women, Summer took Jenny by the hand and swept her into the pantry, which was cool and dark, the shelves filled with dried goods and fermented foods in mason jars.

'What did Thomas do to you in the bunk room?' Summer asked, her tone gentle yet adamant.

Jenny said nothing, only trembled in the darkness.

'Did he hurt you? Did he make threats?'

She could hear the girl quietly weeping, but Summer knew if she quit pressing her now, she might never get an answer.

'I know you're scared, but boys like Thomas think they can do what they want to any girl they choose. It's not right, Jenny. If he hurt you, then something needs to be done about it before he does it to you again, or any of the other girls.'

'I'm fine,' Jenny managed to say between faltering breaths. 'Nothing happened.'

'I'm sorry, but I don't believe that. I saw the way you came out of there. I saw the bruises on your arm. I saw how rejected and angry he looked when he followed you. Angry men are men to be feared, Jenny. Don't protect him.'

'I'm not. And it doesn't matter what happened, anyway. It's over now.'

'Of course it does. It matters a lot, which is why you and I are going to see Mother, and you're going to tell her what Thomas did to you, so she can put a stop to it.'

Jenny lunged out and grabbed Summer's hand, gripping it

tightly. 'Please, don't. We can't go to Mother. She'll only get mad and tell Father.'

'And so she should. Thomas needs a good talking to. More than that, if you ask me.'

'No, you don't understand. She'll get mad at *me*.'

She was sobbing hard now, her tiny frame shivering in the shadows.

'What do you mean? Why the hell would she be angry at you?'

But Jenny would not elaborate. Instead, she wiped her face with the back of her hand and pushed open the pantry door. She stopped and stared back at Summer. When she spoke, her voice was cold and brittle.

'Don't say anything to Mother.'

'But—'

'Mind your own fucking business, outsider.'

And then she was gone, back to the kitchen to wash dishes. Summer remained in the pantry a moment longer, feeling the coolness on her skin and the darkness all around. What had Jenny meant? Mother, of all people in this community, was the one that women and girls were meant to turn to when they needed help, especially if she was adopting the role of the Triple Goddess. For the Triple Goddess was the guardian of all women.

If Jenny was right, that Mother would be angry with her for rejecting Thomas's advances—despite the fact she was just fourteen years old, and below the legal age of consent—then Fortunate Keep was not the paradise it claimed to be.

Now, Jenny was gone, vanished in the middle of the night while everyone else had slept. And Summer was angry at herself for not pressing further, for not leaving the dining hall and going straight to Mother, with or without Jenny's blessing.

Where was she?

None of the other women or children in the bunk house

recalled seeing Jenny leave in the middle of the night, which Summer found surprising; surely someone had to be a light sleeper.

Joni was an emotional wreck, pacing up and down between the beds with tears welling in her eyes. The rest of the women seemed unconcerned. Perhaps Jenny had got up early, one suggested, and gone to start preparations in the kitchen, even though it was not her day for kitchen duty. Perhaps she was working in the vegetable garden, or perhaps she was bathing, or in the laundry room. All valid suggestions. Until Summer had checked each site, with Joni close on her heels, and found no trace of Jenny anywhere.

'I'm really worried. Really, really worried,' Joni said, as the two came to a halt in front of the meeting house.

It was still very early morning, but the sun was already warming the ground and making Summer tug at the collar of her T-shirt.

'Let's check the paddocks,' she said.

She began making her way to the back of the compound. Some of the women were emerging from the bunk room and heading towards the bath house. On the right side of the compound, the men's bunk room was still and quiet. None of the women seemed worried about Jenny. Unlike Joni, whose behaviour was bordering on manic.

'Jenny won't be there,' she said. 'Girls don't work in the paddocks. Besides, she doesn't like to make friends with the animals because she knows we end up eating them.'

'Then where else is there to look? Because that only leaves the men's quarters, and Mother and Father's house.' Summer paused to shoot a quick glance over her shoulder. 'Unless . . .'

'What? What is it?'

'Do you think maybe she ran away?'

Joni's eyes grew wide and round, and she began furiously

shaking her head. 'No way. Jenny would never leave this place. She hates the outside world! She told me she would rather die than go back there. Even if she wanted to run away, which she doesn't, Father keeps the gates locked at night, so none of the outsiders can break in and steal from us when we sleep. So you see, Jenny has to be here somewhere. She has to be!'

The tears that had been threatening to spill finally escaped Joni's eyes. She quickly swept them from her cheeks and sucked in a pitiful sob.

'It's all right. We'll find her,' Summer said.

They got moving again, passing the meeting house and coming upon the paddocks, which were currently empty, all the animals shut away in their shelters. Summer could hear them shuffling about and occasionally bleating. The faecal smell wafting out from the shelters was sharp and acrid.

'I told you Jenny wouldn't be here,' Joni said. 'Where *is* she?'

Summer scanned her surroundings. The three vehicles that were usually parked next to the paddocks were present and accounted for. In the far corner was the storage hut with its strange sloping roof, and over on the right was Mother and Father's house. The curtains appeared to be drawn in every window, the front door closed. No one was out sunning themselves on the porch, or enjoying the small rose garden that grew in front.

Any minute now, Fortunate Keep would come alive with men and women going about their morning chores before sitting down together for lunch. Then there would be more chores or leisure time, depending on the rota, followed by the daily meeting and dinner, then conversation and bed. The day would continue on, oblivious to Jenny's whereabouts.

She had to be at Mother and Father's house. It was the only place. Because the gates were locked at night and the fences were far too high to climb. And even if Jenny could make it to the top, she would have to negotiate thick coils of vicious razor wire.

Lowering her head, Summer began walking towards Mother and Father's house. Girls did not simply vanish in the middle of the night. And if they did, it was for nefarious reasons beyond their control.

'Wait, what are you doing?' Hands flapping, Joni struggled to keep up. 'You can't disturb Mother and Father, not at this hour! It's not allowed!'

'I don't give a shit.'

Summer pressed on, arms swinging, legs pumping like pistons. She would pull Father out of bed if she had to. Jenny was missing, and she would not rest until she was found.

'Please, Summer. You'll get us both into terrible trouble.'

'No one is forcing you to be here, Joni. Go back to bed if you're worried.'

But Joni did not leave. Instead, she quickened her pace until they were side-by-side.

'Last night, I asked Jenny about what Thomas did to her,' Summer said. 'She denied it at first, but when I said I would tell Mother, she said that Mother would be mad at her for not letting Thomas have his way. Is that true? Would Mother really be angry?'

As she walked, Joni kept her eyes fixed firmly on the ground and began twisting her fingers into knots.

'I don't know anything about that. And if Thomas tried to touch Jenny, she never told me. Which means it's probably not true because Jenny tells me everything.'

'Oh, grow up, Joni. If you couldn't see something was wrong with Jenny last night, then you're not a very good friend. And I know what I saw when Jenny came out of the bunk house yesterday.'

Joni's face was flushed and blotchy. 'Maybe they had an argument. Thomas is always teasing the girls.'

'This wasn't just teasing.'

'How can you be so sure?'

'Because I've been where Jenny was yesterday, and it was far worse than just teasing.'

Summer slid to a halt. Joni came up beside her, shocked eyes fixed on hers.

'Oh,' she said.

'Yes. Oh.'

They were standing at the foot of Mother and Father's porch steps. Summer peered up at the front door, then back at Joni. The anxiousness she had felt that first day, when she'd climb those steps to introduce herself to Mother, suddenly returned.

'Are you coming?'

Joni took a faltering step back. 'I'll—I'll wait here.'

'Fine.'

'And Summer?'

'Yes?'

'I *am* a good friend to Jenny. I'm a very good friend.'

'I know.'

Summer turned and sucked in a trembling breath. Then she was climbing the steps and reaching for Mother and Father's door.

28

She found Kenver sitting in darkness, with his back pressed against the bridge's railings and a trail of vomit staining his T-shirt. An empty vodka bottle lay on the ground next to him. Below, the A30 dual carriageway stretched out into the night in both directions. A fall, or a jump, from up here would end in one of two ways, neither of them good. At first, Blake thought Kenver was either dead or passed out. But as she shone torchlight at his face, he slowly raised a hand to shield his eyes.

Blake approached him, awash with shock and worry, but mostly anger. For now, she kept the latter in check. She hurried towards him and dropped to her knees, careful to avoid the pool of vomit next to him.

'What the fuck, Kenver?' she said. 'You've really gone and done it this time.'

Kenver's head rolled on his neck. He opened his eyes and squeezed them shut again, as if the outside world was too great to bear. He tried to speak, but his words were slurred and indecipherable.

'Come on. Let's get your drunken ass on its feet.'

Pocketing her torch, Blake hooked her cousin's arm around her shoulders. Holding onto his forearm, she hoisted him up and wrapped her free arm around his waist. She had always thought Kenver too skinny, which had more to do with his metabolism than a lack of food, seeing as how he could eat enough for two people and still go back for more. But now she was glad for it because the lack of weight made it easier to manoeuvre him, even if his lack of coordination and semi-consciousness were siding against her.

Reaching the end of the bridge, she dragged him along the path that cut through a copse and led towards her Corsa, which she had parked illegally on the roadside. She unlocked the doors with the car key fob and proceeded to bundle Kenver into the passenger seat. As she leaned over him to secure the seat belt, the stench of vomit made her stomach churn.

'Kenver Quick, you're going to owe me for this. Big time,' she muttered.

With her cousin secured, she opened the car boot, removed a large bottle of water, locked all the doors, then returned to the bridge, where she dumped the water over Kenver's vomit and picked up the empty vodka bottle. She hated littering; there was just no excuse for it.

Hurrying back to the car, she found Kenver fast asleep. The question now was what did she do with him? She couldn't take him to his place because he couldn't be left alone. She couldn't take him to his mother's because the last thing Aunt Hester needed to see right now was her son in such a pitiful state. And she couldn't take him to her parents' because Ed would have an aneurysm.

Blake swore under her breath as she started the engine and rolled down the windows. It had been more than twenty years since she'd had to babysit her cousin; she'd never expected to have to do it again now they were both adults.

She pulled away from the kerbside, the open windows doing little to erase the smell of vomit. As soon as Kenver was awake and sober, they would be having a serious talk about his alcohol dependence—and his reasons for leaving London. That was, if Blake didn't murder him in his sleep first.

29

Before Summer could knock on the door, it swung open to reveal Mother. She was dressed in an ankle length green nightgown and wore her long silver hair in a single braid. She looked tired, as if she'd been awake just long enough to put on a pair of slippers and start brewing a pot of coffee, the earthy aroma of which filled the air around her. She did not look pleased to see Summer.

'Well?' Mother said, her voice still gravelly with sleep. 'Are you just going to stand there in silence or are you going to explain to me why you're here? Judging by the racket you were just making, I presume you think it's important enough to break Father's rules.'

Mother peered over Summer's shoulder to see Joni standing at the foot of the steps with her head bowed and her hands clasped.

'You should know better than to come here at this hour, Joni,' Mother said. 'The problem with you is that you're weak minded. You need to build a backbone and a mind of your own, instead of following bad influences.'

Joni lowered her head even further. 'Yes, Mother. Sorry, Mother.'

The older woman returned her steely gaze to Summer. 'I'm still waiting.'

Summer cleared her throat. 'Jenny is missing.'

'What do you mean, missing?'

'She was there when we went to bed last night. When we woke up, she was gone. We've looked everywhere for her, except for the men's quarters and your house. She's gone.'

If Mother was worried, her face didn't show it. If anything, she looked more annoyed. 'Well, she's certainly not here. And she certainly won't be in the men's quarters. Father does not allow that kind of behaviour.'

'Maybe he doesn't.' Summer chose her words carefully. 'But it didn't stop Thomas from being in the women's bunk house yesterday afternoon.'

'What on earth are you talking about, girl? Thomas would never break Father's rules. You're mistaken.'

'I'm not. And if Jenny was here, she could show you the bruises on her arm that he gave her.'

A flicker of something crossed Mother's face. Was it concern? Or disbelief?

'What bruises?'

Drawing in a breath, Summer described to Mother how she had yesterday witnessed Jenny running from the bunk house in a state of upset, with Thomas emerging soon after.

'Jenny ran to Joni and the other women working in the vegetable garden. She hid behind them until Thomas went away. They all saw how terrified she was.'

A crease appeared on Mother's lined forehead. Glancing over Summer's shoulder, she peered down at Joni. 'Is what she says true?'

Joni nodded while keeping her gaze fixed on the ground.

'You saw it with your own eyes?'

Another nod, this one more hesitant.

For a long moment, no one spoke. The aroma of coffee grew stronger, reaching through the doorway to tease Summer's taste buds. At the foot of the steps, Joni nervously scuffed at the ground with her right foot.

At last, Mother shrugged her bony shoulders. 'It's probably all a misunderstanding. Jenny will be around here somewhere. She can be quite the sulk when she wants to be, particularly when she doesn't get her own way. Likes to take herself off to mope until she gets it out of her system. Why don't you have another look around? You may have missed her the first time.'

What the hell?

Her jaw slackening, Summer stared, wide-eyed, at Mother. 'Is this some kind of joke?'

'There's nothing amusing about this situation. Why would I laugh about one of my children being in distress? So perhaps you could be a good sister and run along to find Jenny and offer her some comfort.'

Summer was speechless. She twisted around to see if Joni shared the same shocked expression. But Joni was still staring at the ground as if her life depended on it. Forks of lightning shot through Summer's brain. She turned back to Mother.

'I want to talk to Father,' she said, crossing her arms in front of her stomach.

In the doorway, Mother smiled. 'No, I don't think so. Father is still asleep. He was working late last night and needs to rest.'

'I don't care. Wake him up.'

'And I don't care for your tone. The answer is still no.'

Summer leaned in closer. Her skin itched. 'A fourteen-year-old girl is missing. Yesterday, one of your men clearly tried to assault her. Yet you're telling me that's not important enough to wake Father from his beauty sleep?'

The smile faded from Mother's lips, and a hardness seeped into her features, turning them into resin.

'Might I remind you that you're a guest in our home. You will talk to me with respect. I am Mother!'

'Then might I remind *you*, that as *Mother*, you have a responsibility to care for your children. So, if I'm telling you that one of them is missing, you should be concerned. You should be taking action to find them, not throwing your authority around like you're in a dick swinging contest.'

Behind her, Joni audibly gasped. Mother grew impossibly still, her eyes suddenly the colour of night.

Summer held up her hands in mock defeat.

'Forget it,' she said. 'I'll look again, but this time I'll be checking the men's quarters. And if Jenny isn't there, I'll be coming straight back to search your house.'

Slowly, a smile returned to Mother's face, but this time her jaw was clenched so tightly that Summer thought her teeth might break.

Without waiting for a response from the woman, she turned and stomped down the steps. Then she was striding away from Mother and Father's house, fists swinging through the air. A fire was ablaze inside her, burning out of control. She didn't know how to put it out, or if she wanted to.

'Joni, come on!' she yelled, as she circled the paddocks.

The teenager was still standing at the foot of the porch steps, her head bowed and her body trembling. She peered up at Mother, who still wore the same terrible grin on her lips. Then Joni scurried away like a frightened dormouse, helplessly following Summer.

30

They sat in Blake's kitchen, mugs of black coffee between them. It was 3 AM. Outside, the world was dark and silent. Birds huddled together under leafy tree canopies, soon to awake with the early dawn. Below the surface of the nearby Argal Reservoir, huge carp cut through the water, feeding under the protection of night.

Upon returning home, Blake had dragged Kenver's semi-conscious form upstairs and into the bathroom, where she dumped him, fully clothed, into the shower and turned on the cold water. Kenver woke with a cry and immediately tried to get up, but Blake pinned him with her foot on his chest and let the water do its job.

Now, they were both dressed in jogging bottoms and clean T-shirts, Kenver's soiled clothing spinning in the washing machine. He looked dreadful, his complexion the colour of wet cement. Dark shadows circled his heavy eyes, which were jittery and unfocused. They had been sitting at the kitchen table for fifteen minutes, silence shrouding them like an itchy blanket. Kenver still hadn't touched his coffee.

'Just so you know,' Blake said, 'I've spent countless hours on night-time stakeouts, so if you're expecting me to give up and go to bed before you talk, you're sorely mistaken.'

Kenver's gaze floated up to meet hers then drifted away. He wrapped trembling fingers around his mug of coffee and dragged it towards him.

Anger bubbled in the pit of Blake's stomach. She tried to force it down; Kenver didn't need her fury right now, even if he deserved it.

'Come on, Kenver. Don't make me bring out bad cop.'

Kenver took a slow sip of coffee and winced as it burned his lips.

'You might want to work on your good cop routine first,' he said. 'It needs more good in it.'

'Well, it's three in the morning and I've had to rescue your sorry ass from a bridge while getting covered in your puke. So, excuse me if I'm not Little Miss Sunshine. Now talk. What the hell is going on with you? And before you deny it, I know this is about leaving London because you already said so on the phone. Do you remember that?'

Kenver put his coffee down and lowered his head.

Squeezing her eyes shut, Blake sucked in a breath. She held it for a count of four, before letting it out. When she opened her eyes again, she felt a little calmer.

'If you continue to bottle this up, it's going to destroy you. Please, Kenver. You're my cousin. I care about you. Maybe I can help you with whatever's going on. So tell me, why did you leave London?'

Silent tears fell from Kenver's eyes and splashed on the table. For a long time, he simply sat there, listless and devastated. And then he shook his head and stared into the shadows of the kitchen.

'I think I killed someone,' he said, in a deathly quiet voice. His shoulders trembled. 'I think I'm a killer.'

She had been expecting something bad, something like huge unpaid credit card debt. But not this. Not the taking of a life. Did killing really run in the family?

'Who do you think you killed?'

'Some guy.'

'I'm going to need more than that, Kenver. What guy? What happened? Did he try to hurt you? Was it self-defence?'

More tears slipped from his eyes. He peered down into his coffee, didn't like what he saw, and pushed it away.

'I don't know his name. Maybe John something.'

'And how did you know this John?'

'I didn't. Not really. I met him at a club. We got chatting and one thing led to another. I ended up going back to his place. I was wasted. We both were.'

'Did you have sex?' Blake asked.

'I think so.'

'What does that mean?'

'It means I was so wasted I don't exactly remember. But I think so.'

'Did you use protection?'

'I'm always very careful,' Kenver snapped. 'Don't get all high and mighty on me. You straight people are as promiscuous as the rest of us, if not more.'

'This isn't about sexuality or shaming, Kenver. This is about DNA and trace evidence.' Although Blake thought it impossible, Kenver's complexion turned a shade greyer. She waved a dismissive hand. 'So you went home with this guy, John something, possibly had sex, hopefully protected, and then what?'

A haunted look drifted over Kenver's face. His left eye twitched. 'I woke up in the morning, wondering where the hell I was and how I got there. I felt someone next to me. I turned. And there he was. Naked, with the sheets pulled back. Dead.'

'How did you know he was dead?'

'Because he wasn't breathing. Do you know how dying works or not?'

Blake let the sarcasm pass. She had a terrible feeling in her gut, a twisting of her stomach that refused to relax. She waited for Kenver to continue.

'At first, I thought he was awake and staring into space, probably waiting for me to get up and leave. But then I noticed the colour of his skin, and that he wasn't blinking. Or breathing. I touched his arm and it was stone cold.' The trembling in Kenver shoulders spread to his arms and torso. 'I panicked. I didn't know what to do. I knew it was too late to try resuscitation, not that I knew how to do it back then. All I could think about was that I was lying in bed with a dead man. I got this random thought in my head. That the longer I lay in that bed, the greater chance of me dying too, like the guy had some sort of killer virus. I know it was stupid, that it was just my brain trying to make sense of what my eyes were seeing while kick-starting my survival instinct. But it was all I could suddenly think about. So I jumped up, threw my clothes on, and I left. Found the nearest tube station and went straight home.'

The screech of a bird of prey flying over the cottage startled them both.

'Please tell me you called the police,' Blake said.

Like a scolded child, Kenver turned away. 'I got scared. I thought they'd arrest me.'

'Jesus, Kenver . . .'

'I know, okay? I know.'

'People would have seen you leaving the club with him. Then there's CCTV footage in the streets, which would have captured you both walking to his place, and you leaving alone the next morning, from the sounds of it, in a state of panic.' Blake pressed her hands to her face, then ran them through her hair. 'What happened after you went back to your flat?'

'I don't remember much, it was kind of a blur. I called in sick to work, and mostly I just freaked out. I kept waiting for the police to come knocking. After a couple of days, they still hadn't. But I knew they would eventually. I decided I didn't want to be there when they did. So I came back to Cornwall.'

He wouldn't look at her now, the shame he carried too great to bear.

'Why were you so afraid the police would arrest you for his death? We don't even know how he died. For all you know, he could have been sick. Young people die all the time. Maybe he had a brain tumour or a bad heart. Just because you had the misfortune of sleeping with him on the night he died doesn't make you responsible, Kenver. Does it? So why were you convinced the police would charge you?'

Still Kenver would not look at her. Now his entire body was shaking. He wedged his hands between his arms and his sides.

Blake leaned forward. 'You're not telling me something. What is it?'

Kenver violently shook his head.

'Damn it, Kenver. I can't help you if you don't tell me the whole story.'

'I gave him drugs, okay?' The words fired from his mouth like bullets. 'He said he'd never done anything like that before. Only booze and weed. He wanted to try. So, in the toilets at the club I gave him some G. And when we went back to his place he wanted more. I shouldn't have given it to him, but I did. He must've had a seizure while I was passed out, and choked on his own vomit.' Kenver froze, his face twisted in a terrible grimace.

'That's why I didn't go to the police. Because I killed him and I was scared.'

Blake wanted to scream at Kenver. To slap his face and shake him hard, until he threw up again. Instead, she sat as calmly as possible and stared at him.

'What is G?' she asked.

'GHB. Gamma hydroxybutyrate. It makes you euphoric and increases your sex drive.'

'And apparently kills people. For Christ's sake, Kenver! I don't know what to do with this. Did you ever try to find out about the guy? About John?'

'I kept an eye on the news, but there was nothing about him. Or if there was, it was small enough for me to miss.'

'Which means the medical examiner would have likely concluded death by drug misuse. Stories like that don't make the papers anymore. But death by misuse makes sense. He voluntarily took the drug, which means no signs of being forced.'

'I would never—'

'And no signs of sexual assault. But there would be questions around consent. Such as, while under the influence, was John fully able to give consent?'

'Fuck, Blake! I was wrecked too. You know I would never do anything like that!'

'But the police don't know that. And you fled the scene! That immediately makes you a person of interest. Even if the cause of death is established as an overdose, the police will be interested in how John got the drugs and who gave them to him. Which means they would trace John's movements from the night before, and that means interviewing friends and family, and checking text messages and social media. And when they discover he went to a club, they request the CCTV footage from that night. Perhaps his friends have described the stranger they saw him leave the club with—a very memorable stranger covered in tattoos—and so the police then start searching street cameras for the pair of you. And when they find you went back to his place and then left alone in the morning, it's only a matter of time before they discover your identity and track you down.'

Kenver clutched his stomach. 'I think I'm going to puke again.'

'Except this all happened, what, two, two and a half years ago? And no one has come to arrest you. Which means, somewhere along the chain of investigation, they ran into a brick wall.'

'What does that mean?'

'It could mean a few things. One, that John's cause of death was something other than an overdose. Two, that there was a lack of traceable digital or forensic evidence that would lead them to you. Or three, rising knife crime and homicide on the streets of London takes precedence over an accidental overdose, especially when resources and department budgets are strained.' Blake held up her hands. 'Which in all likelihood means you're off the hook.'

Kenver stared at her, open-mouthed. 'Off the hook?'

'Probably, yes. But maybe never go back to London. Just in case.'

'But I killed someone.'

'Possibly. But if you did it was done indirectly. You didn't force the guy to take anything. He was a grown adult who made an unfortunate choice. One that you now have to live with for the rest of your life. Because you may not have been the one to kill him but you did provide the means.' Blake paused. 'If, of course, his death was determined to be an overdose.'

Kenver tilted his head and glared at her, as if she'd gone mad.

'I killed a man,' he said. 'Why are you taking it so calmly?'

Blake picked up her coffee mug and warmed her hands.

'Because I know how it feels to take a life. And I know that feeling will never leave me, no matter how much I might try to forget. So, you don't need any more shit from me than I've already given you, because you're about to give yourself an entire lifetime of it. If you want to feel better about what you did, you could always turn yourself over to the police for questioning. But then you risk charges of involuntary manslaughter or reckless endangerment, possibly even sexual assault. Not to mention the fact that letting two years pass before going to the police makes you look guilty as hell. So, my advice would be to accept your part in a man's accidental death, or choose to believe he died of something else and that you're entirely innocent. Either way, I want to know why you were taking something as dangerous as GHB in the first place.'

Across the table, Kenver's body went rigid and heavy lines creased his brow.

'Because I'm fucking miserable,' he said. 'Because living in a world where you're made to feel shame for being anything but straight is exhausting. And I don't want to hear, "Oh, but it's better now. You can get married." So fucking what? If that's true then tell me why queer kids are still cutting themselves, or worse, ending their lives because of constant bullying from both straight kids *and* adults? Things may be better on the outside, but all that shame and hatred that's been forced upon us over the years is still festering inside. And none of you ever apologise for it! That's why I took G and everything else. That's why I drink. Because when I do the shame goes away. At least it did, until that John guy died.'

He looked up at Blake, and she had never seen him so sad. Getting up, she went to Kenver and threw her arms around him.

'I'm sorry,' she said. 'I had no idea you felt like that.'

'Why would you? You're too busy living your boring heterosexual life.'

'Hey, I kissed a girl once.'

'Right. I bet you were fifteen and it was while playing spin the bottle.'

'Something like that.' Blake rested her chin on the top of Kenver's head. 'It's late. You're staying with me for a few days. We can talk some more, if you want, but right now we both need to sleep.'

Kenver said nothing, just leaned into her and closed his eyes.

~

An hour later, Blake sat in bed watching the first rays of daylight seep through the curtains and listening to the first birdsong. Kenver's terrible confession played on her mind. She hoped that she'd given him the right advice, but only Kenver could decide how he lived the rest of his life, and if some of it was spent behind bars. She hoped he would choose wisely. Thinking of Kenver's deep unhappiness left her feeling somewhat guilty, and she resolved to support him as much as she could, or he would allow. But his unhappiness also got her thinking about the Teague family, as well as Carrie Killigrew and her son, Cal. And that, in turn, pulled her back to her current investigation, which had been paused at the discovery of Cal's mysterious Bone Man at Trevelyan Wood.

Everything about the Teague case had been sending her back into the past, not forward. Until now, Blake had been dismissive, believing it was due to a distinct lack of evidence. But what if she was wrong? What if to move forward she first had to go back? Perhaps later today she would take a trip to Trevelyan Wood and see what she might find. Perhaps she would take Kenver with her —nature was nothing if not healing. Until then, she would try to sleep, even if sleep tried to evade her. It was her nightly dalliance.

31

The rage that Summer felt was beginning to scare her. She felt as if she'd been holding it in for years, wrapping her arms around its circumference, holding on to it with all of her strength, while it writhed and squirmed, trying to break free from her grasp. But now, she was struggling to keep it under control. Fortunate Keep was a sham. A twisted lie. And everyone who had been sucked in by it was a mindless fool. She included herself among them, because she had been close to believing in Father's vision of utopia. But Father was no god on earth, no vessel for the Horned One. He was a narcissist ruling over a fool's paradise. Nothing more.

As for Mother, the woman had no business playing such a role. It was clear to Summer now, as she stalked across the compound, heading straight for the men's quarters, that Mother was as indoctrinated as the rest of them, choosing to believe in Thomas's dedication to Father's rules rather than the eyewitness testimonies that contested quite the opposite. No, Fortunate Keep was not governed equally by Mother and Father. This was a man's kingdom, a Fortunate Isle of Father's making to do with what he pleased, like a boy playing in a sandbox.

Summer was almost at the men's quarters. She was looking forward to hearing what Thomas had to say for himself. Behind her, Joni was struggling to catch up. Since Summer's outburst, the teen had paled to the colour of milk and had been unusually quiet. Until now.

'You shouldn't have spoken to Mother like that,' she called, in between gulps of air. 'You disrespected her. Now she's going to tell Father, and we're both going to be in big trouble.'

Summer scoffed. 'Oh, fuck Mother. And fuck Father too. Don't you see the only thing they care about is how much people worship them? And Mother certainly doesn't care about Jenny. If she did, she would have woken Father up without even questioning it.'

'That's not true! Mother cares about all of us. And maybe she's right. Maybe Jenny is hiding somewhere and we missed her the first time.'

'We didn't miss her. Jenny is gone.'

They reached the men's bath house. Without hesitating, Summer threw open the door and stepped inside. Joni froze in the doorway. A man in his late twenties, who Summer believed was called Alain, was naked and about to climb into a bath of water. Upon seeing Summer, he froze but made no attempt to cover himself.

'You're not allowed to be in here,' he said.

'I know, but it's urgent. Jenny is missing. Have you seen her?'

Alain removed his leg from the bath and stood up, his genitals on full display.

'What do you mean, missing?'

'I mean she's missing. As in gone. Why does no one understand the meaning of that word around here?'

'Have you tried the kitchen?'

'I've looked everywhere. Which is why I'm now looking in places I'm not supposed to.'

She stepped forward and to the left, scanning the bath house.

Joni remained in the doorway, eyes almost bulging out of their sockets as she stared at Alain's nakedness. She blushed and quickly turned her back on him.

Alain peered down at his bath, where the water was already beginning to cool.

'Clearly Jenny isn't in here,' he said.

Ignoring him, Summer moved further into the bath house, checking each tub and finding them empty. When she reached the end of the room, she instinctively turned to her right, where the entrance to the laundry room was found in the women's bath house. But here in the men's, there were only more bathtubs for bathing.

'May I have my bath now?' Alain said, heaving his shoulders.

Summer glared at him. 'Sure, why not? Clearly a bath is more important to you than a missing girl.'

She made her way outside, pushing past Joni, then headed straight for the men's bunk house. Stopping at the door, she listened for signs of life. Then she pushed it open and stepped inside. This time, Joni stayed back.

As Summer's eyes adjusted to the gloom, gasps and muted laughter filled the air. Some of the men were in the throes of getting up, while others still lay in bed, some awake, some still sleeping. Heads were turned in Summer's direction, each face a picture of shock and surprise.

'I'm looking for Jenny,' she called. 'Have you seen her?'

One of the men called back: 'You're not supposed to be in here. It's forbidden.'

Summer stepped forward to check under the nearest beds and the space in between.

'Didn't you hear me?' the man said, more forcefully this time. 'You have to leave.'

She ignored him. 'Jenny? It's Summer. Are you here?'

Another man, this one younger and possibly still a teenager, giggled nervously as Summer stooped to check beneath his bed.

'Have you seen Jenny?' she asked him, to which he shook his head and continued to laugh. Getting back on her feet, she addressed the rest of the men. 'Someone must have seen her. People don't just disappear.'

'She's clearly not in here. So leave,' a voice called out.

From the shadows, Thomas appeared. He was naked except for his underwear, his lean, muscled body illuminated by daylight seeping through the window. There was an arrogant smirk on his lips, which only fuelled Summer's fury. She marched up to him and leaned in, until their noses were almost touching.

'What did you do to Jenny yesterday? And don't give me any bullshit. I saw the bruises on her arm. She was terrified.'

The smug smile transformed into a sneer. 'I didn't do anything she didn't ask for. And I don't need to answer to you.'

More laughter rippled around the room.

Summer clenched her jaw. 'You do realise rape gets you fifteen years behind bars in this country, don't you? And even if consent was given, which I'm certain it wasn't, Jenny is under age. Which makes you a paedophile, you sick little fuck.'

Spittle flew from her mouth as she spat out the words, and landed on Thomas's face. Outwardly, he appeared unbothered, almost amused by her outrage. But this close up, Summer could see deep into his eyes, and what she saw scared her.

As they continued to glower at each other, Summer sensed

movement on her left. Matthew appeared, hands raised in pleading and eyes flitting to the doorway.

'Summer, you really can't be in here,' he said. 'Please. You'll get into awful trouble.'

'What are they going to do, Matthew? Kick me out? Fine, I'll come back with the police in tow, and they can pull this place apart until they find Jenny.'

More movement, this time on her right. Summer turned to see Kane, the man who had driven her to Fortunate Keep and whose silence had been unnerving. There was something deeply unpleasant about his hulking appearance and cold, shark-like eyes. And there was a strange smell about him, which Summer had noticed back in the car, and was even more pungent now—an odour that made her think of rotten apples.

'You stay where you are, or you lose a testicle,' she warned, soliciting yet more laughter from some of the younger men. She turned on them. 'This isn't funny! Jenny is missing. Why isn't anyone taking this seriously? People don't vanish in a puff of smoke —surely one of you knows where she is.'

'You're making a scene,' Thomas said. 'If you're so convinced something has happened to Jenny, go and talk to Father. I'm sure he can offer a perfectly reasonable explanation.'

Summer stared at him, at all the male faces surrounding her. Someone in this room knew something about Jenny's whereabouts. The lack of concern, the laughing and joking, and the smugness on Thomas's face, all but confirmed it. Yet, it was clear that neither Thomas nor the others were going to tell her anything.

'Fine,' she said. 'I'll talk to Father. I've already told Mother what I saw yesterday, so don't think for a second you've got away with what you did. I hope they nail you to the wall.'

Thomas smiled. 'If I'm guilty of anything, the Horned One will deal out my punishment, and I will accept it. Until then, I answer to no one. Especially not to a homeless slut who thought she could get a free ride.'

Summer moved in closer to him, pressing her forehead against his. 'Go fuck yourself, Thomas. Because no one else is going to.'

She turned, ready to wage war on Mother and Father's house. But, as she soon saw, the fight had been brought to her. Father stood before Summer, still dressed in his nightgown, a mixture of tiredness and disappointment in his eyes.

'You and I,' he said, with a slow shake of his head, 'need to have a little chat about how things work around here.'

32

Trevelyan Wood was approximately three miles long and populated by a mix of conifers and wide-leaved trees, including western hemlock, Scots pine, oak, alder, ash and eucalyptus. Inhabiting the woodland was an equally diverse wildlife. Red deer, otters, badgers and even the humble water shrew could be spotted by patient nature lovers. A popular spot for hikers and dog walkers, weekends in Trevelyan Wood were often a hive of activity. But with the day heating up in spite of the shade provided by the canopies, most responsible dog owners had walked their pets earlier and already returned home. Which left Trevelyan Wood strangely quiet.

Blake had managed to sleep a few hours, waking just after 10 AM. She'd left Kenver to sleep in the spare room while she showered and dressed, then emptied two bottles of red wine and a half bottle of bourbon down the kitchen sink. It pained her to do it, but with Kenver staying for the next few days, she could not risk putting temptation in his path. Bringing him a mug of coffee, she shook him awake and informed him they'd be leaving the house in just over an hour.

'I can't go anywhere,' he moaned, pulling the duvet over his head. 'I think I'm dying.'

Looking at her cousin, Blake could well believe it. His skin was sallow, almost green, and the alcohol still seeping from his pores smelled like formaldehyde.

'You're lucky you're not dead already. And whether you like it or not, you're coming with me. After last night, you can't be trusted alone.'

A hand slipped out from under the duvet and reached for the coffee on the nightstand.

'Where are we going?'

'To the woods. You'll love it. There's nothing like getting out in nature to cure a hangover.'

'You know what's better? Twelve hours of uninterrupted sleep.'

Now it was just after 2 PM. Blake and Kenver made their way from the gravel car park, where Blake's Corsa was just one of three vehicles, and entered Trevelyan Wood. Blake had wanted to get here earlier, but as soon as Kenver had attempted to dress, he'd run to the toilet and promptly vomited. Blake had been tempted to leave him at her cottage while she drove to the wood by herself. But she had meant what she'd said: she did not feel safe leaving him alone. At least, not until he convinced her that he wouldn't attempt anything stupid.

'Isn't this nice?' Blake said, as they walked along a winding path surrounded by towering firs. All around, birdsong filled the air, while a gentle breeze darted between the tree trunks.

Kenver was dawdling behind. A little colour had returned to his face since he'd managed to keep down two slices of buttered toast, but that wasn't to say he looked close to human. Blake thought it lucky they weren't in the throes of a zombie apocalypse, or Kenver could easily be mistaken for one of the undead and end up with a bullet between his eyes.

'Remind me why we're here,' he said, in a voice full of sawdust.

'I told you, to enjoy nature. And I'm following a lead.'

'What lead?'

'Ever heard of the Bone Man?'

'I have a feeling I'm about to.'

'Oh, you'll like this one. It's right up your street.'

The path turned. They passed a clearing where a fallen tree had been sawn into several sections. Up ahead, the firs began to blend with silver birch. Taking a sip of water from her flask, Blake relayed the chilling tale of the Bone Man of Trevelyan Wood.

Back in the seventeenth century, there had lived a wealthy landowner named Lord Trevelyan. Trevelyan was feared by the local villagers. Not only was he a cruel man, but they believed he had made a pact with the Devil in exchange for immortality. For Lord Trevelyan never aged.

A keen huntsman, he would spend many an hour on the back of his steed, stalking through the woodland with his bow and arrow, in search of red deer. But deer were not the only prey that felt the prick of Trevelyan's arrowheads. Every second month, by the light of a full moon, one of the villagers would disappear, only to find themselves racing through the woodland, with Lord Trevelyan hunting them like an animal. When death came, it was slow and savage.

Felling his victim with an arrow through the leg, Trevelyan would sling the body over the back of his horse, and then ride to the centre of the wood, where a tall and crooked tree stood on its own in a clearing, not a single leaf on its gnarled branches. The locals called it the Devil's tree, for the ground around it was ash black and devoid of life, and the sap that flowed from within it was the colour of blood. It was before this tree that Lord Trevelyan would flay his victims alive and hang their skin over its branches, where he would butcher their bodies and place the bones inside a hollow of the tree trunk. The flayed skin was a warning to the villagers of what would happen if they dared interfere with his work. The bones were an offering to the Devil, in exchange for Lord Trevelyan's immortality. And each time he brought a new victim to the Devil's tree, the hollow would always be empty and waiting.

One day, no longer able to tolerate Lord Trevelyan's barbarous ways, the villagers planned to put an end to his murderous behaviour. Creeping into the wood, they ambushed the nobleman as he prepared for his latest hunt. They first slew his horse, then dragged him to the Devil's tree, where they hanged him from its branches and flayed him alive, taking first the skin, then the meat and organs, until he was nothing more than a bloody skeleton.

A bone man.

But instead of offering his bones up to the hollow, they left Lord Trevelyan's body hanging, as a warning to anyone else considering a deal with the Devil in exchange for the villagers' lives.

But Lord Trevelyan's reign of terror did not end there. For it is said that, even today, the Bone Man can be heard rattling as he swings high above your head. And if you dare to look up, he'll reach down with skeletal fingers to take your skin and wear it as his own. And then the Bone Man will rise once again to continue his murderous hunt . . .

Blake and Kenver walked deeper into the woodland. The path was becoming more overgrown and harder to follow. Despite having seen two other vehicles in the car park, they had yet to stumble upon another person.

'So, what do you think? Scary or what?' Blake smiled devilishly at Kenver, who shrugged a shoulder.

'Cool story, bro. Can we go home now?'

'You suck. And no, we cannot.'

Blake walked on, almost tripping over an exposed tree root as she lost sight of the path once more. Above her head, the tree canopies grew thicker, the light dimmer. The chorus of birdsong that had followed them all the way suddenly grew more cautious. She stopped in her tracks, searching the ground ahead for the path.

Kenver caught up to her and held out his hand. She passed him her flask.

'So are we on a ghost hunt or something?' he asked, after taking a long drink of water.

Taking back her flask, Blake wiped the rim with her sleeve and brought it to her lips.

'Not exactly. To be honest, I don't really know what I'm looking for.'

'That's good to know as we continue to get lost in the forest.'

'We're not lost. The path is right there. See?'

Blake pointed to the narrow trail coiling between the trees three metres to her left. They started walking again, stepping over fallen branches and skirting a large holly bush, its berries already beginning to turn red, which was unusual but not unheard of at this time of year.

What *was* she looking for? Signs of the Dawn Children's old encampment, where she would find a clue that pointed in the direction of the Teague twins? No. She was neither an optimist nor an idealist. All she knew was that Cal Anderson's terror of the Bone Man had compelled her to come here. The ghostly story had clearly been used by the leaders of the Dawn Children to frighten and to control. Because what child wouldn't be afraid of such a terrifying spectre, especially when camping out beneath those bony, skin laden branches? It had obviously had a lasting effect on Cal, who was now twenty-three years old and still afraid.

The path grew narrower, the woodland denser, trees leaning in from all sides. The birdsong had all but fallen away, leaving just a solo voice to sing a haunting melody. Behind Blake, Kenver slapped at his neck, crushing a bloodthirsty midge and leaving a scarlet smear on his skin.

Why was she here? She honestly didn't know.

But twenty minutes later, when they'd lost the path for real and were tripping over raw foliage, and Kenver was cursing Blake's name, she saw a flash of something in the distance, between the trees.

Blake froze and held up a silencing hand.

'What is it? Is it homeless people? Because I've watched *Hobo with a Shotgun*, and you don't want to mess with them.'

'Kenver, I don't even want to know what you're talking about. Just be quiet.'

Blake advanced a few steps. Taking out her phone, she activated the camera, then pinched the screen to zoom in. Kenver leaned in over her shoulder.

'Is that a tent?' he asked.

'Looks like it. I'm going to take a closer look.'

She moved forward but Kenver grabbed her arm. 'This is the part in horror films when the brunette always makes a stupid decision like going to check out a random tent in the middle of the forest, and ends up getting hacked to pieces. What do you think you're doing?'

Blake glared at Kenver's hand. He released his grip.

'What I'm doing,' she said, 'is my job. If it's too much for you, you're welcome to stay here or go back to the car and wait for me. What you're not going to do is interfere.'

'Then why did you bring me along?'

'I'm beginning to ask myself that same question.'

She started forward, picking her way through the dense undergrowth. Despite the dry ground, it was slow going; stealth was never easy in a woodland filled with debris that snapped and crunched underfoot.

Shooting a brief glance over her shoulder, she saw that Kenver had chosen to stay put. Good, she thought. She was still angry with him. Still horrified by what he'd done. And she worried about what he would do next. He was a grown adult in charge of making his own life choices, but he was also in trouble. Did she suggest rehab? Or joining a local AA group? Or at the very least, talking to his GP? And then there was the matter of the dead man, John "Something", as he was now known in Blake's head. What did she do about him?

If Kenver did decide to turn himself in to the police, he was seriously looking at time in prison, his life and reputation destroyed. Blake knew what Kenver did was wrong, but it had been John Something's decision as a consenting adult to take the drug. And he would have known the risks. Even so, neither of them could have predicted what had happened next.

Blake drew closer to the tent. Life might feel terrible to Kenver right now, she thought, but at least he'd woken up that morning and wasn't rotting in the ground, his family and friends still trying to make sense of how he'd ended up there.

The trees parted and Blake found herself in a small clearing. The tent was a green, one-person backpacking tent, the kind that was designed to be durable yet lightweight, and easily disassembled for quick getaways. The entrance to the tent was currently zipped up, with a small padlock in place that told Blake its occupant was currently elsewhere. A metre and a half in front of the tent was a makeshift campfire, surrounded by a circle of stones. A metal cooking tripod stood over the remains of the fire, with a blackened pot attached to it. Blake peered inside and saw the leftovers of some kind of stew. A couple of flies were crawling over it. She touched the pot, which was still warm but cooling.

Hanging from a low tree branch on the edge of the clearing were wet clothes. Men's clothes, Blake noted, as she stepped closer. They smelled clean too, as if recently laundered. Which meant there had to be a river nearby. And the wetness of the clothes implied that they'd been washed very recently—which told Blake that whoever the clothes belonged to was not far from home.

The hairs on the back of Blake's neck stood up. She heard Kenver shout something then start running towards her.

She sensed the man before she felt the tip of his knife, cold and sharp against the back of her neck.

Slowly, Blake raised her hands and turned around.

Kenver reached the edge of the clearing and skidded to a halt, his eyes wide and his chest heaving up and down.

'Everything's fine, Kenver,' she said. 'Stay where you are.'

The man standing before her shot a glare in Kenver's direction before returning his attention to Blake. The blade of his kitchen knife was just centimetres from her face. He was wild looking, dressed in nothing but dirty denim shorts. His light brown hair was untamed and matted, as if it hadn't seen a brush in years, and his long beard was tangled with knotty clumps. His eyes, which were sea green and beautiful, had seen more than their share of horrors.

'What are you doing?' he said to Blake, his upper lip peeling back in an animalistic snarl.

She was surprised at how young his voice sounded; from his feral appearance and pained eyes, she'd thought him to be at least in his thirties. But as Blake attempted to see past the beard and unkempt hair, she was struck by how familiar the man seemed. Had she met him somewhere before?

At the edge of the clearing, Kenver gently slid one foot forward. Then the other.

The man waved the knife in Blake's face. 'I asked you a question. What are you doing here?'

Realisation hit Blake hard, as if she'd slammed into a tree.

'My God, it's you,' she said. 'I need to show you something.'

Lowering her hands, she pulled her backpack from her shoulder and slowly delved inside. The man watched her, bringing the tip of the blade even closer. Kenver was two steps behind him now, ready to pounce.

From the bag, Blake removed a sheet of paper. She held it up for the man to see. He stared at it with confused eyes. Ripples appeared on his brow. Then realisation hit him too.

Standing just behind the man, Kenver saw that Blake was holding up one of the flyers they'd circulated in Bournemouth.

'It's you,' Blake repeated, this time with a smile on her lips. 'You're Morgan Teague.'

33

They walked to Mother and Father's house in silence, with Summer trying not to march ahead while Father dawdled behind, his stick tapping the ground. He was a heavy man, and even a brief walk such as this left him struggling for breath. Summer wondered if he had a medical condition, or if this self-created lifestyle, in which the only time he needed to lift a finger was to wipe his own arse, had left him desperately unhealthy.

Joni had been ordered back to the women's sleeping quarters, where she was to stay until Father was ready to speak to her. As for Thomas, he was allowed to go about his day as if he were an innocent victim. Which enraged Summer further. She wanted to lash out at Thomas, to strike him hard in the face and make his nose bleed. And she wanted to do it in front of the other men because she knew that being struck down by a waif of a girl would be his ultimate humiliation. Summer also had a desire to commit violence against Father. Thomas was nothing but a badly behaved dog. And behind every badly behaved dog was a badly behaved owner.

They reached the house. Summer waited for Father to climb the steps, which he did with a sweaty red face and clammy palms. Reaching the porch, he opened the door and turned to her.

'Don't keep me waiting, child.'

Seething at his hypocrisy, Summer took her time on the steps before following him inside. She found Father standing next to the great totem of the Horned One, one hand pressed against the wall and breathing heavily.

'Be a good daughter and fetch me a glass of water,' he said.

Summer played along, filling a glass from a jug in the kitchenette and handing it to Father.

'Thank you, child.'

She watched him drain it, then hand the empty glass back to her. She crouched down and put the glass on the floor.

Father stared at it, an amused smile on his lips.

'So, tell me exactly why you felt the need to cause such chaos this morning. You've turned Fortunate Keep upside down.'

'Jenny is missing,' Summer said. 'But you already know that. Mother told you.'

She looked around, suddenly aware that Mother was not here. Unless she'd been sent to one of the back rooms.

Father moved away from the wall to stand in front of the fireplace. This was clearly not a conversation for sitting.

'Ah, yes. Dearest Jenny. I believe Mother told you that Jenny can be a bit of a sulk and has been known to squirrel herself away in the past. You may think you've looked everywhere for her, but I assure you there are all sorts of nooks and crannies a child of her age can squeeze into. I'm sure she'll turn up soon. So you see, there really was no need for you to wake everyone with all your yelling and thinly veiled threats. That's not how we do things around here.'

The anger inside Summer was dangerously close to erupting.

Then, like a volcano, it would become an unstoppable force of nature, destroying everything in its path.

'Jenny isn't hiding anywhere,' she said, her words slow and deliberate. 'And she hasn't run away either; you lock the gates at night and those fences are at least four metres tall and topped with razor wire. Jenny is gone. Something bad has happened, I can feel it. And I won't stop looking until I find her.'

Leaning his stick against the wall, Father placed his hands upon his large stomach and let out a heavy sigh. 'And what terrible fate do you believe has fallen upon Jenny?'

'I don't know. But I'm willing to bet Thomas does.'

'Ah yes, Thomas. Mother says you believe he assaulted Jenny yesterday. How can you be so sure?'

'Because, like I told Mother, I saw Jenny come running out of the women's bunk house. She was crying, she had bruises on her arms, and her dress was pulled down. Thomas came out moments later, looking angry.'

'So you didn't witness any kind of assault with your own eyes?'

'I didn't need to. It's obvious what happened.'

'To you, perhaps. But it could be, and stick with me here, that you were seeing what you wanted to see. That part of you is desperate to expose Fortunate Keep as a loathsome, terrible place, somewhere so awful that you couldn't possibly stay on and live a peaceful, harmonious existence with the rest of the community. Because that would mean letting go of all your anger and mistrust, and it would mean embracing happiness. You've been on your own for so long now, Summer. Do you think it's entirely possible that you've just come to expect the worst? Could it be that you saw a lovers' quarrel and turned it into an assault?'

'Lovers' quarrel?' Summer was so aghast that she couldn't help but laugh. 'Jenny is fourteen years old, for fuck's sake! Thomas is in his twenties. That's not a lover's quarrel. It's rape.'

'And those are very strong accusations you're making.' Father's face suddenly softened. 'Am I right to believe that you have been a victim of sexual assault?'

Summer froze. Awful memories flooded her mind, which she tried to shut out. 'That's got nothing to do with what's happening to Jenny. You need to find her. And you need to deal with Thomas. It's not okay for him to be walking around without a care in the world after what he's done. But that's typical of this place, isn't it? It's one rule for the masses, and another for you and your favourites.'

'I don't believe that's true. Everyone is treated well here. I just happen to believe that hard work should be paid in rewards. For example, take Thomas and the other boys, who have to face the hardship of the outside world every time they go to sell the women's trinkets and spread our word. No one forces them to go out there. Each one of them volunteers. They endure that hardship so others don't have to. So that the rest of us may benefit. Their selflessness deserves to be rewarded, don't you think?'

'Not if the rewards include attempted assault on a minor. And by the way, if you reward some and not others, that's not utopia. That's capitalism.'

'Clearly you misunderstand our ways, which is a shame. Nevertheless, I will talk to Thomas and hear what he has to say. And if I find that he has committed such a heinous act as you have described, he will be duly punished.'

'And Jenny? In case you've forgotten, she's still missing.'

Father sucked in a heavy breath and let it out. Summer was clearly wearing him down. Good, she thought.

'You say you've searched everywhere? Including the men's quarters?'

'That's right. Everywhere except your house and the storage hut near the paddocks.'

'You won't find Jenny in there. It's kept under lock and key to make sure our grains aren't tampered with. She couldn't get in even if she wanted to. As for my house . . .' Father waved his hand in a theatrical gesture. 'If you believe Mother and I have something to do with Jenny's disappearance, then you'll be wanting to look around. You have my consent. Go forth and explore.'

Summer stared at him, her mouth half open. She had been expecting Father to put up a fight or give a hundred reasons why she could not trespass on his sacred space. Yet here he was, practically offering her a tour, as if he were an estate agent and she a prospective buyer.

He laughed at her. 'What? Did you think me so monstrous that I wouldn't aid in the search for one of my children? You hurt my feelings.'

It was a test. That's what it was. If Summer chose to violate Mother and Father's home, where no one was ever allowed to go, then she would be showing the greatest disrespect to them and would be forced to leave. But if she refused Father's invitation, she would have to admit she was wrong about Jenny. Worse still, she'd have to admit she was wrong about Thomas. Which Summer knew she was not.

She stared at the open door on the right that led to Mother and Father's private quarters. If Father had something to hide, why would he give her full access to his home? It made no sense. *Was* Summer wrong about Jenny? Would the teenager suddenly reappear and admit she had been tucked away somewhere, licking her wounds?

No. Something didn't feel right. Yet Summer still had to make a choice.

Staring silently at Father, she brushed past him and stepped through the doorway into a dimly lit passage. Father did not follow. As her eyes slowly adjusted to the gloom, she saw two doors, one on her left and one straight ahead.

She tried the door on the left, which opened onto a small bathroom. Inside, she was surprised to find the floor and walls were tiled. There was a sink on her left and a ceramic bathtub on her right, below a large window with a view of the woodland beyond. Both the sink and bathtub had taps. But an even bigger surprise was the toilet in the corner, which looked like any other toilet you'd find in the average house, and a world apart from the disgusting latrines that Summer and the others were forced to use.

Moving over to the sink, Summer tried the cold water tap. At first nothing happened. Then, through the wall, she heard a mechanical pumping sound. A second later, a thin but steady stream of water spouted from the tap. Shocked, Summer ran her fingers through the stream, as if she couldn't quite believe what she was seeing. She switched off the tap and dried her hand on a towel, which, unlike the threadbare ones they used in the bath house, was soft and fluffy. Her gaze returned to the toilet. She reached for the handle to see if it would flush, then stopped. She wasn't here to play like a child. She was here to find Jenny.

Returning to the passage, she closed the bathroom door, then opened the remaining door up ahead. Summer entered Mother and Father's bedroom. It was a large space, with a king-sized bed at its centre, which was topped with pristine white sheets and fat, springy pillows. Bedside cabinets sat on either side. An ornately carved trunk rested at the foot of the bed, while a dressing table and chair stood in the far corner and a chaise longue sat below a large picture window.

Summer stared at it all in disbelief. The people of Fortunate Keep were living incredibly modest lives, sharing dirty bathwater and pissing in holes in the ground. Meanwhile, Mother and Father were living lives of luxury in comparison. The volcano inside her began to spit out lava. Again, she reminded herself of why she was here.

A pair of built-in wardrobes stood on the left. Summer opened the doors and peered inside. The interior was narrow and filled with hanging clothes of similar cloth and colours as those worn by the rest of Fortunate Keep. Father's ceremonial robes excepted, it was the one facet of modesty he and Mother could not escape from without courting cries of hypocrisy. Sweeping the clothes to one side, Summer felt around, patting the back walls and then the floors. But she found no secret doors or hidden compartments. And she did not find Jenny.

She got to her feet and regarded the room, her gaze landing on the large trunk at the foot of the bed. Kneeling before it, she made quick work of the clasp. Inside was more bedding. On top of it was a closed shoe box. Fishing it out, she shot a look at the open bedroom door, then removed the lid. The shoe box contained bundles of papers. She took them out and sifted through them, her eyes growing wider by the second.

Summer was looking at receipts and statements of bank transactions, all depositing sums of money from various personal accounts into one single account under the name of Edward Culver. Most of the transactions left the original accounts empty. There were wills here too. Most of them had been drawn up in recent years. All had revoked any previous wills, and stated that the sole beneficiary to any inheritance would now be one Edward Culver.

Summer leaned back on her haunches and caught her breath. She had been right about Fortunate Keep all along. This place was no sanctuary. It was not a paradisiacal commune, where all were equal, living out their days in a perceived heaven on earth. Fortunate Keep was a scam—hand over all your money and we'll free you from a world of pain! But worse than that, Fortunate Keep was a cult.

If Summer was honest, she'd known it since that first day, when the SUV had mounted the hill and she'd seen the tall, imposing fence surrounding the compound. But now she had evidence that Fortunate Keep was nothing more than a pyramid scheme, with Mother and Father perched at the top.

A question formed on her lips, one that she could not answer. If members had to pay their way into Fortunate Keep, why had she, a homeless, destitute young woman, been taken in for free?

Returning the papers, she shoved the box back into the trunk with trembling fingers. She had to leave this place. Now. Because Father had allowed her to search his home, knowing that she would look in every corner. He knew that she'd find the trunk and look inside. Which meant Summer had been wrong. This wasn't a test. It was a trap.

Her chest growing tight, Summer shut the lid of the trunk. She was about to get to her feet, when she heard a sudden thud. She froze. The sound came again, louder this time.

It had come from under the bed.

Scooting around to the side, Summer got on her knees, placed a hand on top of the mattress, and bent down to peer into the shadows.

She gasped.

A large, coffin-like wooden box lay under the bed. A knocking came from within it, followed by a muffled cry.

Summer's hand flew to her mouth. 'Jenny? Jesus Christ, is that you?'

The crying grew more intense.

'Don't worry. I'm here. I'm going to get you out.'

She lunged forwards, fingers scrabbling at the side of the box, trying to gain purchase. But Summer's arms were not long enough, and her chest and shoulders kept pressing into the mattress, preventing her from reaching further.

Panicking, she lay down on her back, slipped her legs under the bed, then held onto the mattress with both hands while placing her feet at the centre of the box's side. She pushed with her legs. The box began to shift, noisily scraping against the wooden floorboards.

Inside it, the crying rose to a crescendo.

'Hold on!' Summer hissed through clenched teeth.

She continued to push. The box shifted and tilted, its top half emerging on the other side of the bed.

Summer could no longer reach it. Scrabbling to her feet, she circled the bed and crouched down. Taking the end of the box in both hands, she pulled with all her strength. Slowly, the box revealed itself in all its horror.

Summer stared at it, barely able to comprehend that a person had been placed inside and hidden away under the bed. She winced at the awful crying coming through the wood. At the kicking and punching.

The lid had a strong yet simple clasp. She quickly unfastened it and pulled up the lid. The sharp stench of stale urine hit her nostrils as she peered inside the box.

A young woman lay inside, her feet and wrists bound with twine, her dress soiled, and her mouth gagged with a cloth. It was only luck that had prevented her from choking to death in a coal-black prison. She stared at Summer with wild, half mad eyes, the whites on display like a spooked horse.

For a long moment, Summer was so shocked that she could do nothing but stare. Because this wasn't Jenny. It was a woman she'd never seen before.

Coming to her senses, she pulled the cloth from the woman's mouth and began untying her hands.

'It's okay,' she said, working at the knot. 'I'm going to get you out of this place.'

The woman tried to sit up as she gasped for air. Daylight invaded her eyes, forcing her to squeeze them shut. As Summer pulled at the twine, she stole a glance at the woman. She looked to be around the same age as Summer, with light brown hair growing past her shoulders, hazel eyes, and elfin-like features that were twisted with terror.

'Please,' she managed to say, before sucking in another ragged breath.

'Don't talk. Just focus on breathing. I'll have you free in a minute.'

The knot was stubborn. Summer picked at it with her fingers.

'You mustn't—' An explosion of coughs cut off the woman's sentence.

'Relax. I'm almost there. Just a few more seconds.'

The twine came away from the woman's wrists. Summer went to work on her feet, but the woman grabbed her hands.

'You have to go. They'll be here soon.'

'No. I won't leave you, and I have to find Jenny.' Summer looked to the open door, then back at the woman. 'What's your name?'

The woman's grip tightened on Summer's hands. 'You have to put me back.'

'What? No!'

'This is my punishment. I was wrong to panic when I heard you come into the room. I should have stayed quiet. Please. If you free me, they'll hurt you.'

Summer wrenched her hands free from the woman's grip and reached for the twine binding her feet.

'I'd like to see them try,' she said.

A voice from behind her chilled her blood.

'Oh, you'll see us try, all right,' Thomas said. 'And you'll wish you hadn't.'

Summer spun around to see Father's hulking form blocking the doorway. Standing at his sides were Thomas and Kane.

Father smiled. 'Ah, I see you've met Sandy.'

'You're animals!' Summer spat. 'All of you, animals!'

She sprang to her feet, ready to pounce on Father. Before she could move, Kane flew at her.

Summer raised her hands in defence, but Kane was faster. His fist struck her hard in the face, knocking her tiny frame to the floor.

She lay there, lightning strikes of white hot pain shooting through her body, the room spinning like a kaleidoscope. Summer managed to pull herself onto an elbow.

And saw Kane's booted foot swinging fast and hard towards her head.

34

Morgan stared at Blake, the blade still wavering in her face. His hands were trembling, his pupils dilated. Slowly, his gaze lowered to the flyer. His brow furrowed and his eyes narrowed, as if he were trying to work out how he knew the man in the picture. Was it . . . him? Blake wondered if it had been so long since he'd looked in a mirror that he no longer recognised himself, especially without the tangled mass of hair and beard. The picture *looked* like him, but it clearly wasn't a real photograph. So, how did she get it? More importantly, how did she find him?

'Who are you?' he demanded.

'My name is Blake Hollow. I'm a private investigator.' From her backpack, Blake removed her wallet, fished out her licence card, and held it up. 'I was following another lead, hoping it might take me to you and your sister. But I had no idea I'd find you right here.'

Wrinkling his brow, Morgan peered at the card. He kept the knife pointed at Blake. 'Who sent you? Was it Father? Because I'm not going back there.'

'It was your mother *and* your father. They hired me on your twenty-first birthday, one last attempt to find you and Sandy after all these years. I didn't think it was possible, but clearly I was wrong.'

'Mum and Dad? Not Father?'

He saw Blake frown in confusion, then shoot a subtle glance over his shoulder and give the barest shake of her head. Morgan whipped around to see the tattooed man advancing. He turned the knife on him.

'Don't you fucking move!'

'It's all right, Morgan,' Blake said. 'This is my cousin Kenver. He's not going to hurt you, are you Kenver? He's just worried about you waving a knife. Do you think you could put it down?'

But Morgan refused to lower the blade, and instead swung it from Blake to Kenver and back again, as he took a step back.

Blake dropped her bag to the ground and held up her hands. 'Please, Morgan. We're not here to harm you, I swear. I came here looking for the Bone Man, but I found you instead. Your parents are going to be so happy. But we don't need to see them straight away, or at all, if you don't want to. Maybe we can sit and talk for a little bit? Maybe you can tell me where you've been.'

A single tear slipped from Morgan's right eye, leaving a pink streak on his dirty cheek.

'My parents sent you?' he said. 'My real parents? Not him? Not Mother and Father?'

'Your real parents, yes. Bronwen and Owen. Who else are you talking about?'

'You're not lying to me? How do I know this isn't one of Father's tricks to make me come back? But I won't, even if Sandy's still there.'

'I don't know who Father is, Morgan. I only know your

parents. Please, can you lower the knife? I can send Kenver away if it makes you feel better, and the two of us can sit and talk.'

Morgan shot a glance at Kenver, who had returned to the edge of the clearing. Blake still had her hands up in surrender.

'No, he stays here. I need you both where I can see you.' He pointed the knife at a partial tree trunk lying on the other side of the clearing. 'Over there.'

Blake nodded at Kenver, who cautiously circled Morgan and sat down on the trunk. She joined him, lowering her hands and placing them on her lap.

The knife trembled in Morgan's hand as he stood, half naked and staring warily at the strangers. With the blade still aimed at them, he backed away until he was by his tent. He entered the code to unlock the padlock, and unzipped the entrance. He shot a look at the strangers to make sure they hadn't moved, then reached inside and pulled out a T-shirt. He slipped it carefully over his head, switching the knife from one hand to the other, and returned to the centre of the clearing.

He stared at the strangers for a long time. Slowly, he lowered the knife.

'You were looking for the Bone Man?' he said. 'You know that's just a story to scare kids.'

Blake nodded. 'A boy called Cal told me about it. Do you remember him, from when you were a kid yourself?'

Morgan's eyes went blank, as if the life had left his body. He let out a trembling breath.

'Yeah, I remember him. The one who never spoke. Jacob's favourite.'

'That's right. Cal told me he first met you and your sister here, before the Dawn Children moved to Burnt House Farm.'

'I don't want to talk about that. Or them.'

'That's all right, we don't have to. Let's talk about something else.' Blake glanced around the clearing, at Morgan's tent and the campfire. 'How long have you been living here in Trevelyn Wood?'

'A while.'

'And where were you before?'

'Around. Different places.'

'Like Bournemouth?'

Morgan's grip on the knife tightened. He was still standing, unable to relax in the presence of the strangers.

'How do you know that?'

'Because I'm a private investigator. And your mum told me you called her from a payphone in Bournemouth three years ago.' Blake paused, watching the shock spread over Morgan's face. 'The police can trace things like that. They went looking for you in Bournemouth, hoping to find you and your sister so they could bring you back home. But you were already gone.'

Next to her on the log, Kenver leaned in and whispered, 'Ask him about the boys he was with.'

Blake shot him a withering glare before returning her attention to Morgan.

'People saw you in Bournemouth Square, with a few other young men. They said you were selling homemade jewellery and handing out leaflets, and that all of you were dressed in grey. Is that who you've been with all this time? Who are they?'

Morgan swayed on his feet, his eyes fixed on the empty space between him and the strangers.

'You really weren't sent by Father?' he asked, his voice small and childlike.

'Unless you're talking about your dad, Owen Teague, I swear to you, I don't know who you're talking about.'

He shook his head and sank to the ground, slipping into a

cross-legged position, with his left hand resting in his lap and his right still gripping the knife.

He was silent for a long time. Then he said, 'They call themselves the Fortunate and Blessed. Mother and Father are their leaders, but really it's just Father. He pretends to be good and kind, and says he's building a home for those of us who are treated cruelly by a mad world. A paradise, he calls it, where we can live in peace and free from harm. But it's bullshit.

'Father isn't good *or* kind. He's the worst of them all. He lies to everyone, tells them he's their saviour. The truth is he doesn't care about a single one of them. All he cares about is the power he holds over them, and how much they adore him. They worship him, you know. Like he's some sort of god. But Father punishes them when they don't follow his rules or get something wrong. As for the women, he . . . Put it this way, Father is nothing but a selfish man who takes what he wants. But if he doesn't get what he wants, if people stand up to him and say no, then the real Father comes out. And you don't want to meet the real Father, like I did. Because he's a bad man.'

Blake was quiet, listening to Morgan talk. She had been right: the Teague twins had escaped one cult only to fall into the hands of another. It seemed unfair, almost comical in some ways, but Morgan and Sandy had been young and impressionable, their minds warped by the Dawn Children's insane rhetoric. After their escape from Devil's Cove, they would have felt lost and frightened, unable to cope with the atrocities they had witnessed. And then along came the Fortunate and Blessed. Along came this charlatan, Father, promising salvation from a world Morgan and Sandy Teague were drowning in.

Blake pictured the twins running into Father's open arms without a moment's hesitation. That was how cults operated, preying on vulnerable people who were at their absolute lowest.

Getting up from the log, Blake moved to the centre of the clearing and sat on the ground opposite Morgan. He stared at her, warily at first. At last, his shoulders slumped and his grip loosened on the blade.

'Where is your sister?' Blake asked.

'She's with the Fortunate and Blessed. With him.'

'Father?'

'I tried to get her to leave. To understand that Father wasn't who he said he was, that it was all a lie. But Sandy wouldn't listen. Father had already worked his magic on her. She didn't want to see the truth, no matter how much I tried to persuade her. She loved him.'

'This was in Bournemouth?'

Morgan nodded. 'We moved around a lot. Father was always looking for the right place for us to call home. He would tell us about his plan to build a sanctuary where the outside world couldn't get in. By the time we arrived in Bournemouth, I'd had enough and I wanted to leave. But I couldn't, not without my sister. So I thought that maybe if I could speak to my parents, and let them know we were still alive and wanted to come home, Mum and Dad would come and get us. That's when I tried to call from the pay phone. But the others came for me before I could even say a word.'

'But you did say a word.' The sadness pouring from Morgan's body was almost unbearable. Blake felt it like a physical manifestation, a disease eating into her organs and bones. 'You said, "Mum". That one word spoken three years ago led me to find you. Without it, we wouldn't be sitting here right now, talking. And if I was able to find you, even if it was through a weird chain of coincidences, maybe I can also find your sister and bring her back home.'

'You'd be wasting your time. When Father gets his hooks in people, it's impossible to free them.'

'And yet you got away.'

'That's because he never had his hooks in me. I knew exactly what he was like from day one. I'd seen it before, with the Dawn Children. I knew the Fortunate and Blessed would be more of the same, but I still went with them. After what happened at Devil's Cove, then to Julia in London—which we had nothing to do with, I swear to God—where else was there for us to go?'

'You could have gone home to your parents. Why didn't you?'

Lowering his head, Morgan began to weep. 'Because we weren't their children anymore. Not in the way they remembered us. Because we did terrible things that can never be forgiven. Because if Mum and Dad knew what we'd been a part of, they'd wish we stayed lost forever.'

Releasing the knife, he covered his face with his hands and continued to sob. Blake glanced over her shoulder at Kenver, who only shrugged.

'That's why you stay here at Trevelyan Wood,' she said. 'Because even though it's the first place the Dawn Children kept you, it means you can stay close to your parents, maybe even sneak out and watch them from time to time, even though that comes with the risk of being seen.'

Morgan's shoulders shook as he cried. Blake reached out and placed a hand on his arm.

'Tell me where I can find your sister.'

'I don't know,' Morgan said, choking back a sob. 'After I tried to call Mum, the others brought me to Father. I told him I wanted to leave, and that I was taking Sandy with me. He said I was free to go, that the Fortunate and Blessed had never been a prison. But he said I couldn't force Sandy to leave if she didn't want to go. He summoned her and told her what I was planning. And you know what my sister said? She told me that she was going nowhere, and if I left that I would no longer have a sister.' More tears spilled from his eyes as he stared into the past. 'But I told her I was leaving, anyway.'

'I'm sorry.' Blake had never been close with her own brother, but she had heard that the bond between twins was often preternaturally strong. For Morgan's sister to sever that bond must have felt like losing a limb.

'The last time I saw Sandy was when Father had Thomas and Kane drive me away from the place we were staying. She just stood on the doorstep, watching me go. She didn't even wave goodbye.'

'And then you came here?'

'Eventually. But not until after Father tried to kill me. You see, he may have told me I was free to leave, but Thomas and Kane didn't drive me to the train station like I'd asked. They drove me out to the middle of nowhere, to a wood just like this one, where they'd already dug a grave. The only reason I managed to escape was because I knew Father wouldn't let me go freely—that would mean admitting he'd lost—and so I was ready to run as soon as Kane opened the car door. It was dark, and my time with the Dawn Children had taught me to be fast on my feet and how to fight. I lost them soon enough, along with my sister. Or so she thinks.'

Blake looked at him. 'What does that mean?'

'It means that if she thinks I've given up on her, she's as brainwashed as the others.' Morgan smiled to himself. 'Before I left, there were rumours that one of the Fortunate and Blessed had signed over a piece of land to Father. That's what he did—reel in vulnerable people and take any assets they had in the name of creating paradise. Everyone was excited because it meant Father could finally build his fortress from the outside world. His Fortunate Keep, as he called it.'

Blake's mind raced alongside her heart. She leaned in closer, until their foreheads were almost touching.

'And where is this piece of land, Morgan? Where is Fortunate Keep?'

Morgan's expression hardened as he met her gaze.

'It's right here,' he said. 'In Cornwall.'

35

They sat in Blake's car in front of a three bedroom terraced house on a leafy, residential street in Newquay. Blake was behind the wheel, with Kenver in the rear and Morgan Teague in the passenger seat. A radical transformation had occurred since yesterday afternoon. Gone were Morgan's ragged, unkempt beard and knotty mass of hair. Now he had a buzz cut and was clean-shaven. He was visibly trembling, his right knee furiously jigging up and down as he watched the house. This was hard for him, Blake knew. Maybe it even felt impossible. But it was what Morgan had desperately wanted for years—to come home.

It had taken Blake several hours to convince Morgan to leave Trevelyan Wood and come home with her, where he could shower and wash his clothes, get a decent meal and a warm bed for the night. Then, come Monday morning, Blake would drive him to the house he grew up in, where his parents would be waiting with open arms. Morgan had refused, over and over. It was shame that prevented him, Blake recognised. Over time, he had convinced himself that his parents had stopped loving him because of what had happened at Devil's Cove. Even if he hadn't taken a life, there was no way of proving it to them, or to anyone else. But proof didn't matter either way because he had been there that day, and brainwashed or not, it meant he was still party to the horrific events that had unfolded.

Blake had finally convinced Morgan by asking him a simple question: 'If your parents stopped loving you, why did they hire me to find you and your sister on your twenty-first birthday?'

Morgan had flinched. 'I'm twenty-one?'

He'd thought he was much younger.

Helping him pack up his tent and belongings, Blake and Kenver had escorted him to the car. Blake had first driven to Wheal Marow, so Kenver could pick up enough clothes for himself for a few days, his laptop and electric shaver. Despite Blake's continued reassurance, Morgan had been skittish in the car, jerking and twisting like a rescued stray animal. But as they arrived at her cottage, his anxiety began to ebb, the isolated location and the surrounding countryside a tonic for his nerves.

Inside, Morgan had showered while Blake put his filthy clothing in the washing machine. Kenver showed Morgan how to use his shaver, then watched in astonishment as the years fell away, along with Morgan's matted hair.

After a late dinner, Blake gave her bedroom to Kenver and put Morgan in the spare room, while she took the sofa. Giving up her room wasn't a mere act of kindness—bedding down on the sofa with the living room door open gave Blake a good view of the hallway and any attempts Morgan might make to escape in the night. But come the morning, Morgan was still asleep.

Now, here they were, parked outside his childhood home on Monday afternoon. Blake had phoned Morgan's parents early that morning while he'd slept. They were due to meet in her office at 11

AM, but she'd instead suggested they meet at Bronwen's house in the early afternoon.

'There's been a development,' she told them. 'It's better if I come over and we talk face to face.'

She'd left those words hanging, a teaser for the surprise that would soon land on Bronwen's doorstep. In truth, she hadn't wanted to tell them over the phone that she'd found their son and was bringing him home—because what if Morgan suddenly got scared and changed his mind? Blake didn't want to be responsible for the devastation caused by a false promise.

She turned to Morgan, whose gaze was frozen on his former home.

'Are you ready?' When he didn't respond, she placed a hand on his shoulder. 'It's going to be fine. Overwhelming maybe, but fine. Just remember they love you.'

Morgan nodded, but made no move to leave the car. In the back, Kenver unbuckled his seat belt.

'You're staying here,' Blake told him.

Kenver huffed. 'Then why didn't you leave me at your place?'

'You know why, or do I have to spell it out?'

Glowering, Kenver grumbled under his breath and stared out of the window.

Blake opened the driver's door and climbed out. It was another fine day of blue skies and radiant sunshine, with a cooling breeze drifting up from the nearby ocean. Morgan was still inside the car. Blake walked around to the passenger side and opened the door. She held out her hand.

'Come on.'

Morgan peered up at her with wide, frightened eyes. Slowly, he unfastened his seat belt, climbed out, and took her hand.

They walked towards the house together. A shadow appeared in the ground floor window. Morgan stopped dead.

Blake squeezed his hand.

She stepped forward but Morgan did not move. His breathing had become erratic, his chest heaving up and down. His grip on Blake's hand grew painfully tight as he looked both ways down the street.

He's going to run, Blake thought. Damn it, he's going to run.

But before either of them could move, the front door of the house flew open, and Bronwen Lander stood on the threshold, frozen like a statue, her skin turning white and her mouth falling open. Owen Teague appeared behind her. At first, his expression was one of confusion. But as he realised who was standing in the street before him, his brow crumpled and he shook his head in disbelief.

Morgan's grip grew even tighter, making Blake wince.

'Oh my God . . .' The words fell from Bronwen's mouth like stones. She took a faltering step into the street, staring at her son. 'Is that my baby boy?'

Tears came, flooding her cheeks, as she rushed forward with her arms outstretched. Morgan flinched as his mother embraced him, but still he wouldn't let go of Blake's hand.

'Morgan. My boy!' Bronwen sobbed, pulling his rigid body closer to hers. 'It's you. It's really you!'

Owen Teague was still paralysed, a single tear slipping down his face. He stared at his ex-wife, at the son whom he thought he would never see again. His legs crumbled beneath him and he slid to the floor, his back pressed up against the doorjamb. He began to weep.

Blake was growing uncomfortable. This should have been a private moment between Morgan and his parents, but his grip on her hand was like iron. And now curtains were twitching in windows, curious neighbours wondering who was making such a fuss on a quiet Monday afternoon.

'I can't believe it's you!' Bronwen continued to sob. 'You've grown so much and you look so different. It is you, isn't it? Of course it is. What am I saying? And where's your sister?' Her arms still around Morgan's neck, Bronwen peered at Blake, sudden panic in her eyes. 'Where's Sandy? Why isn't she here?'

Blake glanced at Owen, who was still slumped in the doorway, staring at his son, then at Morgan, who was as rigid as a corpse in the throes of rigor mortis, and who still hadn't said a word. Finally, her gaze fell upon Bronwen, in whose eyes she saw a maelstrom of joy and overwhelm, of fear and confusion.

'Why don't we go inside?' Blake said, softly. 'We have a lot to talk about.'

From the back seat of the car, Kenver watched Owen Teague pick himself up from the floor, then Blake and the family disappear inside the house. He rubbed his knuckles against his chin and tried to push down the thirst that had taken hold of him.

36

Later that afternoon, Blake found herself back in her office, with Kenver in tow. The day had grown almost unbearably hot, yet there was much work to be done. She had left Morgan with his parents, all three present members of the family awash with tears and heightened emotions. And there were questions—so many questions from Bronwen that Morgan had become overwhelmed, and Owen had quietly intervened. The biggest question on both parents' lips, however, was about their daughter. Where was she?

Blake had been the one to deliver the news. 'Sandy is with a group calling themselves the Fortunate and Blessed. Morgan says she doesn't want to come home, which presents a problem. Your daughter is twenty-one years old, which means if she doesn't want to come home there's nothing you can legally do about it.'

Both parents stared at each other in shock.

Owen broke the silence. 'What about illegally?'

'Short of kidnapping her, I don't know. But I strongly advise against it—the police won't be on your side. In any case, we're still not exactly sure where to find this group. Morgan believes they've set up camp somewhere in Bodmin Moor. He's been searching, but so far has failed to find them, which isn't surprising—Bodmin Moor covers seventeen thousand acres of land.'

Bronwen was clutching Morgan with both hands, as if afraid she would lose him again. 'There must be something we can do. Sandy's clearly been brainwashed—are we just meant to sit back and let that continue?'

'I'm afraid without proof, your hands are tied. But there's one potential way in, if we can find the place. Morgan says the leader of the group tried to have him killed when he left. That warrants a police investigation.'

On the sofa, Morgan flinched. His mother's eyes grew round and wide, his father's dark and violent.

'Killed?' Bronwen gasped. 'Oh my God!'

Her grasp on her son grew tighter.

Blake told them she had friends in the police force who might be able to help. But first they would want to talk to Morgan, not only about the circumstances of his disappearance but his involvement with the Dawn Children and the massacre at Devil's Cove. Deep lines of worry creased Bronwen and Owen's brows. Morgan visibly trembled.

'It's nothing to be afraid of,' said Blake. 'Morgan claims he never hurt anyone that day, and had been trying to get away from the Dawn Children for a long time. There's no incriminating evidence against him. In fact, there isn't even proof he was there that day. But the police still need to interview him—far too many people lost their lives.'

Now, sitting behind her desk, with Kenver taking up space on the other side and the fan in the corner of the room doing little to dispel the heat, Blake was busy scouring Bodmin Moor using Google Maps, which she'd set to satellite mode. She had been at it for over an hour now, dragging the mouse pointer across the screen as she searched for small holdings and unusual structures. But the sheer size of the moor was making it an impossible task.

Morgan believed the Fortunate and Blessed had relocated to Bodmin Moor within the last few years. But even if it was true, and they had constructed Fortunate Keep—their leader's dream compound—it still didn't mean it would show up on Google Maps. Images of remote terrain such as Bodmin Moor were only updated every three to five years, much less frequently than their urban counterparts, which also benefited from more detailed images of places of interest that the user could zoom in on.

Blake leaned back in her chair and stretched her aching spine. She peered across the desk at Kenver, who was pale and perspiring, partly from the heat and partly from the continuing effects of alcohol poisoning.

'How are you doing?' she asked.

Kenver screwed up his face. 'I found plenty of farms and small-holdings on the outskirts, but who's to say which one, if any, belong to our cultist friends. It's like trying to find the one sane person at a conspiracy theory convention.'

'I didn't think there were any.' Blake smiled. 'And I meant how are you doing personally?'

'Oh. Sweating like a pig and sick to my stomach. You know, I really don't need babysitting. I'll be fine at home, and I've got to go back to work at some point—I can only call in sick for so many days.'

Blake's gaze returned to her laptop screen. 'We can talk about that later. Let's keep focused. The Teague family needs our help and we don't want to let them down.'

'Nice dodge,' said Kenver. 'You get bonus points for emotional blackmail.'

Blake stared at the satellite map of Bodmin Moor, then minimised the browser window and brought up a second. Another option to explore was searching land registries for any changes in ownership within the past three years. The main resource for doing so was the HM Land Registry Map Search Tool, which allowed users to browse an interactive map of England and Wales, and click on pockets of land to view ownership details. But there were three barriers preventing Blake from getting what she needed.

The first, that the search tool was best utilised when knowing which specific pocket of land you were looking for. Since Blake had no idea, it would mean clicking on every single pocket of land in and around Bodmin Moor, of which there were many, until she found the right one. Which led to problem number two: the name of the cult leader. Morgan didn't know it, and Blake doubted the land bequeathed to him was registered under the name of "Father".

The final issue was that, to access the search tool, Blake needed to apply for an online account, which required completing a twenty-minute online questionnaire and waiting three to five business days for the account to be approved. It was the lesser of the three problems, but Blake didn't like waiting, especially when a vulnerable young woman was at risk of harm. Nonetheless, she filled in the questionnaire and submitted her application; such a tool could prove useful for future cases.

Puffing out her cheeks, she brought up Google Maps again.

'What we need,' she said, 'are up-to-date satellite maps with the ability to zoom in close. Is there such a thing available to the public?'

On the other side of the desk, Kenver ran his fingers over his laptop keyboard.

'Actually, there is. A few, in fact, but for what you need your best bet is Maxar Technologies.' His shoulders drooped as his eyes scanned the screen. 'But to get up-to-date images of Bodmin Moor in its entirety, or even of just its outskirts, you're looking at a price tag of thousands of pounds and anything up to two weeks waiting time. I guess state-of-the-art satellite imagery hasn't gone mainstream yet?'

'I don't think the twins' parents have that kind of money lying around.' Blake pinched the bridge of her nose and blew out a stream of air. There has to be another way, she thought. Something that didn't cost the earth or take weeks to get results.

She sat up. 'Blake, you bloody idiot.'

'Hey, that's my line.'

'The men in grey,' she said. 'Morgan and the others used to go from town to town, selling their wares to make money and handing out leaflets to bring in new recruits. Which means, if the Fortunate and Blessed are somewhere in Bodmin Moor, those boys will be working in the surrounding towns.'

'Maybe you do know how to do your job after all,' Kenver said. 'But are you proposing we go from town to town, searching the streets in the hope we stumble upon them? If that's the case you may as well wait for the land registry map application to come through.'

Blake was furiously typing, her eyes darting left and right as they locked on the laptop screen.

'The good thing about technology in the twenty-first century is that to find something, you don't even need to leave the comfort of your office.'

'Except comfort left your office a long time ago.'

For the next twenty minutes, Blake had Kenver compile a list of every medium to large town within a thirty mile radius of

Bodmin Moor. Villages and hamlets were ignored because they were far too small to warrant the boys selling their trinkets—or attempting to recruit members without bringing unwanted attention.

The final list came to a total of twelve towns, including Bodmin, Tavistock, and Liskeard. With the summer holiday season in full swing, the financial opportunities for the Fortunate and Blessed were great, which meant it was entirely possible, even likely, the men in grey would be out selling their trinkets to tourists every day of the week.

With the list of towns complete, Kenver's next task was to log in to Facebook and find community groups for each location. Most towns had one these days as a means for locals to share events, ask questions that could be easily Googled, and complain about the amount of dog excrement soiling the streets. Blake stayed away from them. She did have a Facebook account, as well as a few other social media accounts, but she used them for running background checks on potential clients or persons of interest she'd been hired to investigate. That being said, even Blake was susceptible to the occasional adorable puppy picture—although she'd kill before admitting it in public.

Now that she had a list of relevant Facebook community groups, Blake set about writing a post, asking if anyone had seen a group of young men dressed in grey selling lovely handmade bracelets on the street. She was desperate to get her hands on one as a gift, and had heard they were moving around different towns in the local area. By chance, had anyone seen them lately? Oh, and they were handing out leaflets with the following design . . .

Blake uploaded the post to each of the twelve community groups, along with the design based on the description given to her by the old man in Bournemouth.

'What now?' Kenver asked, wiping beads of sweat from his forehead.

'Now we wait. And get ice cream.'

∼

Outside, the streets were rammed with both residents and tourists. Blake and Kenver weaved their way between the bodies, along Market Strand and onto the Prince of Wales pier, passing under strings of colourful bunting. The pier was busier than the street, although there were few locals here. The temperature was sweltering. Even the breeze skimming over the harbour waters and teasing the sails of yachts was warm and clammy.

Blake joined the long queue in front of the ice cream vendor, while Kenver squeezed himself into the nearest shadow like a vampire trapped in daylight. The queue was slow-moving, so Blake took out her phone and moved onto the next task on her to-do list: calling DS Turner. To her surprise, he answered. He'd only recently given her his personal number—a sign their days of animosity had come to an end, as long as Blake didn't push it—but when she'd phoned him before, the call had almost always gone to voicemail. It was nothing personal; detective sergeants rarely had time for non-case-related calls while on duty. At least, that was what Blake told herself.

'I found him, Turner,' she said, before the word "Hello" had fully left the man's mouth. 'I found Morgan Teague.'

Turner replied with stunned silence. Followed by: 'How the hell did you manage that?'

'Believe it or not, by tracking down Cal's Bone Man.'

As the ice cream queue shortened, Blake relayed her discovery of Morgan in Trevelyan Wood, of reuniting him with his parents. She told him of the Fortunate and Blessed, of Morgan's claims of punishments and abuse, and that the leader had tried to have him killed.

'That on its own warrants a police investigation, doesn't it?' Blake said. 'And if we can find their compound on Bodmin Moor, then perhaps we can convince Sandy to come home. Or, at the very least, speak to her parents.'

'We'll want to talk to her too,' Turner replied. 'As we will her brother. There are gaps needing to be filled, questions answered. Not just about what happened to them and where they've been, but about—'

'Devil's Cove. I've told the twins' parents to expect a visit from the police. Morgan says he was there at the cove that day, but he had nothing to do with what happened, and had been trying to escape from the Dawn Children.'

'Do you believe him?'

'I think so. But I've only known him for five minutes, so who knows? About the compound, Turner—I'm close to finding it, I'm sure. Perhaps if you put a team on it, we'd find it in double time. Then you and I can go out there and—'

'Slow down, Blake. Have you forgotten I'm a detective sergeant, not a detective inspector. Although I do have a degree of authority, I don't get to make those kinds of decisions. I can put in requests, which I may well do once we've talked to Morgan Teague. And if we do find this compound, if it exists, and we decide to pay it a visit, I'm afraid it will be a police investigation. Which means no civilians allowed.'

'You're fucking kidding me.' Blake had reached the ice cream vendor, who arched his eyebrows. She apologised and ordered two ice cream cones, one mint chocolate, one vanilla. As the man prepared her order, Blake lowered her voice to a seething whisper. 'This is *my* case. The twins' parents came to me. I was the one to find Morgan. And now you're going to shut me out?'

Turned expelled a heavy sigh. 'It's nothing personal. It's proce-dure. We can't have civilians running around and tearing up the place.'

'If you say "civilian" one more time, I swear I'll break your legs.'

'Fair enough. Look, I'll see what I can do. I'll talk to my boss, but even if she agrees you can come along, which I doubt, it will be strictly from an observational standpoint.'

The ice cream vendor handed Blake the cones. She paid him and stomped away.

'Okay, fine. Just do me a favour, Turner. Give Morgan a few more hours before you go barging in there. He's completely over-whelmed.'

'It won't be me going to see him, and we can't risk him running away again before we can question him.'

'I saw his face when his parents came out the door. That boy isn't going anywhere.'

Another sigh filtered into Blake's ear. To her surprise, Turner said, 'You should have joined the police force. You'd have made one hell of a detective.'

'I *am* one hell of a detective,' Blake said. She hung up.

Pushing her way through the crowd, she found Kenver and handed him the mint chocolate ice cream.

'Payment for your assistance today,' she said.

Kenver laughed, a smile lighting up his face. It was nice to see him do more than scowl. If only Blake could say the same for herself. *Civilian.* She hated the word. It made her feel powerless, even if she was one.

She nodded to Kenver and they turned away from the pier, heading back to the office.

'So what's next?' he asked.

'We go home, and we wait to hear from the Facebook groups.'

'And when you say go home you mean . . .'

'Back to my place. You and I still need to have a talk about your future.'

'God, I need a drink.'

'What you need is shooting.'

Kenver stared at his ice cream cone and heaved his shoulders. 'Don't we all, Blake? Don't we all?'

37

It didn't take long for the general public to work their magic and find the men in grey. By the time Blake got back to her cottage, there were three comments on her Facebook post, placing them that very afternoon in Aylmer Square in St Austell, just in front of the White River Place shopping centre—a perfect location to sell their wares and spread propaganda. Blake wanted to jump in her car and drive to the town, but it was already past five o'clock. The majority of shoppers would have already gone home for the day, which meant the men would have too.

Tomorrow then. She would get up early and stake out the square. She would wait there all day if she had to. And if the boys moved on to another town, Blake was confident she would hear about it.

She spent the rest of the evening talking with Kenver, attempting to persuade him to get help with his drinking, suggesting an AA meeting or seeing a therapist. Kenver was not in the mood to talk but Blake persisted.

'I love you,' she told him. 'I don't want to step over you one day lying in the gutter.'

Kenver countered that his alcohol dependence was not that bad.

Blake had simply responded, 'Maybe not yet, but it's a slippery slope.'

Finally, Kenver had relented and agreed to speak to a therapist. He wasn't ready for something like an AA meeting—he didn't feel comfortable sharing his problems with a group of strangers. Especially one problem in particular.

John Something. What was to be done about him? Kenver couldn't think about it right now. Blake, however, resolved to use her resources, once her present case was over, to discover the truth about the dead man, and to see if Kenver truly was in trouble.

~

Located on the south coast, and with a population of around twenty thousand people, St Austell was one of Cornwall's larger towns and the beating heart of its China clay industry. Upon arriving in St Austell, the first point of interest to catch a visitor's eye was not the golden beach with its stunning ocean views, but the mountainous white peaks of the clay pits dominating the skyline; peaks that were known locally as the Cornish Alps, as China clay was the colour of snow.

Blake had arrived early and set herself up at a table in front of the Costa in Aylmer Square. To the casual passerby, she was just another self-employed freelancer taking advantage of the good weather and stretching out the single coffee she'd ordered. The square itself was nothing special; a drab concrete space surrounded by high-street shops, which formed part of the White River Place shopping centre. When Blake first sat down, only a handful of shoppers had been present. Now, an hour later, the square was buzzing with noise and bodies. But there was still no sign of the men in grey.

Half an hour passed. Blake ordered a second coffee then texted Kenver, who was back at her cottage. After last night's conversation, she had agreed to ease up on the babysitting routine. But only a little. Blake hoped Kenver would stay true to his word and get in touch with a therapist. If he didn't, there was more drastic action Blake could take, such as involving the rest of the family. She hoped it didn't come to that, yet she also knew when it came to any kind of dependency, the user had to *want* to change. If they didn't, any help offered was rendered futile.

Another ten minutes ticked by. Blake jigged her knee up and down beneath the table. Picking up her phone, she checked the Facebook posts from yesterday, looking to see if the men had moved on to another town. But there were no more notifications.

Shouldn't they have been here already? With the square as busy as it was, the men were missing out on a lucrative opportunity. Maybe they had moved on to another town after all. But which one? Did it mean that Blake would now have to drive to each town on Kenver's list and scour the streets?

Grumbling, she finished her coffee and tossed her laptop inside her bag. She got up from the table and tucked her chair in. She was about to leave when she saw a flash of grey amid a sea of summer colours. And then there they were: the young men from the Fortunate and Blessed, dressed in grey trousers and tunics, and smart shoes, although Blake noted that one of the young men's shoes were scuffed and worn.

She watched them as they set up a table at the edge of the square. There were three of them in total: the young man with the worn shoes, who looked to be around eighteen years old; a man in his early twenties with a shaved head and a muscular body, whose eyes were cold and hard; and another man of similar age, who was generically good-looking, with dark hair and eyes and a square jaw. He was clearly the leader of the three, giving out directions while the other two set up the table and laid out handmade bracelets, pendants, and sheer scarves. The last items placed on the table were a bright red cash box and a small white container. From the container, the younger man with the worn shoes removed a wad of leaflets. He took up position to the right of the table, leaflets poised in hand.

The more muscular of the three stood behind the table, his unblinking eyes scanning the crowds. Blake had met young men like him before: cool and silent on the outside, a raging inferno within. She would need to watch him closely.

With the table now ready for business, the leader of the trio checked everything was in place and joined the others.

Blake waited for a few interested customers to flock before making her move. Slipping in between two women, she glanced at the men behind the table, then made an act of browsing the various bracelets on sale.

'These are nice,' she said, making eye contact with the trio's leader. 'Did you make them yourself?'

The man smiled. 'I wish I was that skilled. I'm afraid, we're only the sellers.'

'Then who makes them?'

'A group of talented women.'

'Do you have a card for them? Or a website?' Blake picked up one of the bracelets, made of azure-coloured thread, with a central line of tiny green beads. She thought it was very bohemian.

'No card or website, I'm afraid. Jewellery making is more of a sideline for them.'

'That's a shame. Do you know if they take custom orders?

There's a design in my head I'd love to see brought to life. But I'm no jewellery maker. Perhaps I could hire their services.'

One of the customers handed the man an elegant pendant carved from wood and attached to a thin leather thread. Blake stepped to one side. The younger man with the worn shoes tried to hand a leaflet to a departing shopper, but he and the leaflet were ignored.

With the transaction complete, the man behind the table glanced at Blake. As did the muscular, silent one.

'I'm afraid the women don't take custom orders,' he said. 'As I mentioned, jewellery making is only a small part of what they do. Almost a hobby, you could say.'

'That's a shame.' Blake nodded at the young man with the leaflets. 'What are those about?'

The leader of the group shifted his weight from one foot to the other.

'We belong to a small community who believe in peace and harmony for all, without the need for government rules or rhetoric. We believe in the old ways and the power of nature.'

'The power of nature . . .' Blake mused. 'Sounds fascinating. And I'm always up for socking it to the man—down with capitalism and all that! Where are you based?'

The stiff smile on the man's face made it clear he was not used to his customers asking so many questions.

'If you're interested in learning more, please take a leaflet,' he said. 'If not, perhaps you'd consider making a purchase.'

'I believe I'll take a leaflet *and* this rather lovely bracelet,' she said, grabbing one at random and handing it over with a twenty pound note.

As the man dealt with the transaction, Blake regarded his quiet, intimidating colleague beside him.

'Nice day, isn't it?' she said.

The man did not reply, only stared at her.

'Here you go.'

The group leader handed Blake her change. He'd put the bracelet in a small, hand-stitched purse with drawstrings. It was a nice addition, Blake thought, that would make customers remember them kindly and come back for more. But what the man hadn't given her was one of the leaflets. The omission felt deliberate, as if he could sense something awry about the middle-aged woman and her probing questions.

Blake smiled at him. 'Thank you. Well, have a nice day and enjoy the sunshine. I hope your jewellery maker friends change their minds about custom designs.'

'They won't. But thank you for your custom.'

Leaving the table, Blake stopped by the younger man with worn shoes and plucked a leaflet from his fingers. She gave its cover a cursory glance. The design she had drawn based on the old man's description had been surprisingly accurate.

Blake thanked him and walked away. As she moved through the crowd, she could feel at least two pairs of eyes burning holes into her back. The Fortunate and Blessed were nothing if not guarded.

38

Thomas sat in the passenger seat of the SUV, Matthew in the rear, as Kane drove them back to Fortunate Keep. It had been a good day—the Horned One had blessed them with many sales, if not potential recruits. But that was fine; Father had already said Fortunate Keep was close to full, and soon they would either have to build more sleeping quarters or turn newcomers away. Unless, of course, they were offering generous donations. Those types of newcomers were always welcome.

In spite of the money made today, Thomas was distracted.

That woman. The one who had asked questions about custom jewellery and the location of the community. Something about her had left Thomas on edge. He didn't like the way she looked at him, or the way she smiled as if she were keeping secrets. And even though she'd made a purchase, she had done so at random, which didn't make sense. If she'd truly admired the pieces as she claimed, she would have taken her time to pick out the right one, not just pluck a bracelet from the table without even looking.

No. There was something about that woman that didn't feel

right. Perhaps Thomas would mention her to Father when they returned. He'd want to know—there had been enough recent trouble at Fortunate Keep without someone else causing them problems.

Bodmin Moor appeared up ahead on both sides of the road, ominous and brooding despite the early evening sunshine. As ever, Kane was quiet behind the wheel. In the rear seat, Matthew had removed his shoes and was massaging the ball of his right foot. A minute later, Kane was turning off the dual carriageway and onto a thin, winding B road. They would be home soon, in time for evening thanks. Father would be pleased with Thomas when he saw how much money they'd made. More money meant more resources for Fortunate Keep, and more resources kept everyone happy.

Next to him, Kane glanced in the rear-view mirror and frowned. A moment later, he looked again. On either side of the road, the land grew barren and rocky as they drove deeper into the moor.

'What is it?' Thomas asked.

Kane's eyes flicked back to the mirror. 'That car. I think it's following us.'

Whenever Kane spoke, which was rare, Thomas was always taken aback by his deep, undulating voice.

'For how long?'

'A while.'

Thomas turned and peered at the left wing mirror. An old blue Corsa was two hundred metres behind them and in no hurry to catch them up. It was unusual to see another car on this road, which acted as an access road to the A30 for several farms and smallholdings, with the other end petering out in the middle of nowhere. The car behind them was not the type farmers tended to drive, and Thomas could tell, even from this distance, that its exterior was far too clean; most vehicles kept on farms were always covered in layers of dirt.

The mouth of a much narrower lane appeared on the right. Kane turned the vehicle into it and drove on, thick tyres running in and out of potholes.

Thomas kept his gaze fixed on the passenger wing mirror. Just as the lane curved to the left, he saw the Corsa appear in the entrance. Then it was gone from view as the SUV took the corner.

'Stop the car,' he said. Kane glanced at him but kept driving. 'I said stop it now!'

In the rear seat, Matthew furrowed his brow. 'What's happening?'

Kane hit the brakes. The SUV lurched to a halt.

Thomas held his breath and watched the wing mirror.

The Corsa came around the corner. Seeing the SUV blocking the lane, the driver slammed the brakes, and the car screeched to a halt.

Throwing open the passenger door, Thomas jumped out and turned to face the car behind. Kane quickly followed. Matthew remained in the rear seat.

It was her. The woman from earlier today. She was staring at him through her windscreen, that secretive smile on her lips.

Rage fired through Thomas's veins. Who was she? What did she want from them? And how did she have the nerve to think she could follow them without consequence?

Nodding to Kane, he started forwards, taking large strides towards the Corsa. As he approached, the woman reached for the gear stick and put the car in reverse. She began backing away quickly, expertly rounding the corner and continuing on, driving backwards towards the B road. Back to whichever hole she'd crawled out of.

Thomas stood, watching the car disappear in the distance, taking its troubling passenger with it.

'Who is she?' asked Kane, his voice vibrating through Thomas's body.

Thomas didn't answer.

They returned to the vehicle and drove on in silence, until they soon reached the gates of Fortunate Keep. Thomas's stomach churned. This woman had come close to discovering their sanctuary. Far too close.

They drove through the gates, children waving as they entered. Perhaps that was the point, he thought. Not to reach Fortunate Keep. But to come close enough to find it.

Thomas swallowed. He needed to speak to Father.

∾

As she rounded the corner and almost slammed into the back of the SUV, Blake felt a jolt of exhilaration. Not because she had nearly crashed her car. Not because the men had caught her following them; on a road as lonely as this discovery was inevitable.

As two of the men climbed out of the SUV and started towards her, the desire to inflict violence darkening their eyes, Blake tapped the screen of her mobile phone, sticking a red pin into a digital map. She tapped the save button, threw the phone into the cup holder, and put the car into reverse.

She drove away, her eyes fixed on the rear-view mirror, and a smug smile on her lips.

The men did not follow.

The exhilaration returned. Blake was now one large step closer to finding Fortunate Keep.

39

Father was troubled. He had delivered the evening sermon with his usual pomp and grace, and had coasted through dinner with his usual jovial veneer. But now, sitting in his living room, surrounded by candles and with Mother already retired to bed, he sipped from a glass of single malt whisky and thought about the woman Thomas had described. Who was she? What did she want? All he knew was that it could be nothing good. People didn't just hear about Fortunate Keep. It was a closely guarded secret, shared only when Thomas had come to Father with news of a potential follower who fit his criteria. But this woman clearly already knew about their sanctuary—why else would she have followed Thomas and the others?

Was she somehow connected to that ungrateful heathen, Summer? Father's newest recruit had tried to bring trouble raining down on his peaceful haven. But she had failed. Father's followers were gullible sheep who believed without question every word he told them. And so he'd told them that Jenny had not vanished but had come to him and Mother in the middle of the night and asked to leave. The child had sadly lost her way, growing doubtful of their ways and longing to see the outside world in all its terrible glory. Father and Mother had tried to warn her of the dangers, but she insisted. And so Father consulted with the Horned One, for he was his conduit, and the Horned One commanded that Jenny be set free because Fortunate Keep was no prison. Father could only hope that Jenny would quickly see how rotten the outside world truly was, and would soon return.

It was a ludicrous story. One he'd invented on the spot, with virtually no connection to what had happened between Jenny and Thomas in the women's bunk house—although Father insisted Thomas had merely been trying to convince Jenny not to leave. Yet his people smiled and nodded, and prayed to the Horned One for Jenny's safe return. Convincing them had been easy, such was Father's sway.

Joni had been the only one to concern him. She and Jenny were close, and when Father had told the congregation of Jenny's plight, deep lines had appeared on Joni's brow. She had not believed straight away. Not until Father had taken her aside and explained how the Horned One felt about doubters. He wasn't worried about Joni now—the child was a pathetic little thing, with a mind like marshmallow—easily moulded. And now that Father had taken care of Summer, he knew Joni lacked the confidence to go searching for answers herself.

What a troublesome, selfish whore Summer was. It was always the same whenever they brought the homeless into the fold, which was why they rarely did. Yet Thomas had believed Summer would serve Father well. What they hadn't expected was the girl's grit and driving anger. It was obvious to Father now that Summer had been hurt by men before. It was why she had refused to accept Jenny's disappearance.

Well, Summer could relax now. She and Jenny had been reunited.

As far as the others were aware, Summer had been cast out of Fortunate Keep and would never return. They had all witnessed the chaos she had caused, the disrespect she had shown to Father. And so enraged was the Horned One by the woman's ugly contempt that He instantly cursed her to live the rest of her life in eternal damnation—such was the punishment for unbelievers.

But the outsider woman who had followed Thomas and the others, what did he do about her? Until he had made a decision, Father had ordered a temporary pause on trips into town.

He peered up at the great carving of the Horned One.

'What do you think?' he said, sipping his whisky. He'd already finished half a bottle and was halfway to drunk. 'Should we find out who she is, then bury her in the ground? Or should we bring her to Fortunate Keep and make her our pet?'

He smiled to himself as he continued to stare at the carving. 'Why so quiet tonight? Cat got your tongue? Or is it because you don't exist unless I say you do. I made you, you horny son of a bitch. Just remember that.'

Father threw back his head and drained the rest of his whisky. Setting the glass down on the coffee table, he wiped his mouth with his sleeve, then hauled himself to his feet. His gait was unsteady as he zigzagged his way to the bathroom, where he urinated and flushed the toilet, before stumbling into the bedroom.

A kerosene lantern sat on his nightstand, the flickering flame making shadows dance on the wall. Mother was already asleep, or at least pretending to be, her back turned to him. Father curled his upper lip. Mother served her purpose well enough, welcoming new followers and picking out suitable girls, while providing a maternal presence for Father's followers. But that was where her role ended.

She had long ago refused Father's touch, except when in the presence of his followers. Father was perfectly happy to oblige her wishes—her ageing, saggy flesh was of no interest. Not when he had his special girls.

Peeling off his clothes, Father pulled a nightgown over his mountainous form and climbed into bed beside Mother, who did not stir. He lay for a moment in his alcoholic fuzz, thinking about Jenny and Summer, and the woman stranger. Perhaps he should perform a ritual in the name of the Horned One and burn them like witches. He wondered if his followers would enjoy that, or if it would be a step too far for their fragile minds. A sacrifice had never been required because Father's followers had always been compliant. There had been punishments, yes—a finger here, a thumb there—but that had been in the early days when unruly members had stirred up trouble and Father had still been figuring out the mythology of it all.

It was fortunate that Summer's wilful disruption had only caused ripples among his people. But perhaps someone still needed to lose an eye, maybe even a hand, just to remind them that the Horned One was all-seeing, and just one person's defiance could bring His hellfire raining down upon the entire community.

Father would sleep on it.

Putting out the lantern, he briefly wondered about installing a generator so that he could finally have electricity. But how would he justify that to the others, who would remain in candlelight, without upsetting the status quo? Father would sleep on that too.

He rolled onto his side, his back turned to Mother, and stared into the darkness. Slipping a hand from beneath the covers, he reached over the side of the mattress and stroked the edge of the large box beneath the bed.

'Goodnight, Sandy,' he whispered.

The box remained silent.

Perhaps when they uncovered the identity of the stranger woman, he would make space under the bed for her too.

40

Father did not have to wait long to discover the identity of the mystery woman. Following her encounter with the three men in grey, Blake had driven to Truro police station, where she'd shown Turner the pinned location she'd saved on Google Maps and requested he use the resources at his disposal to find the compound. It had to be close by—the men were already heading deep into the moor when Blake had caught up with them.

Turner told Blake that police officers had interviewed Morgan Teague that morning. He had given a detailed account of his time with the Fortunate and Blessed, describing the leader of the cult, a man known only as Father, as a dangerous sociopath who bathed in the adoration of his followers while subjecting them to a stream of subtle psychological torture. Morgan had tried to convince his sister Sandy to leave with him, but she'd refused, even though she knew women were occasionally vanishing in the middle of the night. When questioned about their disappearances, Father would always give the same excuse—the women had sadly decided to return to the outside world. Morgan knew it was a lie. When he'd been caught phoning his mother and subsequently cast out of the group, he had confronted Father and threatened to go to the police. It was why, Morgan believed, Father had ordered his murder.

Armed with Blake's pinned map location and Morgan's statement, Turner had gone to his boss and requested he further investigate the Fortunate and Blessed, with the aim of pinpointing their location. His request was granted, along with a minimal budget that funded access to a commercial satellite imagery service. Using the map location provided by Blake, it wasn't long before Turner had located a compound of several single-storey buildings on the outskirts of the moors, which appeared to be a hive of human activity.

Despite the details of Morgan Teague's statement, Turner's application for a search warrant had been denied on the grounds of Morgan's questionable credibility as a former member of not one but two cults, and the fact he could not identify any of the women who had allegedly disappeared beyond first names and vague physical descriptions.

It was decided that Turner would instead take a small team and head out to the compound known as Fortunate Keep, where they would make contact and request to search the premises. If anything of a suspicious nature was noted, or if they were denied entry without good reason, then a warrant could be requested again.

And so it was that Blake now found herself in the back of a police-issue 4x4, awkwardly wedged in between Police Constable Alison Rhodes and Detective Constable Rory Angove, whom she'd known since childhood and still deeply cared for, even though her feelings had ceased to be of a romantic nature several years ago. She had told him so quite explicitly last year, during the Porthenev harbour case, where their investigative paths had crossed amid a series of particularly brutal murders. Rory had already known Blake did not share his affections, despite them occasionally sleeping together, but hearing her speak it out loud had been like sealing a tomb on his feelings. Since then, the drunken sex had ceased, and Rory had resolved to be amiable enough whenever they saw each other. But Blake couldn't deny their friendship had irrevocably changed. Rory had also finally started dating again, which she thought was healthy and about time.

Since leaving Truro twenty minutes ago, conversation between the two had been polite yet scant, but that was more to do with the seriousness of the case than any animosity between them.

Blake wasn't even supposed to be there. Turner had known that any request for a civilian to join an investigation, private investigator or otherwise, would be flatly denied. Yet he also knew that without Blake's help they would still be searching for the location of Fortunate Keep. So Turner had quietly added her to the team, telling himself that by keeping her close he could call on her for advice if they uncovered anything directly related to Sandy Teague.

He had also made it clear that her role was strictly observational, which meant she was not permitted to interact with anyone at the compound and would stay under the watchful eye of DC Angove at all times. Any bending of the rules would not only potentially compromise an active police investigation, but could also see Turner reprimanded for breaking protocol.

Blake was grateful for Turner allowing her to come along. She was also surprised; the detective sergeant was such a stickler for the rules that she couldn't quite believe he had finally broken one. Perhaps he'd been inspired by her constant wilfulness. Whatever the reason, Blake was glad to be aboard. She just hoped she could keep her word and prevent Turner from getting into trouble.

The rocky slopes of Bodmin Moor appeared before them. Soon, they were turning off the A30 and driving along narrower lanes, then onto the moor itself, the 4x4 easily handling the rough terrain. A minute later, they came upon existing tyre tracks that were worn into the ground, a sign of the same journey taken many times. They followed the tracks and the GPS location on the sat-nav, the gradient of the moors steepening, until they were climbing a granite hill peppered with gorse and heather. The driver, a police constable named Deepak Anand, changed gear. The 4x4 lurched forwards.

'We're almost there,' Turner called from the front seat.

Blake felt Rory tense beside her.

'You okay?' she asked.

He nodded. 'Just as long as you behave yourself.'

'When haven't I?'

'Is that a joke? Are you a comedian now?'

Blake arched an eyebrow.

They crested the hill. From her position in the back seat, Blake could see little. But Turner saw Fortunate Keep looming in the distance, its tall fences topped with razor wire glinting in the sunshine.

'This should be interesting,' he said, as PC Anand drove up to the gates and ground the vehicle to a halt. 'I hope you all remembered to bring your tinfoil hats.'

41

As they exited the 4x4, Turner leading with the two uniformed officers in tow, and Blake and Rory at the back, pandemonium was unfolding on the other side of the fence. Bodies dressed in earthy colours flitted left and right. Most ran towards log cabins and shut the doors. Some fled into the distance, disappearing behind a tall barn-like construction that stood at the centre of the compound. Within seconds, Fortunate Keep became a ghost town.

'I guess they don't get visitors often,' Turner said, examining the double gates of the fence, which were sealed together from the inside with an impressive heavy duty padlock.

Blake could see little from behind, so she stepped to one side for a better view. Rory glanced at her, a pained look on his face. Now she could see what Turner was seeing: a collection of simple log cabins and outbuildings surrounding a larger central building, with healthy looking vegetable gardens over on the left and a crude well on the right. The compound seemed to stretch out in the distance, but it was hard to see what lay beyond.

It was curious how quickly the people of Fortunate Keep had scattered, Blake thought, almost as if they'd practised such a manoeuvre many times before.

'What do we do now, Sarge?' PC Alison Rhodes said, as she peered through the gaps in the fence.

Turner rattled the gate. 'Let's give it a minute.'

'I should have brought my wire cutters,' Blake said, earning scowls from Turner and Rory. The PCs both smirked.

Cupping his hands around his mouth, Turner bellowed, 'Hello? My name is Detective Sergeant Turner. I'm with Devon and Cornwall Police. I'd like to talk to whoever is in charge here.'

Silence. Then, from one of the cabins, a young child began to cry and was quickly silenced.

Blake glanced at Rory, who shook his head.

'Why are they all hiding?' he said. 'It's not like we're here to arrest them.'

'They don't know that,' said Turner. He cupped his mouth and tried again. 'We're not here to cause trouble. We're looking for a missing person and need to ask some questions.'

All of the cabin doors remained shut, the grounds eerily quiet. Blake craned her neck, thinking she'd seen movement at one of the windows. But all she saw was sunlight glinting off glass.

A noise came to them. A slow and rhythmic *tap*, *tap*, *tap*, growing in volume. All eyes moved past the fence, to the left side of the centre building, which Blake had already decided was a church or a meeting house—no cult was complete without one. A man had appeared and was slowly making his way towards them, leaning his great weight on a sturdy walking stick. As he drew closer, Blake saw he was a white man in his mid to late sixties, with a wide, bearded face, salt and pepper hair, and narrow, furtive eyes that observed his unexpected guests with snake-like precision. He took his time in approaching, his gaze never leaving them. Finally, he reached the gate and stared at the intruders. Beads of perspiration dotted his brow and he was panting slightly. His lips curled into a friendly smile, although Blake noted it didn't reach anywhere near his eyes.

'Gentlemen,' he said. 'Ladies.' His eyes searched the group of police officers and landed on Blake, lingering on her before drifting back to Turner. 'I apologise for the sudden scattering of folk to the four corners of the earth. We're not used to visitors, and I'm afraid your presence may have caused undue panic.'

He smiled again, his lips spreading large and wide; a big, friendly grin designed to charm and entice.

Turner reached inside his jacket pocket, which he insisted on wearing despite the heat, and removed his ID. He held it up.

'Detective Sergeant Turner. CID. And you are?'

'It's nice to meet you, Detective Sergeant Turner. Around here, people call me Father.'

Turner stared at him. Blake could tell he wasn't happy with the man's reply. But until they had gained access to the compound, Turner would have to play the man's game.

'You're in charge here?' he asked.

Father chuckled. 'That's not how I like to see it. You see, our community is all about living harmoniously as equals. Yes, it needs someone to steer the boat, so to speak, and I suppose you could call me the captain of that boat, but I've never considered myself in any way a leader.' When none of the police officers smiled, Father cleared his throat. 'May I ask why you're here?'

'We're investigating a missing person,' Turner said, putting away his ID. 'We've also heard troubling reports about your community, which concern us. Perhaps you could let us in so we can have a chat.'

Deep lines of concern creased Father's brow. Blake watched him closely. He was good, an experienced conman who could talk the talk and had charm to spare. But she had met plenty of men like him before and all had been caught in the end thanks to the same hardwired flaw—overconfidence.

'A missing person?' Father said, with the right amount of concern in his voice. 'And these reports you mention—I hate to think anything bad has been said of our humble community. We're peaceful people, Detective. No one here would dream of hurting another person.'

'Then perhaps you'd be so good to let us in so we can discuss it.'

Father's gaze made its way back to Blake. There was something about her that had struck his curiosity. She was certainly dressed differently, wearing neither police uniform nor plainclothes suit. But Blake didn't think her black skinny jeans, boots, and T-shirt were what had caught his attention.

'Who's missing?' he asked, still looking at her. 'Because I can assure you all of our community members are accounted for.'

Turner leaned forward. 'Really? Are we going to discuss this through locked gates?'

'Well, it's just that I haven't seen a warrant yet.'

'That's because this is just a friendly visit, with the hope you might help us with our enquiries. Of course, if you'd prefer I had a search warrant, I'll happily come back with one, just as long as you're aware that would mean more disruption and upheaval for your people, and more police officers on site.' Turner smiled pleasantly. 'All I need is to ask you a few questions, which I would prefer not to do through a conspicuously locked gate.'

Father glanced at the heavy duty padlock. 'Well, I'm sure I can oblige. We have nothing to hide here—the lock is to protect us, not to keep you out.'

'Protect you from what?' Turner asked.

Father gave a not so subtle nod. 'From the denizens of the outside world.'

His left hand disappeared in the folds of his clothes, reappearing seconds later with a large bunch of keys. He rifled through them until he eventually located the right key and slipped it into the padlock. A quick snap of his wrist and the gates were open. Father took a few awkward steps back, his stick doing little to help him balance.

'Thank you,' said Turner, as he pushed open the gates. He nodded at the police constable before shooting a warning glance over his shoulder at Blake, who, in turn, looked over her own shoulder in mock confusion. Then the party was entering Fortunate Keep.

42

As Rory shut the gates behind them, Father turned to face the cabins and outbuildings.

'It's all right,' he called. 'There's no need to be afraid. I'm just going to help these police officers with their enquiries. The rest of you may go about your day.'

At first, no one stirred. Then, one by one, doors opened and people stepped out. They were all of different ages—children, adults, the elderly—but they all shared a common trait as they regarded the strangers that had violated the sanctity of their home: distrust.

Blake watched them mill about, some heading back to the vegetable garden, while others meandered into the distance towards the sound of bleating animals.

Father turned back to the visiting party.

'You see, we're a peaceful community here with nothing to hide. Please, why don't you come to my home and I'll have Mother make some tea.'

'Mother?' Turner repeated.

'Why, yes. You can't have Father without Mother.'

Blake scoffed, earning herself glares from both Rory and Turner.

'Please,' Father said, beckoning them forward. He began shuffling away from the gate, his stick creating little dust pools with every tap of the ground.

Turner indicated to Police Constables Anand and Rhodes to remain by the gates. Rory and Blake were to go with him. As they followed Father, the people of Fortunate Keep looked up from their duties and watched them through wary eyes.

Glancing over his shoulder, Father saw the uniformed officers returning to stand by the gates. He stared questioningly at Turner.

'I thought five might be a crowd,' Turner explained.

'I see. You mentioned a missing person?'

Turner nodded. 'Her name is Sandra Teague. She just turned twenty-one. Disappeared when she was twelve years old, along with her twin brother.'

'Sandra . . .' Father frowned and shook his head.

'She also goes by Sandy. We have a picture if you wouldn't mind taking a look. It's a composite by a forensic artist that suggests what she might look like now.'

He motioned to Blake, who removed a copy of one of the age progression images of Sandy from her bag and brought it to him. As she handed it over, she felt Father's eyes upon her.

Turner handed the image to Father, who stopped next to the washing lines, where a group of women were busy hanging wet clothes. A young girl was with them, about thirteen or fourteen years old, with long blonde hair and large green eyes that flicked nervously from stranger to stranger, finally coming to rest on Blake, who had dropped back to walk with Rory again. Blake gave her a slight smile. The girl quickly turned away. In the near distance, a group of children eyed the strangers curiously as they played with a ball.

Father regarded the image. 'A pretty girl. Although I'm not sure she ever passed through our gates. I do hope no harm has come to her.'

'Are you sure you don't recognise her? Perhaps if you took another look.'

Father did what was asked of him. 'No, I don't think so. But to be honest, we've had many people come and go over the years, and we weren't always located here. It took a long time and many places to find our perfect home. I suppose it's possible this poor girl came through our doors in the past, but I really don't recall her.'

He handed the image back to Turner and got walking again, moving away from the washing lines and towards the rear of the compound, with the others close behind.

'So you don't remember Sandy?'

'I can't say I do. But like I said, I'm getting old and we've had lots of girls come and go.'

'Then what about her brother. Morgan Teague? He claims to have spent time with your group. In fact, he says when he left, his sister Sandy was still with you.'

Father ground to a halt again. A strange look came over him, lasting just a second before fading away—but both Blake and Turner saw it. They had reached the rear of the compound, where the smell of livestock thickened the warm air. Blake stepped to one side and saw pens of pigs, sheep, and goats. Vehicles were parked next to the pens, including the SUV she had followed two days ago. Blake had not yet seen the men the vehicle had been carrying and wondered where they were hiding.

Over on the right stood a large cabin with a porch, while in the far left corner was a long shed with a sloping roof. On the other side of the fence was thick woodland, providing perfect cover for Father and his secrets.

'You know, I may have been mistaken,' he said. 'I do remember a Morgan from a few years back, before we came here. Quite the troublemaker if I'm correct. We asked him to leave and never saw him again. Now I think about it, I do recall him having a sister. A quiet thing, like a mouse. Her name was Sandy, you say?'

Turner was staring at him intently. 'That's correct.'

'Well, I'll need to ask Mother, but I'm sure Morgan and his sister left together, or his sister left soon after. It's one or the other. All I know is that both of them are no longer with us, and parted ways before we came to Cornwall and founded Fortunate Keep.' He paused to look at the livestock, catching the curious glances of the man and young boy tending to them. 'Let's keep moving. We're almost there.'

Before turning the corner, Blake peered back towards the front of the compound and the tall double gates. The police constables were gone. She scanned the vegetable garden and the washing lines but saw only Father's people dressed in their earthy colours. But then the door to one of the outbuildings opened and PC Rhodes stepped out. She glanced around before heading towards one of the cabins.

Turner, you sneaky bastard, Blake thought, and decided she liked him even more.

The others had rounded the meeting house and were halfway towards the large cabin with the porch. Blake caught up to Rory, who shot her a questioning look.

'What do you think?' he whispered.

'About what? The fact that Father's lying through his teeth or that this place is giving serious *Wicker Man* meets *Midsommar* vibes?'

'It's not just me then.'

'Most definitely not.'

The party reached the cabin and waited for Father to climb the porch steps before following him into his home. Blake glanced around the airy space but her focus was almost immediately drawn to the large wooden carving of a bipedal stag.

'Bloody hell,' Rory whispered.

Turner regarded it with a practised neutral expression before shooting a quick, bewildered glance in Rory's direction as Father called for Mother.

The woman appeared from a doorway on the right. She was about the same age as father, with long silver hair, tanned skin and many fine lines. At first her eyes were hard and watchful, but as Father introduced the visitors and explained their reasons for being here, Mother's gaze softened.

'I'll make tea,' she said. 'I've only just heated some water, so it won't be long.'

Turner thanked her. He nodded to the comfortable looking sofas and chairs. 'Perhaps we could sit?'

Father waved a consenting hand.

They all sat down, Father in an armchair next to the fireplace, Turner and Rory on one of the sofas. Blake selected an armchair that faced Father and the fireplace. From here she had a perfect view of everyone in the room, as well as Mother making tea in the kitchenette and the closed doorway over on the right.

Father regarded her for a moment before turning his attention to Mother.

'Do you remember a girl called Sandy?' he asked her. 'Detective Sergeant Turner believes she stayed with us for a time, perhaps a few years ago, before we came to Cornwall.'

Mother's hand wavered slightly as she reached for a teapot. 'I'm not sure. What did you say was the girl's name?'

'Sandy Teague. Am I right in thinking she came to us with her brother, Morgan? Do you remember him? He was a rather troubled character. We unfortunately had to ask him to leave.'

Mother slowly nodded. 'Oh, yes. I do remember Morgan. And his sister. They were twins, I believe.'

'That's correct,' Turner said. 'Do you remember what happened to Sandy after her brother left you?'

On the stove, the kettle began to whistle. Mother took a towel and wrapped it around the handle so she could pick up. She peered at Turner, then at Father.

'She left, I think. Isn't that right, Father?'

'Yes, exactly. Although I was trying to remember if she left with her brother or shortly after.'

Mother poured hot water into the teapot and spooned in what looked to be dried herbs.

'Oh, I'm not sure if I recall. Surely, she must have left with her brother. Twins are said to have a strong bond—I can't imagine she would have stayed behind.'

'And yet that's exactly what Morgan Teague claims happened,' Turner said. 'He states that he begged Sandy to leave with him, but she refused. In fact, she insisted she would be going nowhere and staying right here.'

'Oh, I see.' Mother placed the teapot on a tray, along with five teacups, and brought it over to the living area, where she set it down on the oak coffee table. 'We don't have black tea. I hope you'll enjoy a cup of lemon balm instead. It's very soothing.'

Father leaned forward, his great bulk spilling out of the chair. 'When you say Sandy insisted on staying here, you're of course referring to another of our former dwellings. As I mentioned, Morgan and Sandy left us before we came to Fortunate Keep. As for her insisting on staying with us, I'm afraid that's simply not true. Mother and I may be getting on in age, but we would remember. Besides, if it were true she'd be here somewhere, wouldn't she?' He smiled. 'Is Sandy here, Mother?'

'No, I'm afraid she isn't.' Mother poured gold-coloured tea into the cups and handed them out, first to Father, who immediately set his cup down, then to Turner, Rory, and lastly Blake.

Blake thanked her, but the woman did not acknowledge her. She hovered like a bird as her eyes wandered past the fireplace and the monstrous stag carving, to the door on the right.

'Well, if I'm not needed for anything else, I'll leave you in Father's capable hands,' she said, turning to leave.

'Actually, I'd prefer it if you stayed,' said Turner. 'What I have to say next concerns both of you.'

Mother glanced at Father, who nodded. She sat down in the chair next to him, placing her feet neatly together as she smoothed creases from her dress.

Rory took a sip of tea, rolling it around his mouth before swallowing.

'Very nice,' he said. Mother stared at him blankly, as if he'd spoken a foreign language.

Father cleared his throat. 'You mentioned allegations. What kind?'

Turner tried the tea, swallowed hard, and put the cup down. 'Morgan Teague claims the reason he left your group was because there was abuse going on, both physical and psychological. He also claims certain members of your group—young women, to be exact —vanished without trace. But the most serious of his accusations is that you tried to have him killed. Which clearly didn't work because here we are.'

Turner fixed Father with the kind of well-trained glare that would have had lesser criminals squirming. But Father merely blinked. Then he surprised everyone by laughing. It was a deep, throaty sound that swamped the room.

'I'm astonished,' he said. 'Truly astonished. That you would come here based on the ravings of a clearly unstable individual such as Morgan Teague. His time with us was fraught with nothing but trouble. He was unruly, often violent, always ungrateful. I don't know what happened to him and his sister before they found us, but I can only imagine that it left the boy damaged in some way. And why is he deciding to launch this unfounded attack upon us now, nearly three years later?

'There is no abuse here, Detective Sergeant. None at all. As I told you, we are a peaceful community who respect and love each other equally. We abhor violence. In fact, I built this place to help people escape from the very kind of violence you're talking about. To suggest it goes on here is not only deeply offensive but goes against everything we believe in. Everything we've created.'

He leaned back in the chair, a compelling look of hurt in his eyes. Whoever this man was, Blake thought, he was a professional. But still not nearly as clever as he clearly believed.

'As for missing women,' Father said, adding a disbelieving smirk, 'We're not a prison camp, Detective Sergeant Turner. People are free to come and go as they please. If Morgan has distorted people's free will into something nefarious, then I feel sorry for the boy. And I certainly did not try to have him killed. Or anyone else for that matter. I implore you, go outside and speak to anyone you like, and they'll tell you all the good I've done here. I've given these people a home, free from the dangers of your society. Why would I want to destroy all that when my goal has only ever been to bring people together?'

Silence fell over the room. Rory drank more tea, while Turner sat, processing all that Father had said. Blake found her gaze drawn to the closed door that Mother had first appeared from. The same door Mother had been staring at for the past two minutes.

'Is there a toilet I could use?'

Turner caught Blake's eye, before lowering his gaze to her untouched cup of lemon balm tea.

Mother glanced at Father, who grinned.

'Of course,' he said. 'We may live a simple life but we're not heathens. It's through that door and on the left.'

Blake thanked him and got to her feet.

Father held up a hand. 'I meant to ask. You're not in uniform or a suit, so I wonder which rank of police officer are you?'

'She's not,' Turner interjected. 'Blake is working with us in an advisory position on behalf of Morgan Teague and his family.'

'I see. A friend of theirs, are you?'

Blake smiled. 'Something like that.'

She left Father with a question on his lips and made her way through the door on the right and into a darkened passage. There were no light switches, suggesting no electricity, so Blake felt around in the shadows until she found the bathroom door and opened it. Inside was a small room with the usual bathroom furniture, and a large window that let in bright daylight, which spilled into the passage and pushed back the shadows. At the end of the passage, Blake could see another door.

She trod softly towards it, throwing a look over her shoulder as she moved. Out in the living room, Turner was talking in a serious tone, his words muted by the walls.

Blake reached the door, which had been left slightly ajar by Mother after Father had summoned her. She stood for a few seconds, her head cocked as she listened intently. Hearing nothing, she pushed the door open with two fingers and peeked inside.

It was a bedroom. Nothing more. There was no torture chamber. No tied up women. No walls adorned with blades and guns or far-right memorabilia. There was only a bed and other furnishings, including a fancy-looking chaise longue under the window and a storage chest at the foot of the bed.

Blake opened the door a few more inches and slipped inside. Her fingers were itching, longing to open drawers and rifle through their contents. She stared at the bed, then dropped to her knees and peered beneath it. Half hidden in shadows was a long wooden box. She stared at it. A strange thing to have under the bed, she thought, noting its length and depth, and how it sort of resembled a cheap coffin. She reached a hand under the bed.

And then Turner was calling her name, and he didn't sound happy. Blake's eyes lingered on the box. Swearing under her breath, she left the room, making sure to leave the door as she'd found it, and made her way back to the living room.

Turner and Rory were on their feet. Mother had retreated to the kitchen, where she was busy pouring unfinished cups of tea into the sink. Father stood in front of the giant stag carving, leaning his weight on his stick.

But there were others here too. Standing close to Father were two young men. Blake recognised them instantly—the two men in grey who had leapt from the SUV she'd been following. They both glowered at her.

'Everything all right, Turner?' Blake said, keeping the men in her sights.

'Everything's fine,' he replied. 'We're leaving now.'

Father took a lumbering step forward. 'You know, Detective Sergeant, rather than have your people sneak around like thieves in the night, you could have simply asked to take a look, and I likely would have said yes.'

So that was it. The PCs had been caught in the act.

'Before you go, I have a question for you,' Father continued. 'You say that Morgan Teague made these clearly false accusations. Yet he and his sister left us long before we came to Cornwall and built Fortunate Keep. So, indulge me, how did you know where to find us?'

'What can I say? I'm one hell of a detective.' Turner thanked Mother for the tea, and nodded to Blake and Rory. Reaching the front door, which had been left open, he paused and turned back to Father. 'Incidentally, can I assume that your land ownership deeds are all in order for this place? And that you have the correct planning permission for constructing what looks like homes? And, of course, taxes need to be paid, even in a place like this. I'm assuming your payments are up to date?'

Any good cheer Father had previously exerted was now gone.

'I'll happily share any relevant paperwork,' he said, 'when I'm presented with a search warrant.'

Turner gave a half smile. 'Thank you for your time, *Father*.'

He made his way out to the porch and descended the steps. Rory quickly followed. Blake lingered for a moment, staring at the men in grey.

'It's nice to see you again,' she said. Then she nodded goodbye to Father and followed the detectives outside.

∾

She found Rory and Turner at the bottom of the steps, talking with Police Constables Anand and Rhodes.

'We searched everywhere we could, but there's no sign of Sandy Teague,' Anand said.

'And no signs of anything unusual,' Rhodes added. 'Well, except for the entire place. But you know what I mean, Sarge.'

'Unfortunately, I do,' Turner said.

Blake walked away from them, coming to a stop in front of the livestock pens. Ignoring the bleats of the animals and the curious eyes of the man and boy caring for them, she jabbed a finger in the direction of the long storage shed in the far corner.

'What about there?' she said. 'Did you look inside?'

PC Anand shook his head. 'It was locked.'

'It's just storage,' the man with the livestock called. 'It's full of tools and sacks of grain. Nothing special.'

'So why is it locked?'

'To stop birds and rats getting at the grain.'

Blake's gaze wandered back to the shed.

'You do know rats can tunnel through the ground?' she said.

'Not in there they can't.'

Turner called to Blake. 'Leave the man alone. It's time to go.'

She was about to turn and say something sarcastic, when she noticed Father's men in grey standing on the porch, watching her.

'But we're not done here yet,' she said.

Turner, Rory, and the police constables began walking away from Father's cabin, heading back in the direction of the gates.

'We are,' Turner said. 'For now.'

Blake caught up with them. 'What do you mean "for now"? Come on, Father's full of shit! He went from not knowing Sandy to vaguely knowing Morgan to having very specific memories about him. He knows more than he's saying. Mother too. Surely you saw that, Turner.'

'I did. But you heard Anand and Rhodes—they searched the place and found nothing.'

'Well did they ask anyone if they knew Sandy?'

'We tried,' said Rhodes. 'But hardly anyone would speak to us, and those who did said they didn't know her.'

They cleared the corner of the meeting house and were now passing the washing lines and outbuildings. Behind them, the men in grey slowly followed, no doubt on Father's instruction, to ensure their guests departed without causing further trouble.

'So, that's it?' Blake said. 'We couldn't find anything, so we just give up?'

Turner massaged his left temple. 'No one said that. But I can't get a search warrant without any kind of evidence. So we have to try a different way.'

'You mean by catching Father not paying his taxes? How does that find Sandy?'

'Have you considered that Father might be telling the truth about Sandy?' Rory said. 'That she left a long time ago? I mean, she isn't here.'

Blake snorted. 'Maybe she's in that shed. Maybe he already killed her after failing to kill Morgan.'

'Why would he do that? His beef was with her brother.'

'I don't know. Because he's a psychopath. Maybe she didn't want to bear his children—or did no one else notice how most of the kids around here look a lot like Father?'

Rhodes raised her hand. 'I did.'

They were almost at the exit. Two men were by the gates, watching them. As they approached, the men opened the gates and stood like sentries, waiting for the party to exit.

'It's not good enough, Turner.' Blake said, as they reached the 4x4. 'You might not get a chance like this again. What if Sandy really is here somewhere, being held against her will? Why would Morgan lie about those other women disappearing? About Father trying to kill him? It doesn't make sense.'

Turner opened the passenger door and expelled a weary breath.

'I can only do what the rule book allows me to. I already broke protocol so you could come along today, and again with Rhodes and Anand conducting an unsanctioned search. There's nothing here, Blake. I'm not saying I disagree with you. I believe Father is lying—but we have to somehow catch him in the lie. Now, I could invite him in for questioning, but I don't think he'll give us much more than he already has. I can't arrest him and I can't do any more here without a warrant—and I already told you that's not going to happen, no matter how much we want it. So, we have to find another angle. And I know that's going to take time, and I know it's frustrating, but my hands are tied.'

He ducked his head and climbed inside the vehicle. Anand was already in the driver's seat, Rhodes in the back. Rory stood, waiting for Blake to get in. But she was pinned to the ground, weighed down with anger and frustration.

Anand started the engine. Before them, the gates of Fortunate Keep swung shut and the padlock was snapped into place. Through the chain link, the men in grey watched Blake with unblinking eyes.

'We should go,' Rory said, gently.

Blake glared at him.

She climbed in the back of the 4x4, quickly followed by Rory. Rhodes gave her a sympathetic glance, and then they were driving away from Fortunate Keep. Away from Father and his men in grey. Away from Sandy Teague.

43

From down in the dark, she could hear voices. They were muffled and unfamiliar, coming from somewhere above her feet. She could not open her mouth to scream for help. She could not move her limbs or hands to escape from her confines. She could only hang there, upside down, in the pitch black, bound with rope, and with a sackcloth tied over her head and neck. She wept silently to herself; crying out loud was forbidden, and the last time she'd tried to scream had led to a savage beating. Father had chosen that punishment over losing a finger—he did not wish to look upon mutilated hands when he was with his girls, his great weight heaving on top of them. Not that he'd had his way with her yet, but she knew he soon would. Because that was why she had been brought here—to satisfy Father's needs.

She was not alone down here. In this blackened, musty void she was blind, but her hearing had become fine tuned, like that of a nocturnal prey animal. Another girl was somewhere in the darkness, hanging from her feet just like she was. She heard her silent tears like mighty waves crashing on rocks. She heard her trembling breath like a thunderous rainstorm. She could not call out to this other girl, to tell her she was not alone. Nor could she reach out a hand to soothe her like her mother had once done, when she'd been a child afraid of the dark.

All she could do was hang, the blood in her body filling her skull like a chalice of wine, while listening to the voices from above. She focused on them, trying and failing to hear their words, but even nocturnal prey animals had their limits. So instead, she willed the voices to find her in the dark abyss. To set her free.

But the voices began to drift away, growing quieter with each passing second. Until silence returned. Except it wasn't real silence. Not when there were rainstorms and crashing waves.

Summer closed her eyes and prayed to the Triple Goddess, begging for a quick death. But she already knew that Father liked to take things slow.

44

Father tightened his grip on his stick as he raised it high above his head and drove it downwards to strike Thomas's bare flesh. The young man clenched his teeth but he did not cry out. He knew better than that. He lay naked and foetal on the floor of Father's living room, his hands covering his face as the beating continued.

'You lied to me!' Father raged. 'And you kept that lie for three years.'

The stick came down again, hitting Thomas in the lower back, turning his vision white.

'You told me Morgan was dead. That you'd taken care of it. So explain to me why the fucking police have visited our fucking home, making all sorts of FUCKING ACCUSATIONS!'

The stick sliced through the air again, battering Thomas's shins.

Father staggered backwards from the impact, his great chest heaving up and down as he sucked in large breaths of air.

'You're a liar, Thomas,' he said. 'I can never trust you again.

And now I have a problem to deal with that would never have happened if you'd just told me the truth.'

Thomas lay motionless on the ground, arms wrapped around his body. Tears stung his eyes but he would not let them fall. It was against the rules.

'Do you see the position you've put me in?' Father said, as he removed a handkerchief from the folds of his clothing and dabbed his brow. 'You may think me a monster. Perhaps you're even wondering why I haven't brought Kane in here and done the same to him. But you are my son, Thomas. My firstborn. If I cannot trust my own son, tell me who I can trust!'

Father raised the stick once more. Then lowered it, exhausted. Stooping to pick up Thomas's clothes, he bunched them up and held them over his son.

'I've a good mind to make you walk naked from here, to parade you around to show our people the shame you've brought upon this house. But I'm tired.'

He dropped the clothes onto his son's naked body, then slumped into an armchair, his stick still in hand. As Thomas slowly began to move, uncurling fingers and toes, bending elbows and knees to check if they were broken, Father fell into a sudden depression.

What should he do? How did he prevent the police from returning? Because they would return—Detective Sergeant Turner had made that abundantly clear.

The truthful answer was that he could not stop them from returning, which meant he would instead have to ensure his house was in order. How long he would have to achieve that, he didn't know. What he did know was that Thomas would make up for his lies and deceit. He may not have been able to make Morgan Teague disappear for good, but now he would have a second chance with Sandy.

Not tonight though, Father decided. Thomas would need time to recover from his punishment, and Father would need time to say goodbye to his sweet girl.

As for that whore who had led the police to them, Father vowed to track her down and let Kane have his way with her. Because even though Kane was not his biological son, he shared Father's anger and rage. And unlike Thomas, he was not afraid to unleash it.

Thomas was on his knees now, his clothes clutched to his chest, black, swollen bruises already showing on his back and legs.

'You can go now,' said Father. 'But first say goodnight to Mother. There will be no meeting tonight, I need time to think. Tell the others. And you make sure you apologise to Mother for your despicable behaviour. She will be just as disappointed as I am.'

Staggering to his feet, his clothes still gripped in his hands, Thomas nodded painfully. 'Yes, Father. Sorry, Father. I won't let you down again.'

A sneer twisted Father's lips as he turned away from his son's naked form. 'No, you won't. Because next time, I'll put you in the fucking ground.'

45

Night fell. A kaleidoscope of stars shimmered across an expanse of black sky. Fortunate Keep was still and calm. At the front of the compound, the men and women's bunk houses were dark and quiet. At the rear, the animals slept inside their shelters, occasional soft snorts punctuating the cool air. In the cabin on the right, Mother and Father lay in their bed with their backs turned to each other. Father snored loudly, while Mother slept a dreamless sleep, induced by her nightly dose of Valerian root.

No one was aware of the stranger emerging from the woodland, dressed in black. Nor did they hear her approach the fence, remove the backpack from her shoulders, and crouch down. Only when she removed a pair of wire cutters and gripped the fence between its jaws, causing it to tremble, did one of the animals stir.

Blake held her breath as the goat emitted a curious bleat. Silence fell once more. She waited a full minute and then began to cut.

After departing with Turner and the others earlier, Blake's foul mood had only grown worse. She was fully aware that Turner's hands were tied by red tape and procedure, but it hadn't tempered her frustration towards him. Or towards Rory, who had done nothing to deserve her ire except wear the suit of a police detective. The man calling himself Father was a liar. The woman, Mother, was a liar too; although the way she'd looked to Father for approval before answering Turner's questions made it clear there was only one person in charge at Fortune Keep.

After leaving Turner and the others, she had visited Morgan Teague and his parents to tell them of meeting Father. Morgan had flown into a rage, screaming that Father was a murderer who didn't deserve to live. He'd begged Blake to disclose the location of Fortunate Keep, but she had refused. It was for his own good, she told him, because he had only just been reunited with his parents. Why throw that into jeopardy now, when the police could use the full force of the law to prosecute Father and find Sandy, hopefully unharmed?

Blake was aware of the irony of her words, as she snipped a human-sized hole in the fence surrounding Fortunate Keep. But she had not just returned from the dead, and there were no questions hanging over her head about whether she was capable of murder. Because although the police had interviewed Morgan about the events at Devil's Cove, and had so far found no proof of criminal wrongdoing, it didn't mean they had dropped their investigation. Any wrong move by Morgan now would immediately see him in handcuffs and back in an interview room at the police station.

Which was why Blake was here now—because neither Turner nor Morgan could afford to be.

No matter the web of lies he had tried to spin, Father knew Sandy Teague, and exactly where to find her. Whether that was hidden somewhere within the grounds of Fortunate Keep or buried in a shallow grave at an undisclosed location, Blake didn't know. All she knew was that she'd seen alarm in Father's eyes when Turner had mentioned land ownership deeds and taxes, and that his fear went beyond the risk of getting fined. So it didn't matter how much Kenver had tried to talk Blake out of coming here alone tonight—because when Turner finally came back with a search warrant, he would find Fortunate Keep cleansed of incriminating evidence, including any trace of Sandy Teague.

The section of fence that Blake had been cutting fell away. She caught it before it could hit the dirt with a clang, and laid it gently on the ground. She put the wire cutters away, slung the bag over her shoulder, and climbed through the hole in the fence.

Now that she was inside the compound, blood rushed in her ears. Despite the lack of light pollution and it being summer, the darkness up here on the moors was intimidating. She could make out the shapes of buildings, their rooftops silhouetted against the starry sky. Beyond that she was half blind. There was a penlight in her trouser pocket, which had helped her find her way through the trees, but using it inside Fortunate Keep would have to be reserved for desperate situations.

The animals were stirring inside their shelters, aware of Blake's presence. She kept low and quiet as she flanked the fence, moving past the paddocks and towards the locked storage shed. She was certain Father was hiding something inside. The police constables had searched the rest of the buildings and found nothing, while Blake had taken care of Mother and Father's house. And the shed was the only building that Father kept locked.

'Rats, my ass,' Blake whispered, as she reached the shed door. From her bag she removed a pair of bolt cutters, then examined the padlock securing the door with her fingers. She had been expecting a high security padlock, but to her surprise it felt like a standard padlock that required a unique but simple key and had a shackle of medium thickness. Easy work for her bolt cutters.

Blake fitted the jaws of the cutters around the shackle. She hesitated. Did the simple nature of the lock mean she was wrong about the storage shed, that Father was not hiding anything nefarious inside? Or did it mean that his influence over his followers was so great that not one of them was interested in looking inside? There was only one way to find out.

Squeezing with all her strength, Blake made quick work of the padlock, severing the shackle with a loud *snap*. The lock hit the ground with a clatter. Blake snatched it up and spun around. Her heart thumped in her chest as she scanned the shadows, waiting for a door to open, or a lantern to appear. Over in the shelters, the animals grew restless. But no one came.

Thankful the main living quarters were at the front of the compound, Blake slipped the cutters and broken padlock inside her bag. She quietly pulled back the bolt on the door. Then, casting one more wary glance over the area, she stepped inside the storage shed and bolted the door.

Pure darkness swarmed around her. At first, she panicked. But realising the storage shed was windowless, she removed the penlight from her pocket. Before switching it on, she first sniffed the air, smelling a stale, plant-like odour. And then she listened. When all she heard was her beating heart, she activated the penlight, and a cold beam cut through the darkness.

The storage shed was long and narrow, about a metre and a half wide and two metres tall where Blake stood. But as she stepped forward, the roof quickly began to slope, forcing her to crouch the further she advanced.

Shelves lined both walls of the shed, upon which sat jars of preserved and fermented foods. Beneath the shelves, lined up on the ground, were several large hessian sacks. Blake poked one with a finger, felt something soft. She tried another, this time removing the twine that sealed the neck. Her shoulders sagged as she shone the torch beam inside, illuminating harvested grains of wheat.

Had the lock been to keep out rats, after all?

Blake dropped to her knees and pointed the penlight at the floor, which was covered in dried straw.

No. There were no other hiding places. This shed had to be hiding a secret.

She continued searching. And five minutes later, after dragging heavy sacks of grain back and forth and brushing aside handfuls of straw, Blake found it.

A steel trapdoor.

It was square in shape and about a metre wide, with another padlock securing it in place. Blake stared at it, her stomach twisting in knots. Setting the penlight on the ground so the beam pointed at the trapdoor, she retrieved the bolt cutters and tested the shackle. It was thicker than that of the other padlock, which meant it would be harder to cut. And this padlock did not require a key but a combination code, so it could not be picked.

Crouching on her knees, Blake gripped the padlock between the bolt cutter's jaws. She clenched her teeth and squeezed. The shackle held. She rested for a few seconds, then squeezed again, her muscles screaming until she gave in and released her grip. The cutters had damaged the shackle but not sliced all through the way through.

Panting and swearing, Blake leaned back on her haunches. A minute passed by. She picked up the cutters and tried again. Tendons popped in her neck. Veins throbbed in her temples.

'Come on!' she hissed.

The shackle snapped and the lock clattered noisily on the trapdoor. Blake collapsed over it, gasping for air. When she could breathe again, she scooted back, tossed the broken lock to one side, then glanced behind her at the shed door and listened.

Still no one came.

Grabbing the penlight, Blake pulled open the trapdoor.

She peered down into icy blackness. A terrible smell hit her: the acrid stench of human decay.

A ladder reached down into the darkness. Holding her breath, Blake leaned into the hole and pointed the beam of the penlight downwards. She could see the ground, poured concrete covered in filth, about three metres below. Not too far to climb, but far enough to cause a wave of anxiety to rush over her as she lowered herself into the hole and tested the rungs of the ladder with her feet. The rungs held.

Blake hovered for a moment, attempting to block out the nauseating odour.

She had no idea what was waiting down there. Or who. What if this was all an elaborate trap set by Father, who knew people like Blake well enough to pre-empt her return tonight? What if someone was crouched just outside the shed, waiting for her to climb down into the darkness so they could slam the door over her head and trap her inside with a new lock? Blake shuddered. Fear was seeping into her skin and gnawing at her bones.

'It's fine,' she whispered. 'Everything is fine.'

Placing the penlight between her teeth, she gripped the ladder with both hands and began to descend.

46

Darkness swelled around her, rushing in and out like waves. The smell of human waste climbed up her nostrils and down her throat, threatening to make her vomit. Blake held her breath as she quickly descended. She was on the ground in seconds, reversing away from the ladder and swinging the torch through the dark. Her back slammed into a wall, knocking the breath from her lungs and piercing her spine with damp cold.

Terrified, she spun in a half circle. And froze. The beam of the penlight began to flicker as it illuminated the horror before her.

The chamber was small, two metres wide by four metres long, with the ladder at one end and a metal rail running along the centre of the ceiling. Attached to the railing were large meat hooks. Attached to two of the hooks were short lengths of rope.

And attached to the ropes, hanging upside down, were a woman and a girl.

Blake could only stare at them, observing the twine binding their ankles, wrists, and arms. Hoods made of sackcloth were pulled over their heads and secured at the neck with more twine.

The bodies were unmoving; the girl and the woman strung up like cuts of beef in a butcher's window. Except these women were not on display. They were vile, nasty secrets that had to be kept hidden in a dank pit, away from the people of Fortunate Keep, for fear they saw just how grotesque and abominable their leader truly was.

A shudder wracked Blake's body. Were these just two of Morgan's disappearing women? Was one of them his sister?

Blake stepped forward, the penlight still trembling in her grip. She reached out her free hand, then quickly drew it back.

'Hello?' she whispered.

And the woman burst into life like a corpse brought back from the grave.

Startled, Blake leapt back.

The woman thrashed and writhed on the hook. She was trying to say something, but the sackcloth buried her words.

Beside her, the girl remained deathly still.

Coming to her senses, Blake tore off her backpack and pulled out a penknife.

'I'm going to free you,' she said, as she crouched down. 'But I need you to keep still while I cut the twine around your neck.'

The woman continued to buck and moan.

'Please. You need to keep still or I'm going to cut you.'

But it was as if the woman couldn't hear her.

Swearing, Blake put the woman in a headlock. She began carefully sawing at the twine, while the woman continued to shriek. The twine snapped. Blake released her and removed the hood from her head. A gag was stuffed in the woman's mouth. She pulled it out, and the woman dragged in a breath.

'You're okay,' Blake said. 'I'm not going to hurt you. I'm here to get you out.'

The woman sucked in air, choked on it and began to cry. She

was young, Blake noted. Maybe in her early twenties, although it was hard to be sure due to the dirt on her face and the fact she was hanging upside down.

Blake made quick work of severing the bindings around her arms and wrists. The woman's limbs fell limp at the sides of her head.

Whirling around, Blake spied a stepladder leaning against the wall. She grabbed it and set it up next to the woman.

'I'm going to free your ankles now. You're going to fall a little bit, so if you can, use your hands to protect your head.'

Blake climbed the ladder, clamped the penlight between her teeth, and began cutting the twine.

'Get ready,' she called.

The woman wailed. The twine snapped. She dropped to the ground like a stone, landing hard on her left shoulder.

Descending the ladder, Blake helped the woman into a sitting position.

'I've got you,' she said. 'We're going to get out of here. What's your name?'

The woman cradled her injured shoulder. In between her rattling sobs, she managed to say, 'My name is Summer.'

'Well, Summer, my name is Blake. I'm sorry to have met you in such shitty circumstances, but it will all be over soon. Do you think you can stand? I might need your help to free this girl.'

'Her name is Jenny,' Summer said. 'She's fourteen years old.'

Blake peered up at the limp body. *Fourteen years old.* Nausea bubbled in her stomach. She pushed it back down and held out a hand to Summer, who took it in a weak grip. She heaved the woman to her feet.

Summer stood for a second, wobbling to and fro, before collapsing again.

'I can't feel my ankles,' she said, and began rubbing them furiously.

'You've been hanging upside down for a while. The blood will come back to them; you just need to give it a minute.'

Blake shuffled the stepladder over to Jenny's body. She would have to take a chance, try to catch the girl as she fell.

Climbing the rungs, Blake gripped the penlight between her teeth once more and began to cut the twine. The blade sliced through the threads, splitting them open.

The twine suddenly broke.

Jenny fell.

Blake lunged, grabbing the girl's ankle but dropping the penlight. It bounced off the bottom rung of the ladder and hit the ground. The bulb, by some miracle, remained intact.

Jenny slammed into the stepladder, which shuddered beneath Blake's feet. Tossing the penknife, she grabbed Jenny's other ankle.

Summer had managed to get on her hands and knees, and had crawled over. Picking up the penlight, she reached up with both hands.

'Drop her,' she said.

'You'll catch her?'

'I will.'

'You're sure?'

'Just do it!'

Blake released her grip on Jenny's ankles. The girl fell, slamming into Summer's chest and knocking her to the floor.

Jumping from the stepladder, Blake dropped to her knees, grabbed the penlight, and pulled the girl off Summer.

'Are you okay?' she asked.

Summer arched her back and winced. 'Fuck, no. But I'll live. Can we please leave now?'

Jenny was waking up in Blake's arms. As her eyes snapped open, her instinctive reaction was to scream. Blake clasped a hand over her mouth.

'You're safe,' she said. 'I'm Blake. Summer is next to me. We're going to take you away from here just as soon as you can walk.'

She slowly removed her hand from Jenny's mouth. Summer sat up and leaned over the girl.

'Hey. Remember me?'

Jenny started to cry.

Retrieving the penlight, Blake pointed the torch at the ladder leading up to the shed. 'How are those ankles, Summer?'

'Coming back.'

'Then we're going to be leaving soon. I've cut a hole in the fence nearby. We'll go through the wood. My car is parked about half a mile away. I'm afraid we'll have to walk.'

She peered down at Jenny, who seemed to be drifting in and out of reality. It was shock, she supposed, then wondered just how long Summer and Jenny had been left hanging down here in the dark. It was a question for another time, when they were far from here, where no one could hurt them.

'Actually, we can't leave yet,' Summer said. 'There's another girl. Mother and Father have her kept in a box, under their fucking bed.'

A terrible chill ran the length of Blake's spine. She had seen that box. She had crouched close enough to reach out and touch it.

'We can't leave her in there,' Summer was saying. 'We have to go and get her.'

Blake stared at the woman. She was so young, and had been through hell and was still not out of it. Yet her strength crackled like electricity.

'What's the girl's name?'

'I think she said it was Sandy. But she's lost her mind. Who wouldn't, trapped in a coffin like that?'

Sandy. She had been here all along.

Blake glanced down at Jenny, who peered up at her with an eerie, serene expression.

'Okay,' she said. 'Let's go get Sandy. But first we need to put this one somewhere safe.'

47

Kenver paced Blake's living room, repeatedly rubbing his knuckles against his chin. He hadn't been able to sit still since Blake had left the cottage in a swirl of angry determination. She was furious that the police could do nothing about the cult without playing it safe and abiding by the rules—a notion that was completely alien to her.

She was certain something nefarious was happening behind the walls of that compound, and Kenver thought she was right; nothing good ever came from fanatic cult mentality. One only needed to turn to the history books—or YouTube in Kenver's case —to see just how destructive they could be. Jonestown, Heaven's Gate, Waco, and the Order of the Solar Temple, were just a few examples where cults had come to horrible ends, involving mass suicide and brutal murder. And then of course there was Devil's Cove. Kenver had not been living in Cornwall at the time, but the Dawn Children's bloody wave had been felt far and wide.

And now Blake was going after another cult, one which little was known about, but was displaying all the classic signs of yet another narcissistic leader ruling over his brainwashed followers with violence and abuse. Kenver was worried. He knew Blake was great at her job, and that she was driven by finding the good in all the shit the world continued to drown in. But for fuck's sake, just for once in her life couldn't she play by the rules like Detective Sergeant Turner had suggested? One of these days Blake was going to end up dead on a mortuary table, and she would only have herself to blame.

She was also something of a hypocrite. Because she'd gone on and on about Kenver having a problem with alcohol, insisting that he was dependent, possibly addicted, if there was even a difference. And yet here Blake was, diving headfirst into potentially deadly circumstances without a moment's thought for her own safety. And it wasn't the first time. No, Kenver was not the only one with a dependency problem. Whether she would admit it or not, Blake was addicted to danger, and the thrill of the chase was her high. It was undeniably self-destructive in Kenver's mind.

But he was still worried, his anxiety growing by the minute. What was she expecting to do? Break into their compound and take on the entire cult by herself? Kenver stopped pacing. That was exactly what she was planning to do. Of course it was.

Hurrying over to the sofa, he scooped up his mobile phone and found Rory's phone number. He had never called Rory before; they weren't exactly friends, although Kenver had nothing against the man, apart from his questionable taste in women. Rory had given Kenver his number years ago, back when he and Blake had been on more intimate terms. Kenver had thought it odd at the time, but perhaps by giving his phone number to members of Blake's family, Rory was able to pretend their non-relationship was something more genuine.

Poor Rory, Kenver thought. He really did need to get over Blake.

Hitting the call button on his phone, Kenver waited for the line to connect and for Rory to answer.

48

Jenny watched the women cut through the darkness from the other side of the fence. The feeling in her feet and ankles was slowly returning. She couldn't quite walk yet without stumbling everywhere, but pacing up and down at the treeline seemed to be helping her circulation.

She was scared here outside of the compound, the woodland shifting and creaking ominously at her back. She still remembered the day they had all entered Fortunate Keep. She had crossed the threshold with her hand in her birth mother's, the gates had closed, and they had never stepped outside again. Until now.

Father had told them the outside world was a cruel and terrible place that would devour them all alive. Jenny had always believed it. But recently she'd discovered that cruelty could transcend any barrier, no matter how tall you built your fences or how much razor wire you put on top. Because cruelty, it seemed, lived within everyone. Take Father, for example, who had always shown Jenny nothing but kindness, making her laugh with his silly jokes or putting an arm around her if she ever felt sad. Then Jenny had turned thirteen and started to bleed down there. That was when Father stopped being so kind. He would look at her differently, like how sometimes she'd seen the dogs stare at the baby lambs in spring. It wasn't anger, exactly. Or hatred. It was more like hunger. All Jenny knew was the way Father looked at her made her feel dirty.

And then along came Thomas, who was younger than Father but still too old to call Jenny his girlfriend. That's what he did when he got her alone, in between trying to touch her. She'd told him to stop many times. She'd told him she didn't like it. But Thomas liked it and that was all that mattered.

That day in the bunk house, when he had followed her in and pushed her roughly onto the bed, Jenny had feared for her life. She had kicked him hard, right between the legs, and had run to the women working in the vegetable garden. Thomas had been furious, but instead of coming after her, he'd gone straight to Father. Jenny had thought Father would beat Thomas for his actions, but to Jenny's surprise, Father was angry with her.

'You're of age now,' he'd told her. 'Which means you have womanly duties to uphold.'

Jenny had been shocked. She knew she bled down there, but she also knew she was too young for what Father was insinuating. Her birth mother had made sure of that, long before they'd entered Fortunate Keep.

'Boys only want one thing,' she told a younger Jenny. 'Some will try to trick you into giving it to them, whether you're ready or not. But until the law says you're old enough to decide for yourself, you keep away from those boys.'

Jenny was sure fourteen years old was not old enough to decide for herself. But Father had struck her anyway. Mother had sat back and watched. And when she insisted Jenny do Father's bidding, Jenny ran away and hid in the pantry.

They came for her that night; she didn't remember how. One minute, she'd been in her bed, softly crying so as not to wake the others. The next she had awoken in that terrible dark pit, hanging by her feet and screaming so loudly her throat had bled.

It was her punishment, Thomas had told her, ordered by Father to teach her a lesson—because it was only the Horned One, speaking through Father, who decided which paths we walked. And if the Horned One had decided that Jenny was ready to uphold womanly duties, then Jenny had no choice but to comply.

But Jenny did have a choice, and she was making it now. She was going to leave Fortunate Keep and never come back.

She was walking a little better now, in spite of the pain that pulsated through her ankles. Soon, she would be able to run. She peered through the hole in the fence, wondering how Summer and the outsider woman were going to free Sandy.

Jenny had known Sandy from before. She had always been kind and friendly, if perhaps a little too persistent in her seeking of Father's attention. But she hadn't seen Sandy for a long time, not since that first year they'd arrived at Fortunate Keep, which had been a while after Sandy's brother had left.

Now Jenny wondered if Sandy had been in that box all this time, tucked away beneath Mother and Father's bed like an old suitcase. And she wondered what had really happened to Sandy's brother because she knew Morgan had hated Father in the end, and had begged his sister to leave with him. Jenny hadn't understood Morgan's hatred at the time. But now she did. It burned through her like wildfire.

She was going to leave this place and never look back.

Jenny froze.

If she left, what would become of Joni? She was the same age as Jenny, and although she was more immature and perhaps not as pretty, it wouldn't be long before Father came looking for her, expecting her to perform her own womanly duties.

Jenny turned to stare into the dark wood, then back at Fortunate Keep. Perhaps she could convince Joni to come with her. If she explained to her what Father had done, if she showed Joni the terrible pit where she'd been kept, surely she would realise that Fortunate Keep was a place built on lies.

Moving unsteadily on her feet, Jenny crouched and pushed her way through the hole in the fence. She stole past the animal paddocks, making sure to keep the storage shed out of her sight, then hurried alongside the meeting house.

She wondered what Father had told the others about where she'd gone. There were other girls that had vanished in the night, just like Jenny. Now she wondered if they had been taken to the same nightmarish place. And if it was true, where were they now? Were they all in boxes under Mother and Father's bed? Jenny didn't want to think about it.

She reached the women's bunk house. Stopping outside, she searched the darkness for signs of danger. When she saw none, she slipped through the door and tiptoed between the beds of sleeping women and children.

Moonlight spilled through the windows, pooling on the floor. Reaching her own bed, Jenny's hands flew to her mouth. The mattress was bare, the sheets and pillow removed, as if she had never existed.

Tears stung her eyes, but this was no time for weeping.

Joni was asleep on her back in the next bed, one hand tucked beneath her head. Jenny leaned over her.

'Joni, wake up,' she whispered, then glanced up to see if any of the women had heard her. Joni did not stir, so Jenny reached down and gave her a gentle shake. 'Wake up, Joni. It's me. I'm back. In fact, I never left.'

She watched as Joni slowly woke up. At first, she seemed confused and disorientated. But then, as she became more conscious, her eyes grew wide and round.

'Get up,' Jenny said. 'We have to go. This is a bad place, Joni. If we stay here, horrible things are going to happen.'

Joni sat up. 'Jenny? Is that really you? Father told everyone you left.'

'Father is a liar. I didn't go anywhere. He put me in a hole in the ground and hung me upside down from a hook, all because I wouldn't let Thomas touch me.'

'Don't say things like that!' Joni hissed. The woman asleep in the next bed over rolled onto her side. 'Why would you tell lies like that? Father is good and kind. He loves us. He would never hurt you.'

Jenny took her by the arm and began pulling her out of bed. 'But he did hurt me, Joni. I could have died down there and no one would have ever known. He put Summer down there too. But a woman rescued us. We're leaving with her, and we're never coming back. You need to come with us, before Father hurts you too.'

Joni was on her feet now, staring open-mouthed at Jenny. 'There's an outsider here?'

'That's right. She cut a hole in the fence and we're going to escape through it.'

Jenny began dragging her along, but Joni wrenched free of her grip

'Stop it!' she cried. 'Stop trying to make me leave!'

All around them, bodies began to stir. A woman sat up, her bed close to the door. Jenny glanced at her, then back at Joni. She was finding it hard to breathe.

'Please, Joni. Don't do this. You have no idea what Father is really like. He pretends to love us but he's cruel and selfish. And I don't believe the Horned One speaks through him at all. I think Father makes it all up to get what he wants.'

'You can't say that!' Joni gasped.

More women were sitting up now. One was getting out of bed.

'What are you two up to?' she said. 'You're waking the children.'

The tears Jenny had been holding back sprang from her eyes.

'Please, Joni. I'm begging you. Come with me.'

Joni took a step back.

'You've gone mad,' she said. 'I don't know why you're saying the things you are. The Jenny I know loves Father, and she would never betray him. Not like you are now.'

'You're just like I was,' Jenny said, tears choking her. 'You won't see the truth until it's too late.'

And then, to her horror, Joni sucked in a deep breath and bellowed at the top of her lungs: 'An outsider is here! Jenny let her in!'

A flurry of gasps flew about the room. Jenny turned and saw all the women staring at her. It had been a mistake coming here. She should have listened to the outsider woman and stayed on the other side of the fence.

'Someone wake up the men!' one of the women cried.

'I'll go get Father!' another yelled.

Jenny turned and ran.

She had made it halfway to the door, when her right ankle spasmed painfully. She went down, hitting the floor hard.

The women were on top of her before she could even catch her breath.

49

Standing on the porch of Mother and Father's house, Blake pressed her ear to the front door and listened. She heard nothing. Behind her, Summer shifted her weight from one foot to the other as she gripped Blake's penknife. Blake gave her a nod—*be ready*—and reached for the door handle. The door popped open, which was no real surprise: who would dare enter Father's domain without his consent? Besides, locks and bolts had no place in a community allegedly built on safety and serenity. Unless Father decided to imprison you in his underground hellhole.

Blake stepped inside. The living room was cast in darkness, the great totem of the Horned God lurking in the shadows. Summer followed, her muscles taut and her breaths shallow. For someone who had been hanging from a hook just fifteen minutes ago, she was making a remarkable recovery. Blake wasn't surprised. One look into Summer's eyes revealed a woman who had endured horrors long before coming to Fortunate Keep. Whatever had been done to her had left her hardened—a survivor.

What did surprise Blake was that she had so far managed to

break into Fortunate Keep, rescue Summer and Jenny, and infiltrate Mother and Father's house without alerting anyone. But now she had no choice but to wake them.

Father's heavy snoring was coming through the passage door. Blake crept forwards and pushed it open. She entered the passage, Summer on her heels. Darkness swarmed about them. Blake felt along the wall, one hand outstretched in front of her. Father's snoring grew to a crescendo, as if they had stepped into the heart of a violent storm.

They reached the bedroom door. Blake's skin prickled with unease as she peered over her shoulder, into the darkness.

'Ready?' she whispered.

'Ready,' Summer replied.

Blake turned the door handle.

Tiptoeing inside the darkened room, she saw Father's mammoth form, his chest heaving up and down in time with his snores. Mother lay next to him with her back turned, perfectly still.

Blake advanced, one foot slowly sliding in front of the other. Summer came in behind her and circled around to the foot of the bed.

She glanced at Blake, who sucked in a nervous breath, let it out, then gave her a sharp nod.

Summer pounced, leaping onto the bed and landing on top of Father. He woke with a start, had just enough time to gasp before sharp metal bit into his neck.

'You try anything and I slit your throat like a pig,' Summer whispered in his ear. On the bed next to Father, Mother had woken up and was pressing herself against the headboard. 'The same goes for you, bitch. You're no better than he is.'

Blake dropped to the floor, then lay on her back and slipped her feet beneath the bed. She felt the hard wood of the box against the soles of her boots, and began to push.

Father tried to free himself. Summer pushed the tip of the blade into his flesh, producing a thin black line of blood that trickled down his neck and onto the pillow.

'You must have a death wish, old man. Didn't you hear what I said?'

'There's no need for violence,' Father managed to say, in between frightened breaths. 'Why don't you just leave now? I'll give you the key to the gates and you can leave before anyone gets hurt.'

'I don't need your key, Father. We have our own special way out. And the only people who are in serious danger of getting hurt before I leave are you and your wife. So if I were you I wouldn't say another word.'

'Please,' Father said.

Summer raised the penknife and plunged it into his cheek, feeling the tip of the blade glance off his teeth.

Father howled like an animal. Summer pulled the knife from the wound and slipped it back under his chin. Thick blood ran down Father's face. Next to him, Mother stared in horror.

On the floor, Blake gave the box one last shove with her feet, then jumped up and moved to the other side of the mattress. She crouched down and pulled the box from under the bed, shuffling backwards with her jaw clenched.

Summer had Father's arms pinned between her thighs, so he could do nothing about his wound, which bled freely down his cheek and dripped into the back of his throat, making him cough.

'I should kill you after what you did to me and Jenny,' Summer hissed. 'She's just a kid, you fucking sadist. I can't wait for all of your brainwashed little sheep to find out exactly what kind of depraved, perverted man they have for a leader. They'll look at you in disgust, like the piece of shit you are. And when they turn their backs on you and walk away, there'll be nothing left for you. Even Mother will leave you. And then you'll be alone. I hope you die that way, you monster. I hope you drown in a pool of your own piss and tears.'

She pressed the knife into his neck, carving a thin black line; not deep enough to cause serious injury but enough to make him shriek.

'Please, child,' Mother whispered. 'There's no need to do this.'

Summer ignored her. Rage was burning inside her, years of pain and anguish igniting like dry tinder. Her grip on the penknife was impossibly tight. All she had to do was press down a little harder to sever through sinews and arteries. Then Father's life would be snuffed out. But would Summer's anguish?

Over by the window, Blake was breathing hard. Sinking to her knees, she pulled open the lid of the box, switched on her penlight, and peered inside.

Sandy Teague stared up at her with dull, lifeless eyes. Then blinked in the light. Her ankles were tied, as were her wrists, which rested upon her stomach. Blake reached inside her bag and removed a second penknife; if she'd learned anything in her years of private investigation, it was to always carry a spare of her most essential tools.

She cut at the twine binding Sandy's limbs. When the young woman was free, she took her by the arms and gently pulled her into a sitting position.

'Let's get you out of this box and back to your family,' Blake said.

On the bed, Father wailed. 'You can't take her! She's mine.'

Summer raised a fist and struck him hard on the bridge of his nose. Mother began to cry.

Throwing Sandy's arm around her shoulder, Blake hoisted the woman to her feet.

'There we go,' she said. 'Now can you step out of the box?'

Slowly, Sandy raised her left foot and placed it on the floor. Her right foot came next, wobbling as she set it down.

'Excellent. Now we're going to take a slow walk to the door.'

Blake spoke words of encouragement as Sandy shuffled unsteadily forwards, her body leaning into Blake's.

'Summer, we're leaving.'

'I'm right behind you.'

Fingers itching to cut open Father's flesh, Summer leaned over him and spat in his face.

'You don't deserve to live,' she said.

Shooting Mother a warning glance, she sprang from Father and onto her feet. Blake and Sandy had reached the bedroom door.

Summer pointed the knife at Mother and Father.

'Enjoy your freedom while it lasts,' she said. 'Which won't be very long.'

Sandy's feet were slipping out from under her. Blake heaved her up again and wrapped an arm tightly around her ribcage.

Summer came up behind them, the blade still pointed towards the bed. Mother was on her knees and pressing a handkerchief over Father's ruined cheek. Father was motionless, glowering at the escaping women.

Stumbling into the passage, Blake dragged Sandy through the darkness and into the living room. Sandy's gait was becoming more unsteady, her feet tripping over themselves.

'I need your help,' Blake called to Summer.

'I'm coming.'

Summer came up beside her and took Sandy's other arm.

Together, they pulled her shell-shocked form towards the front door.

'Almost there,' Blake said.

She reached for the door handle, wrenched the door open.

And saw the entire community of Fortunate Keep racing towards her.

Blake stumbled back into the room, almost toppling Sandy and Summer.

Two men burst through the doorway. Then four, then seven. Women followed, carrying lanterns as they pushed their way in to surround the intruders. More people flooded in, until Mother and Father's living room was tightly packed.

Summer gasped.

Blake was silent, staring at a sea of angry faces.

Behind them, the passage door opened and Father staggered into the room, fresh blood oozing from the hole in his cheek. Despite the blinding pain it caused, he smiled at his people. His Fortunate and Blessed. But the smile quickly turned sour.

Mother appeared behind him, still clutching her bloody hand-kerchief. Father gave her a cursory glance.

'Put Sandy back to bed. The rest of us will go to the meeting house. The Horned One is furious. He demands retribution for this gross violation.'

He turned to stare at Summer and Blake, who were powerless against an entire cult.

'The Horned One demands blood,' he said.

50

Turner sat in the passenger seat of the police-issue 4x4, as it raced along the A30. PC Anand was once again behind the wheel, while DC Angove sat in the rear seat next to PC Rhodes. It was late, the roads clear, so the police siren remained inactive. Turner was quietly furious. Not with Blake, but himself. Of course Blake had decided to take on the entire cult alone. He'd seen it in her eyes the moment he'd told her there was nothing more to be done without a warrant. He should have handcuffed her then, he thought. Made up some random crime and charged her with it.

A voice in Turner's mind kept asking the same question: Had he wanted Blake to go after them?

He didn't want her to get hurt, but he did want justice. Playing by the rules, no matter how much he believed in them, could often be frustrating, especially in circumstances like these, when it was obvious the man calling himself Father was lying through his teeth, and that something was very wrong at Fortunate Keep. There was no evidence, just a bad feeling in his gut—but bad feelings didn't count as reasonable grounds for issuing a search warrant. So Turner's hands were tied, relegated to searching land registries and tax records, in the hope of finding a fraudulent offence that might grant a more official return to the compound.

That was why he had let Blake go—his moral crown had momentarily slipped and fallen into the hands of exasperation and envy. That was why he was furious at himself. Because he had knowingly let Blake walk into danger.

Still, he reminded himself that Blake Hollow was a force of nature, who would have found a way to Fortunate Keep tonight even if he'd thrown her into a police cell and swallowed the key.

In the rear seat, Rory cleared his throat and leaned forward. 'How far away are we?'

Turner glanced at the sat-nav. 'ETA seventeen minutes.'

'Seventeen minutes? Jesus, can we put our foot down?'

'Any faster and we'll be no good to anyone. Try to stay calm, Rory. Knowing Blake, I'd be more worried about Father and his followers.'

Rory leaned back again and stared at the dark landscape on the other side of the window.

'She's out there,' he said, after a while.

'I know.'

Silence resumed. The vehicle shot through the blackness, a sliver of light in a fathomless void.

51

Every bench in the meeting house was full, sleepy children wedged between the adults, who all thrummed with anticipation of what was to come. For now, the stage was empty except for the two giant totems of the Horned One, which stared down at the congregation, a myriad of flickering candle flames bringing their colossal forms to life.

Joni sat at the back. Occasionally, she glanced at the empty space beside her, where Jenny once sat, before shame made her hang her head and look away.

Anxiety filled the air. People were afraid. The Horned One had been angered and demanded recompense. No one here had besmirched Him, yet it didn't mean they were safe. For the Horned One was a vengeful god.

A chorus of whispers resounded from the front rows. Father entered through the stage door and took his place behind the lectern, his walking stick nowhere in sight. There would be no pomp tonight, no ceremonial robes. Father stared at his people. The makeshift dressing on his cheek was already dark with blood.

He said nothing for a long time, simply gazed at the rows of faces that were aglow in the candlelight. At last he spoke.

'Tonight, we were violated in the worst kind of way. An outsider desecrated our sacred space by first destroying our fences, our protection from the outside world, then spoiling most of our grain, which means we will go hungry this winter.'

Gasps of horror rose up from the congregation. One of the younger children began to cry.

Father leaned over the lectern, his injured face a nightmarish vision.

'This outsider was not alone,' he said. 'Summer was with her. We all remember Summer, don't we? The unbeliever. The liar and thief who made a mockery of our ways. I can only imagine it was Summer who brought this outsider into our midst, because how else did she know where to find us? This outsider, who just the other day followed Thomas and the others, who brought the police into our home this very afternoon. This outsider, who not only brought Summer back with her, but Jenny too. Dear, sweet Jenny, who chose the sins of the outside world over her own people. Who clearly fell under the spell of wicked influence, then dared to return to bring ruin upon those who love her.'

Father held out his hands to form the shape of a cross. He turned his gaze up to the rafters.

'The Horned One is enraged,' he said, his voice loud and commanding. 'This is His paradise, and we are His humble servants. A violation of our home is a violation of His spirit. Of His righteousness. And there will be a reckoning!'

Lowering his arms, he turned towards the stage door and gave a sharp nod. The men in grey appeared, Kane, Matthew, and Thomas, dragging Father's captives by lengths of rope. Kane had Blake, who pulled and thrashed at the rope binding her wrists, while Matthew had Summer. Thomas, who was limping and wincing with every step, trailed behind with Jenny.

'Bring them forward so we may all look upon their sinful faces,' commanded Father.

Kane yanked Blake to the front of the stage, then shoved her forward. She fell at Father's feet, tried to stand, and was rewarded by a sharp burst of pain as Kane grabbed her by her hair and forced her onto her knees.

Next came Summer, whose left eye was bruised and swollen, her nose broken and bloody. Matthew tugged the rope and she stumbled forwards, past Father, until she was on the other side of him. She too was brought to her knees and held there by her hair, facing the audience.

Lastly came Jenny, who went willingly with Thomas, her head bowed so low that her hair covered her face. Father beckoned. Thomas brought Jenny to him, handing over the length of rope, before backing painfully away to the rear of the stage.

Father stared down at the teenager and shook his head. 'Jenny, Jenny, Jenny . . . What are we to do with you? It wasn't so long ago that you sat on the back bench next to darling Joni, singing your little heart out in praise of our beloved Horned One. And now here you are, a traitor among us, filled with rancour and deceit.'

He pushed her chin up with the tip of his index finger, forcing her to stare at him. 'Is it my fault? Did I expect too much of you too soon? Or is it that you've lost your faith in both your family and our God? What should I do with you, Jenny? The Horned One believes you are young and easily led. He is undecided whether you should be returned to the fold and given the opportunity to atone for your sins, or if you should be made an example of. What do you think? If you were to return, would you atone or would you continue to work against us?'

Tears escaped from Jenny's eyes. In the candlelight, she looked gaunt and pale, like the ghost of a child who had died too young.

Father was waiting for her answer.

'Well?' he said. 'What's it to be? And choose well, for the Horned One is always listening.'

A sob escaped Jenny's lips. Slowly, she sank to her knees.

'I'll atone,' she said, choking back more tears. 'Forgive me, Father. I beg you to let me return.'

She continued to weep, her shoulders quaking, until Father could stand it no more.

'Oh, enough, sweet child. The Horned One has spoken. He grants your return. Your atonement will commence immediately.' Father motioned to Thomas, who limped forward. 'Jenny needs time to think about what she's done. Take her somewhere she can do that. Somewhere she won't be disturbed. Somewhere she can *hang* alone with her thoughts.'

Jenny's eyes grew impossibly large. She shook her head violently. 'No! Please, Father! Please, don't make me go there. Please, I'm begging you!'

But Father was already turning his back on her. Thomas took the rope that bound Jenny's wrists and wrenched her forwards. She stumbled and tripped, hitting the floor hard. Thomas dragged her across the stage and through the door, until Jenny was gone and only her screams remained. But soon they too had vanished.

'Now we're left with the true deceivers,' Father told his people. 'And the Horned One has been very clear on what should be done with them.'

He signalled to Kane and Matthew, who each wore a leather sheath attached to their belts. Unbuttoning them, both took out a ceremonial looking knife with a black handle and a curved silver blade upon which several runes were engraved.

Seeing the blade, Summer began to struggle. Blake was unmoving, her eyes fixed on the paling faces before her.

'Sacrifice,' Father said, as whispers rose from the crowd. 'It is a frightening word, and one we are unfamiliar with here at Fortunate Keep. But our sanctuary has been breached and made unclean. These heathens have let the outside world into our home and poisoned it with disease. The Horned One demands sacrifice as retribution. And when He has it, He will purify us all.'

'Then He must have his sacrifice!' a man shouted from the front row.

From somewhere near the middle, a woman's voice rang out. 'Yes, sacrifice in exchange for purity!'

Other voices quickly joined in, bowing to the Horned One's demands. But not all voices. Many of the congregation remained silent, nervously staring at each other.

And then a woman in her thirties stood and raised a hand.

'What about Sandy, Father? I thought she had left us a long time ago, but she was there tonight. You told Mother to put her back to bed. Has she been here all this time?'

The congregation fell deathly silent. Even Summer stopped struggling.

Father brought his hands together and fixed his eyes on the woman. Anger flashed in them, at her blatant defiance. He held out a hand and motioned for her to sit. The woman did as he asked, but her accusatory gaze did not waver.

'You are right to ask about Sandy,' he said. 'Most of you knew her well and loved her, long before we came to Fortunate Keep. After the trouble we had with Sandy's sinful brother Morgan, she stayed on for a while but eventually decided to leave us, to go in search of her twin. As was her right. What I didn't tell you, with good reason, is that Sandy returned to us in the middle of the night a few weeks ago. She was in a bad way. Hurt and unstable, the outside world having taken its toll on her. Thomas found her at the gates and summoned Mother and I. Sandy begged us to bring her back into the fold. She told us she had been wrong to search for Morgan, that he was lost to her forever, and that her real family was right here at Fortunate Keep.

'Mother and I made a decision. We chose to let Sandy return, but only under our care and discretion, until we deemed she was well enough to be reunited with you. I'm afraid that time has yet to come. You saw her tonight, how despondent and detached she is. I fear for Sandy's mind. I fear the outside world broke her, possibly beyond repair. That is why I chose to keep her return a secret. Why Sandy stays within the confines of our home, with Mother caring for her as best she can. So you will forgive me for keeping Sandy's presence from you, but you will understand why.'

Faces peered up at Father. He stared at the woman who had challenged him. She bowed her head.

'He's lying,' Summer suddenly cried. 'They keep Sandy in a wooden box beneath their bed. Father isn't helping her. He keeps her as his pet—a plaything he brings out when he chooses then puts away when he's done.'

Murmurs rippled through the rows.

Father was momentarily paralysed. Then he was striding towards Summer, his face turning the colour of nightshade.

Summer continued to plead with the congregation. 'You have to help her. She's lost her mind because they keep her inside a fucking coffin. You have to free her! You have to get her out!'

Father towered over Summer and Matthew, who had grown pale and uncertain, the knife trembling in his hand.

'Kill her,' Father commanded. 'Cut her throat and let her blood spill over this stage. The Horned One commands it.'

Matthew stared up at him, his dewy brown eyes filling with tears. 'I—I can't do that.'

'You can, and you will. Cut her open, Matthew, or you'll be next in line.'

The teenager flinched and stared at Summer. 'I don't think I can.'

Father bore down on him, showing his teeth. The makeshift dressing slipped from his face, exposing the bloody wound.

'You kill her now or I will have Kane tear you open, right in front of these people,' he hissed. 'He'll split you from gullet to groin, and pull out your insides, and he'll keep you alive while he does it. So take that knife and put it to her neck and bleed her fucking dry!'

Tears leaked from Matthew's eyes. He pulled Summer's head back and placed the blade against her neck.

She stared up at him, fires burning in her eyes.

'Fuck you,' she said. 'You're all going to hell.'

Father signalled to Kane, who still had Blake's hair gripped tightly in his hand, and his knee pressed into her back. He brought the blade to her throat and smiled.

'In the name of our beloved Horned One,' Father boomed, his hands in the air, 'We give flesh, blood, and bone. Let it cleanse the earth of impurity and cast out the sickness seeping through our veins, so that we may bathe in His love again.'

His hands dropped to his sides. He nodded first to Matthew, then to Kane.

'Do it,' he said. 'Kill them both.'

52

Mother stood over the box lying next to the bed. Sandy had climbed in without fuss and lain down without a word of complaint. And Mother had suddenly turned and vomited on the floor. At first she wondered if she'd ingested too much Valerian root, and had poisoned herself. But vomiting had made her feel no better, only worse.

She stared at the woman in the box, who was waiting patiently for the lid to be closed upon her, to be pushed back under the bed until it was time to feed her or let her go to the toilet, or for Father to have his way. And Mother realised why she'd been sick—she was rotten to the core, and disgusted by her own compliance. It had taken a stranger to break into Fortunate Keep to tear Mother from her medicated dream, but she was awake now. And she didn't like what she saw.

Mother had been with Father since the beginning, when he had genuinely cared about politics and the human condition. But as the years had passed, he had grown cynical and bitter, realising he had no control in a world where only a few reigned supreme.

And so he had created his own world in which he had full control —over Mother, and over the others.

She had loved him at the start. They had met young, when she was a painfully shy thing who could barely look in a mirror. But Father had made her feel special. He had called her beautiful and clever. He had called her Mother. And the name had lasted so long now that she barely remembered her own.

Sandy was still lying there. Still waiting.

Mother felt faint. She teetered on her feet. Holding onto the wall, she waited until the dizziness had passed.

Father had once been a good man. Or at least she'd thought so. Yet somewhere along the way, a poison had found its way inside him, seeping into his veins and travelling up to his brain, corrupting him. Father was sick. Mother knew she was sick too. That the name 'Mother' was nothing more than a mask to hide her depravity.

She stared down at Sandy.

'For God's sake, get to your feet.'

Sandy did as she was told. She watched Mother with curious eyes. Something was different. Something was changing.

'Go on,' Mother said, leaning against the wall. 'Leave before he comes back.'

But Sandy just stood there, like a dumb animal.

Mother slapped her face. 'Didn't you hear me? You're free. So go!'

When Sandy still didn't move, Mother took her by the arm and dragged her from the room, through the passage and into the living area. Throwing open the door, she pushed Sandy onto the porch and shoved her down the steps. Sandy fell on the grass. She lay in the darkness, unmoving. Then she slowly got to her knees and stood up.

Mother watched her for a minute, guilt and hatred tearing at her insides. From her pocket, she took out a key and threw it down to Sandy. It landed at her feet but she made no move to retrieve it.

'For the gate,' Mother said.

She shut the door and went to the kitchen. She stood, hovering listlessly, for what seemed like an hour, the sickness in her gut spreading to her limbs, her torso, her head.

Staggering, she pulled open a kitchen drawer and removed a pair of scissors. She examined the blades, tested the sharpness.

No. Now that she was awake, she didn't like what she saw—because what she saw was what she had become. And what she had become was a monster.

Mother let out a desperate wail. She plunged the blades of the scissors first into her left eye, then the right. And she saw nothing at all.

53

A terrible silence fell over the meeting house, in which no one breathed or moved. Blake saw looks of horror, of anticipation and excitement. She peered up into Kane's eyes and saw a terrible, vast emptiness devoid of humanity. Of all the ways she had pictured herself dying, being sacrificed to a god had not been among them. Yet there she was, having finally found Sandy Teague, only to end up on stage in front of a room full of broken people, with her life about to be brutally snuffed out. *Why of all places a stage?* she thought. Theatricality had always been Kenver's thing, not hers.

Kenver . . . She hoped he would find a way to forgive himself for what he'd done. He had always been more of a brother to her than Alfie, who was more interested in making money than his family. Even so, she wished her sibling well, and that his child grew up healthy and strong, free from the curse of generational trauma.

As for Blake's mother, she knew her death would hit Mary the worst, and so she hoped she would find solace in the arms of Blake's father, even if Blake could still not forgive Ed for his past misdeeds, even with a knife biting into her throat. But she wished him a long life anyway. And then there was dear Judy Moon, her closest friend, whom she had neglected lately because work kept getting in the way, and Judy had responsibilities that Blake didn't have or want—like children and a husband. In another life, Blake would have made more time for her friends and family. But there was no other life. Only this one. And it was about to come to a violent end.

The blade pressed into Blake's throat. She squeezed her eyes shut and waited for the swish of metal, a sharp sting, and the letting of blood.

But it didn't come.

She opened her eyes again.

Something was happening. Something to cause a panic. People were at the windows, peering out at the night and muttering to each other.

'What is it?' Father called, his voice weak with uncertainty.

Blake saw it a second later. A flash of orange, lighting up the dark.

Someone screamed.

Another shouted, 'The women's bunk house is on fire!'

More people jumped from the benches and rushed to the windows. Father remained where he was, scratching his head, the black hole in his cheek still oozing blood.

A man ran to the double doors and threw them open.

'The vegetable garden is burning too!' a woman cried.

And then something whistled through the air and smashed against the man, who immediately burst into flames.

Terrified screams filled the air.

The man staggered back, shrieking in pain. The floor around him caught alight.

Blake thought she saw someone dash past the meeting house.

A second later, glass exploded inwards as a ball of fire burst through a window and smashed onto the stage, close to Father's feet. Blake stared at it while Father stumbled away. It was a broken lantern. Kerosene was pouring out and catching instantly ablaze.

The flames began to spread. Matthew was already backing away from Summer, his frightened eyes fixed on the fire. Blake peered up at Kane, who still had the knife to her throat and her hair in his hand, but his grip on both had loosened. Like Matthew, his gaze was flickering between the flames and Father, who was escaping through the stage door.

By the main doors, the man who had caught fire writhed on the grounds, legs kicking, hands grasping at air. No one helped him. The flames continued to spread around him, reaching towards the doors.

'This is the outsider's fault!' someone shrieked. 'The Horned One is punishing us all!'

Blake sucked in a breath. Then clenched her jaw and slammed the back of her skull into Kane's groin.

The man went down, his face flushing red as he dropped the knife and writhed in agony.

Blake was on her feet in seconds, swooping down to snatch the blade, before hurrying over to Summer, who was still on her knees, a look of stunned confusion lining her face. Below them, people ran in all directions. The fire was spreading quickly.

'Get up!' Blake shouted, startling Summer from her daze. The woman got to her feet. 'Now run!'

Blake flew across the stage, heading through the door at the end, with Summer close behind. They descended a short flight of steps and found themselves in a pitch-black corridor. Blake raced along it, crashing into the wall before tripping over something on the floor. Summer collided with her. Fortunately neither fell.

They got moving again, passing a window, then coming to a

door. Someone was behind them, closing in fast. Blake shouldered the door open and ran outside.

The night air flooded her lungs, heavy with the taste of smoke. Summer ran up beside her.

They had exited at the right side of the meeting house, next to the kitchen and dining hall, which was also ablaze, thick plumes of smoke rising up to the stars. Blake didn't know who had started the fires, but she was grateful to them.

'Where do we go?' Summer said. Her eyes were bulging in their sockets, her head turning left and right.

Blake saw people bursting through the side door. Kane was among them. His dark eyes fell upon her.

'The fence,' she said, and took off running.

Summer followed, their bound wrists swinging to and fro, slowing them down.

Blake shot a glance over her shoulder, but it seemed Kane had chosen self-preservation over retribution, and had fled in a different direction.

They reached the back of the meeting house, heard the screams coming from inside and saw flames licking the windows. They turned the corner and Blake slid to halt.

Father's house was an inferno, flames as tall as trees shooting through the roof. The heat was overwhelming. It seared Blake's skin.

Father was kneeling in front of his home, Mother cradled gently in his arms. She was dead, her eyes gone. Heat blisters bubbled on Father's neck and face, but he was oblivious, as he quietly sobbed while rocking back and forth.

There had been love there once, Blake saw, a long time ago, before Father had sold his soul to the Horned One. Before he'd betrayed love for control.

Her gaze lingered on the blazing house. She hoped Sandy had

not suffered, that smoke inhalation had killed her quickly before the box had caught ablaze. Blake shuddered. What a terrible way to die.

Summer tugged on her arm. 'Blake! We have to go.'

So they ran on, past the inferno, leaving Father and his dead wife behind. Past the paddocks and the livestock shelters, which had all been opened and the animals set free. Past the storage shed and its abominable pit of horrors that would haunt Blake's dreams for nights to come, but not for as long as it would haunt Summer's. They ran until they came upon the hole in the fence and climbed through, Blake first, quickly followed by Summer.

Using the ceremonial knife she'd taken from Kane, Blake freed Summer's wrists, then waited patiently as Summer freed hers. They stood for a long time, shell-shocked and mesmerised, as they watched Fortunate Keep burn to the ground and listened to the screams of its people, who were burning in their own personal hell.

A face flashed in Blake's mind and she gasped in horror.

'Jenny!'

She started back towards the fence. Summer gripped her arm.

'It's too late,' she said.

Blake tried to throw her off, but Summer had strength to spare.

'Let go of me!'

'If you go back in there you won't come back out. You'll burn like the others.'

'I'll take my chances. Now let me go!'

Summer released Blake's arm.

And another hand emerged from the shadows of the trees to wrap fingers around Blake's hand.

'I'm here,' Jenny said.

Blake stared at the teenager, her jaw going slack.

Blood matted Jenny's hair and soaked the front of her dress. Her haunted blue eyes peered out from a tear-streaked scarlet sea.

'I had to do it,' she wept. 'He was going to hurt me. I had to do it.'

She collapsed into Blake's arms and sobbed uncontrollably. Blake held her to her chest, feeling Thomas's blood seeping into her clothes.

'We need to leave,' she said. 'Find our way through the trees and back to my car.'

Summer peered into the wood. 'We don't have a torch. How are we going to see? And what about your car keys? Were they in your bag?'

A loud *crack* shattered the night. They turned in time to see Mother and Father's house collapse in on itself.

'I always keep a spare,' said Blake. 'It's under the bumper in a magnetic case.'

'Someone's going to find that one day,' Summer said. 'Then you'll be sorry.'

Blake shrugged. 'You haven't seen my car.'

They turned away from the fence and the fires beyond. Part of Blake wanted to stay, to help the others get out, but Summer was right—to go back in risked burning with the others. She hoped at least some of them would find the hole she had left.

As they reached the treeline, Blake paused and wondered again who had started the blaze.

'Was it you?' she asked Jenny. 'Did you set fire to it all?'

Jenny squeezed her hand and peered into the trees.

'No,' she said.

'Do you know who did?'

The girl shook her head and quickly looked away.

Blake took one last look at the burning buildings. For a second, she thought she saw someone on the other side of the fence. A woman, walking slowly, as if in a daze. But then the darkness shifted, and Summer and Jenny were pulling Blake into the trees, away from Fortunate Keep.

⁓

As the 4x4 screeched to a halt outside of the main gates, Turner and the others stared in horror. Rory was out of the vehicle first, racing to the back to pull open the boot and dive into the toolbox. Removing a pair of hydraulic bolt cutters, he dashed towards the gates, where men, women, and children were pressed into the mesh, shrieking with terror as Fortunate Keep burned behind them.

Turner raced up next to him, followed by the police constables.

Feeding the cutters through the fence, Rory slipped its jaws around the shackle of the padlock and squeezed. The lock snapped and fell away. The gates flew open and the people came rushing out.

Turner was momentarily stunned by the scene before him. They had only visited the compound that afternoon, but now Fortunate Keep was a ravaged hellscape. He glanced at the people, who were swarming about the uniformed officers, all crying and talking over each other.

'Radio for back up, and for fire and ambulance,' he called to Anand and Rhodes. 'And keep this lot contained.'

He nodded to Rory and they both entered Fortunate Keep, the heat burning their skin. They made their way through the compound, staring in disbelief at burning buildings and charred bodies, while hysterical people ran to and fro, without any real direction.

Choking on smoke, they reached the rear of the compound, where Father's house was a burning pyre. He was still sitting in front of it, his dead wife in his arms, flames flickering in his eyes.

Turner and Rory ran to him.

'Where is she?' Rory demanded. 'What have you done to Blake?'

Father stared at the detectives, then at the blazing buildings.

'What a waste' he said, shaking his head. 'No matter how much I try, the outside world always finds its way in.'

Turner reached around and removed a pair of handcuffs from a pouch on his belt.

'Well, you won't need to worry about it anymore. Because where you're going, no one's getting in.'

Rory continued searching while Turner watched over Father. He found the ragged hole in the fence a few minutes later. He stared through it, at the dark wood beyond.

And somehow he knew Blake had made it out alive.

54

Blake slowed the car to a halt in front of the barricade and switched off the engine. She turned to her passenger, who had been silent for the past ten minutes.

'I guess we're walking from here. Are you sure you still want to do this?'

'I'm sure,' he said.

Together, Blake and Morgan stepped out of the car and peered down the long, sloping road that led to the town of Devil's Cove.

A week had passed since Fortunate Keep had been razed to the ground. Twelve people were dead, killed in the blaze. Father was in police custody. Other cult members were under investigation. Jenny was safe and well. Her birth mother had survived the fire, and with nowhere else to go they had been placed in emergency accommodation.

Jenny's police interview had proved crucial in bringing several charges against Father, whose real identity had been revealed as sixty-seven year old Edward Culver, a former university professor who had taught political science and had a previous criminal conviction for assaulting his first wife. With Jenny's help—and the help of a string of female followers who had since come forward—Father was likely to spend the rest of his life in prison.

As for Summer, who had spent a night in hospital, then two more in Blake's spare room, once the police had finished with their interviews, she vanished. Blake had found a note on her kitchen counter, thanking her for saving Summer from that dank, awful pit, for which she would be forever grateful. But Summer wanted to put as much distance between herself and the remnants of Fortunate Keep as possible. Maybe she would even return to her native Scotland and try to settle down. Although she was doubtful she would contact her mother, who was beyond forgiveness.

And then there was Sandy. No human remains had been found inside the shell of Mother and Father's house, which led Blake to believe either Sandy had escaped or Mother had set her free. And once she'd known Sandy had survived the fire, it was quickly clear who had started it. No one knew how long Sandy had been kept prisoner in that box beneath Mother and Father's bed, but Blake knew that even a day spent confined in a pitch-black space where she couldn't move her arms or legs, or even sit up, would be enough to make her lose her mind.

Blake had learned from Jenny that Sandy had been at Fortunate Keep at least for that first year, perhaps even longer. And then she'd disappeared. Father had spun his old tale of another young woman heading into the outside world to fall into ruin. They had all believed him, including Jenny. No one knew if the story Father had told the night of the fire was true. Had Sandy arrived in the middle of the night a few weeks ago, begging to return to Fortunate Keep? Or had she been kept in that box for over a year, maybe even two, let out only on Father's say so, but never outside the confines of his home?

Why had Father kept Sandy in that box? It was one of the

cruellest punishments Blake could think of. On the night Blake had tried to free Sandy, Father had cried out: 'You can't take her! She's mine!' Had he been in love with her? Or what he believed was love, but in reality was an obsession that had driven him to treat Sandy like property, his to take out and put her away whenever he wanted? Blake wondered if they'd ever know the real answer. For now, Father wasn't talking to anyone. And Sandy was still missing.

Blake was sure it was her she'd seen that night, walking through the flames as if in a dream. Wherever she was now, it was not among the dead. Perhaps she had found her way through the hole in the fence and vanished into the trees. Maybe she was still there, hiding like her twin brother had done for so long at Trevelyan Wood.

Morgan. He stood beside Blake, so young looking now all that wild hair was gone. His gaze flitted past the barrier blocking the road, moving downhill, where the town of Devil's Cove had once stood.

Blake gave him a gentle nudge.

'We can always turn around,' she said.

Morgan shook his head, then deftly grabbed the top of the concrete barrier and swung himself over. Blake was not so graceful, but managed to scale the barricade and jump down to the other side.

They walked in silence, the road sloping sharply under their feet, running downhill to loop around the town like a hangman's noose. As they drew closer to the blackened ruins, Morgan's breathing became fast and shallow. His eyes darted everywhere, his pupils dilated.

Passing rows of burned out houses, Blake could only think of Fortunate Keep. But what had happened here at Devil's Cove was on a far greater scale of horror. Morgan had been present for it, not as victim but as perpetrator, although he swore he'd never harmed anyone. All he'd wanted was to get away from the Dawn Children and their insane rhetoric, but Sandy had already been indoctrinated and Morgan couldn't leave without her.

He'd called Blake two days ago, asking if she could give him a ride. She had thought it an odd request, when both of his parents had a car and Blake was a near stranger to him. But then he told her where he wanted to go. She asked him why he wanted to return there, and Morgan said he didn't know, only that he needed to. Blake wondered if Morgan was in need of catharsis, and that perhaps walking the ruined streets of Devil's Cove would give it to him.

The smell of smoke still lingered in the air, even though years had passed. They reached the town square, where shop facades were scorched and blackened, their names illegible. And then Blake and Morgan were stepping through a small alleyway and emerging onto Cove Road, where a long promenade of pink flagstones stretched out in both directions on the other side. Crossing the road, they stepped onto the promenade and came to a rest in front of the iron railings. Below them was a golden brushstroke of deserted beach, where the remnants of a collapsed beach bar was slowly sinking beneath the sand. This was the place where Cal Anderson had disappeared fifteen years ago, while playing in the waves. The same place he had mysteriously returned eight years later, triggering a series of catastrophic events.

On either side of the beach were two sheer cliffs. On the right was a lighthouse and Briar Wood. On the left, an empty space where a pristine white hotel had once stood, staring out to sea.

Morgan leaned against the promenade railings, staring out at the cobalt waters, which were calm and glistening, not a ship or boat in sight. Blake stood next to him. Will Turner entered her thoughts. She wondered if he had witnessed Devil's Cove burning, if the fire at Fortunate Keep had triggered terrible memories. She thought about calling him, then decided against it. Both Turner and Rory were still furious with her for once again ignoring their pleas and charging into a dangerous situation, only to leave a trail of carnage in her wake. Perhaps she would give it a few days before checking in on them both. Or perhaps a few months.

Blake heaved her shoulders. With her eyes pointed towards the ocean and her back turned on Devil's Cove, it was easy to forget the death and destruction that had been inflicted upon the town and its people.

'Why are we here Morgan?' she asked.

The young man drew in a long breath. He shook his head. When he spoke, he did so with his eyes fixed firmly on the horizon.

'She killed someone, you know.'

Despite the heat, Blake felt a chill slip beneath her clothes. 'You mean Sandy?'

'We came down here with the rest of them, mingling with the crowds, wearing those stupid masks. When everyone started dying, I got scared. I lost sight of Sandy. It was hard to keep track of anyone with all the running and screaming. And the masks. Then the fires started and I thought I was going to die. So I ran.

'I found her in a street. She was frozen, watching a house burn, while the Dawn Children killed people all around her. I tried to make her leave but it was like she was in a trance. I said to her, 'Do you want to die?' And she just shrugged. I looked down and I saw the blood on her clothes and the knife in her hand. There was blood on the blade. Not a lot. But enough for me to know what she'd done.

'I asked her about it, months later. She told me she'd killed a man. Stabbed him in the stomach when he'd come running around the corner. He fell to his knees and she stabbed him in the throat.

She'd said it had been easy with the mask on, that she'd done what had been expected of her. But Sandy was changed after that. She never looked anyone in the eye again. Not even me.'

Morgan paused. He glanced at Blake, who tried to mask her horror.

'I think that's why she stayed with Father,' he said. 'I think that's why she let him do the things he did to her. Why she's disappeared again. Because deep down, under all that damage, all she feels is guilt.'

Blake watched a flock of gulls swoop over the shoreline. She didn't know what to say, so she remained silent. A breeze drifted in from the ocean, cooling her skin. At last, she turned to Morgan and placed a hand on his shoulder.

'I think your sister set the fire at Fortunate Keep, which killed twelve people,' she said. 'The police are looking for her. If they find her, she'll be charged with arson and multiple counts of murder, or at the very least voluntary manslaughter. But the question is, is she guilty? You were part of the Dawn Children, and then the Fortunate and Blessed. You know how these groups operate. They may not have worked on you, you may have only stayed for your sister, but they destroyed her. When I pulled Sandy from that box, it was like she had nothing left inside. So think of it this way: Sandy didn't kill that man—the Dawn Children did. And Sandy didn't burn all those people—that's on Father. That's how you separate your sister from what she did. Because you don't want to remember her the other way. It'll ruin you.'

Morgan stared at her, his ocean-coloured eyes tinged with grey at the edges, like the calm before a storm.

'Sandy's gone,' he said. 'My sister is never coming home.'

A sob escaped him and he collapsed into Blake's arms.

Blake felt his body shudder against hers as the grief came. There was nothing she could say to console him, and she did not want to give him false hope. And so she held him for the longest time, until clouds began to drift across the blue sky, and the breeze grew stronger.

When Morgan was done crying, they walked back to the car in silence. All around them, the town of Devil's Cove continued its slow decay into ash and ruin.

And up in the hills of Bodmin Moor, a young woman with sea-green eyes emerged from the wood and drifted through the heather and gorse, until she stood at the edge of Dozmary Pool. She seemed to exist in a liminal space, neither of this world or the next. One moment she was there, watching clouds drift across the pool's surface.

And then she was gone, leaving only ripples in her wake.

A Note from Malcolm

Thank you for reading *The Devil's Hand.* If you enjoyed the book, I'd be grateful if you could leave a short review on the website you purchased it from. Reviews encourage new readers to try my books, which helps me to earn a living and write more books for you to read.

In case you weren't aware, *The Devil's Hand* crosses over into another of my series, *The Devil's Cove Trilogy,* which tells the story of Cal Anderson and the terrifying Dawn Children cult. If you would like to read it, you can find the eBook, paperback, large print and hardcover editions at most online bookstores, as well as at your local library. If you purchase the series—or any other book —direct from my website, you can get 15% OFF at checkout by using the code **THRILLER15.** This includes physical books.

Visit: www.malcolmrichardsauthor.com/books

Acknowledgements

Thank you to my editor Natasha Orme for your insight and wisdom, and your unwavering enthusiasm for Blake and her often gruesome world. Thank you to Devon and Cornwall Police, and to *copsandwriters.com*—any aspiring crime writers out there should listen to their podcast, or at the very least join their invaluable Facebook group. Thanks also go to my family and friends, my wonderful readers, and, as always, to Xander.

Books I read in preparation for this novel included *Wicca: A Comprehensive Guide to the Old Religion in the Modern World* by Vivianne Crowley and *Traditional Witchcraft: A Cornish Book of Ways* by Gemma Gary. For research into cults I read the seminal text *Cults in Our Midst: The Hidden Menace in Our Everyday Lives* by Margaret Singer & Janja Lalich, and *Seductive Poison: A Jonestown Survivor's Story of Life and Death in the Peoples Temple* by Deborah Layton. I also watched the chilling documentaries *Going Clear: Scientology and the Prison of Belief* and *Keep Sweet: Prey and Obey*.

Any factual errors made in this book are mine alone.

Milton Keynes UK
Ingram Content Group UK Ltd.
UKHW040940081224
452111UK00015B/259/J

9 781914 452635